The Daisy Chain; or, Aspirations - Part 2

Charlotte M. Yonge

PART II

CHAPTER I.

Now have I then eke this condicion
That above all the flouris in the mede;
Then love I most these flouris white and rede,
Soche that men callin daisies in our town.
To them have I so great affection,
As I said erst, when comin is the Maie,
That in my bed there dawith me no daie
That I am up and walking in the mede,
To see this floure agenst the sunne sprede.—CHAUCER.

"That is better!" said Margaret, contemplating a butterfly of the penwiper class, whose constitution her dexterous needle had been rendering less rickety than Blanche had left it.

Margaret still lay on the sofa, and her complexion had assumed the dead white of habitual ill-health. There was more languor of manner, and her countenance, when at rest, and not under the eye of her father, had a sadness of expression, as if any hopes that she might once have entertained were fading away. The years of Alan Ernescliffe's absence that had elasped had rather taken from her powers than added to them. Nevertheless, the habit of cheerfulness and sympathy had not deserted her, and it was with a somewhat amused glance that she turned towards Ethel, as she heard her answer by a sigh.

These years had dealt more kindly with Etheldred's outward appearance. They had rounded her angles, softened her features, and tinged her cheeks with a touch of red, that took off from the surrounding sallowness. She held herself better, had learned to keep her hair in order, and the more womanly dress, plain though it was, improved her figure more than could have been hoped in the days of her lank, gawky girlhood. No one could call her pretty, but her countenance had something more than ever pleasing in the animated and thoughtful expression on those marked features. She was sitting near the window, with a book, a dictionary, and pencil, as she replied to Margaret, with the sigh that made her sister smile.

1

"Poor Ethel! I condole with you."

"And I wonder at you!" said Ethel, "especially as Flora and Mrs. Hoxton say it is all for your sake;" then, nettled by Margaret's laugh, "Such a nice occupation for her, poor thing, as if you were Mrs. Hoxton, and had no resource but fancy-work."

"You know I am base enough to be so amused," said Margaret; "but, seriously, Ethel dear, I cannot bear to see you so much hurt by it. I did not know you were really grieved."

"Grieved! I am ashamed—sickened!" cried Ethel vehemently. "Poor Cocksmoor! As soon as anything is done there, Flora must needs go about implying that we have set some grand work in hand, and want only means—"

"Stop, Ethel; Flora does not boast."

"No, she does not boast. I wish she did! That would be straightforward and simple; but she has too good taste for that—so she does worse—she tells a little, and makes that go a long way, as if she were keeping back a great deal! You don't know how furious it makes me!"

"Ethel!"

"So," said Ethel, disregarding, "she stirs up all Stoneborough to hear what the Miss Mays are doing at Cocksmoor. So the Ladies' Committee must needs have their finger in! Much they cared for the place when it was wild and neglected! But they go to inspect Cherry and her school—Mrs. Ledwich and all—and, back they come, shocked— no system, no order, the mistress untrained, the school too small, with no apparatus! They all run about in despair, as if we had ever asked them to help us. And so Mrs. Hoxton, who cares for poor children no more than for puppy-dogs, but who can't live without useless work, and has filled her house as full of it as it can hold, devises a bazaar—a field for her trumpery, and a show-off for all the young ladies; and Flora treats it like an inspiration! Off they trot, to the old Assembly Rooms. I trusted that the smallness of them would have knocked it on the head; but, still worse, Flora's talking of it makes Mr. Rivers think it our pet scheme; so, what does he do but offer his park, and so we are to have a regular fancy fair, and

Cocksmoor School will be founded in vanity and frivolity! But I believe you like it!"

"I am not sure of my own feeling," said Margaret. "It has been settled without our interposition, and I have never been able to talk it over calmly with you. Papa does not seem to disapprove."

"No," said Ethel. "He will only laugh, and say it will spare him a great many of Mrs. Hoxton's nervous attacks. He thinks of it nearly as I do, at the bottom, but I cannot get him to stop it, nor even to say he does not wish Flora to sell."

"I did not understand that you really had such strong objections," said Margaret. "I thought it was only as a piece of folly, and —"

"And interference with my Cocksmoor?" said Ethel. I had better own to what may be wrong personal feeling at first."

"I can hardly call it wrong," said Margaret tenderly, "considering what Cocksmoor is to you, and what the Ladies' Committee is."

"Oh, Margaret, if the lawful authority—if a good clergyman would only come, how willingly would I work under him! But Mrs. Ledwich and—it is like having all the Spaniards and savages spoiling Robinson Crusoe's desert island!"

"It is not come to that yet," said Margaret; "but about the fancy fair. We all know that the school is very much wanted."

"Yes, but I hoped to wait in patience and perseverance, and do it at last."

"All yourself?"

"Now, Margaret! you know I was glad of Alan's help."

"I should think so!" said Margaret. "You need not make a favour of that!"

"Yes, but, don't you see, that came as almsgiving, in the way which brings a blessing. We want nothing to make us give money and work to Cocksmoor. We do all we can already; and I don't want to get a fine bag or a ridiculous pincushion in exchange!"

"Not you, but—"

"Well, for the rest. If they like to offer their money, well and good, the better for them; but why must they not give it to Cocksmoor— but for that unnatural butterfly of Blanche's, with black pins for horns, that they will go and sell at an extortionate rate."

"The price will be given for Cocksmoor's sake!"

"Pooh! Margaret. Do you think it is for Cocksmoor's sake that Lady Leonora Langdale and her fine daughter come down from London? Would Mrs. Hoxton spend the time in making frocks for Cocksmoor children that she does in cutting out paper, and stuffing glass bottles with it? Let people be honest—alms, or pleasure, or vanity! let them say which they mean; but don't make charity the excuse for the others; and, above all, don't make my poor Cocksmoor the victim of it."

"This is very severe," said Margaret, pausing, almost confounded. "Do you think no charity worth having but what is given on unmixed motives? Who, then, could give?"

"Margaret—we see much evil arise in the best-planned institutions; nay, in what are not human. Don't you think we ought to do our utmost to have no flaw in the foundation? Schools are not such perfect places that we can build them without fear, and, if the means are to be raised by a bargain for amusement—if they are to come from frivolity instead of self-denial, I am afraid of them. I do not mean that Cocksmoor has not been the joy of my life, and of Mary's, but that was not because we did it for pleasure."

"No!" said Margaret, sighing, "you found pleasure by the way. But why did you not say all this to Flora?"

"It is of no use to talk to Flora," said Ethel; "she would say it was high-flown and visionary. Oh! she wants it for the bazaar's own sake, and that is one reason why I hate it."

"Now, Ethel!"

"I do believe it was very unfortunate for Flora that the Hoxtons took to patronising her, because Norman would not be patronised. Ever since it began, her mind has been full of visitings, and parties, and county families, and she has left off the home usefulness she used to care about."

"But you are old enough for that," said Margaret. "It would be hard to keep Flora at home, now that you can take her place, and do not care for going out. One of us must be the representative Miss May, you know, and keep up the civilities; and you may think yourself lucky it is not you."

"If it was only that, I should not care, but I may as well tell you, Margaret, for it is a weight to me. It is not the mere pleasure in gaieties—Flora cares for them, in themselves, as little as I do—nor is it neighbourliness, as a duty to others, for, you may observe, she always gets off any engagement to the Wards, or any of the town folk, to whom it would be a gratification to have her—she either eludes them, or sends me. The thing is, that she is always trying to be with the great people, the county set, and I don't think that is the safe way of going on."

Margaret mused sadly. "You frighten me, Ethel! I cannot say it is not so, and these are so like the latent faults that dear mamma's letter spoke of—"

Ethel sat meditating, and at last said, "I wish I had not told you! I don't always believe it myself, and it is so unkind, and you will make yourself unhappy too. I ought not to have thought it of her! Think of her ever-ready kindness and helpfulness; her pretty courteous ways to the very least; her obligingness and tact!"

"Yes," said Margaret, "she is one of the kindest people there is, and I am sure that she thought the gaining funds for Cocksmoor was the best thing to be done, that you would be pleased, and a great deal of pleasant occupation provided for us all."

"That is the bright side, the surface side," said Ethel.

"And not an untrue one," said Margaret; "Meta will not be vain, and will work the more happily for Cocksmoor's sake. Mary and Blanche, poor Mrs. Boulder, and many good ladies who hitherto have not known how to help Cocksmoor, will do so now with a good will, and though it is not what we should have chosen, I think we had better take it in good part."

"You think so?"

"Yes, indeed I do. If you go about with that dismal face and strong disapproval, it will really seem as if it was the having your dominion muddled with that you dislike. Besides, it is putting yourself forward to censure what is not absolutely wrong in itself, and that cannot be desirable."

"No," said Ethel, "but I cannot help being sorry for Cocksmoor. I thought patience would prepare the way, and the means be granted in good time, without hastiness—only earnestness."

"You had made a picture for yourself," said Margaret gently. "Yes, we all make pictures for ourselves, and we are the foremost figures in them; but they are taken out of our hands, and we see others putting in rude touches, and spoiling our work, as it seems; but, by-and-by, we shall see that it is all guided."

Ethel sighed. "Then having protested to my utmost against this concern, you think I ought to be amiable about it."

"And to let poor Mary enjoy it. She would be so happy, if you would not bewilder her by your gloomy looks, and keep her to the hemming of your endless glazed calico bonnet strings."

"Poor old Mary! I thought that was by her own desire."

"Only her dutiful allegiance to you; and, as making pincushions is nearly her greatest delight, it is cruel to make her think it, in some mysterious way, wrong and displeasing to you."

Ethel laughed, and said, "I did not think Mary was in such awe of me. I'll set her free, then. But, Margaret, do you really think I ought to give up my time to it?"

"Could you not just let them have a few drawings, or a little bit of your company work—just enough for you not to annoy every one, and seem to be testifying against them? You would not like to vex Meta."

"It will go hard, if I do not tell Meta my mind. I cannot bear to see her deluded."

"I don't think she is," said Margaret; "but she does not set her face against what others wish. As papa says of his dear little humming-bird, she takes the honey, and leaves the poison."

"Yes; amid all that enjoyment, she is always choosing the good, and leaving the evil; always sacrificing something, and then being happy in the sacrifice!"

"No one would guess it was a sacrifice, it is so joyously done—least of all Meta herself."

"Her coming home from London was exactly a specimen of that sacrifice—and no sacrifice," said Ethel.

"What was that?" said Norman, who had come up to the window unobserved, and had been listening to their few last sentences.

"Did not you hear of it? It was a sort of material turning away from vanity that made me respect the little rival Daisy, as much as I always admired her.

"Tell me," said Norman. "When was it?"

"Last spring. You know Mr. Rivers is always ill in London: indeed, papa says it would be the death of him; but Lady Leonora Langdale thinks it dreadful that Meta should not go to all the gaieties; and last year, when Mrs. Larpent was gone, she insisted on her coming to stay with her for the season. Now Meta thought it wrong to leave her father alone, and wanted not to have gone at all, but, to my surprise, Margaret advised her to yield, and go for some short fixed time."

"Yes," said Margaret; "as all her elders thought it right, I did not think we could advise her to refuse absolutely. Besides, it was a promise."

"She declared she would only stay three weeks, and the Langdales were satisfied, thinking that, once in London, they should keep her. They little knew Meta, with her pretty ways of pretending that her resolution is only spoiled-child wilfulness. None of you quite trusted her, did you, Margaret? Even papa was almost afraid, though he wanted her very much to be at home; for poor Mr. Rivers was so low and forlorn without her, though he would not let her know, because Lady Leonora had persuaded him to think it was all for her good."

"What did they do with her in London?" asked Norman.

"They did their utmost," said Ethel. "They made engagements for her, and took her to parties and concerts—those she did enjoy very much and she had lessons in drawing and music, but whenever she wanted to see any exhibitions, or do anything, they always said there was time to spare. I believe it was very charming, and she would have been very glad to stay, but she never would promise,and she was always thinking of her positive duty at home. She seemed afterwards to think of her wishes to remain almost as if they had been a sin; but she said—dear little Meta—that nothing had ever helped her so much as that she used to say to herself, whenever she was going out, 'I renounce the world.' It came to a crisis at last, when Lady Leonora wanted her to be presented—the Drawing-Room was after the end of her three weeks—and she held out against it; though her aunt laughed at her, and treated her as if she was a silly, shy child. At last, what do you think Meta did? She went to her uncle, Lord Cosham, and appealed to him to say whether there was the least necessity for her to go to court."

"Then she gained the day?" said Norman.

"He was delighted with that spirited, yet coaxing way of hers, and admired her determination. He told papa so himself—for you must know, when he heard all Meta had to say, he called her a very good girl, and said he would take her home himself on the Saturday she had fixed, and spend Sunday at Abbotstoke. Oh! he was perfectly won by her sweet ways. Was not it lucky? for before this Lady Leonora had written to Mr. Rivers, and obtained from him a letter, which Meta had the next day, desiring her to stay for the Drawing-Room. But Meta knew well enough how it was, and was not to be conquered that way; so she said she must go home to entertain her uncle, and that if her papa really wished it, she would return on Monday."

"Knowing well that Mr. Rivers would be only too glad to keep her."

"Just so. How happy they both did look, when they came in here on their way from the station where he had met her! How she danced in, and how she sparkled with glee!" said Margaret, "and poor Mr. Rivers was quite tremulous with the joy of having her back, hardly able to keep from fondling her every minute, and coming again into the room after they had taken leave, to tell me that his little girl had preferred her home, and her poor old father, to all the pleasures in London. Oh, I was so glad they came! That was a sight that did one good! And then, I fancy Mr. Rivers is a wee bit afraid of his brother-in-law, for he begged papa and Flora to come home and dine with them, but Flora was engaged to Mrs. Hoxton."

"Ha! Flora!" said Norman, as if he rather enjoyed her losing something through her going to Mrs. Hoxton. "I suppose she would have given the world to go!"

"I was so sorry," said Ethel; "but I had to go instead, and it was delightful. Papa made great friends with Lord Cosham, while Mr. Rivers went to sleep after dinner, and I had such a delightful wandering with Meta, listening to the nightingales, and hearing all about it. I never knew Meta so well before."

"And there was no more question of her going back?" said Norman.

"No, indeed! She said, when her uncle asked in joke, on Monday morning, whether she had packed up to return with him, Mr. Rivers was quite nervously alarmed the first moment, lest she should intend it."

"That little Meta," said Margaret. "Her wishes for substantial use have been pretty well realised!"

"Um!" said Ethel.

"What do you mean?" said Norman sharply. "I should call her present position the perfection of feminine usefulness."

"So perhaps it is," said Ethel; "but though she does it beautifully, and is very valuable, to be the mistress of a great luxurious house like that does not seem to me the subject of aspirations like Meta's."

"Think of the contrast with what she used to be," said Margaret gently, "the pretty, gentle, playful toy that her father brought her up to be, living a life of mere accomplishments and self-indulgence; kind certainly, but never so as to endure any disagreeables, or make any exertion. But as soon as she entered into the true spirit of our calling, did she not begin to seek to live the sterner life, and train herself in duty? The quiet way she took always seemed to me the great beauty of it. She makes duties of her accomplishments by making them loving obedience to her father."

"Not that they are not pleasant to her?" interposed Norman.

"Certainly," said Margaret, "but it gives them the zest, and confidence that they are right, which one could not have in such things merely for one's own amusement."

"Yes," said Ethel, "she does more; she told me one day that one reason she liked sketching was, that looking into nature always made psalms and hymns sing in her ears, and so with her music and her beautiful copies from the old Italian devotional pictures. She says our papa taught her to look at them so as to see more than the mere art and beauty."

"Think how diligently she measures out her day," said Margaret;

"getting up early, to be sure of time for reading her serious books, and working hard at her tough studies."

"And what I care for still more," said Ethel, "her being bent on learning plain needlework and doing it for her poor people. She is so useful amongst the cottagers at Abbotstoke!"

"And a famous little mistress of the house," added Margaret. "When the old housekeeper went away two years ago, she thought she ought to know something about the government of the house; so she asked me about it, and proposed to her father that the new one should come to her for orders, and that she should pay the wages and have the accounts in her hands. Mr. Rivers thought it was only a freak, but she has gone on steadily; and I assure you, she has had some difficulties, for she has come to me about them. Perhaps Ethel does not believe in them?"

"No, I was only thinking how I should hate ordering those fanciful dinners for Mr. Rivers. I know what you mean, and how she had difficulties about sending the maids to church, and in dealing with the cook, who did harm to the other servants, and yet sent up dinners that he liked, and how puzzled she was to avoid annoying him. Oh! she has got into a peck of troubles by making herself manager."

"And had she not been the Meta she is, she would either have fretted, or thrown it all up, instead of humming briskly through all. She never was afraid to speak to any one," said Margaret, "that is one thing; I believe every difficulty makes the spirit bound higher, till she springs over it, and finds it, as she says, only a pleasure."

"She need not be afraid to speak," said Ethel, "for she always does it well and winningly. I have seen her give a reproof in so firm and kind a way, and so bright in the instant of forgiveness."

"Yes," said Margaret, "she does those disagreeable things as well as Flora does in her way."

"And yet," said Ethel, "doing things well does not seem to be a snare to her."

"Because," whispered Margaret, "she fulfils more than almost any one—the—'Whatsoever ye do, do all to the glory of God.'"

"Do you know," said Norman suddenly, "the derivation of Margarita?"

"No further than those two pretty meanings, the pearl and the daisy," said Ethel.

"It is from the Persian Mervarid, child of light," said Norman; and, with a sudden flush of colour, he returned to the garden.

"A fit meaning for one who carries sunshine with her," said Margaret. "I feel in better tune for a whole day after her bright eyes have been smiling on me."

"You want no one to put you in tune," said Ethel fondly—"you, our own pearl of light."

"No, call me only an old faded daisy," said Margaret sadly.

"Not a bit, only our moon, la gran Margarita" said Ethel.

"I hear the real Daisy coming!" exclaimed Margaret, her face lighting up with pleasure as the two youngest children entered, and, indeed, little Gertrude's golden hair, round open face, fresh red and white complexion, and innocent looks, had so much likeness to the flower, as to promote the use of the pet name, though protests were often made in favour of her proper appellation. Her temper was daisy—like too, serene and loving, and able to bear a great deal of spoiling, and resolve as they might, who was not her slave?

Miss Winter no longer ruled the schoolroom. Her sway had been brought to a happy conclusion by a proposal from a widowed sister to keep house with her; and Ethel had reason to rejoice that Margaret had kept her submissive under authority, which, if not always judicious, was both kind and conscientious.

Upon the change, Ethel had thought that the lessons could easily be managed by herself and Flora; while Flora was very anxious for a finishing governess, who might impart singing to herself, graces to Ethel, and accomplishments to Mary and Blanche.

Dr. May, however, took them both by surprise. He met with a family of orphans, the eldest of whom had been qualifying herself for a governess, and needed nothing but age and finish; and in ten minutes after the project had been conceived, he had begun to put it in execution, in spite of Flora's prudent demurs.

Miss Bracy was a gentle, pleasing young person, pretty to look at, with her soft olive complexion, and languid pensive eyes, obliging and intelligent; and the change from the dry, authoritative Miss Winter was so delightful, that unedifying contrasts were continually being drawn. Blanche struck up a great friendship for her at once;

Mary, always docile, ceased to be piteous at her lessons, and Ethel moralised on the satisfaction of having sympathy needed instead of repelled, and did her utmost to make Miss Bracy feel at home—and like a friend—in her new position.

For herself, Ethel had drawn up a beautiful time-table, with all her pursuits and duties most carefully balanced, after the pattern of that which Margaret Rivers had made by her advice, on the departure of Mrs. Larpent, who had been called away by the ill-health of her son. Meta had adhered to hers in an exemplary manner, but she was her own mistress in a manner that could hardly be the lot of one of a large family.

Margaret had become subject to languor and palpitations, and the head of the household had fallen entirely upon Flora, who, on the other hand, was a person of multifarious occupations, and always had a great number of letters to write, or songs to copy and practise, which, together with her frequent visits to Mrs. Hoxton, made her glad to devolve, as much as she could, upon her younger sister; and, "Oh, Ethel, you will not mind just doing this for me," was said often enough to be a tax upon her time.

Moreover, Ethel perceived that Aubrey's lessons were in an unsatisfactory state. Margaret could not always attend to them, and suffered from them when she did; and he was bandied about between his sisters and Miss Bracy in a manner that made him neither attentive nor obedient.

On her own principle, that to embrace a task heartily renders it no longer irksome, she called on herself to sacrifice her studies and her regularity, as far as was needful, to make her available for home requirements. She made herself responsible for Aubrey, and, after a few battles with his desultory habits, made him a very promising pupil, inspiring so much of herself into him, that he was, if anything, overfull of her classical tastes. In fact, he had such an appetite for books, and dealt so much in precocious wisdom, that his father was heard to say, "Six years old! It is a comfort that he will soon forget the whole."

Gertrude was also Ethel's pupil, but learning was not at all in her line; and the sight of "Cobwebs to catch Flies," or of the venerated "Little Charles," were the most serious clouds, that made the Daisy pucker up her face, and infuse a whine into her voice.

However, to-day, as usual, she was half dragged, half coaxed, through her day's portion of the discipline of life, and then sent up for her sleep, while Aubrey's two hours were spent in more agreeable work, such as Margaret could not but enjoy hearing—so spirited was Ethel's mode of teaching—so eager was her scholar.

His play afterwards consisted in fighting o'er again the siege of Troy on the floor, with wooden bricks, shells, and the survivors of a Noah's ark, while Ethel read to Margaret until Gertrude's descent from the nursery, when the only means of preventing a dire confusion in Aubrey's camp was for her elder sisters to become her playfellows, and so spare Aubrey's temper. Ethel good-humouredly gave her own time, till their little tyrant trotted out to make Norman carry her round the garden on his back.

So sped the morning till Flora came home, full of the intended bazaar, and Ethel would fain have taken refuge in puzzling out her Spanish, had she not remembered her recent promise to be gracious.

The matter had been much as she had described it. Flora had a way of hinting at anything she thought creditable, and thus the Stoneborough public had become aware of the exertions of the May family on behalf of Cocksmoor.

The plan of a fancy fair was started. Mrs. Hoxton became more interested than was her wont, and Flora was enchanted at the opening it gave for promoting the welfare of the forlorn district. She held a position which made her hope to direct the whole. As she had once declared, with truth, it only had depended on themselves, whether she and her sisters should sink to the level of the Andersons and their set, or belong to the county society; and her tact had resulted in her being decidedly—as the little dressmaker's apprentice amused Ethel by saying—"One of our most distinguished patronesses"—a name that had stuck by her ever since.

Margaret looked on passively, inclined to admire Flora in everything, yet now and then puzzled; and her father, in his simple-hearted way, felt only gratitude and exultation in the kindness that his daughter met with. As to the bazaar, if it had been started in his own family, he might have weighed the objections, but, as it was not his daughter's own concern, he did not trouble himself about it, only regarding it as one of the many vagaries of the ladies of Stoneborough.

So the scheme had been further developed, till now Flora came in with much to tell. The number of stalls had been finally fixed. Mrs. Hoxton undertook one, with Flora as an aide-de-camp, and some nieces to assist; Lady Leonora was to chaperon Miss Rivers; and a third, to Flora's regret, had been allotted to Miss Cleveland, a good-natured, merry, elderly heiress, who would, Flora feared, bring on them the whole "Stoneborough crew." And then she began to reckon up the present resources—drawings, bags, and pincushions. "That chip hat you plaited for Daisy, Margaret, you must let us have that. It will be lovely, trimmed with pink."

"Do you wish for this?" said Ethel, heaving up a mass of knitting.

"Thank you," said Flora; "so ornamental, especially the original performance in the corner, which you would perpetrate, in spite of my best efforts."

"I shall not be offended if you despise it. I only thought you might have no more scruple in robbing Granny Hall than in robbing Daisy."

"Pray, send it. Papa will buy it as your unique performance."

"No; you shall tell me what I am to do."

"Does she mean it?" said Flora, turning to Margaret. "Have you converted her? Well done! Then, Ethel, we will get some pretty batiste, and you and Mary shall make some of those nice sun-bonnets, which you really do to perfection."

"Thank you. That is a more respectable task than I expected. People may have something worth buying," said Ethel, who, like all the world, felt the influence of Flora's tact.

"I mean to study the useful," said Flora. "The Cleveland set will be sure to deal in frippery, and I have been looking over Mrs. Hoxton's stores, where I see quite enough for mere decoration. There are two splendid vases in potichomanie, in an Etruscan pattern, which are coming for me to finish."

"Mrs. Taylor, at Cocksmoor, could do that for you," said Ethel. "Her two phials, stuffed with chintz patterns and flour, are quite as original and tasteful."

"Silly work," said Flora, "but it makes a fair show."

"The essence of Vanity Fair," said Ethel.

"It won't do to be satirical over much," said Flora. "You won't get on without humouring your neighbours' follies."

"I don't want to get on."

"But you want—or, at least, I want—Cocksmoor to get on."

15

Ethel saw Margaret looking distressed, and, recalling her resolution she said, "Well, Flora, I don't mean to say any more about it. I see it can't be helped, and you all think you intend it for good; so there's an end of the matter, and I'll do anything for you in reason."

"Poor old King Ethel!" said Flora, smiling in an elder-sisterly manner. "You will see, my dear, your views are very pretty, but very impracticable, and it is a work-a-day world after all—even papa would tell you so. When Cocksmoor school is built, then you may thank me. I do not look for it before."

CHAPTER II.

Knowledge is second, not the first;
A higher Hand must make her mild,
If all be not in vain, and guide
Her footsteps, moving side by side,
With wisdom; like the younger child,
For she is earthly of the mind,
But knowledge heavenly of the soul. —In Memoriam.

Etheldred had not answered her sister, but she did not feel at all secure that she should have anything to be thankful for, even if the school were built.

The invasion of Cocksmoor was not only interference with her own field of action, but it was dangerous to the improvement of her scholars. Since the departure of Mr. Wilmot, matters at Stoneborough National School had not improved, though the Misses Anderson talked a great deal about progress, science, and lectures.

The Ladies' Committee were constantly at war with the mistresses, and that one was a veteran who endured them, or whom they could endure beyond her first half-year. No mistress had stayed a year within the memory of any girl now at school. Perpetual change prevented any real education, and, as each lady held different opinions and proscribed all books not agreeing thereto, everything "dogmatical" was excluded; and, as Ethel said, the children learned nothing but facts about lions and steam-engines, while their doctrine varied with that of the visitor for the week. If the ten generals could only have given up to Miltiades, but, alas! there was no Miltiades. Mr. Ramsden's health was failing, and his neglect told upon the parish in the dreadful evils reigning unchecked, and engulfing many a child whom more influential teaching might have saved. Mental arithmetic, and the rivers of Africa, had little power to strengthen the soul against temptation.

The scanty attendance at the National School attested the indifference with which it was regarded, and the borderers voluntarily patronised Cherry Elwood, and thus had, perhaps, first aroused the emulation that led Mrs. Ledwich on a visit of inspection, to what she chose to consider as an offshoot of the National School.

The next day she called upon the Misses May. It was well that Ethel was not at home. Margaret received the lady's horrors at the sight of the mere crowded cottage kitchen, the stupid untrained mistress, without an idea of method, and that impertinent woman, her mother! Miss Flora and Miss Ethel must have had a great deal to undergo, and she would lose no time in convening the Ladies' Committee, and appointing a successor to "that Elwood," as soon as a fit room could be erected for her use. If Margaret had not known that Mrs. Ledwich sometimes threatened more than she could accomplish, she would have been in despair. She tried to say a good word for Cherry, but was talked down, and had reason to believe that Mrs. Elwood had mortally offended Mrs. Ledwich.

The sisters had heard the other side of the story at Cocksmoor. Mrs. Elwood would not let them enter the school till she had heard how that there Mrs. Ledwich had come in, and treated them all as if it was her own place—how she had found fault with Cherry before all the children, and as good as said she was not fit to keep a school. She had even laid hands on one of the books, and said that she should take it home, and see whether it were a fit one for them to use; whereupon Mrs. Elwood had burst out in defence—it was Miss Ethel May's book, and should not be taken away—it was Miss Ethel as she looked to; and when it seemed that Mrs. Ledwich had said something disparaging of Miss Ethel, either as to youth, judgment, or doctrine, Mrs. Elwood had fired up into a declaration that "Miss Ethel was a real lady—that she was! and that no real lady would ever come prying into other folk's work and finding fault with what wasn't no business of theirs," with more of a personal nature, which Flora could not help enjoying, even while she regretted it.

Cherry was only too meek, as her mother declared. She had said not a word, except in quiet reply, and being equally terrified by the attack and defence, had probably seemed more dull than was her wont. Her real feelings did not appear till the next Sunday, when, in her peaceful conference with Margaret, far from the sound of storms, she expressed that she well knew that she was a poor scholar, and that she hoped the young ladies would not let her stand in the children's light, when a better teacher could be found for them.

"I am sure!" cried Ethel, as she heard of this, "it would be hard to find such a teacher in humility! Cherry bears it so much better than I, that it is a continual reproof!"

As to the dullness, against which Ethel used to rail, the attacks upon it had made her erect it into a positive merit; she was always comparing the truth, honesty, and respectful demeanour of Cherry's scholars with the notorious faults of the National School girls, as if these defects had been implanted either by Mrs. Ledwich, or by geography. It must be confessed that the violence of partisanship did not make her a pleasant companion.

However, the interest of the bazaar began somewhat to divert the current of the ladies' thoughts, and Ethel found herself walking day after day to Cocksmoor, unmolested by further reports of Mrs. Ledwich's proceedings. Richard was absent, preparing for ordination, but Norman had just returned home for the Long Vacation, and, rather than lose the chance of a conversation with her, had joined her and Mary in a walk to Cocksmoor.

His talk was chiefly of Settlesham, old Mr. Wilmot's parish, where he had been making a visit to his former tutor, and talking over the removal to Eton of Tom, who had well responded to the care taken of him, and with his good principles confirmed, and his character strengthened, might be, with less danger, exposed to trial.

It had been a visit such as to leave a deep impression on Norman's mind. Sixty years ago, old Mr. Wilmot had been what he now was himself—an enthusiastic and distinguished Balliol man, and he had kept up a warm, clear-sighted interest in Oxford throughout his long life. His anecdotes, his recollections, and comments on present opinions had been listened to with great eagerness, and Norman had felt it an infinite honour to give the venerable old man his arm, as to be shown by him his curious collection of books. His parish, carefully watched for so many years, had been a study not lost upon Norman, who detailed particulars of the doings there, which made Ethel sigh to think of the contrast with Stoneborough. In such conversation they came to the entrance of the hamlet, and Mary, with a scream of joy, declared that she really believed that he was going to help them! He did not turn away.

"Thank you!" said Ethel, in a low voice, from the bottom of her heart.

She used him mercifully, and made the lessons shorter than usual, but when they reached the open air again, he drew a long breath;

and when Mary eagerly tried for a compliment to their scholars, asked if they could not be taught the use of eyelids.

"Did they stare?" said Ethel. "That's one advantage of being blind. No one can stare me out of countenance."

"Why were you answering all your questions yourself?" asked Mary.

"Because no one else would," said Norman.

"You used such hard words," replied Ethel.

"Indeed! I thought I was very simple."

"Oh!" cried Mary, "there were derive, and instruction, and implicate, and—oh, so many."

"Never mind," said Ethel, seeing him disconcerted. "It is better for them to be drawn up, and you will soon learn their language. If we only had Una M'Carthy here!"

"Then you don't like it?" said Mary, disappointed.

"It is time to learn not to be fastidious," he answered. "So, if you will help me—"

"Norman, I am so glad!" said Ethel.

"Yes," said Norman, "I see now that these things that puff us up, and seem the whole world to us now, all end in nothing but such as this! Think of old Mr. Wilmot, once carrying all before him, but deeming all his powers well bestowed in fifty years' teaching of clowns!"

"Yes," replied Ethel, very low. "One soul is worth—" and she paused from the fullness of thought.

"And these things, about which we are so elated, do not render us so fit to teach—as you, Mary, or as Richard."

"They do," said Ethel. The ten talents were doubled. Strength tells in power. The more learning, the fitter to teach the simplest thing."

"You remind me of old Mr. Wilmot saying that the first thing he learned at his parish was, how little his people knew; the second, how little he himself knew."

So Norman persevered in the homely discipline that he had chosen for himself, which brought out his deficiency in practical work in a manner which lowered him in his own eyes, to a degree almost satisfactory to himself. He was not, indeed, without humility, but his nature was self-contemplative and self-conscious enough to perceive his superiority of talent, and it had been the struggle of his life to abase this perception, so that it was actually a relief not to be obliged to fight with his own complacency in his powers. He had learned not to think too highly of himself—he had yet to learn to "think soberly." His aid was Ethel's chief pleasure through this somewhat trying summer, it might be her last peaceful one at Cocksmoor.

That bazaar! How wild it had driven the whole town, and even her own home!

Margaret herself, between good nature and feminine love of pretty things, had become ardent in the cause. In her unvaried life, it was a great amusement to have so many bright elegant things exhibited to her, and Ethel was often mortified to find her excited about some new device, or drawn off from "rational employments," to complete some trifle.

Mary and Blanche were far worse. From the time that consent had been given to the fancy-work being carried on in the schoolroom, all interest in study was over. Thenceforth, lessons were a necessary form, gone through without heart or diligence. These were reserved for paste-board boxes, beplastered with rice and sealing-wax, for alum baskets, dressed dolls, and every conceivable trumpery; and the governess was as eager as the scholars.

If Ethel remonstrated, she hurt Miss Bracy's feelings, and this was a very serious matter to both parties.

The governess was one of those morbidly sensitive people, who cannot be stopped when once they have begun arguing that they are injured. Two women together, each with the last-word instinct, have no power to cease; and, when the words are spent in explaining—not in scolding—conscience is not called in to silence them, and nothing but dinner or a thunder-storm can check them. All Ethel's good sense was of no avail; she could not stop Miss Bracy, and, though she might resolve within herself that real kindness would be to make one reasonable reply, and then quit the subject, yet, on each individual occasion, such a measure would have seemed mere impatience and cruelty. She found that if Miss Winter had been too dry, Miss Bracy went to the other extreme, and demanded a manifestation of sympathy, and return to her passionate attachment that perplexed Ethel's undemonstrative nature. Poor good Miss Bracy, she little imagined how often she added to the worries of her dear Miss Ethel, all for want of self-command.

Finally, as the lessons were less and less attended to, and the needs of the stall became more urgent, Dr. May and Margaret concurred in a decision, that it was better to yield to the mania, and give up the studies till they could be pursued with a willing mind.

Ethel submitted, and only laughed with Norman at the display of treasures, which the girls went over daily, like the "House that Jack built," always starting from "the box that Mary made." Come when Dr. May would into the drawing-room, there was always a line of penwipers laid out on the floor, bags pendent to all the table-drawers, antimacassars laid out everywhere.

Ethel hoped that the holidays would create a diversion, but Mary was too old to be made into a boy, and Blanche drew Hector over to the feminine party, setting him to gum, gild, and paste all the contrivances which, in their hands, were mere feeble gimcracks, but which now became fairly sound, or, at least, saleable.

The boys also constructed a beautiful little ship from a print of the Alcestis, so successfully, that the doctor promised to buy it; and Ethel grudged the very sight of it to the bazaar.

Tom, who, in person, was growing like a little shadow or model of Norman, had, unlike him, a very dexterous pair of hands, and made himself extremely useful in all such works. On the other hand, the Cleveland stall seemed chiefly to rely for brilliance on the wit of Harvey Anderson, who was prospering at his college, and the pride of his family. A great talker, and extremely gallant, he was considered a far greater acquisition to a Stoneborough drawing-room than was the silent, bashful Norman May, and rather looked down on his brother Edward, who, having gone steadily through the school, was in the attorney's office, and went on quietly and well, colouring up gratefully whenever one of the May family said a kind word to him.

CHAPTER III.

Any silk, any thread,
Any toys for your head,
Of the newest and finest wear-a?
Come to the pedlar,
Money's a medlar.
That doth utter all men's ware-a.
Winter's Tale.

"This one day and it will be over, and we shall be rational again," thought Ethel, as she awoke.

Flora was sleeping at the Grange, to be ready for action in the morning, and Ethel was to go early with Mary and Blanche, who were frantic to have a share in the selling. Norman and the boys were to walk at their own time, and the children to be brought later by Miss Bracy. The doctor would be bound by no rules.

It was a pattern day, bright, clear, warm, and not oppressive, perfect for an out-of-doors fete; and Ethel had made up her mind to fulfil her promise to Margaret of enjoying herself. In the brilliant sunshine, and between two such happy sisters, it would have been surly, indeed, not to enter into the spirit of the day; and Ethel laughed gaily with them, and at their schemes and hopes; Blanche's heart being especially set on knowing the fate of a watch-guard of her own construction.

Hearing that the ladies were in the gardens, they repaired thither at once. The broad, smooth bowling-green lay before them; a marquee, almost converted into a bower, bounding it on either side, while in the midst arose, gorgeous and delicious, a pyramid of flowers— contributions from all the hot-houses in the neighbourhood—to be sold for the benefit of the bazaar. Their freshness and fragrance gave a brightness to the whole scene, while shrinking from such light, as only the beauteous works of nature could bear, was the array accomplished by female fingers.

Under the wreathed canopies were the stalls, piled up with bright colours, most artistically arranged. Ethel, with her over-minute knowledge of every article, could hardly believe that yonder glowing Eastern pattern of scarlet, black, and blue, was, in fact, a judicious mosaic of penwipers that she remembered, as shreds begged from the tailor, that the delicate lace-work consisted of Miss Bracy's perpetual antimacassars, and that the potichomanie could look so dignified and Etruscan.

"Here you are!" cried Meta Rivers, springing to meet them. "Good girls, to come early. Where's my little Daisy?"

"Coming in good time," said Ethel. "How pretty it all looks!"

"But where's Flora?—where's my watch-guard?" anxiously asked Blanche.

"She was here just now," said Meta, looking round. "What a genius she is, Ethel! She worked wonders all yesterday, and let the Miss Hoxtons think it was all their own doing, and she was out before six this morning, putting finishing touches."

"Is this your stall?" said Ethel.

"Yes, but it will not bear a comparison with hers. It has a lady's-maid look by the side of hers. In fact, Bellairs and my aunt's maid did it chiefly, for papa was rather ailing yesterday, and I could not be out much."

"How is he now?"

"Better; he will walk round by-and-by. I hope it will not be too much for him."

"Oh, what beautiful things!" cried Mary, in ecstasy, at what she was forced to express by the vague substantive, for her imagination had never stretched to the marvels she beheld.

"Ay, we have been lazy, you see, and so Aunt Leonora brought down all these smart concerns. It is rather like Howell and James's, isn't it?"

In fact, Lady Leonora's marquee was filled with costly knick-knacks, which, as Meta justly said, had not half the grace and appropriate air that reigned where Flora had arranged, and where Margaret had worked, with the peculiar freshness and finish that distinguished everything to which she set her hand.

Miss Cleveland's counter was not ill set-out, but it wanted the air of ease and simplicity, which was even more noticeable than the perfect taste of Flora's wares. If there had been nothing facetious, the effect would have been better, but there was nothing to regret, and the whole was very bright and gay.

Blanche could hardly look; so anxious was she for Flora to tell her the locality of her treasure.

"There she is," said Meta at last. "George is fixing that branch of evergreen for her."

"Flora! I did not know her," cried each sister amazed; while Mary added, "Oh, how nice she looks!"

It was the first time of seeing her in the white muslin, and broad chip hat—which all the younger saleswomen of the bazaar had agreed to wear. It was a most becoming dress, and she did, indeed, look strikingly elegant and well dressed. It occurred to Ethel, for the first time, that Flora was decidedly the reigning beauty of the bazaar—no one but Meta Rivers could be compared to her, and that little lady was on so small a scale of perfect finish, that she seemed fit to act the fairy, where Flora was the enchanted princess.

Flora greeted her sisters eagerly, while Meta introduced her brother—a great contrast to herself, though not without a certain comeliness, tall and large, with ruddy complexion, deep lustreless black eyes, and a heavy straight bush of black moustache, veiling rather thick lips. Blanche reiterated inquiries for her watch-guard.

"I don't know,"—said Flora. "Somewhere among the rest."

Blanche was in despair.

"You may look for it," said Flora, who, however hurried, never failed in kindness, "if you will touch nothing."

So Blanche ran from place to place in restless dismay, that caused Mr. George Rivers to ask what was the matter.

"The guards! the guards!" cried Blanche; whereupon he fell into a fit of laughter, which disconcerted her, because she could not understand him, and made Ethel take an aversion to him on the spot.

However, he was very good-natured; he took Blanche's reluctant hand, and conducted her all along the stall, even proceeding to lift her up where she could not command a view of the whole, thus exciting her extreme indignation. She shook herself out when he set her down, surveyed her crumpled muslin, and believed he took her for a little girl! She ought to have been flattered when the quest was successful, and he insisted on knowing which was the guard, and declared that he should buy it. She begged him to do no such thing, and he desired to know why—insisting that he would give five shillings—fifteen—twenty-five for that one! till she did not know whether he was in earnest, and she doing an injury to the bazaar.

Meantime, the hour had struck, and Flora had placed Mrs. Hoxton in a sheltered spot, where she could take as much or as little trouble as she pleased. Lady Leonora and Miss Langdale came from the house, and, with the two ladies'-maids in the background, took up their station with Miss Rivers. Miss Cleveland called her party to order, and sounds of carriages were heard approaching.

Mary and Blanche disbursed the first money spent in the "fancy fair;" Mary, on a blotting-book for Harry, to be placed among the presents, to which she added on every birthday, while Blanche bought a sixpenny gift for every one, with more attention to the quantity than the quality. Then came a revival of her anxieties for the guards, and while Mary was simply desirous of the fun of being a shopwoman, and was made happy by Meta Rivers asking her help, Blanche was in despair, till she had sidled up to their neighbourhood, and her piteous looks had caused good-natured Mrs. Hoxton to invite her to assist, when she placed herself close to the precious object.

A great fluttering of heart went to that manoeuvre, but still felicity could not be complete. That great troublesome Mr. George Rivers had actually threatened to buy nothing but that one watch-chain, and Blanche's eye followed him everywhere with fear, lest he should come that way. And there were many other gentlemen—what could they want but watch-guards, and of them—what—save this paragon?

Poor Blanche; what did she not undergo whenever any one cast his eye over her range of goods? and this was not seldom, for there was an attraction in the pretty little eager girl, glowing and smiling. One old gentleman actually stopped, handled the guards themselves, and asked their price.

"Eighteen-pence," said Blanche, colouring and faltering, as she held up one in preference.

"Eh! is not this the best?" said he, to the lady on his arm.

"Oh! please, take that instead?" exclaimed Blanche, in extremity.

"And why?" asked the gentleman, amused.

"I made this," she answered.

"Is that the reason I must not have it?"

"No, don't tease her," the lady said kindly; and the other was taken.

"I wonder for what it is reserved!" the lady could not help saying, as she walked away.

"Let us watch her for a minute or two. What an embellishment children are! Ha! don't you see—the little maid is fluttering and reddening—now! How pretty she looks! Ah! I see! here's the favoured! Don't you see that fine bronzed lad—Eton—one can see at a glance! It is a little drama. They are pretending to be strangers. He is turning over the goods with an air, she trying to look equally careless, but what a pretty carnation it is! Ha! ha! he has come to it—he has it! Now the acting is over, and they are having their laugh out! How joyously! What next! Oh! she begs off from keeping shop—she darts out to him, goes off in his hand—I declare that is the prettiest sight in the whole fair! I wonder who the little demoiselle can be?"

The great event of the day was over now with Blanche, and she greatly enjoyed wandering about with Hector and Tom. There was a post-office at Miss Cleveland's stall, where, on paying sixpence, a letter could be obtained to the address of the inquirer. Blanche had been very anxious to try, but Flora had pronounced it nonsense; however, Hector declared that Flora was not his master, tapped at

28

the sliding panel, and charmed Blanche by what she thought a most witty parody of his name as Achilles Lionsrock, Esquire. When the answer came from within, "Ship letter, sir, double postage," they thought it almost uncanny; and Hector's shilling was requited by something so like a real ship letter, that they had some idea that the real post had somehow transported itself thither. The interior was decidedly oracular, consisting of this one line, "I counsel you to persevere in your laudable undertaking."

Hector said he wished he had any laudable undertaking, and Blanche tried to persuade Tom to try his fortune, but he pronounced that he did not care to hear Harvey Anderson's trash—he knew his writing, though disguised, and had detected his shining boots below the counter. There Mr. George Rivers came up, and began to tease Blanche about the guards, asking her to take his fifteen shillings—or five-and-twenty, and who had got that one, which alone he wanted; till the poor child, after standing perplexed for some moments, looked up with spirit, and said, "You have no business to ask," and, running away, took refuge in the back of Mrs. Hoxton's marquee, where she found Ethel packing up for Miss Hoxton's purchasers, and confiding to her that Mr. George Rivers was a horrid man, she ventured no more from her protection. She did, indeed, emerge, when told that papa was coming with Aubrey and Daisy and Miss Bracy, and she had the pleasure of selling to them some of her wares. Dr. May bargaining with her to her infinite satisfaction; and little Gertrude's blue eyes opened to their full width, not understanding what could have befallen her sisters.

"And what is Ethel doing?" asked the doctor.

"Packing up parcels, papa," and Ethel's face was raised, looking very merry.

"Packing parcels! How long will they last tied up?" said Dr. May, laughing.

"Lasting is the concern of nothing in the fair, papa," answered she, in the same tone.

For Ethel was noted as the worst packer in the house; but, having offered to wrap up a pincushion, sold by a hurried Miss Hoxton, she became involved in the office for the rest of the day—the same which Bellairs and her companion performed at the Langdale counter.

Flora was too ready and dexterous to need any such aid, but the Misses Hoxton were glad to be spared the trouble; and Blanche, whose fingers were far neater than Ethel's, made the task much easier, and was kept constant to it by her dread of the dark moustache, which was often visible near their tent, searching, she thought, for her.

Their humble employment was no sinecure; for this was the favourite stall with the purchasers of better style, since the articles were, in general, tasteful, and fairly worth the moderate price set on them. At Miss Cleveland's counter there was much noisy laughter—many jocular cheats—tricks for gaining money, and refusals to give change; and it seemed to be very popular with the Stoneborough people, and to carry on a brisk trade. The only languor was in Lady Leonora's quarter—the articles were too costly, and hung on hand; nor were the ladies sufficiently well known, nor active enough, to gain custom, excepting Meta, who drove a gay traffic at her end of the stall, which somewhat redeemed the general languor.

Her eyes were, all the time, watching for her father, and, suddenly perceiving him, she left her trade in charge of the delighted and important Mary, and hastened to walk round with him, and show him the humours of the fair.

Mary, in her absence, had the supreme happiness of obtaining Norman as a customer. He wanted a picture for his rooms at Oxford, and water-coloured drawings were, as Tom had observed, suitable staple commodities for Miss Rivers. Mary tried to make him choose a brightly-coloured pheasant, with a pencil background; and, then, a fine foaming sea-piece, by some unknown Lady Adelaide, that much dazzled her imagination; but nothing would serve him but a sketch of an old cedar tree, with Stoneborough Minster in the distance, and the Welsh hills beyond, which Mary thought a remarkable piece of bad taste, since—could he not see all that any day of his life? and was it worth while to give fourteen shillings and sixpence for it? But he said it was all for the good of Cocksmoor, and Mary was only too glad to add to her hoard of coin; so she only marvelled at his extravagance, and offered to take care of it for him; but, to this, he would not consent. He made her pack it up for him, and had just put the whitey-brown parcel under his arm, when Mr. Rivers and his daughter came up, before he was aware. Mary proudly advertised Meta that she had sold something for her.

"Indeed! What was it?"

"Your great picture of Stoneborough!" said Mary.

"Is that gone? I am sorry you have parted with that, my dear; it was one of your best," said Mr. Rivers, in his soft, sleepy, gentle tone.

"Oh, papa, I can do another. But, I wonder! I put that extortionate price on it, thinking no one would give it, and so that I should keep it for you. Who has it, Mary?"

"Norman, there. He would have it, though I told him it was very dear."

Norman, pressed near them by the crowd, had been unable to escape, and stood blushing, hesitating, and doubting whether he ought to restore the prize, which he had watched so long, and obtained so eagerly.

"Oh! it is you?" said Mr. Rivers politely. "Oh, no, do not think of exchanging it. I am rejoiced that one should have it who can appreciate it. It was its falling into the hands of a stranger that I disliked. You think with me, that it is one of her best drawings?"

"Yes, I do," said Norman, still rather hesitating. "She did that with C—, when he was here last year. He taught her very well. Have you that other here, that you took with him, my dear? The view from the gate, I mean."

"No, dear papa. You told me not to sell that."

"Ah! I remember; that is right. But there are some very pretty copies from Prout here."

While he was seeking them, Meta contrived to whisper, "If you could persuade him to go indoors—this confusion of people is so bad for him, and I must not come away. I was in hopes of Dr. May, but he is with the little ones."

Norman signed comprehension, and Meta said, "Those copies are not worth seeing, but you know, papa, you have the originals in the library."

Mr. Rivers looked pleased, but was certain that Norman could not prefer the sketches to this gay scene. However, it took very little persuasion to induce him to do what he wished, and he took Norman's arm, crossed the lawn, and arrived in his own study, where it was a great treat to him to catch any one who would admire his accumulation of prints, drawings, coins, etc.; and his young friend was both very well amused and pleased to be setting Miss Rivers's mind at ease on her father's account. It was not till half-past four that Dr. May knocked at the door, and stood surprised at finding his son there. Mr. Rivers spoke warmly of the young Oxonian's kindness in leaving the fair for an old man, and praised Norman's taste in art. Norman rose to take leave, but still thought it incumbent on him to offer to give up the picture, if Mr. Rivers set an especial value on it. But Mr. Rivers went to the length of being very glad that it was in his possession, and added to it a very pretty drawing of the same size, by a noted master, which had been in the water-colour exhibition, and, while Norman walked away, well pleased, Mr. Rivers began to extol him to his father, as a very superior and sensible young man, of great promise, and began to wish George had the same turn.

Norman, on returning to the fancy fair, found the world in all the ardour of raffles. Lady Leonora's contributions were the chief prizes, which attracted every one, and, of course, the result was delightfully incongruous. Poor Ethel, who had been persuaded to venture a shilling to please Blanche, who had spent all her own, obtained the two jars in potichomanie, and was regarding them with a face worth painting. Harvey Anderson had a doll, George Rivers a wooden monkey, that jumped over a stick; and, if Hector Ernescliffe was enchanted at winning a beautiful mother-of-pearl inlaid workbox, which he had vainly wished to buy for Margaret, Flora only gained a match-box of her own, well known always to miss fire, but which had been decided to be good enough for the bazaar.

By fair means or foul, the commodities were cleared off, and, while the sunbeams faded from the trodden grass, the crowds disappeared, and the vague compliment, "a very good bazaar," was exchanged between the lingering sellers and their friends.

Flora was again to sleep at the Grange, and return the next day, for a committee to be held over the gains, which were not yet fully ascertained. So Dr. May gathered his flock together, and packed them, boys and all, into the two conveyances, and Ethel bade Meta good-night, almost wondering to hear her merry voice say, "It has been a delightful day, has it not? It was so kind of your brother to take care of papa."

"Oh, it was delightful!" echoed Mary, "and I took one pound fifteen and sixpence!"

"I hope it will do great good to Cocksmoor," added Meta, "but, if you want real help, you know, you must come to us."

Ethel smiled, but hurried her departure, for she saw Blanche again tormented by Mr. George Rivers, to know what had become of the guard, telling her that, if she would not say, he should be furiously jealous.

Blanche hid her face on Ethel's arm, when they were in the carriage, and almost cried with indignant "shamefastness." That long-desired day had not been one of unmixed happiness to her, poor child, and Ethel doubted whether it had been so to any one, except, indeed, to Mary, whose desires never soared so high but that they were easily fulfilled, and whose placid content was not easily wounded. All she was wishing now was, that Harry were at home to receive his paper-case.

The return to Margaret was real pleasure. The narration of all that had passed was an event to her. She was so charmed with her presents, of every degree; things, unpleasant at the time, could, by drollery in the relating, be made mirthful fun ever after; Dr. May and the boys were so comical in their observations—Mary's wonder and simplicity came in so amazingly—and there was such merriment at Ethel's two precious jars, that she could hardly wish they had not come to her. On one head they were all agreed, in dislike of George Rivers, whom Mary pronounced to be a detestable man, and, when gently called to order by Margaret, defended it, by saying that Miss Bracy said it was better to detest than to hate, while Blanche coloured up to the ears, and hid herself behind the arm-chair; and Dr. May qualified the censure by saying, he believed there was no great harm in the youth, but that he was shallow-brained and extravagant, and, having been born in the days when Mr. Rivers had been working himself up in the world, had not had so good an education as his little half-sister.

"Well, what are you thinking of?" said her father, laying his hand on Ethel's arm, as she was wearily and pensively putting together the scattered purchases before going up to bed.

"I was thinking, papa, that there is a great deal of trouble taken in this world for a very little pleasure."

"The trouble is the pleasure, in most cases, most misanthropical miss!"

"Yes, that is true; but, if so, why cannot it be taken for some good?"

"They meant it to be good," said Dr. May. "Come, I cannot have you severe and ungrateful."

"So I have been telling myself, papa, all along; but, now that the day has come, and I have seen what jealousies, and competitions, and vanities, and disappointments it has produced—not even poor little Blanche allowed any comfort—I am almost sick at heart with thinking Cocksmoor was the excuse!"

"Spectators are more philosophical than actors, Ethel. Others have not been tying parcels all day."

"I had rather do that than— But that is the 'Fox and the Grapes,'" said Ethel, smiling. "What I mean is, that the real gladness of life is not in these great occasions of pleasure, but in the little side delights that come in the midst of one's work, don't they, papa? Why is it worth while to go and search for a day's pleasuring?"

"Ethel, my child! I don't like to hear you talk so," said Dr. May, looking anxiously at her. "It may be too true, but it is not youthful nor hopeful. It is not as your mother or I felt in our young days, when a treat was a treat to us, and gladdened our hearts long before and after. I am afraid you have been too much saddened with loss and care—"

"Oh, no, papa!" said Ethel, rousing herself, though speaking huskily. "You know I am your merry Ethel. You know I can be happy enough—only at home—"

And Ethel, though she had tried to be cheerful, leaned against his arm, and shed a few tears.

"The fact is, she is tired out," said Dr. May soothingly, yet half laughing. "She is not a beauty or a grace, and she is thoughtful and quiet, and so she moralises, instead of enjoying, as the world goes by. I dare say a night's rest will make all the difference in the world."

"Ah! but there is more to come. That Ladies' Committee at Cocksmoor!"

"They are not there yet, Ethel. Good-night, you tired little cynic."

CHAPTER IV.

Back then, complainer...
Go, to the world return, nor fear to cast
Thy bread upon the waters, sure at last
In joy to find it after many days. —Christian Year.

The next day Ethel had hoped for a return to reason, but behold, the world was cross! The reaction of the long excitement was felt, Gertrude fretted, and was unwell; Aubrey was pettish at his lessons; and Mary and Blanche were weary, yawning and inattentive; every straw was a burden, and Miss Bracy had feelings.

Ethel had been holding an interminable conversation with her in the schoolroom, interrupted at last by a summons to speak to a Cocksmoor woman at the back door, and she was returning from the kitchen, when the doctor called her into his study.

"Ethel! what is all this? Mary has found Miss Bracy in floods of tears in the schoolroom, because she says you told her she was ill-tempered."

"I am sure you will be quite as much surprised," said Ethel, somewhat exasperated, "when you hear that you lacerated her feelings yesterday."

"I? Why, what did I do?" exclaimed Dr. May.

"You showed your evident want of confidence in her."

"I? What can I have done?"

"You met Aubrey and Gertrude in her charge, and you took them away at once to walk with you."

"Well?"

"Well, that was it. She saw you had no confidence in her."

"Ethel, what on earth can you mean? I saw the two children dragging on her, and I thought she would see nothing that was

36

going on, and would be glad to be released; and I wanted them to go with me and see Meta's gold pheasants."

"That was the offence. She has been breaking her heart all this time, because she was sure, from your manner, that you were displeased to see them alone with her—eating bon-bons, I believe, and therefore took them away."

"Daisy is the worse for her bon-bons, I believe, but the overdose of them rests on my shoulders. I do not know how to believe you, Ethel. Of course you told her nothing of the kind crossed my mind, poor thing!"

"I told her so, over and over again, as I have done forty times before but her feelings are always being hurt."

"Poor thing, poor thing! no doubt it is a trying situation, and she is sensitive. Surely you are all forbearing with her?"

"I hope we are," said Ethel; "but how can we tell what vexes her?"

"And what is this, of your telling her she was ill-tempered?" asked Dr. May incredulously.

"Well, papa," said Ethel, softened, yet wounded by his thinking it so impossible. "I had often thought I ought to tell her that these sensitive feelings of hers were nothing but temper; and perhaps—indeed I know I do—I partake of the general fractiousness of the house to-day, and I did not bear it so patiently as usual. I did say that I thought it wrong to foster her fancies; for if she looked at them coolly, she would find they were only a form of pride and temper."

"It did not come well from you, Ethel," said the doctor, looking vexed.

"No, I know it did not," said Ethel meekly; "but oh! to have these janglings once a week, and to see no end to them!"

"Once a week?"

"It is really as often, or more often," said Ethel. "If any of us criticise anything the girls have done, if there is a change in any arrangement, if she thinks herself neglected—I can't tell you what little matters suffice; she will catch me, and argue with me, till— oh, till we are both half dead, and yet cannot stop ourselves."

"Why do you argue?"

"If I could only help it!"

"Bad management," said the doctor, in a low, musing tone. "You want a head!" and he sighed.

"Oh, papa, I did not mean to distress you. I would not have told you if I had remembered—but I am worried to-day, and off my guard—"

"Ethel, I thought you were the one on whom I could depend for bearing everything."

"These were such nonsense!"

"What may seem nonsense to you is not the same to her. You must be forbearing, Ethel. Remember that dependence is prone to morbid sensitiveness, especially in those who have a humble estimate of themselves."

"It seems to me that touchiness is more pride than humility," said Ethel, whose temper, already not in the smoothest state, found it hard that, after having long borne patiently with these constant arguments, she should find Miss Bracy made the chief object of compassion.

Dr. May's chivalrous feeling caused him to take the part of the weak, and he answered, "You know nothing about it. Among our own kith and kin we can afford to pass over slights, because we are sure the heart is right—we do not know what it is to be among strangers, uncertain of any claim to their esteem or kindness. Sad! sad!" he continued, as the picture wrought on him. "Each trifle seems a token one way or the other! I am very sorry I grieved the poor thing yesterday. I must go and tell her so at once."

He put Ethel aside, and knocked at the schoolroom door, while Ethel stood, mortified. "He thinks I have been neglecting, or speaking harshly to her! For fifty times that I have borne with her maundering, I have, at last, once told her the truth; and for that I am accused of want of forbearance! Now he will go and make much of her, and pity her, till she will think herself an injured heroine, and be worse than ever; and he will do away with all the good of my advice, and want me to ask her pardon for it—but that I never will. It was only the truth, and I will stick to it."

"Ethel!" cried Mary, running up to her, then slackening her pace, and whispering, "you did not tell Miss Bracy she was ill-tempered."

"No—not exactly. How could you tell papa I did?"

"She said so. She was crying, and I asked what was the matter, and she said my sister Ethel said she was ill-tempered."

"She made a great exaggeration then," said Ethel.

"I am sure she was very cross all day," said Mary.

"Well, that is no business of yours," said Ethel pettishly. "What now? Mary, don't look out at the street window."

"It is Flora—the Grange carriage," whispered Mary, as the two sisters made a precipitate retreat into the drawing-room.

Meanwhile, Dr. May had been in the schoolroom. Miss Bracy had ceased her tears before he came—they had been her retort on Ethel, and she had not intended the world to know of them. Half disconcerted, half angry, she heard the doctor approach. She was a gentle, tearful woman, one of those who are often called meek, under an erroneous idea that meekness consists in making herself exceedingly miserable under every kind of grievance; and she now had a sort of melancholy satisfaction in believing that the young ladies had fabricated an exaggerated complaint of her temper, and that she was going to become injured innocence. To think herself accused of a great wrong, excused her from perceiving herself guilty of a lesser one.

"Miss Bracy," said Dr. May, entering with his frank, sweet look, "I am concerned that I vexed you by taking the children to walk with me yesterday. I thought such little brats would be troublesome to any but their spoiling papa, but they would have been in safer hands with you. You would not have been as weak as I was, in regard to sugar-plums." Such amends as these confused Miss Bracy, who found it pleasanter to be lamentable with Ethel, than to receive a full apology for her imagined offence from the master of the house. Feeling both small and absurd, she murmured something of "oh, no," and "being sure," and hoped he was going, so that she might sit down to pity herself, for those girls having made her appear so ridiculous.

No such thing! Dr. May put a chair for her, and sat down himself, saying, with a smile, "You see, you must trust us sometimes, and overlook it, if we are less considerate than we might be. We have rough, careless habits with each other, and forget that all are not used to them."

Miss Bracy exclaimed, "Oh, no, never, they were most kind."

"We wish to be," said Dr. May, "but there are little neglects—or you think there are. I will not say there are none, for that would be answering too much for human nature, or that they are fanciful—for that would be as little comfort as to tell a patient that the pain is only nervous—"

Miss Bracy smiled, for she could remember instances when, after suffering much at the time, she had found the affront imaginary.

He was glad of that smile, and proceeded. "You will let me speak to you, as to one of my own girls? To them, I should say, use the only true cure. Don't brood over vexations, small or great, but think of them as trials that, borne bravely, become blessings."

"Oh! but Dr. May!" she exclaimed, shocked; "nothing in your house could call for such feelings."

"I hope we are not very savage," he said, smiling; "but, indeed, I still say it is the safest rule. It would be the only one if you were really among unkind people; and, if you take so much to heart an unlucky neglect of mine, what would you do if the slight were a true one?"

"You are right; but my feelings were always over-sensitive;" and this she said with a sort of complacency.

"Well, we must try to brace them," said Dr. May, much as if prescribing for her. "Will not you believe in our confidence and esteem, and harden yourself against any outward unintentional piece of incivility?"

She felt as if she could at that moment.

"Or at least, try to forgive and forget them. Talking them over only deepens the sense of them, and discussions do no good to any one. My daughters are anxious to be your best friends, as I hope you know."

"Oh! they are most kind—"

"But, you see, I must say this," added Dr. May, somewhat hesitating, "as they have no mother to—to spare all this," and then, growing clearer, he proceeded, "I must beg you to be forbearing with them, and not perplex yourself and them with arguing on what cannot be helped. They have not the experience that could enable them to finish such a discussion without unkindness; and it can only waste the spirits, and raise fresh subjects of regret. I must leave you—I hear myself called."

Miss Bracy began to be sensible that she had somewhat abused Ethel's patience; and the unfortunate speech about the source of her sensitiveness did not appear to her so direfully cruel as at first. She hoped every one would forget all about it, and resolved not to take umbrage so easily another time, or else be silent about it, but she was not a person of much resolution.

The doctor found that Meta Rivers and her brother had brought Flora home, and were in the drawing-room, where Margaret was hearing another edition of the history of the fair, and a by-play was going on, of teasing Blanche about the chain.

George Rivers was trying to persuade her to make one for him; and her refusal came out at last, in an almost passionate key, in the midst of the other conversation— "No! I say-no!"

"Another no, and that will be yes."

"No! I won't! I don't like you well enough!"

Margaret gravely sent Blanche and the other children away to take their walk, and the brother and sister soon after took leave, when

Flora called Ethel to hasten to the Ladies' Committee, that they might arrange the disposal of the one hundred and fifty pounds, the amount of their gains.

"To see the fate of Cocksmoor," said Ethel.

"Do you think I cannot manage the Stoneborough folk?" said Flora, looking radiant with good humour, and conscious of power. "Poor Ethel! I am doing you good against your will! Never mind, here is wherewith to build the school, and the management will be too happy to fall into our hands. Do you think every one is as ready as you are, to walk three miles and back continually?"

There was sense in this; there always was sense in what Flora said, but it jarred on Ethel; and it seemed almost unsympathising in her to be so gay, when the rest were wearied or perturbed. Ethel would have been very glad of a short space to recollect herself, and recover her good temper; but it was late, and Flora hurried her to put on her bonnet, and come to the committee. "I'll take care of your interests," she said, as they set out. "You look as doleful as if you thought you should be robbed of Cocksmoor; but that is the last thing that will happen, you will see."

"It would not be acting fairly to let them build for us, and then for us to put them out of the management," said Ethel.

"My dear, they want importance, not action. They will leave the real power to us of themselves."

"You like to build Cocksmoor with such instruments," said Ethel, whose ruffled condition made her forget her resolution not to argue with Flora.

"Bricks are made of clay!" said Flora. "There, that was said like Norman himself! On your plan, we might have gone on for forty years, saving seven shillings a year, and spending six, whenever there was an illness in the place."

"You, who used to dislike these people more than even I did!" said Ethel.

"That was when I was an infant, my dear, and did not know how to deal with them. I will take care—I will even save Cherry Elwood for you, if I can. Alan Ernescliffe's ten pounds is a noble weapon."

"You always mean to manage everything, and then you have no time!" said Ethel, sensible all the time of her own ill-humour, and of her sister's patience and amiability, yet propelled to speak the unpleasant truths that in her better moods were held back.

Still Flora was good-tempered, though Ethel would almost have preferred her being provoked; "I know," she said, "I have been using you ill, and leaving the world on your shoulders, but it was all in your service and Cocksmoor's; and now we shall begin to be reasonable and useful again."

"I hope so," said Ethel.

"Really, Ethel, to comfort you, I think I shall send you with Norman to dine at Abbotstoke Grange on Wednesday. Mr. Rivers begged us to come; he is so anxious to make it lively for his son."

"Thank you, I do not think Mr. George Rivers and I should be likely to get on together. What a bad style of wit! You heard what Mary said about him? and Ethel repeated the doubt between hating and detesting.

"Young men never know how to talk to little girls," was Flora's reply.

At this moment they came up with one of the Miss Andersons, and Flora began to exchange civilities, and talk over yesterday's events with great animation. Her notice always gave pleasure, brightened as it was by the peculiarly engaging address which she had inherited from her father, and which, therefore, was perfectly easy and natural. Fanny Anderson was flattered and gratified, rather by the manner than the words, and, on excellent terms, they entered the committee-room, namely, the schoolmistress's parlour.

There were nine ladies on the committee—nine muses, as the doctor called them, because they produced anything but harmony. Mrs. Ledwich was in the chair; Miss Rich was secretary, and had her pen and ink, and account-book ready. Flora came in, smiling and greeting; Ethel, grave, earnest, and annoyed, behind her, trying to be perfectly civil, but not at all enjoying the congratulations on the successful bazaar. The ladies all talked and discussed their yesterday's adventures, gathering in little knots, as they traced the fate of favourite achievements of their skill, while Ethel, lugubrious and impatient, beside Flora, the only one not engaged, and, therefore, conscious of the hubbub of clacking tongues.

At last Mrs. Ledwich glanced at the mistress's watch, in its pasteboard tower, in Gothic architecture, and insisted on proceeding to business. So they all sat down round a circular table, with a very fine red, blue, and black oilcloth, whose pattern was inseparably connected, in Ethel's mind, with absurdity, tedium, and annoyance.

The business was opened by the announcement of what they all knew before, that the proceeds of the fancy fair amounted to one hundred and forty-nine pounds fifteen shillings and tenpence.

Then came a pause, and Mrs. Ledwich said that next they had to consider what was the best means of disposing of the sum gained in this most gratifying manner. Every one except Flora, Ethel, and quiet Mrs. Ward, began to talk at once. There was a great deal about Elizabethan architecture, crossed by much more, in which normal, industrial, and common things, most often met Ethel's ear, with some stories, second-hand, from Harvey Anderson, of marvellous mistakes; and, on the opposite side of the table, there was Mrs. Ledwich, impressively saying something to the silent Mrs. Ward, marking her periods with emphatic beats with her pencil, and each seemed to close with "Mrs. Perkinson's niece," whom Ethel knew to be Cherry's intended supplanter. She looked piteously at Flora, who only smiled and made a sign with her hand to her to be patient. Ethel fretted inwardly at that serene sense of power; but she could not but admire how well Flora knew how to bide her time, when, having waited till Mrs. Ledwich had nearly wound up her discourse on Mrs. Elwood's impudence, and Mrs. Perkinson's niece, she leaned towards Miss Boulder, who sat between, and whispered to her, "Ask Mrs. Ledwich if we should not begin with some steps for getting the land."

Miss Boulder, having acted as conductor, the president exclaimed, "Just so, the land is the first consideration. We must at once take steps for obtaining it." Thereupon Mrs. Ledwich, who "always did things methodically," moved, and Miss Anderson seconded, that the land requisite for the school must be obtained, and the nine ladies held up their hands, and resolved it.

Miss Rich duly recorded the great resolution, and Miss Boulder suggested that, perhaps, they might write to the National Society, or Government, or something; whereat Miss Rich began to flourish one of the very long goose quills which stood in the inkstand before her, chiefly as insignia of office, for she always wrote with a small, stiff metal pen.

Flora here threw in a query, whether the National Society, or Government, or something, would give them a grant, unless they had the land to build upon?

The ladies all started off hereupon, and all sorts of instances of hardness of heart were mentioned, the most relevant of which was, that the Church Building Society would not give a grant to Mr. Holloway's proprietary chapel at Whitford, when Mrs. Ledwich was suddenly struck with the notion that dear Mr. Holloway might be prevailed on to come to Stoneborough to preach a sermon in the Minster, for the benefit of Cocksmoor, when they would all hold plates at the door. Flora gave Ethel a tranquillising pat, and, as Mrs. Ledwich turned to her, asking whether she thought Dr. May, or Dr. Hoxton, would prevail on him to come, she said, with her winning look, "I think that consideration had better wait till we have some more definite view. Had we not better turn to this land question?"

"Quite true!" they all agreed, but to whom did the land belong?— and what a chorus arose! Miss Anderson thought it belonged to Mr. Nicolson, because the wagons of slate had James Nicolson on them, and, if so, they had no chance, for he was an old miser—and six stories illustrative thereof ensued. Miss Rich was quite sure some Body held it, and Bodies were slow of movement. Mrs. Ledwich remembered some question of enclosing, and thought all waste lands were under the Crown; she knew that the Stoneborough people once had a right to pasture their cattle, because Mr. Southron's cow had tumbled down a loam-pit when her mother was a girl. No, that was on Far-view down, out the other way! Miss Harrison was positive that Sir Henry Walkinghame had some right there, and would not Dr. May apply to him? Mrs. Grey thought it ought to be part of the Drydale estate, and Miss Boulder was certain that Mr. Bramshaw knew all about it.

Flora's gentle voice carried conviction that she knew what she was saying, when, at last, they left a moment for her to speak—(Ethel would have done so long ago). "If I am not mistaken, the land is a copyhold of Sir Henry Walkinghame, held under the manor of Drydale, which belongs to M— College, and is underlet to Mr. Nicolson."

Everybody, being partially right, was delighted, and had known it all before; Miss Boulder agreed with Miss Anderson that Miss May had stated it as lucidly as Mr. Bramshaw could. The next question was, to whom to apply? and, after as much as was expedient had been said in favour of each, it was decided that, as Sir Henry Walkinghame was abroad, no one knew exactly where, it would be best to go to the fountain-head, and write at once to the principal of the college. But who was to write? Flora proposed Mr. Ramsden as the fittest person, but this was negatived. Every one declared that he would never take the trouble, and Miss Rich began to agitate her pens. By this time, however, Mrs. Ward, who was opposite to the Gothic clock-tower, began to look uneasy, and suggested, in a nervous manner, that it was half-past five, and she was afraid Mr. Ward would be kept waiting for his dinner. Mrs. Grey began to have like fears, that Mr. Grey would be come in from his ride after banking hours. The other ladies began to think of tea, and the meeting decided on adjourning till that day next week, when the committee would sit upon Miss Rich's letter.

"My dear Miss Flora!" began Miss Rich, adhering to her as they parted with the rest at the end of the street, "how am I to write to a principal? Am I to begin Reverend Sir, or My Lord, or is he Venerable, like an archdeacon? What is his name, and what am I to say?"

"Why, it is not a correspondence much in my line," said Flora, laughing.

"Ah! but you are so intimate with Dr. Hoxton, and your brothers at Oxford! You must know—"

"I'll take advice," said Flora good-naturedly. "Shall I come, and call before Friday, and tell you the result?"

"Oh, pray! It will be a real favour! Good-morning—"

"There," said Flora, as the sisters turned homewards, "Cherry is not going to be turned out just yet!"

"How could you, Flora? Now they will have that man from Whitford, and you said not a word against it!"

"What was the use of adding to the hubbub? A little opposition would make them determined on having him. You will see, Ethel, we shall get the ground on our own terms, and then it will be time to settle about the mistress. If the harvest holidays were not over, we would try to send Cherry to a training-school, so as to leave them no excuse."

"I hate all this management and contrivance. It would be more honest to speak our minds, and not pretend to agree with them."

"My dear Ethel! have I spoken a word contrary to my opinion? It is not fit for me, a girl of twenty, to go disputing and dragooning as you would have me; but a little savoir faire, a grain of common sense, thrown in among the babble, always works. Don't you remember how Mrs. Ward's sister told us that a whole crowd of tottering Chinese ladies would lean on her, because they felt her firm support, though it was out of sight?"

Ethel did not answer; she had self-control enough left not to retort upon Flora's estimate of herself, but the irritation was strong; she felt as if her cherished views for Cocksmoor were insulted, as well as set aside, by the place being made the occasion of so much folly and vain prattle, the sanctity of her vision of self-devotion destroyed by such interference, and Flora's promises did not reassure her. She doubted Flora's power, and had still more repugnance to the means by which her sister tried to govern; they did not seem to her straightforward, and she could not endure Flora's complacency in their success. Had it not been for her real love for the place and people, as well as the principle which prompted that love, she could have found it in her heart to throw up all concern with it, rather than become a fellow-worker with such a conclave.

Such were Ethel's feelings as the pair walked down the street; the one sister bright and smiling with the good humour that had endured many shocks all that day, all good nature and triumph, looking forward to success, great benefit to Cocksmoor, and plenty of management, with credit and praise to herself; the other, downcast and irritable, with annoyance at the interference with her schemes, at the prospects of her school, and at herself for being out of temper, prone to murmur or to reply tartly, and not able to recover from her mood, but only, as she neared the house, lapsing into her other trouble, and preparing to resist any misjudged, though kind attempt of her father, to make her unsay her rebuke to Miss Bracy. Pride and temper! Ah! Etheldred! where were they now?

Dr. May was at his study door as his daughters entered the hall, and Ethel expected the order which she meant to question; but, instead of this, after a brief inquiry after the doings of the nine muses, which Flora answered, so as to make him laugh, he stopped Ethel, as she was going upstairs, by saying, "I do not know whether this letter is intended for Richard, or for me. At any rate, it concerns you most."

The envelope was addressed to the Reverend Richard May, D. D., Market Stoneborough, and the letter began, "Reverend Sir." So far Ethel saw, and exclaimed, with amusement, then, with a long-drawn "Ah!" and an interjection, "My poor dear Una!" she became absorbed, the large tears—yes, Ethel's reluctant tears gathering slowly and dropping.

The letter was from a clergyman far away in the north of England, who said he could not, though a stranger, resist the desire to send to Dr. May an account of a poor girl, who seemed to have received great benefits from him, or from some of his family, especially as she had shown great eagerness on his proposing to write.

He said it was nearly a year since there had come into his parish a troop of railwaymen and their families. For the most part, they were completely wild and rude, unused to any pastoral care; but, even on the first Sunday, he had noticed a keen-looking, freckled, ragged, unmistakably Irish girl, creeping into church with a Prayer-book in her hand, and had afterwards found her hanging about the door of the school. "I never saw a more engaging, though droll, wild expression, than that with which she looked up to me." (Ethel's cry of delight was at that sentence—she knew that look too well, and had yearned after it so often!) "I found her far better instructed than her appearance had led me to expect, and more truly impressed with the spirit of what she had learned than it has often been my lot to find children. She was perfect in the New Testament history" —("Ah! that she was not, when she went away!")—"and was in the habit of constantly attending church, and using morning and evening prayers." ("Oh! how I longed, when she went away, to beg her to keep them up! Dear Una.") "On my questions, as to how she had been taught, she always replied, 'Mr. Richard May,' or 'Miss Athel.' You must excuse me if I have not correctly caught the name from her Irish pronunciation." ("I am afraid he thinks my name is Athaliah! But oh! this dear girl! How I have wished to hear of her!") "Everything was answered with 'Mr. Richard,' or 'Miss Athel'; and, if I inquired further, her face would light up with a beam of gratitude, and she would run on, as long as I could listen, with instances of their kindness. It was the same with her mother, a wild, rude specimen of an Irishwoman, whom I never could bring to church herself, but who ran on loudly with their praises, usually ending with 'Heavens be their bed,' and saying that Una had been quite a different girl since the young ladies and gentleman found her out, and put them parables in her head.

"For my own part, I can testify that, in the seven months that she attended my school, I never had a serious fault to find with her, but far more often to admire the earnestness and devout spirit, as well as the kindness and generosity apparent in all her conduct. Bad living, and an unwholesome locality, have occasioned a typhus fever among the poor strangers in this place, and Una was one of the first victims. Her mother, almost from the first, gave her up, saying she knew she was one marked for glory; and Una has been lying, day after day, in a sort of half-delirious state, constantly repeating hymns and psalms, and generally, apparently very happy, except when one distress occurred again and again, whether delirious or sensible, namely, that she had never gone to wish Miss May good-bye, and thank her; and that maybe she and Mr. Richard thought her ungrateful; and she would sometimes beg, in her phraseology, to go on her bare knees to Stoneborough, only to see Miss Athel again.

"Her mother, I should say, told me the girl had been half mad at not being allowed to go and take leave of Miss May; and she had been sorry herself, but her husband had come home suddenly from the search for work, and, having made his arrangements, removed them at once, early the next morning—too early to go to the young lady; though, she said, Una did—as they passed through Stoneborough—run down the street before she was aware, and she found her sobbing, fit to break her heart, before the house." ("Oh, why, why was I not up, and at the window! Oh, my Una! to think of that!") "When I spoke of writing to let Miss May hear how it was, the poor girl caught at the idea with the utmost delight. Her weakness was too great to allow her to utter many words distinctly, when I asked her what she would have me say, but these were as well as I could understand:—'The blessing of one, that they have brought peace unto. Tell them I pray, and will pray, that they may walk in the robe of glory—and tell Mr. Richard that I mind what he said to me, of taking hold on the sure hope. God crown all their crosses unto them, and fulfil all their desires unto everlasting life.' I feel that I am not rendering her words with all their fervour and beauty of Irish expression, but I would that I could fully retain and transmit them, for those who have so led her must, indeed, be able to feel them precious. I never saw a more peaceful frame of penitence and joy. She died last night, sleeping herself away, without more apparent suffering, and will be committed to the earth on Sunday next, all her fellow-scholars attending; and, I hope, profiting by the example she has left.

"I have only to add my most earnest congratulations to those whose labour of love has borne such blessed fruit; and, hoping you will pardon the liberty, etc."

Etheldred finished the letter through blinding tears, while rising sobs almost choked her. She ran away to her own room, bolted the door, and threw herself on her knees, beside her bed—now confusedly giving thanks for such results—now weeping bitterly over her own unworthiness. Oh! what was she in the sight of Heaven, compared with what this poor girl had deemed her—with what this clergyman thought her? She, the teacher, taught, trained, and guarded, from her infancy, by her wise mother, and by such a father! She, to have given way all day to pride, jealousy, anger, selfish love of her own will; when this poor girl had embraced, and held fast, the blessed hope, from the very crumbs they had brought her! Nothing could have so humbled the distrustful spirit that had been working in Ethel, which had been scotched into silence—not killed—when she endured the bazaar, and now had been indemnifying itself by repining at every stumbling-block. Her own scholar's blessing was the rebuke that went most home to her heart, for having doubted whether good could be worked in any way, save her own.

She was interrupted by Mary trying to open the door, and, admitting her, heard her wonder at the traces of her tears, and ask what there was about Una. Ethel gave her the letter, and Mary's tears showered very fast—they always came readily. "Oh, Ethel, how glad Richard will be!"

"Yes; it is all Richard's doing. So much more good, and wise, and humble, as he is. No wonder his teaching—" and Ethel sat down and cried again.

Mary pondered. " It makes me very glad," she said; "and yet I don't know why one cries. Ethel, do you think"—she came near, and whispered—"that Una has met dear mamma there?"

Ethel kissed her. It was almost the first time Mary had spoken of her mother; and she answered, "Dear Mary, we cannot tell—we may think. It is all one communion, you know."

Mary was silent, and, next time she spoke, it was to hope that Ethel would tell the Cocksmoor children about Una.

Ethel was obliged to dress, and go downstairs to tea. Her father seemed to have been watching for her, with his study door open, for he came to meet her, took her hand, and said, in a low voice, "My dear child, I wish you joy. This will be a pleasant message, to bid poor Ritchie good speed for his ordination, will it not?"

"That it will, papa—"

"Why, Ethel, have you been crying over it all this time?" said he, struck by the sadness of her voice.

"Many other things, papa. I am so unworthy—but it was not our doing—but the grace—"

"No, but thankful you may be, to have been the means of awakening the grace!"

Ethel's lips trembled. "And oh, papa! coming to-day, when I have been behaving so ill to you, and Miss Bracy, and Flora, and all.

"Have you? I did not know you had behaved ill to me."

"About Miss Bracy—I thought wrong things, if I did not say them. To her, I believe, I said what was true, though it was harsh of me to say it, and—"

"What? about pride and temper? It was true, and I hope it will do her good. Cure a piping turkey with a peppercorn sometimes. I have spoken to her, and told her to pluck up a little spirit; not fancy affronts, and not to pester you with them. Poor child! you have been sadly victimised to-day and yesterday. No wonder you were bored past patience, with that absurd rabble of women!"

"It was all my own selfish, distrustful temper, wanting to have Cocksmoor taken care of in my own way, and angry at being interfered with. I see it now—and here this poor girl, that I thought thrown away—"

"Ay, Ethel, you will often see the like. The main object may fail or fall short, but the earnest painstaking will always be blessed some way or other, and where we thought it most wasted, some fresh green shoot will spring up, to show it is not we that give the increase. I suppose you will write to Richard with this?"

"That I shall."

"Then you may send this with it. Tell him my arm is tired and stiff to-day, or I would have said more. He must answer the clergyman's letter."

Dr. May gave Ethel his sheet not folded. His written words were now so few as to be cherished amongst his children.

"Dear Richard,—

"May all your ministerial works be as blessed as this, your first labour of love. I give you hearty joy of this strengthening blessing. Mine goes with it—'Only be strong and of a good courage!'

—Your affectionate father, R. May.

"PS.—Margaret does not gain ground this summer; you must soon come home and cheer her."

CHAPTER V.

As late, engaged by fancy's dream,
I lay beside a rapid stream,
I saw my first come gliding by,
Its airy form soon caught my eye;
Its texture frail, and colour various,
Like human hopes, and life precarious.
Sudden, my second caught my ear,
And filled my soul with constant fear;
I quickly rose, and home I ran,
My whole was hissing in the pan. — Riddle.

Flora revised the letter to the principal, and the Ladies' Committee approved, after having proposed seven amendments, all of which Flora caused to topple over by their own weakness.

After interval sufficient to render the nine ladies very anxious, the principal wrote from Scotland, where he was spending the Long Vacation, and informed them that their request should he laid before the next college meeting.

After the committee had sat upon this letter, the two sisters walked home in much greater harmony than after the former meeting. Etheldred had recovered her candour, and was willing to own that it was not art, but good sense, that gave her sister so much ascendancy. She began to be hopeful, and to declare that Flora might yet do something even with the ladies. Flora was gratified by the approval that no one in the house could help valuing; "Positively," said Flora, "I believe I may in time. You see there are different ways of acting, as an authority, or as an equal."

"The authority can move from without, the equal must from within," said Ethel.

"Just so. We must circumvent their prejudices, instead of trying to beat them down."

"If you only could have the proper catechising restored!"

"Wait; you will see. Let me feel my ground."

"Or if we could only abdicate into the hands of the rightful power!"

"The rightful power would not be much obliged to you."

"That is the worst of it," said Ethel. "It is sad to hear the sick people say that Dr. May is more to them than any parson; it shows that they have so entirely lost the notion of what their clergyman should be."

"Dr. May is the man most looked up to in this town," said Flora, "and that gives weight to us in the committee, but it is all in the using."

"Yes," said Ethel hesitatingly.

"You see, we have the prestige of better birth, and better education, as well as of having the chief property in the town, and of being the largest subscribers, added to his personal character," said Flora;

"so that everything conspires to render us leaders, and our age alone prevented us from assuming our post sooner."

They were at home by this time, and entering the hall, perceived that the whole party were in the lawn. The consolation of the children for the departure of Hector and Tom, was a bowl of soap-suds and some tobacco pipes, and they had collected the house to admire and assist, even Margaret's couch being drawn close to the window.

Bubbles is one of the most fascinating of sports. There is the soft foamy mass, like driven snow, or like whipped cream. Blanche bends down to blow "a honeycomb," holding the bowl of the pipe in the water; at her gurgling blasts there slowly heaves upwards the pile of larger, clearer bubbles, each reflecting the whole scene, and sparkling with rainbow tints, until Aubrey ruthlessly dashes all into fragments with his hand, and Mary pronounces it stiff enough, and presents a pipe to little Daisy, who, drawing the liquid into her mouth, throws it away with a grimace, and declares that she does not like bubbles! But Aubrey stands with swelled cheeks, gravely puffing at the sealing-waxed extremity. Out pours a confused assemblage of froth, but the glassy globe slowly expands the little branching veins, flowing down on either side, bearing an enlarging miniature of the sky, the clouds, the tulip-tree. Aubrey pauses to exclaim! but where is it? Try again! A proud bubble, as Mary calls it, a peacock, in blended pink and green, is this transparent sphere, reflecting and embellishing house, wall, and shrubs! It is too beautiful! It is gone! Mary undertakes to give a lesson, and blows deliberately without the slightest result. Again! She waves her disengaged hand in silent exultation as the airy balls detach themselves, and float off on the summer breeze, with a tardy, graceful, uncertain motion. Daisy rushes after them, catches at them, and looks at her empty fingers with a puzzled "All gone!" as plainly expressed by Toby, who snaps at them, and shakes his head with offended dignity at the shock of his meeting teeth, while the kitten frisks after them, striking at them with her paw, amazed at meeting vacancy.

Even the grave Norman is drawn in. He agrees with Mary that bubbles used to fly over the wall, and that one once went into Mrs. Richardson's garret window, when her housemaid tried to catch it with a pair of tongs, and then ran downstairs screaming that there was a ghost in her room; but that was in Harry's time, the heroic age of the May nursery.

He accepts a pipe, and his greater height raises it into a favourable current of air—the glistening balloon sails off. It flies, it soars; no, it is coming down! The children shout at it, as if to drive it up, but it wilfully descends—they rush beneath, they try to waft it on high with their breath—there is a collision between Mary and Blanche—Aubrey perceives a taste of soapy water—the bubble is no more—it is vanished in his open mouth!

Papa himself has taken a pipe, and the little ones are mounted on chairs, to be on a level with their tall elders. A painted globe is swimming along, hesitating at first, but the dancing motion is tending upwards, the rainbow tints glisten in the sunlight—all rush to assist it; if breath of the lips can uphold it, it should rise, indeed! Up! above the wall! over Mrs. Richardson's elm, over the topmost branch—hurrah! out of sight! Margaret adds her voice to the acclamations. Beat that if you can, Mary! That doubtful wind keeps yours suspended in a graceful minuet; its pace is accelerated—but earthwards! it has committed self-destruction by running foul of a rose-bush. A general blank!

"You here, Ethel?" said Norman, as the elders laughed at each other's baffled faces.

"I am more surprised to find you here," she answered.

"Excitement!" said Norman, smiling; "one cause is as good as another for it."

"Very pretty sport," said Dr. May. "You should write a poem on it, Norman."

"It is an exhausted subject," said Norman; "bubble and trouble are too obvious a rhyme."

"Ha! there it goes! It will be over the house! That's right!"

Every one joined in the outcry.

"Whose is it?"

"Blanche's—"

"Hurrah for Blanche! Well done, white Mayflower, there!" said the doctor, "that is what I meant. See the applause gained by a proud bubble that flies! Don't we all bow down to it, and waft it up with the whole force of our lungs, air as it is; and when it fairly goes out of sight, is there any exhilaration or applause that surpasses ours?"

"The whole world being bent on making painted bubbles fly over the house," said Norman, far more thoughtfully than his father. "It is a fair pattern of life and fame."

"I was thinking," continued Dr. May, "what was the most unalloyed exultation I remember."

"Harry's, when you were made dux," whispered Ethel to her brother.

"Not mine," said Norman briefly.

"I believe," said Dr. May, "I never knew such glorification as when Aubrey Spencer climbed the poor old market-cross. We all felt ourselves made illustrious for ever in his person."

"Nay, papa, when you got that gold medal must have been the grandest time?" said Blanche, who had been listening.

Dr. May laughed, and patted her. "I, Blanche? Why, I was excessively amazed, that is all, not in Norman's way, but I had been doing next to nothing to the very last, then fell into an agony, and worked like a horse, thinking myself sure of failure, and that my mother and my uncle would break their hearts."

"But when you heard that you had it?" persisted Blanche.

"Why, then I found I must be a much cleverer fellow than I thought for!" said he, laughing; "but I was ashamed of myself, and of the authorities, for choosing such an idle dog, and vexed that other plodding lads missed it, who deserved it more than I."

"Of course," said Norman, in a low voice, "that is what one always feels. I had rather blow soap-bubbles!"

"Where was Dr. Spencer?" asked Ethel.

"Not competing. He had been ready a year before, and had gained it, or I should have had no chance. Poor Spencer! what would I not give to see him, or hear of him?"

"The last was—how long ago?" said Ethel.

"Six years, when he was setting off, to return from Poonshedagore," said Dr. May, sighing. "I gave him up; his health was broken, and there was no one to look after him. He was the sort of man to have a nameless grave, and a name too blessed for fame."

Ethel would have asked further of her father's dear old friend, but there were sounds, denoting an arrival, and Margaret beckoned to them as Miss Rivers and her brother were ushered into the drawing-room; and Blanche instantly fled away, with her basin, to hide herself in the schoolroom.

Meta skipped out, and soon was established on the grass, an attraction to all the live creatures, as it seemed; for the kitten came, and was caressed till her own graceful Nipen was ready to fight with the uncouth Toby for the possession of a resting-place on the skirt of her habit, while Daisy nestled up to her, as claiming a privilege, and Aubrey kept guard over the dogs.

Meta inquired after a huge doll—Dr. Hoxton's gift to Daisy, at the bazaar.

"She is in Margaret's wardrobe," was the answer, "because Aubrey tied her hands behind her, and was going to offer her up on the nursery grate."

"Oh, Aubrey, that was too cruel!"

"No," returned Aubrey; "she was Iphigenia, going to be sacrificed."

"Mary unconsciously acted Diana," said Ethel, "and bore the victim away."

"Pray, was Daisy a willing Clytemnestra?" asked Meta.

"Oh, yes, she liked it," said Aubrey, while Meta looked discomfited.

"I never could get proper respect paid to dolls," said Margaret; "we deal too much in their natural enemies."

"Yes," said Ethel, "my only doll was like a heraldic lion, couped in all her parts."

"Harry and Tom once made a general execution," said Flora; "there was a doll hanging to every baluster—the number made up with rag."

George Rivers burst out laughing—his first sign of life; and Meta looked as if she had heard of so many murders.

"I can't help feeling for a doll!" she said. "They used to be like sisters to me. I feel as if they were wasted on children, that see no character in them, and only call them Dolly."

"I agree with you," said Margaret. "If there had been no live dolls, Richard and I should have reared our doll family as judiciously as tenderly. There are treasures of carpentry still extant, that he made for them."

"Oh, I am so glad!" cried Meta, as if she had found another point of union. "If I were to confess—there is a dear old Rose in the secret recesses of my wardrobe. I could as soon throw away my sister—"

"Ha!" cried her brother, laying hold of the child, "here, little Daisy, will you give your doll to Meta?"

"My name is Gertrude Margaret May," said the little round mouth. The fat arm was drawn back, with all a baby's dignity, and the rosy face was hidden in Dr. May's breast, at the sound of George Rivers's broad laugh and "Well done, little one!"

Dr. May put his arm round her, turned aside from him, and began talking to Meta about Mr. Rivers.

Flora and Norman made conversation for the brother; and he presently asked Norman to go out shooting with him, but looked so amazed on hearing that Norman was no sportsman that Flora tried to save the family credit by mentioning Hector's love of a gun, which caused their guest to make a general tender of sporting privileges;

"Though," added he, with a drawl, "shooting is rather a nuisance, especially alone."

Meta told Ethel, a little apart, that he was so tired of going out alone, that he had brought her here, in search of a companion.

"He comes in at eleven o'clock, poor fellow, quite tired with solitude," said she, "and comes to me to be entertained."

"Indeed," exclaimed Ethel. "What can you do?"

"What I can," said Meta, laughing. "Whatever is not 'a horrid nuisance' to him."

"It would be a horrid nuisance to me," said Ethel bluntly, "if my brothers wanted me to amuse them all the morning."

"Your brothers, oh!" said Meta, as if that were very different; "besides, you have so much more to do. I am only too glad and grateful when George will come to me at all. You see I have always been too young to be his companion, or find out what suited him, and now he is so very kind and good-natured to me."

"But what becomes of your business?"

"I get time, one way or another. There is the evening, very often, when I have sung both him and papa to sleep. I had two hours, all to myself, yesterday night," said Meta, with a look of congratulation, "and I had a famous reading of Thirlwall's 'Greece.'"

"I should think that such evenings were as bad as the mornings."

"Come", Ethel, don't make me naughty. Large families, like yours, may have merry, sociable evenings; but, I do assure you, ours are very pleasant. We are so pleased to have George at home; and we really hope that he is taking a fancy to the dear Grange. You can't think how delighted papa is to have him content to stay quietly with us so long. I must call him to go back now, though, or papa will be kept waiting."

When Ethel had watched the tall, ponderous brother help the bright fairy sister to fly airily into her saddle, and her sparkling glance, and wave of the hand, as she cantered off, contrasting with his slow bend, and immobility of feature, she could not help saying that Meta's life certainly was not too charming, with her fanciful, valetudinarian father, and that stupid, idealess brother.

"He is very amiable and good-natured," interposed Norman.

"Ha! Norman, you are quite won by his invitation to shoot! How he despised you for refusing—as much as you despised him."

"Speak for yourself," said Norman. "You fancy no sensible man likes shooting, but you are all wrong. Some of our best men are capital sportsmen. Why, there is Ogilvie—you know what he is. When I bring him down here, you will see that there is no sort of sport that he is not keen after."

"This poor fellow will never be keen after anything," said Dr. May. "I pity him! Existence seems hard work to him!"

"We shall have baby calling him 'the detestable' next," said Ethel.

"What a famous set down she gave him."

"She is a thorough lady, and allows no liberties," said Dr. May.

"Ah!" said Margaret, "it is a proof of what I want to impression you. We really must leave off calling her Daisy when strangers are there."

"It is so much nicer," pleaded Mary.

"The very reason," said Margaret, "fondling names should be kept for our innermost selves, not spread abroad, and made common. I remember when I used to be called Peg-top—and Flora, Flossy—we were never allowed to use the names when any visitor was near; and we were asked if we could not be as fond of each other by our proper names. I think it was felt that there was a want of reserve in publishing our pet words to other people."

"Quite true," said Dr. May; "baby-names never ought to go beyond home. It is the fashion to use them now; and, besides the folly, it seems, to me, an absolute injury to a girl, to let her grow up, with a nickname attached to her."

"Ay!" chimed in Norman, "I hear men talking of Henny, and Loo, and the like; and you can't think how glad I have been that my sisters could not be known by any absurd word!"

"It is a case where self-respect would make others behave properly," said Flora.

"True," said Dr. May; "but if girls won't keep up their own dignity, their friends' duty is to do it for them. The mischief is in the intimate friends, who blazon the words to every one."

"And then they call one formal, for trying to protect the right name," said Flora. "It is, one-half of it, silliness, and, the other, affectation of intimacy."

"Now, I know," said Mary, "why you are so careful to call Meta Miss Rivers, to all the people here."

"I should hope so!" cried Norman indignantly.

"Why, yes, Mary," said Margaret, "I should hope lady-like feelings

would prevent you from calling her Meta before—"

"The Andersons!" cried Ethel, laughing. "Margaret was just going to say it. We only want Harry, to exact the forfeit! Poor dear little humming-bird! It gives one an oppression on the chest, to think of her having that great do-nothing brother on her hands all day."

"Thank you," said Norman, "I shall know where I am not to look when I want a sister."

"Ay," said Ethel, "when you come yawning to me to find amusement for you, you will see what I shall do!"

"Stand over me with a stick while I print A B C for Cocksmoor, I suppose," said Norman.

"Well! why not? People are much better doing something than nothing."

"What, you won't even let me blow bubbles!" said Norman.

"That is too intellectual, as papa makes it," said Ethel. "By the bye, Norman," she added, as she had now walked with him a little apart, "it always was a bubble of mine that you should try for the Newdigate prize. Ha!" as the colour rushed into his cheeks, "you really have begun!"

"I could not help it, when I heard the subject given out for next year. Our old friend, Decius Mus."

"Have you finished?"

"By no means, but it brought a world of notions into my head, such as I could not but set down. Now, Ethel, do oblige me, do write another, as we used in old times."

"I had better not," said Ethel, standing thoughtful. "If I throw myself into it, I shall hate everything else, and my wits will be woolgathering. I have neither time nor poetry enough."

"You used to write English verse."

"I was cured of it."

"How?"

"I wanted money for Cocksmoor, and after persuading papa, I got leave to send a ballad about a little girl and a white rose to that school magazine. I don't think papa liked it, but there were some verses that touched him, and one had seen worse. It was actually inserted, and I was in high feather, till, oh, Norman! imagine Richard getting hold of this unlucky thing, without a notion where it came from! Margaret put it before him, to see what he would say to it."

"I am afraid it was not like a young lady's anonymous composition in a story."

"By no means. Imagine Ritchie picking my poor metaphors to pieces, and weighing every sentimental line! And all in his dear old simplicity, because he wanted to understand it, seeing that Margaret liked it. He had not the least intention of hurting my feelings, but never was I so annihilated! I thought he was doing it on purpose, till I saw how distressed he was when he found it out; and worse than all was, his saying at the end that he supposed it was very fine, but he could not understand it."

"Let me see it."

"Some time or other; but let me see Decius."

"Did you give up verses because Richard could not understand them?"

"No; because I had other fish to fry. And I have not given them up altogether. I do scrabble down things that tease me by running in my head, when I want to clear my brains, and know what I mean; but I can't do it without sitting up at night, and that stupefies me before breakfast. And as to making bubbles of them, Ritchie has cured me of that!"

"It is a pity! " said Norman.

"Nonsense, let me see Decius. I know he is splendid."

"I wish you would have tried, for all my best ideas are stolen from you."

Ethel prevailed by following her brother to his room, and perching herself on the window-sill, while he read his performance from many slips of paper. The visions of those boyish days had not been forgotten, the Vesuvius scenery was much as Ethel had once described it, but with far more force and beauty; there was Decius's impassioned address to the beauteous land he was about to leave, and the remembrances of his Roman hearth, his farm, his children, whom he quitted for the pale shadows of an uncertain Elysium. There was a great hiatus in the middle, and Norman had many more authorities to consult, but the summing-up was nearly complete, and Ethel thought the last lines grand, as they spoke of the noble consul's name living for evermore, added to the examples that nerve ardent souls to devote life, and all that is precious, to the call of duty. Fame is not their object. She may crown their pale brows, but for the good of others, not their own, a beacon light to the world. Self is no object of theirs, and it is the casting self behind that wins—not always the visible earthly strife, but the combat between good and evil. They are the true victors, and, whether chronicled or forgotten, true glory rests on their heads, the sole true glory that man can attain, namely, the reflected beams that crown them as shadowy types of Him whom Decius knew not—the Prince who gave Himself for His people, and thus rendered death, for Truth's sake, the highest boon to mortal man.

"Norman, you must finish it! When will it be given in?"

"Next spring, if at all, but keep the secret, Ethel. I cannot have my father's hopes raised."

"I'll tell you of a motto," said Ethel. "Do you remember Mrs. Hemans' mention of a saying of Sir Walter Scott— 'Never let me hear that brave blood has been shed in vain. It sends a roaring voice down through all time.'"

"If," said Norman, rather ashamed of the enthusiasm which, almost approaching to the so-called "funny state" of his younger days, had trembled in his voice, and kindled his eye—"if you won't let me put 'nascitur ridiculus mus.'"

"Too obvious," said Ethel. "Depend upon it, every undergraduate has thought of it already."

Ethel was always very happy over Norman's secrets, and went about smiling over Decius, and comparing her brother with such a one as poor Meta was afflicted with; wasting some superfluous pity and contempt on the weary weight that was inflicted on the Grange.

"What do you think of me?" said Margaret, one afternoon. "I have had Mr. George Rivers here for two hours."

"Alone! what could bring him here?"

"I told him that every one was out, but he chose to sit down, and seemed to be waiting."

"How could you get on?"

"Oh! we asked a few questions, and brought out remarks, with great difficulty, at long intervals. He asked me if lying here was not a great nuisance, and, at last, he grew tired of twisting his moustache, and went away."

"I trust it was a call to take leave."

"No, he thinks he shall sell out, for the army is a great nuisance."

"You seem to have got into his confidence."

"Yes, he said he wanted to settle down, but living with one's father was such a nuisance."

"By the bye," cried Ethel, laughing, "Margaret, it strikes me that this is a Dumbiedikes' courtship!"

"Of yourself?" said Margaret slyly.

"No, of Flora. You know, she has often met him at the Grange and other places, and she does contrive to amuse him, and make him almost animated. I should not think he found her a great nuisance."

"Poor man! I am sorry for him!" said Margaret.

"Oh! rejection will be very good for him, and give him something to think of."

"Flora will never let it come to that," said Margaret. "But not one word about it, Ethel!"

Margaret and Etheldred kept their eyes open, and sometimes imagined, sometimes laughed at themselves for their speculations, and so October began; and Ethel laughed, as she questioned whether the Grange would feel the Hussar's return to his quarters, as much as home would the departure of their scholar for Balliol.

CHAPTER VI.

So, Lady Flora, take my lay,
  And if you find a meaning there,
Oh! whisper to your glass, and say,
  What wonder, if he thinks me fair.—Tennyson.

Flora and Norman were dining with one of their county acquaintance, and Dr. May had undertaken to admit them on their return. The fire shone red and bright, as it sank calmly away, and the timepiece and clock on the stairs had begun their nightly duet of ticking, the crickets chirped in the kitchen, and the doctor sat alone. His book lay with unturned pages, as he sat musing, with eyes fixed on the fire, living over again his own life, the easy bright days of his youth, when, without much pains on his own part, the tendencies of his generous affectionate disposition, and the influences of a warm friendship, and an early attachment, had guarded him from evil— then the period when he had been perfectly happy, and the sobering power of his position had been gradually working on him; but though always religious and highly principled, the very goodness of his natural character preventing him from perceiving the need of self-control, until the shock that changed the whole tenor of his life, and left him, for the first time, sensible of his own responsibility, but with inveterate habits of heedlessness and hastiness that love alone gave him force to combat. He was now a far gentler man. His younger children had never seen, his elder had long since forgotten, his occasional bursts of temper, but he suffered keenly from their effects, especially as regarded some of his children. Though Richard's timidity had been overcome, and Tom's more serious failures had been remedied, he was not without anxiety, and had a strange unsatisfactory feeling as regarded Flora. He could not feel that he fathomed her! She reminded him of his old Scottish father-in-law, Professor Mackenzie, whom he had never understood, nor, if the truth were known, liked. Her dealings with the Ladies' Committee were so like her grandfather's canny ways in a public meeting, that he laughed over them—but they were not congenial to him. Flora was a most valuable person; all that she undertook prospered, and he depended entirely on her for household affairs, and for the care of Margaret; but, highly as he esteemed her, he was a little afraid of her cool prudence; she never seemed to be in any need of him, nor to place any confidence in him, and seemed altogether so much older and wiser than he could feel himself—pretty girl as she was—and very pretty were her fine blue eyes and clear skin, set off by her dark brown hair. There arose the vision of eyes as blue, skin as clear, but of light blonde locks, and shorter, rounder, more dove-like form, open, simple, loving face, and serene expression, that had gone straight to his heart, when he first saw Maggie Mackenzie making tea.

He heard the wheels, and went out to unbolt the door. Those were a pair for a father to be proud of—Norman, of fine stature and noble looks, with his high brow, clear thoughtful eye, and grave intellectual eagle face, lighting into animation with his rare, sweet smile; and Flora, so tall and graceful, and in her white dress, picturesquely half concealed by her mantle, with flowers in her hair, and a deepened colour in her cheek, was a fair vision, as she came in from the darkness.

"Well! was it a pleasant party?"

Norman related the circumstances, while his sister remained silently leaning against the mantel-piece, looking into the fire, until he took up his candle, and bade them good-night. Dr. May was about to do the same, when she held out her hand. "One moment, if you please, dear papa," she said; "I think you ought to know it." "

What, my dear?"

"Mr. George Rivers, papa—"

"Ha!" said Dr. May, beginning to smile. "So that is what he is at, is it? But what an opportunity to take."

"It was in the conservatory," said Flora, a little hurt, as her father discovered by her tone. "The music was going on, and I don't know that there could have been—"

"A better opportunity, eh?" said Dr. May, laughing; "well, I should have thought it awkward; was he very much discomposed?"

"I thought," said Flora, looking down and hesitating, "that he had better come to you."

"Indeed! so you shifted the ungracious office to me. I am very glad to spare you, my dear; but it was hard on him to raise his hopes."

"I thought," faltered Flora, "that you could not disapprove—"

"Flora—" and he paused, completely confounded, while his daughter was no less surprised at the manner in which her news was received. Each waited for the other to speak, and Flora turned away, resting her head against the mantel-piece.

"Surely," said he, laying his hand on her shoulder, "you do not mean that you like this man?"

"I did not think that you would be against it," said Flora, in a choked voice, her face still averted.

"Heaven knows, I would not be against anything for your happiness, my dear," he answered; "but have you considered what it would be to spend your life with a man that has not three ideas! not a resource for occupying himself—a regular prey to ennui—one whom you could never respect!" He had grown more and more vehement, and Flora put her handkerchief to her eyes, for tears of actual disappointment were flowing.

"Come, come," he said, touched, but turning it off by a smile, "we will not talk of it any more to-night. It is your first offer, and you are flattered, but we know

'Colours seen by candle-light,
Will not bear the light of day.'

There, good-night, Flora, my dear—we will have a-tete-a-tete in the study before breakfast, when you have had time to look into your own mind."

He kissed her affectionately, and went upstairs with her, stopping at her door to give her another embrace, and to say "Bless you, my dear child, and help you to come to a right decision—"

Flora was disappointed. She had been too highly pleased at her conquest to make any clear estimation of the prize, individually considered. Her vanity magnified her achievement, and she had come home in a flutter of pleasure, at having had such a position in society offered to her, and expecting that her whole family would share her triumph. Gratified by George Rivers's admiration, she regarded him with favour and complacency; and her habit of considering herself as the most sensible person in her sphere made her so regard his appreciation of her, that she was blinded to his inferiority. It must be allowed that he was less dull with her than with most others.

And, in the midst of her glory, when she expected her father to be delighted and grateful—to be received as a silly girl, ready to accept any proposal, her lover spoken of with scorn, and the advantages of the match utterly passed over, was almost beyond endurance. A physician, with eleven children dependent on his practice, to despise an offer from the heir of such a fortune! But that was his customary romance! She forgave him, when it occurred to her that she was too important, and valuable, to be easily spared; and a tenderness thrilled through her, as she looked at the sleeping Margaret's pale face, and thought of surrendering her and little Daisy to Ethel's keeping. And what would become of the housekeeping? She decided, however, that feelings must not sway her—out of six sisters some must marry, for the good of the rest. Blanche and Daisy should come and stay with her, to be formed by the best society; and, as to poor dear Ethel, Mrs. Rivers would rule the Ladies' Committee for her with a high hand, and, perhaps, provide Cocksmoor with a school at her sole expense. What a useful, admirable woman she would be! The doctor would be the person to come to his senses in the morning, when he remembered Abbotstoke, Mr. Rivers, and Meta.

So Flora met her father, the next morning, with all her ordinary composure, in which he could not rival her, after his sleepless, anxious night. His looks of affectionate solicitude disconcerted what she had intended to say, and she waited, with downcast eyes, for him to begin.

"Well, Flora," he said at last, "have you thought?"

"Do you know any cause against it?" said Flora, still looking down.

"I know almost nothing of him. I have never heard anything of his character or conduct. Those would be a subject of inquiry, if you wish to carry this on—"

"I see you are averse," said Flora. "I would do nothing against your wishes—"

"My wishes have nothing to do with it," said Dr. May. "The point is—that I must do right, as far as I can, as well as try to secure your happiness; and I want to be sure that you know what you are about."

"I know he is not clever," said Flora; "but there may be many solid qualities without talent."

"I am the last person to deny it; but where are these solid qualities? I cannot see the recommendation!"

"I place myself in your hands," said Flora, in a submissive tone, which had the effect of making him lose patience.

"Flora, Flora! why will you talk as if I were sacrificing you to some dislike or prejudice of my own! Don't you think I should only rejoice to have such a prosperous home offered to you, if only the man were worthy?"

"If you do not think him so, of course there is an end of it," said Flora, and her voice showed suppressed emotion.

"It is not what I think, in the absence of proof, but what you think, Flora. What I want you to do is this—to consider the matter fairly. Compare him with—I'll not say with Norman—but with Richard, Alan, Mr. Wilmot. Do you think you could rely on him—come to him for advice?" (Flora never did come to any one for advice.) "Above all— do you think him likely to be a help, or a hindrance, in doing right?"

"I think you underrate him," said Flora steadily; "but, of course, if you dislike it—though, I think, you would change your mind if you knew him better—"

"Well," he said, as if to himself, "it is not always the most worthy;" then continued, "I have no dislike to him. Perhaps I may find that you are right. Since your mind is made up, I will do this: first, we must be assured of his father's consent, for they may very fairly object, since what I can give you is a mere nothing to them. Next, I shall find out what character he bears in his regiment, and watch him well myself; and, if nothing appear seriously amiss, I will not

71

withhold my consent. But, Flora, you should still consider whether he shows such principle and right feeling as you can trust to."

"Thank you, papa. I know you will do all that is kind."

"Mind, you must not consider it an engagement, unless all be satisfactory."

"I will do as you please."

Ethel perceived that something was in agitation, but the fact did not break upon her till she came to Margaret, after the schoolroom reading, and heard Dr. May declaiming away in the vehement manner that always relieved him.

"Such a cub!" These were the words that met her ear; and she would have gone away, but he called her. "Come in, Ethel; Margaret says you guessed at this affair!"

"At what affair!" exclaimed Ethel. "Oh, it is about Flora. Poor man; has he done it?"

"Poor! He is not the one to be pitied!" said her father.

"You don't mean that she likes him?"

"She does though! A fellow with no more brains than a turnip lantern!"

"She does not mean it?" said Ethel.

"Yes, she does! Very submissive, and proper spoken, of course, but bent on having him; so there is nothing left for me but to consent—provided Mr. Rivers does, and he should turn out not to have done anything outrageous; but there's no hope of that—he has not the energy. What can possess her? What can she see to admire?"

"He is good-natured," said Margaret, "and rather good-looking—"

"Flora has more sense. What on earth can be the attraction?"

"I am afraid it is partly the grandeur—" said Ethel. She broke off short, quite dismayed at the emotion she had xcited. Dr. May stepped towards her, almost as if he could have shaken her.

"Ethel," he cried, "I won't have such motives ascribed to your sister!"

Ethel tried to recollect what she had said that was so shocking, for the idea of Flora's worldly motives was no novelty to her. They had appeared in too many instances; and, though frightened at his anger, she stood still, without unsaying her words.

Margaret began to explain away. "Ethel did not mean, dear papa—"

"No," said Dr. May, his passionate manner giving way to dejection. "The truth is, that I have made home so dreary, that my girls are ready to take the first means of escaping."

Poor Margaret's tears sprang forth, and, looking up imploringly, she exclaimed, "Oh, papa, papa! it was no want of happiness! I could not help it. You know he had come before—"

Any reproach to her had been entirely remote from his thoughts, and he was at once on his knee beside her, soothing and caressing, begging her pardon, and recalling whatever she could thus have interpreted. Meanwhile, Ethel stood unnoticed and silent, making no outward protestation, but with lips compressed, as in her heart of hearts she passed the resolution—that her father should never feel this pain on her account. Leave him who might, she would never forsake him; nothing but the will of Heaven should part them. It might be hasty and venturesome. She knew not what it might cost her; but, where Ethel had treasured her resolve to work for Cocksmoor, there she also laid up her secret vow—that no earthly object should be placed between her and her father.

The ebullition of feeling seemed to have restored Dr. May's calmness, and he rose, saying, "I must go to my work; the man is coming here this afternoon."

"Where shall you see him?" Margaret asked.

"In my study, I suppose. I fear there is no chance of Flora's changing her mind first. Or do you think one of you could talk to her, and get her fairly to contemplate the real bearings of the matter?" And, with these words, he left the room.

Margaret and Ethel glanced at each other; and both felt the impenetrability of Flora's nature, so smooth, that all thrusts glided off.

"It will be of no use," said Ethel; "and, what is more, she will not have it done."

"Pray try; a few of your forcible words would set it in a new light."

"Why! Do you think she will attend to me, when she has not chosen to heed papa?" said Ethel, with an emphasis of incredulity. "No; whatever Flora does, is done deliberately, and unalterably."

"Still, I don't know whether it is not our duty," said Margaret.

"More yours than mine," said Ethel.

Margaret flushed up. "Oh, no, I cannot!" she said, always timid, and slightly defective in moral courage. She looked so nervous and shaken by the bare idea of a remonstrance with Flora, that Ethel could not press her; and, though convinced that her representation would be useless, she owned that her conscience would rest better after she had spoken. "But there is Flora, walking in the garden with Norman," she said. "No doubt he is doing it."

So Ethel let it rest, and attended to the children's lessons, during which Flora came into the drawing-room, and practised her music, as if nothing had happened.

Before the morning was over, Ethel contrived to visit Norman in the dining-room, where he was wont to study, and asked him whether he had made any impression on Flora.

"What impression do you mean?"

"Why, about this concern," said Ethel; "this terrible man, that makes papa so unhappy."

"Papa unhappy! Why, what does he know against him? I thought the Riverses were his peculiar pets."

"The Riverses! As if, because one liked the sparkling stream, one must like a muddy ditch."

"What harm do you know of him?" said Norman, with much surprise and anxiety, as if he feared that he had been doing wrong, in ignorance.

"Harm! Is he not a regular oaf?"

"My dear Ethel, if you wait to marry till you find some one as clever as yourself, you will wait long enough."

"I don't think it right for a woman to marry a man decidedly her inferior."

"We have all learned to think much too highly of talent," said Norman gravely.

"I don't care for mere talent—people are generally more sensible without it; but, one way or other, there ought to be superiority on the man's side."

"Well, who says there is not?"

"My dear Norman! Why, this George Rivers is really below the average! you cannot deny that! Did you ever meet any one so stupid?"

"Really!" said Norman, considering; and, speaking very innocently, "I cannot see why you think so. I do not see that he is at all less capable of sustaining a conversation than Richard."

Ethel sat down, perfectly breathless with amazement and indignation.

Norman saw that he had shocked her very much. "I do not mean," he said, "that we have not much more to say to Richard; all I meant to say was, merely as to the intellect."

"I tell you," said Ethel, "it is not the intellect. Richard! why, you know how we respect, and look up to him. Dear old Ritchie! with his goodness, and earnestness, and right judgment—to compare him to that man! Norman, Norman, I never thought it of you!"

"You do not understand me, Ethel. I only cited Richard, as a person who proves how little cleverness is needed to insure respect."

"And, I tell you, that cleverness is not the point."

"It is the only objection you have put forward."

"I did wrong," said Ethel. "It is not the real one. It is earnest goodness that one honours in Richard. Where do we find it in this man, who has never done anything but yawn over his self indulgence?"

"Now, Ethel, you are working yourself up into a state of foolish prejudice. You and papa have taken a dislike to him; and you are overlooking a great deal of good safe sense and right thinking. I know his opinions are sound, and his motives right. He has been undereducated, we all see, and is not very brilliant or talkative; but I respect Flora for perceiving his solid qualities."

"Very solid and weighty, indeed!" said Ethel ironically. "I wonder if she would have seen them in a poor curate."

"Ethel, you are allowing yourself to be carried, by prejudice, a great deal too far. Are such imputations to be made, wherever there is inequality of means? It is very wrong! very unjust!"

"So papa said," replied Ethel, as she looked sorrowfully down. "He was very angry with me for saying so. I wish I could help feeling as if that were the temptation."

"You ought," said Norman. "You will be sorry, if you set yourself, and him, against it."

"I only wish you to know what I feel; and, I think, Margaret and papa do," said Ethel humbly; "and then you will not think us more unjust than we are. We cannot see anything so agreeable or suitable in this man as to account for Flora's liking, and we do not feel convinced of his being good for much. That makes papa greatly averse to it, though he does not know any positive reason for refusing; and we cannot feel certain that she is doing quite right, or for her own happiness."

"You will be convinced," said Norman cheerfully. "You will find out the good that is under the surface when you have seen more of him. I have had a good deal of talk with him."

A good deal of talk to him would have been more correct, if Norman had but been aware of it. He had been at the chief expense of the conversation with George Rivers, and had taken the sounds of assent, which he obtained, as evidences of his appreciation of all his views. Norman had been struggling so long against his old habit of looking down on Richard, and exalting intellect; and had seen, in his Oxford life, so many ill-effects of the knowledge that puffeth up, that he had come to have a certain respect for dullness, per se, of which George Rivers easily reaped the benefit, when surrounded by the halo, which everything at Abbotstoke Grange bore in the eyes of Norman.

He was heartily delighted at the proposed connection, and his genuine satisfaction not only gratified Flora, and restored the equanimity that had been slightly disturbed by her father, but it also reassured Ethel and Margaret, who could not help trusting in his judgment, and began to hope that George might be all he thought him.

Ethel, finding that there were two ways of viewing the gentleman, doubted whether she ought to express her opinion. It was Flora's disposition, and the advantages of the match, that weighed most upon her, and, in spite of her surmise having been treated as so injurious, she could not rid herself of the burden.

Dr. May was not so much consoled by Norman's opinion as Ethel expected. The corners of his mouth curled up a little with diversion, and though he tried to express himself glad, and confident in his son's judgment, there was the same sort of involuntary lurking misgiving with which he had accepted Sir Matthew Fleet's view of Margaret's case.

There was no danger that Dr. May would not be kind and courteous to the young man himself. It was not his fault if he were a dunce, and Dr. May perceived that his love for Flora was real, though clumsily expressed. He explained that he could not sanction the engagement till he should be better informed of the young gentleman's antecedents; this was, as George expressed it, a great nuisance, but his father agreed that it was quite right, in some doubt, perhaps, as to how Dr. May might be satisfied.

CHAPTER VII.

Ye cumbrous fashions, crowd not on my head.
　Mine be the chip of purest white,
Swan-like; and, as her feathers light,
　When on the still wave spread;
And let it wear the graceful dress
　Of unadorned simpleness.

Catherine Fanshaw's 'Parody on Grey'.

Nothing transpired to the discredit of Lieutenant Rivers. He had spent a great deal of money, but chiefly for want of something else to do, and, though he was not a subject for high praise, there was no vice in him—no more than in an old donkey—as Dr. May declared, in his concluding paroxysm of despair, on finding that, though there was little to reconcile him to the engagement, there was no reasonable ground for thwarting his daughter's wishes. He argued the matter once more with her, and, finding her purpose fixed, he notified his consent, and the rest of the family were admitted to a knowledge of the secret which they had never suspected.

Etheldred could not help being gratified with the indignation it excited. With one voice, Mary and Blanche declared that they would never give up the title of "the detestable," and would not make him any presents; certainly not watch-chains! Miss Bracy, rather alarmed, lectured them just enough to make them worse; and Margaret, overhearing Blanche instructing Aubrey in her own impertinences, was obliged to call her to her sofa, and assure her that she was unkind to Flora, and that she must consider Mr. George Rivers as her brother.

"Never my brother like Harry!" exclaimed Mary indignantly.

"No, indeed; nor like Alan!" exclaimed Blanche. "And I won't call him George, I am determined, if it is ever so!"

"It will not matter to him what such little girls call him," said Margaret.

Blanche was so annihilated, that the sound of a carriage, and of the door bell, was a great satisfaction to her.

Meta Rivers came flying into the room, her beautiful eyes dancing, and her cheeks glowing with pleasure, as, a little timidly, she kissed Margaret; while Ethel, in a confused way, received Mr. Rivers, in pain for her own cold, abrupt manner, in contrast with his gentle, congratulating politeness.

Meta asked, blushing, and with a hesitating voice, for their dear Flora; Mary offered to call her, but Meta begged to go herself, and thus was spared the awkwardness that ensued. Ethel was almost vexed with herself, as ungrateful, when she saw Mr. Rivers so mildly kind, and so delighted, with the bland courtesy that seemed fully conscious of the favour that Flora had conferred on his son, and thankful to the Mays for accepting him.

Margaret answered with more expression of gratification than would have been sincere in Ethel; but it was a relief when Flora and Meta came in together, as pretty a contrast as could be seen; the little dark-eyed fairy, all radiant with joy, clinging to the slender waist of Flora, whose quiet grace and maidenly dignity were never more conspicuous than as, with a soft red mantling in her fair cheek, her eyes cast down, but with a simple, unaffected warmth of confidence and gratitude, she came forward to receive Mr. Rivers's caressing affectionate greeting.

Stiffness was over when she came in, and Dr. May, who presently made his appearance, soon was much more at his ease than could have been hoped, after his previous declarations that he should never be able to be moderately civil about it to Mr. Rivers. People of ready sympathy, such as Dr. May and Margaret, have a great deal of difficulty with their sincerity spared them, by being carried along with the feelings of others. Ethel could not feel the same, and was bent on avoiding any expression of opinion; she hoped that Meta's ecstasies would all be bestowed upon her future sister-in-law; but Meta was eager for an interview with Ethel herself, and, as usual, gained her point.

"Now then, you are property of my own!" she cried. "May I not take you all for sisters?"

Ethel had not thought of this as a convenience of the connection, and she let Meta kiss her, and owned that it was very nice.

"Ethel," said Meta, "I see, and I wanted to talk to you. You don't think poor George good enough for Flora."

"I never meant to show it," said Ethel.

"You need not mind," said Meta, smiling. "I was very much surprised myself, and thought it all a mistake. But I am so very glad, for I know it will make such a difference to him, poor fellow. I should like to tell you all about him, for no one else can very well, and you will like him better, perhaps. You know my grandfather made his own fortune, and you would think some of our relations very queer. My Aunt Dorothy once told me all about it—papa was made to marry the partner's daughter, and I fancy she could not have been much of a lady. I don't think he could have been very happy with her, but she soon died, and left him with this one son, whom those odd old aunts brought up their own way. By and by, you know, papa came to be in quite another line of society, but when he married again, poor George had been so spoiled by these aunts, and was so big, and old, that my mother did not know what to make of him."

"A great lubberly boy," Ethel said, rather repenting the next moment.

"He is thirteen years older than I am," said Meta, "and you see it has been hard on him altogether; he had not the education that papa would have given him if he had been born later: and he can't remember his mother, and has always been at a loss when with clever people. I never understood it till within the last two or three years, nor knew how trying it must be to see such a little chit as me made so much of—almost thrusting him aside. But you cannot think what a warm-hearted good fellow he is—he has never been otherwise than so very kind to me, and he was so very fond of his old aunt. Hitherto, he has had such disadvantages, and no real, sensible woman has taken him in hand; he does not care for papa's tastes, and I am so much younger, that I never could get on with him at all, till this time; but I do know that he has a real good temper, and all sorts of good qualities, and that he only needs to be led right, to go right. Oh! Flora may make anything of him, and we are so thankful to her for having found it out!"

"Thank you for telling me," said Ethel. "It is much more satisfactory to have no shamming."

Meta laughed, for Ethel's sham was not too successful; she continued, "Dear Dr. May, I thought he would think his beautiful Flora not exactly matched—but tell him, Ethel, for if he once is sorry for poor George, he will like him. And it will really be the making of George, to be thrown with him and your brothers. Oh! we are so glad! But I won't tease you to be so."

"I can like it better now," said Ethel. "You know Norman thinks very highly of your brother, and declares that it will all come out by and by."

Meta clapped her hands, and said that she should tell her father, and Ethel parted with her, liking her, at least, better than ever. There was a comical scene between her and the doctor, trying to define what relations they should become to each other, which Ethel thought did a good deal to mollify her father.

The history of George's life did more; he took to pitying him, and pity was, indeed, akin to love in the good doctor's mind. In fact, George was a man who could be liked, when once regarded as a belonging—a necessity, not a choice; for it was quite true that there was no harm in him, and a great deal of good nature. His constant kindness, and evident liking for Margaret, stood him in good stead; he made her a sort of confidante, bestowing on her his immeasurable appreciation of Flora's perfections, and telling her how well he was getting on with "the old gentleman"—a name under which she failed to recognise her father.

As to Tom, he wrote his congratulations to Ethel, that she might make a wedding present of her Etruscan vases, the Cupids on which must have been put there by anticipation. Richard heard none of the doubts, and gave kind, warm congratulations, promising to return home for the wedding; and Mary and Blanche no sooner heard a whisper about bride's-maids than all their opposition faded away, in a manner that quite scandalised Ethel, while it set Margaret on reminiscences of her having been a six-year-old bride's-maid to Flora's godmother, Mrs. Arnott.

As to the gossip in the town, Ethel quite dreaded the sight of every one without Flora to protect her, and certainly, Flora's unaffected, quiet manner was perfection, and kept off all too forward congratulations, while it gratified those whom she was willing to encourage.

There was no reason for waiting, and Mr. Rivers was as impatient as his son, so an understanding arose that the wedding, should take place near the end of the Christmas holidays.

Flora showed herself sensible and considerate. Always open-handed, her father was inclined to do everything liberally, and laid no restrictions on her preparations, but she had too much discretion to be profuse, and had a real regard for the welfare of the rest. She laughed with Ethel at the anticipations of the Stoneborough ladies that she must be going to London, and, at the requests, as a great favour, that they might be allowed the sight of her trousseau. Her wedding-dress, white silk, with a white cashmere mantle, was, indeed, ordered from Meta's London dressmaker; but, for the rest, she contented herself with an expedition to Whitford, accompanied by Miss Bracy and her two enchanted pupils, and there laid in a stock of purchases, unpretending and in good taste, aiming only at what could be well done, and not attempting the decorative wardrobe of a great lady. Ethel was highly amused when the Misses Anderson came for their inspection, to see their concealed disappointment at finding no under garments trimmed with Brussels lace, nor pocket-handkerchiefs all open-work, except a centre of the size of a crown-piece, and the only thing remarkable was Margaret's beautiful marking in embroidery. There was some compensation in the costly wedding presents—Flora had reaped a whole harvest from friends of her own, grateful patients of her father, and the whole Rivers and Langdale connection; but, in spite of the brilliant uselessness of most of these, the young ladies considered themselves ill-used, thought Dr. May never would have been shabby, and were of opinion that when Miss Ward had married her father's surgical pupil, her outfit had been a far more edifying spectacle.

The same moderation influenced Flora's other arrangements. Dr. May was resigned to whatever might be thought most proper, stipulating only that he should not have to make a speech; but Flora felt that, in their house, a grand breakfast would be an unsuccessful and melancholy affair. If the bride had been any one else, she could have enjoyed making all go off well, but, under present circumstances, it would be great pain to her father and Margaret, a misery to Ethel, and something she dared not think of to the guests.

She had no difficulty in having it dispensed with. George was glad to avoid "a great nuisance." Mr. Rivers feared the fatigue, and, with his daughter, admired Flora for her amiability, and, as to the home party, no words could express their gratitude to her for letting them off. Mary and Blanche did, indeed, look rather blank, but Blanche was consoled, by settling with Hector the splendours in store for Alan and Margaret, and Mary cared the less, as there would be no Harry to enjoy the fun.

The bride-maiden's glory was theirs by right, though Ethel was an unsatisfactory chief for such as desired splendour. She protested against anything incongruous with January, or that could not be useful afterwards, and Meta took her part, laughing at the cruel stroke they were preparing for Bellairs. Ethel begged for dark silks and straw bonnets, and Flora said that she had expected to hear of brown stuff and gray duffle, but owned that they had better omit the ordinary muslin garb in the heart of winter. The baby bride's-maid was, at last, the chief consideration. Margaret suggested how pretty she and Blanche would look in sky-blue merino, trimmed with swan's-down. Meta was charmed with the idea, and though Ethel stuck out her shoulder-blades and poked out her head, and said she should look like the ugly duckling, she was clamorously reminded that the ugly duckling ended by being a swan, and promised that she should be allowed a bonnet of a reasonable size, trimmed with white, for Mr. Rivers's good taste could endure, as little as Dr. May's sense of propriety, the sight of a daughter without shade to her face, Ethel, finally, gave in, on being put in mind that her papa had a penchant for swan's-down, and on Margaret's promising to wear a dress of the same as theirs.

Ethel was pleased and satisfied by Flora's dislike of parade, and attention to the feelings of all. Passing over the one great fact, the two sisters were more of one mind than usual, probably because all latent jealousy of Ethel had ceased in Flora's mind. Hitherto, she had preferred the being the only practically useful person in the family, and had encouraged the idea of Ethel's gaucherie but now she desired to render her sister able to take her place, and did all in her power to put her in good heart.

For Etheldred was terrified at the prospect of becoming responsible housekeeper. Margaret could only serve as an occasional reference. Her morning powers became too uncertain to be depended on for any regular, necessary duty, and it would have oppressed her so much to order the dinners, which she never saw, that, though she offered to resume the office, Flora would not hear of Ethel's consenting. If it were her proper business, Ethel supposed she could do it, but another hour of her leisure was gone, and what would become of them all, with her, a proverb for heedlessness, and ignorance of ordinary details. She did not know that these were more proverbial than actual, and, having a bad name, she believed in it herself. However, Flora made it her business to persuade her that her powers were as good for household matters, as for books, or Cocksmoor; instructed her in her own methodical plans, and made her keep house for a fortnight, with so much success that she began to be hopeful.

In the attendance on Margaret, the other great charge, old nurse was the security; and Ethel, who had felt her self much less unhandy than before, was, to succeed to the abode, in her room—Blanche being promoted from the nursery to the old attic. "And," said Flora consolingly, "if dear Margaret ever should be ill, you may reckon on me."

Miss Flora May made her last appearance at the Ladies' Committee to hear the reply from the principal of the college. It was a civil letter, but declined taking any steps in the matter without more certain intelligence of the wishes of the incumbent of the parish or of the holders of the land in question.

The ladies abused all colleges—as prejudiced old Bodies, and feared that it would be impossible to ask Mrs. Perkinson's niece to take the school while there was neither room nor lodging. So Miss Rich recorded the correspondence, and the vote of censure, by which it was to be hoped the Ladies' Committee of Market Stoneborough inflicted a severe blow on the principal and fellows of M— College.

"Never mind, Ethel," said Flora. "I shall meet Sir Henry Walkinghame in London, and will talk to him. We shall yet astonish the muses. If we can get the land without them, we shall be able to manage it our own way, without obligations."

"You forget the money!"

"We will keep them from dissipating it—or that might be no harm! A hundred pounds will be easily found, and we should then have it in our own hands. Besides, you know, I don't mean to give up. I shall write a polite note to Mrs. Ledwich, begging to subscribe on my own account, and to retain my seat! and you will see what we shall do."

"You mean to come down with the external authority," said Ethel, smiling.

"True! and though my driving in with a pair of horses may make little difference to you, Ethel, depend upon it, Mrs. Ledwich will be the more amenable. Whenever I want to be particularly impressive, I shall bring in that smelling-bottle, with the diamond stopper that won't come out, and you will find that carries all before it."

"A talisman!" said Ethel, laughing. "But I had rather they yielded to a sense of right!"

"So had I," said Flora. "Perhaps you will rule them that way?"

"Not I!" cried Ethel, terrified.

"Then you must come to me, and secondary motives. Seriously—I do mean that George should do something for Stoneborough; and, in a position of influence, I hope to be able to be useful to my poor old town. Perhaps we shall have the minster restored."

Flora did wish it. She did love Stoneborough, and was sincerely interested for Cocksmoor. She thought she worked earnestly for them, and that her situation would be turned to their profit; but there was something for which she worked more earnestly. Had Flora never heard of the two masters whom we cannot serve at the same time?

Richard came home for "a parson's week," so as to include the wedding. He looked very fresh and youthful; but his manner, though still gentle and retiring, had lost all that shrinking diffidence, and had, now, a very suitable grave composure. Everybody was delighted to have him; and Ethel, more than any one, except Margaret. What floods of Cocksmoor histories were poured upon him; and what comparing of notes about his present school-children! He could not enter into the refinements of her dread of the Ladies' Committee, and thought she might be thankful if the school were built by any proper means; for, if Cherry Elwood were retained, and the ladies prevented from doing harm, he did not understand why

Ethel should wish to reject all assistance that did not come in a manner she admired. He never would comprehend — so Ethel gave it up — feared she was again jealous and self-sufficient, and contented herself with the joy that his presence produced at Cocksmoor, where the children smiled, blushed, and tittered, with ecstasy, whenever he even looked at one of them.

Richard was not allowed to have a Sunday of rest. His father apologised for having made an engagement for him — as Mr. Ramsden was unwell, and the school clergy were all absent, so that he could do no otherwise than assist in the service. Richard coloured, and said that he had brought no sermon; and he was, in fact, deprived of much of his sister's company, for composition was not easy to him, and the quantity of time he spent on it, quite alarmed Norman and Ethel, who both felt rather nervous on the Sunday morning, but agreed that preaching was not everything.

Ethel could not see well as far as the reading-desk, but she saw her father glance up, take off his spectacles, wipe them, and put them away; and she could not be displeased, though she looked reproof at Blanche's breathless whisper, "Oh, he looks so nice!" Those white folds did truly suit well with the meek, serious expression of the young deacon's fair face, and made him, as his sisters afterwards said, like one of the solemnly peaceful angel-carvings of the earlier ages.

His voice was sweet and clear, and his reading full of quiet simplicity and devotion, such as was not often heard by that congregation, who were too much used either to carelessness or to pomposity. The sermon made his brother and sister ashamed of their fears. It was an exposition of the Gospel for the day, practical and earnest, going deep, and rising high, with a clearness and soberness, yet with a beauty and elevation, such as Norman and Ethel had certainly not expected — or, rather, they forgot all their own expectations and Richard himself, and only recollected their own hearts and the great future before them.

Even Blanche and Aubrey told Margaret a great deal about it, and declared that, if Richard preached every Sunday, they should like going to church much better.

When Dr. May came in, some time after, he was looking much pleased. "So, Mr. Ritchie," he said, "you have made quite a sensation—every one shaking me by the hand, and thanking me for my son's sermon. You will be a popular preacher at last!"

Richard blushed distressfully, and quoted the saying, that it would be the true comfort to hear that people went home, thinking of themselves rather than of the sermon. This put an end to the subject; but the doctor went over it again, most thoroughly, with his other children, who were greatly delighted.

Flora's last home Sunday! She was pale and serious, evidently feeling much, though seeking no tete-a-tetes; and chiefly engrossed with waiting on Margaret, or fondling little Gertrude. No one saw the inside of her mind—probably, she did not herself. On the outside was a very suitable pensiveness, and affection for all that she was leaving. The only one in the family to whom she talked much was Norman, who continued to see many perfections in George, and contrived, by the force of his belief, to impress the same on the others, and to make them think his great talent for silence such a proof of his discretion, that they were not staggered, even by his shy blundering exclamation that his wedding would be a great nuisance—a phrase which, as Dr. May observed, was, to him, what Est-il-possible was to his namesake of Denmark.

Nobody wished for any misgivings, so Richard was never told of any, though there was a careful watch kept to see what were his first impressions. None transpired, except something about good nature, but it was shrewdly believed that Richard and George, being much alike in shy unwillingness to speak, had been highly satisfied with the little trouble they had caused to each other, and so had come to a tacit esteem.

There was very little bustle of preparation. Excepting the packing, everything went on much as usual, till the Thursday morning, and then the children were up early, refreshing the Christmas hollies, and working up their excitement, only to have it damped by the suppressed agitation of their elders at the breakfast-table.

Dr. May did not seem to know what he was about; and Flora looked paler and paler. She went away before the meal was over, and when Ethel went to the bedroom, shortly after, she found that she had fairly broken down, and was kneeling beside Margaret's sofa, resting her head on her sister's bosom, and sobbing—as Ethel had never seen her weep, except on that dreadful night, after their mother's death.

In a person ordinarily of such self-command as Flora, weeping was a terrible thing, and Margaret was much distressed and alarmed; but the worst had passed before Ethel came up, and Flora was able to speak.

"Oh! Margaret! I cannot leave you! Oh! how happy we have been—"

"You are going to be happier, we trust, dearest," said Margaret fondly.

"Oh! what have I done? It is not worth it!"

Ethel thought she caught those words, but no more. Mary's step was heard, and Flora was on her feet, instantly, composing herself rapidly. She shed no more tears, but her eyelids were very heavy, and her face softened, in a manner that, though she was less pretty than usual, was very becoming under her bridal veil. She recovered calmness and even cheerfulness, while reversing the usual order of things, and dressing her bride's-maids, who would never have turned out fit to be seen, but for the exertions of herself, Margaret, and Miss Bracy. Ethel's long Scotch bones and Mary's round, dumpy shapelessness were, in their different ways, equally hard to overcome; and the one was swelled out with a fabulous number of petticoats, and the other pinched in, till she gasped and screamed for mercy, while Blanche and Gertrude danced about, beautiful to behold, under their shady hats; and presently, with a light tap at the door, Meta Rivers stepped in, looking so pretty, that all felt that to try to attain to such an appearance was vain.

Timid in her affection, she hardly dared to do more than kiss them, and whisper her pretty caressing words to each. There was no more time—Dr. Hoxton's carriage was come to take up the bride.

Ethel did as she was told, without much volition of her own; and she quitted the carriage, and was drawn into her place by Norman, trusting that Meta would not let her do wrong, and relieved that just in front of her were the little ones, over whose heads she could see her father, with Flora's veiled bending figure.

That pause while the procession was getting into order, the slow movement up the centre aisle, the week-day atmosphere of the church, brought back to her thoughts a very different time, and one of those strange echoings on the mind repeated in her ears the words, "For man walketh in a vain shadow, and disquieteth himself in vain—"

There was a little pause—George did not seem to be forthcoming, and Meta turned round, rather uneasily, and whispered something about his having been so nervous. However, there he was, looking exceedingly red, and very sheepish, and disposed to fall back on his best man, Norman, whose countenance was at the brightest—and almost handsome.

Dr. Hoxton performed the ceremony, "assisted by" Richard. It had been Flora's choice; and his loud sonorous voice was thought very impressive. Blanche stood the nearest, and looked happy and important, with Flora's glove. Gertrude held Mary's hand, and gazed straight up into the fretted roof, as if that were to her the chief marvel. Ethel stood and knelt, but did not seem, to herself, to have the power of thinking or feeling. She saw and heard—that was all; she could not realise.

They drew her forward, when it was over, to sign her name, as witness. She took up the pen, looked at the Flora May, written for the last time, and found her hand so trembling, that she said, half smiling, that she could not write. Mary was only too well pleased to supply the deficiency. Dr. May looked at her anxiously, and asked whether she felt overcome.

"No, papa. I did not know my hand was shaky."

He took it into his, and pressed it. Ethel knew, then, how much had been undeveloped in her own mind, catching it, as it were, from his touch and look. The thought of his past joy—the sad fading of hope for Margaret—the fear and doubt for their present bride—above all, the sense that the fashion of this world passeth away; and that it is not the outward scene, but our bearing in it, that is to last for ever.

The bells struck up, each peal ending with a crash that gave Ethel some vague idea of fatality; and they all came back to the house, where Margaret was ready, in the drawing-room, to receive them, looking very pretty, in her soft blue dress, which especially became her fair complexion and light brown hair. Ethel did not quite like the pink colour on her cheeks, and feared that she had been shaken by Flora's agitation in the morning; but she was very calm and bright, in the affectionate greeting with which she held out her hands to the bride and bridegroom, as they came in.

Mr. Rivers and Meta were the only guests, and, while Meta was seized by the children, Margaret lay talking to Mr. Rivers, George standing upright and silent behind her sofa, like a sentinel. Flora was gone to change her dress, not giving way, but nervous and hurried, as she reiterated parting directions about household comforts to Ethel, who stood by the toilette-table, sticking a pin into the pincushion and drawing it out again, as if solely intent on making it always fit into the same hole, while Mary dressed Flora, packed, flew about, and was useful.

As they came downstairs, Ethel found that Flora was trembling from head to foot, and leaning on her; Dr. May stood at the foot of the stairs, and folded his daughter in a long embrace; Flora gave herself up to it as if she would never bear to leave it. Did a flash come over her then, what the father was, whom she had held cheaply? what was the worth of that for which she had exchanged such a home? She spoke not a word, she only clung tightly—if her heart failed her—it was too late. "Bless you! my child!" he said at last. "Only be what your mother was!"

A coming tread warned them to part. There was a tray of luncheon for the two who were about to depart, and the great snow-white cake was waiting for Flora to cut it. She smiled, accomplished that feat steadily, and Norman continuing the operation, Aubrey guided Gertrude in handing round the slices. George did full justice thereto, as well as to the more solid viands. Flora could taste nothing, but she contrived to smile and say it was too early. She was in haste to have it over now, and, as soon as George had finished, she rose up, still composed and resolved, the last kisses were given—Gertrude was lifted up to her, after she was in the carriage for the very last, when George proposed to run away with her also, whereupon Daisy kicked and screamed, and was taken back in haste. The door was shut, and they drove off, bound for the Continent, and then Mary, as if the contingency of losing Flora had only for the first time occurred to her as the consequence of the wedding, broke out into a piteous fit of sobbing—rather too unrestrained, considering her fourteen years.

Poor Mary, she was a very child still! They pulled her into the study, out of the way of Mr. Rivers, and Meta had no sooner said how Flora would soon come home and live at the Grange, and talked of the grand school-feast to which she was at once going to take her friends, than the round rosy face drew out of its melancholy puckers into smiles, as Mary began to tell the delight caused by the invitations which she had conveyed. That was to be a feast indeed — all the Abbotstoke children — all Flora's class at Stoneborough, and as many Cocksmoor scholars as could walk so far, were to dine on Christmas fare, at one o'clock, at the Grange, and Meta was in haste to be at home to superintend the feast.

Mary, Blanche, and Aubrey, went with her, under the keeping of Miss Bracy, the boys were to follow. She had hoped for Ethel, but on looking at her, ceased her coaxing importunity.

"I see," she said kindly; "even schoolchildren will not be so good for you as peace."

"Thank you," said Ethel, "I should like to be quiet till the evening, if you will let me off. It is very kind in you."

"I ought to know how to pity you," said Meta, "I who have gained what you have lost."

"I want to think too," said Ethel. "It is the beginning to me of a new life, and I have not been able to look at it yet."

"Besides, Margaret will want you. Poor Margaret — has it been very trying to her?"

"I fear so, but I shall keep out of her way, and leave her to a quiet afternoon with Richard. It will be the greatest treat to those two to be together."

"Very well, I will carry off the children, and leave the house quiet."

And quiet it was in another hour — Gertrude walking with the nurses, Dr. May gone to his patients, and all the rest at Abbotstoke, except Richard and Margaret downstairs; and Ethel, who, while arranging her properties in her new room, had full leisure to lay out before herself the duties that had devolved on her and to grapple with them. She recalled the many counsels that she had received

from Flora, and they sounded so bewildering that she wished it had
been Conic sections, and then she looked at a Hebrew grammar that
Norman had given her, and gave a sigh as she slipped it into the
shelf of the seldom used. She looked about the room, cleared out the
last piece of brown paper, and burned the last torn envelope, that no
relic of packing and change might distress Margaret's eyes for order;
then feeling at once desolate and intrusive, she sat down in Flora's
fireside chair, opened her desk, and took out her last time-table. She
looked at it for some minutes, laid it aside, and rising, knelt down.
Again seating herself, she resumed her paper, took a blank one,
ruled it, and wrote her rules for each hour of each day in the week.
That first hour after breakfast, when hitherto she had been free, was
one sacrifice; it must go now, to ordering dinner, seeing after stores,
watching over the children's clothes, and the other nondescripts,
which, happily for her, Flora had already reduced to method. The
other loss was the spare time between the walk and tea; she must not
spend that in her own room now, or there would be no one to sit
with Margaret, or keep the little ones from being troublesome to her.
Ethel had often had to give up this space before, when Flora went
out in the evening, and she had seldom felt otherwise than annoyed.
Give it up for good! that was the cure for temper, but it had been
valuable as something of her own. She would have been thankful
could she have hoped to keep regularly to her own rules, but that
she knew was utterly improbable—boys, holidays, callers,
engagements, Dr. May, would all conspire to turn half her days
upside down, and Cocksmoor itself must often depend not only on
the weather, but on home doings. Two or three notes she wrote at
the foot of her paper.

'N. B. These are a standard—not a bed of Procrustes.

MUSTS—To be first consulted.—Mays—last. Ethel May's last of
all. If I cannot do everything—omit the self-chosen.

MEM— Neither hurry when it depends on myself, nor fidget
when it depends on others.

Keep a book going to pacify myself.'

Her rules drawn up, Ethel knelt once more. Then she drew a long
sigh, and wondered where Flora was; and next, as she was fairly
fagged, mind and body, she threw herself back in the armchair, took
up a railway novel that Hector had brought home, and which they

had hidden from the children, and repaired herself with the luxury of an idle reading.

Margaret and Richard likewise spent a peaceful, though pensive afternoon. Margaret had portions of letters from Alan to read to him, and a consultation to hold. The hope of her full recovery had so melted away, that she had, in every letter, striven to prepare Mr. Ernescliffe for the disappointment, and each that she received in return was so sanguine and affectionate, that the very fondness was as much grief as joy. She could not believe that he took in the true state of the case, or was prepared to perceive that she could never be his wife, and she wanted Richard to write one of his clear, dispassionate statements, such as carried full conviction, and to help to put a final end to the engagement.

"But why," said Richard—"why should you wish to distress him?"

"Because I cannot bear that he should be deceived, and should feed on false hopes. Do you think it right, Richard?"

"I will write to him, if you like," said Richard; "but I think he must pretty well know the truth from all the letters to Harry and to himself."

"It would be so much better for him to settle his mind at once," said Margaret.

"Perhaps he would not think so—"

There was a pause, while Margaret saw that her brother was thinking. At last he said, "Margaret, will you pardon me? I do think that this is a little restlessness. The truth has not been kept from him, and I do not see that we are called to force it on him. He is sensible and reasonable, and will know how to judge when he comes home."

"It was to try to save him the pang," murmured Margaret.

"Yes; but it will be worse far away than near. I do not mean that we should conceal the fact, but you have no right to give him up before he comes home. The whole engagement was for the time of his voyage."

"Then you think I ought not to break it off before his return?"

"Certainly not."

"It will be pain spared—unless it should be worse by and by."

"I do not suppose we ought to look to by and by," said Richard.

"How so?"

"Do the clearly right thing for the present, I mean," he said, "without anxiety for the rest. How do we—any of us—know what may be the case in another year?"

"Do not flatter me with hopes," said Margaret, sadly smiling; "I have had too many of them."

"No," said Richard; "I do not think you will ever get well. But so much may happen—"

"I had rather have my mind made up once for all, and resign myself," said Margaret.

"His will is sometimes that we should be uncertain," said Richard.

"And that is the most trying," said Margaret.

"Just so—" and he paused tenderly.

"I feel how much has been right," said Margaret. "This wedding has brought my real character before me. I feel what I should have been. You have no notion how excited and elated I can get about a little bit of dress out of the common way for myself or others," said she, smiling; "and then all the external show and things belonging to station—I naturally care much more for them than even Flora does. Ethel would bear all those things as if they did not exist—I could not."

"They would be a temptation?"

"They would once have been. Yes, they would now," said Margaret. "And government, and management, and influence—you would not guess what dreams I used to waste on them, and now here am I set aside from it all, good for nothing but for all you dear ones to be kind to."

"They would not say so," said Richard kindly.

"Not say it, but I feel it. Papa and Ethel are all the world to each other—Richard, I may say it to you. There has been only one thing more hard to bear than that—don't suppose there was a moment's neglect or disregard; but when first I understood that Ethel could be more to him than I, then I could not always feel rightly. It was the punishment for always wanting to be first."

"My father would be grieved that you had the notion. You should not keep it."

"He does not know it is so," said Margaret; "I am his first care, I fear, his second grief; but it is not in the nature of things that Ethel should not be more his comfort and companion. Oh! I am glad it was not she who married! What shall we do when she goes?"

This came from Margaret's heart, so as to show that if there had once been a jealous pang of mortification, it had been healed by overflowing, unselfish affection and humility.

They went off to praise Ethel, and thence to praise Norman, and the elder brother and sister, who might have had some jealousy of the superiority of their juniors, spent a good happy hour in dwelling on the shining qualities they loved so heartily.

And Richard was drawn into talking of his own deeper thoughts, and Margaret had again the comfort of clerical counsel—and now from her own most dear brother! So they sat till darkness closed in, when Ethel came down, bringing Gertrude and her great favour, very full of chatter, only not quite sure whether she had been bride, bride's-maid, or bridegroom.

The schoolroom set, with Tom and Aubrey, came home soon after, and tongues went fast with stories of roast-beef, plum-pudding, and blind-man's-buff. How the dear Meta had sent a cart to Cocksmoor to bring Cherry herself, and how many slices everybody had eaten, and how the bride's health had been drunk by the children in real wine, and how they had all played, Norman and all, and how Hector had made Blanche bold enough to extract a raisin from the flaming snap-dragon. It was not half told when Dr. May came home, and Ethel went up to dress for her dinner at Abbotstoke, Mary following to help her and continue her narration, which bade fair to entertain Margaret the whole evening.

Dr. May, Richard, and Ethel had a comfortable dark drive to the Grange, and, on arriving, found Hector deep in 'Wild Sports of the West', while Norman and Meta were sitting over the fire talking, and Mr. Rivers was resting in his library.

And when Ethel and Meta spent the time before the gentlemen came in from the dining-room, in a happy tete-a-tete, Ethel learned that the fire-light dialogue had been the pleasantest part of the whole day, and that Meta had had confided to her the existence of Decius Mus—a secret which Ethel had hitherto considered as her own peculiar property, but she supposed it was a pledge of the sisterhood, which Meta professed with all the house of May.

CHAPTER VIII.

The rest all accepted the kind invitation,
And much bustle it caused in the plumed creation;
Such ruffling of feathers, such pruning of coats,
Such chirping, such whistling, such clearing of throats,
 Such polishing bills, and such oiling of pinions,
Had never been known in the biped dominions.

— Peacock at Home.

Etheldred was thankful for that confidence to Meta Rivers, for without it, she would hardly have succeeded in spurring Norman up to give the finishing touches to Decius, and to send him in. If she talked of the poem as the devotion of Decius, he was willing enough, and worked with spirit, for he liked the ideas, and enjoyed the expressing them, and trying to bring his lines to his notion of perfection, but if she called it the "Newdigate," or the "Prize Poem," and declared herself sure it would be successful, he yawned, slackened, leaned back in his chair, and began to read other people's poetry, which Ethel was disrespectful enough not to think nearly as good as his own.

It was completed at last, and Ethel stitched it up with a narrow red and white ribbon—the Balliol colours; and set Meta at him till a promise was extorted that he would send it in.

And, in due time, Ethel received the following note:

"My Dear Ethel,—

"My peacock bubble has flown over the house. Tell them all about it.

—Your affectionate,

N. W. M."

They were too much accustomed to Norman's successes to be extraordinarily excited; Ethel would have been much mortified if the prize had been awarded to any one else, but, as it was, it came rather as a matter of course. The doctor was greatly pleased, and said he should drive round by Abbotstoke to tell the news there, and then laughed beyond measure to hear that Meta had been in the plot, saying he should accuse the little humming-bird of being a magpie, stealing secrets.

By this time the bride and bridegroom were writing that they thought of soon returning; they had spent the early spring at Paris, had wandered about in the south of France, and now were at Paris again. Flora's letters were long, descriptive, and affectionate, and she was eager to be kept fully informed of everything at home. As soon as she heard of Norman's success, she wrote a whole budget of letters, declaring that she and George would hear of no refusal; they were going to spend a fortnight at Oxford for the Commemoration, and must have Meta and Ethel with them to hear Norman's poem in the theatre.

Dr. May, who already had expressed a hankering to run up for the day and take Ethel with him, was perfectly delighted at the proposal, and so was Mr. Rivers, but the young ladies made many demurs. Ethel wanted Mary to go in her stead, and had to be told that this would not be by any means the same to the other parties—she could not bear to leave Margaret; it was a long time since there had been letters from the Alcestis, and she did not like to miss being at home when they should come; and Meta, on her side, was so unwilling to leave her father that, at last, Dr. May scolded them both for a pair of conceited, self-important damsels, who thought nothing could go on without them; and next, compared them to young birds, obliged to be shoved by force into flying.

Meta consented first, on condition that Ethel would; and Ethel found that her whole house would be greatly disappointed if she refused, so she proceeded to be grateful, and then discovered how extremely delightful the plan was. Oxford, of which she had heard so much, and which she had always wished to see! And Norman's glory—and Meta's company—nay, the very holiday, and going from home, were charms enough for a girl of eighteen, who had never been beyond Whitford in her life. Besides, to crown all, papa promised that, if his patients would behave well, and not want him too much, he would come up for the one great day.

Mr. and Mrs. George Rivers came to Abbotstoke to collect their party. They arrived by a railroad, whose station was nearer to Abbotstoke than to Stoneborough, therefore, instead of their visiting the High Street by the way, Dr. May, with Ethel and Mary, were invited to dine at the Grange, the first evening—a proposal, at least, as new and exciting to Mary as was the journey to Oxford to her sister.

The two girls went early, as the travellers had intended to arrive before luncheon, and, though Ethel said few words, but let Mary rattle on with a stream of conjectures and questions, her heart was full of longings for her sister, as well as of strange doubts and fears, as to the change that her new life might have made in her.

"There! there!" cried Mary. "Yes! it is Flora! Only she has her hair done in a funny way!"

Flora and Meta were both standing on the steps before the conservatory, and Mary made but one bound before she was hugging Flora. Ethel kissed her without so much violence, and then saw that Flora was looking very well and bright, more decidedly pretty and elegant than ever, and with certainly no diminution of affection; it was warmer, though rather more patronising.

"How natural you look!" was her first exclamation, as she held Mary's hand, and drew Ethel's arm into hers. "And how is Margaret?"

"Pretty well-but the heat makes her languid—"

"Is there any letter yet?"

"No—"

"I do not see any cause for alarm—letters are so often detained, but, of course, she will be anxious. Has she had pain in the back again?"

"Sometimes, but summer always does her good—"

"I shall see her to-morrow—and the Daisy. How do you all get on?

Have you broken down yet, Ethel?"

"Oh! we do go on," said Ethel, smiling; "the worst thing I have done was expecting James to dress the salads with lamp-oil."

"A Greenland salad! But don't talk of oil—I have the taste still in my mouth after the Pyrennean cookery! Oh! Ethel, you would have been wild with delight in those places!"

"Snowy mountains! Are they not like a fairy-dream to you now? You must have felt at home, as a Scotchwoman's daughter."

"Think of the peaks in the sunrise! Oh! I wanted you in the pass of Roncevalles, to hear the echo of Roland's horn. And we saw the cleft made by Roland's sword in the rocks."

"Oh! how delightful—and Spain too!"

"Ay, the Isle of Pheasants, where all the conferences took place."

"Where Louis XIV. met his bride, and Francois I. sealed his treason with his empty flourish—"

"Well, don't let us fight about Francois I. now; I want to know how Tom likes Eton."

"He gets on famously. I am so glad he is in the same house with Hector."

"Mr. Ramsden—how is he?"

"No better; he has not done any duty for weeks. Tomkins and his set want to sell the next presentation, but papa hopes to stave that off, for there is a better set than usual in the Town Council this year."

"Cocksmoor? And how are our friends the muses? I found a note from the secretary telling me that I am elected again. How have they behaved?"

"Pretty well," said Ethel. "Mrs. Ledwich has been away, so we have had few meetings, and have been pretty quiet, except for an uproar about the mistress beating that Franklin's girl—and what do you think I did, Flora? I made bold to say the woman should show her to papa, to see if she had done her any harm, and he found that it was all a fabrication from one end to the other. So it ended in the poor girl being expelled, and Mary and I have her twice a week, to see if there is any grace in her."

"To reward her!" said Flora. "That is always your way—"

"Why, one cannot give the poor thing quite up," said Ethel.

"You will manage the ladies at last!" cried Flora.

"Not while Mrs. Ledwich is there!"

"I'll cope with her! But, come, I want you in my room—"

"May not I come?" said Meta. "I must see when—"

Flora held up her hand, and, while signing invitation, gave an arch look to Meta to be silent. Ethel here bethought herself of inquiring after Mr. Rivers, and then for George.

Mr. Rivers was pretty well—George, quite well, and somewhere in the garden; and Meta said that he had such a beard that they would hardly know him; while Flora added that he was delighted with the Oxford scheme. Flora's rooms had been, already, often shown to her sisters, when Mr. Rivers had been newly furnishing them, with every luxury and ornament that taste could devise. Her dressing-room, with the large bay window, commanding a beautiful view of Stoneborough, and filled, but not crowded, with every sort of choice article, was a perfect exhibition to eyes unaccustomed to such varieties.

Mary could have been still amused by the hour, in studying the devices and ornaments on the shelves and chiffonieres; and Blanche had romanced about it to the little ones, till they were erecting it into a mythical palace.

And Flora, in her simple, well-chosen dress, looked, and moved, as if she had been born and bred in the like.

There were signs of unpacking about the room-Flora's dressing-case on the table, and some dresses lying on the sofa and ottoman.

Mary ran up to them eagerly, and exclaimed at the beautiful shot blue and white silk.

"Paris fashions?" said Ethel carelessly.

"Yes; but I don't parade my own dresses here," said Flora.

"Whose are they then? Your commissions, Meta?"

"No!" and Meta laughed heartily.

"Your French maid's then?" said Ethel. I dare say she dresses quite as well; and the things are too really pretty and simple for an English maid's taste."

"I am glad you like them," said Flora maliciously. "Now, please to be good."

"Who are they for then?" said Ethel, beginning to be frightened.

"For a young lady, whose brother has got the Newdigate prize, and who is going to Oxford."

"Me! Those! But I have not got four backs," as Ethel saw Meta in fits of laughing, and Flora making affirmative signs. Mary gave a ponderous spring of ecstasy.

"Come!" said Flora, "you may as well be quiet. Whatever you may like, I am not going to have the Newdigate prizeman shown as brother to a scarecrow. I knew what you would come to, without me to take care of you. Look at yourself in the glass."

"I'm sure I see no harm in myself," said Ethel, turning towards the pier-glass, and surveying herself—in a white muslin, made high, a black silk mantle, and a brown hat. She had felt very respectable when she set out, but she could not avoid a lurking conviction that, beside Flora and Meta, it had a scanty, schoolgirl effect. "And," she continued quaintly, "besides, I have really got a new gown on purpose—a good useful silk, that papa chose at Whitford—just the colour of a copper tea-kettle, where it turns purple."

"Ethel! you will kill me!" said Meta, sinking back on the sofa.

"And I suppose," continued Flora, "that you have sent it to Miss Broad's, without any directions, and she will trim it with flame-coloured gimp, and glass buttons; and, unless Margaret catches you, you will find yourself ready to set the Thames on fire. No, my dear tea-kettle, I take you to Oxford on my own terms, and you had better

103

submit, without a fuss, and be thankful it is no worse. George wanted me to buy you a white brocade, with a perfect flower-garden on it, that you could have examined with a microscope. I was obliged to let him buy that lace mantle, to make up to him. Now then, Meta, the scene opens, and discovers—"

Meta opened the folding-doors into Flora's bedroom, and thence came forward Bellairs and a little brisk Frenchwoman, whom Flora had acquired at Paris. The former, who was quite used to adorning Miss Ethel against her will, looked as amused as her mistresses; and, before Ethel knew what was going on, her muslin was stripped off her back, and that instrument of torture, a half made body, was being tried upon her. She made one of her most wonderful grimaces of despair, and stood still. The dresses were not so bad after all; they were more tasteful than costly, and neither in material nor ornament were otherwise than suitable to the occasion and the wearer. It was very kind and thoughtful of Flora—that she could not but feel— nothing had been forgotten, but when Ethel saw the mantles, the ribbons, the collars, the bonnet, all glistening with the French air of freshness and grace, she began to feel doubts and hesitations, whether she ought to let her sister go to such an expense on her account, and privately resolved that the accepting thanks should not be spoken till she should have consulted her father.

In the meantime, she could only endure, be laughed at by her elders, and entertained by Mary's extreme pleasure in her array. Good Mary— it was more than any comedy to her; she had not one moment's thought of herself, till, when Flora dived into her box, produced a pair of bracelets, and fastened them on her comfortable plump arms, her eyes grew wide with wonder, and she felt, at least, two stages nearer womanhood.

Flora had omitted no one. There was a Paris present for every servant at home, and a needle-case even for Cherry Elwood, for which Ethel thanked her with a fervency wanting in her own case.

She accomplished consulting her father on her scruples, and he set her mind at rest. He knew that the outlay was a mere trifle to the Riverses, and was greatly pleased and touched with the affection that Flora showed; so he only smiled at Ethel's doubts, and dwelt with heartfelt delight on the beautiful print that she had brought him, from Ary Scheffer's picture of the Great Consoler.

Flora was in her glory. To be able to bestow benefits on those whom she loved, had been always a favourite vision, and she had the full pleasure of feeling how much enjoyment she was causing. They had a very pleasant evening; she gave interesting accounts of their tour, and by her appeals to her husband, made him talk also. He was much more animated and agreeable than Ethel had ever seen him, and was actually laughing, and making Mary laugh heartily with his histories of the inns in the Pyrennees. Old Mr. Rivers looked as proud and happy as possible, and was quite young and gay, having evidently forgotten all his maladies, in paying elaborate attention to his daughter-in-law.

Ethel told Margaret, that night, that she was quite satisfied about Flora—she was glad to own that she had done her injustice, and that Norman was right in saying there was more in George Rivers than met the eye.

The morning spent at home was equally charming. Flora came back, with love strengthened by absence. She was devoted to Margaret—caressing to all; she sat in her old places; she fulfilled her former offices; she gratified Miss Bracy by visiting her in the schoolroom, and talking of French books; and won golden opinions, by taking Gertrude in her hand, and walking to Minster Street to call on Mrs. Hoxton, as in old times, and take her the newest foreign device of working to kill time.

So a few days passed merrily away, and the great journey commenced. Ethel met the Abbotstoke party at the station, and, with a parting injunction to her father, that he was to give all his patients a sleeping potion, that they might not miss him, she was carried away from Stoneborough.

Meta was in her gayest mood; Ethel full of glee and wonder, for once beyond Whitford, the whole world was new to her; Flora more quiet, but greatly enjoying their delight, and George not saying much, but smiling under his beard, as if well pleased to be so well amused with so little trouble.

He took exceeding care of them, and fed them with everything he could make them eat at the Swindon Station, asking for impossible things, and wishing them so often to change for something better, that, if they had been submissive, they would have had no luncheon at all; and, as it was, Flora was obliged to whisk into the carriage with her last sandwich in her hand.

"I am the more sorry," said he, after grumbling at the allotted ten minutes, "as we shall dine so late. You desired Norman to bring any friend he liked, did you not, Flora?"

"Yes, and he spoke of bringing our old friend, Charles Cheviot, and Mr. Ogilvie," said Flora.

"Mr. Ogilvie!" said Ethel, "the Master of Glenbracken! Oh! I am so glad! I have wanted so much to see him!"

"Ah! he is a great hero of yours?" said Flora.

"Do you know him?" said Meta.

"No; but he is a great friend of Norman's, and a Scottish cousin—Norman Ogilvie. Norman has his name from the Ogilvies."

"Our grandmother, Mrs. Mackenzie, was a daughter of Lord Glenbracken," said Flora.

"This man might be called the Master of Glenbracken at home," said Ethel. "It is such a pretty title, and there is a beautiful history belonging to them. There was a Master of Glenbracken who carried James IV.'s standard at Flodden, and would not yield, and was killed with it wrapped round his body, and the Lion was dyed with his blood. Mamma knew some scraps of a ballad about him. Then they were out with Montrose, and had their castle burned by the Covenanters, and since that they have been Jacobites, and one barely escaped being beheaded at Carlisle! I want to hear the rights of it. Norman is to go, some time or other, to stay at Glenbracken."

"Yes," said Flora, "coming down to times present, this young heir seems worthy of his race. They are pattern people—have built a church, and have all their tenantry in excellent order. This is the only son, and very good and clever—he preferred going to Balliol, that he might work; but he is a great sportsman, George," added she;

"you will get on with him very well, about fishing, and grouse shooting, I dare say."

Norman met them at the station, and there was great excitement at seeing his long nose under his college cap. He looked rather thin and worn, but brightened at the sight of the party. After the question — whether there had been any letters from Harry? he asked whether his father were coming? — and Ethel thought he seemed nervous at the idea of this addition to his audience. He saw them to their hotel, and, promising them his two guests, departed.

Ethel watched collegiate figures passing in the street, and recollected the gray buildings, just glimpsed at in her drive — it was dreamy and confused, and she stood musing, not discovering that it was time to dress, till Flora and her Frenchwoman came in, and laid violent hands on her.

The effect of their manipulations was very successful. Ethel was made to look well-dressed, and, still more, distinguished. Her height told well, when her lankiness was overcome, and her hair was disposed so as to set off her features to advantage. The glow of amusement and pleasure did still more for her; and Norman, who was in the parlour when the sisters appeared, quite started with surprise and satisfaction at her aspect.

"Well done. Flora!" he said. "Why! I have been telling Ogilvie that one of my sisters was very plain!"

"Then, I hope we have been preparing an agreeable surprise for him," said Flora. "Ethel is very much obliged to you. By the bye," she said, in her universal amity, "I must ask Harvey Anderson to dinner one of these days?" Norman started, and his face said "Don't."

"Oh, very well; it is as you please. I thought it would please Stoneborough, and that Edward was a protege of yours. What has he been doing? Did we not hear he had been distinguishing himself? Dr. Hoxton was boasting of his two scholars."

"Ask him," said Norman hurriedly. "At least," said he, "do not let anything from me prevent you."

"Has he been doing anything wrong?" reiterated Flora.

"Not that I know of," was the blunt answer; and, at the same instant, Mr. Ogilvie arrived. He was a pleasant, high-bred looking gentleman, brown-complexioned, and dark-eyed, with a brisk and resolute cast of countenance, that, Ethel thought, might have suited the Norman of Glenbracken, who died on the ruddy Lion of Scotland, and speaking with the very same slight degree of Scottish intonation as she remembered in her mother, making a most home-like sound in her ears.

Presently, the rest of their own party came down, and, soon after, Charles Cheviot appeared, looking as quiet and tame, as he used to be in the schoolboy days, when Norman would bring him home, and he used to be too shy to speak a word.

However, he had learned the use of his tongue by this time, though it was a very soft one; and he stood by Ethel, asking many questions about Stoneborough, while something, apparently very spirited and amusing, was going on between the others.

The dinner went off well—there were few enough for the conversation to be general. The young men began to strike out sparks of wit against each other—Flora put in a word or two—Ethel grew so much interested in the discussion, that her face lighted up, and she joined in it, as if it had been only between her father and brother— keen, clear, and droll. After that, she had her full share in the conversation, and enjoyed it so much that, when she left the dinner-table, she fetched her writing-case to sketch the colloquy for Margaret and her father.

Flora exclaimed at her for never allowing any one to think of rest. Meta said she should like to do the same, but it was impossible now; she did not know how she should ever settle down to write a letter. Ethel was soon interrupted—the gentlemen entered, and Mr. Ogilvie came to the window, where she was sitting, and began to tell her how much obliged to her he and his college were, for having insisted on her brother's sending in his poem. "Thanks are due, for our being spared an infliction next week," he said.

"Have you seen it?" she asked, and she was amused by the quick negative movement of his head.

"I read my friend's poems? But our lungs are prepared! Will you give me my cue—it is of no use to ask him when we are to deafen you. One generally knows the crack passages—something beginning with 'Oh, woman!' but it is well to be in readiness—if you would only forewarn me of the telling hits?"

"If they cannot tell themselves," said Ethel, smiling, "I don't think they deserve the name."

"Perhaps you think what does tell on the undergraduates, collectively, is not always what ought to tell on them."

"I don't know. I dare say the same would not be a favourite with them and with me."

"I should like to know which are your favourites. No doubt you have a copy here—made by yourself;" and he looked towards her paper-case.

There was the copy, and she took it out, peering to see whether Norman were looking.

"Let me see," he said, as she paused to open the MS., "he told me the thoughts were more yours than his own."

"Did he? That was not fair. One thought was an old one, long ago talked over between us; the rest is all his own."

Here Mr. Ogilvie took the paper, and Ethel saw his countenance show evident tokens of surprise and feeling.

"Yes," he said presently, "May goes deep—deeper than most men— though I doubt whether they will applaud this."

"I should like it better if they did not," said Ethel. "It is rather to be felt than shouted at."

"And I don't know how the world would go on if it were felt. Few men would do much without the hope of fame," said Norman Ogilvie.

"Is it the question what they would do?" said Ethel.

"So you call fame a low motive? I see where your brother's philosophy comes from."

"I do not call it a low motive—" Her pause was expressive.

"Nor allow that the Non omnis moriar of Horace has in it something divine?"

"For a heathen—yes."

"And pray, what would you have the moving spring?"

"Duty."

"Would not that end in 'Mine be a cot, beside the rill'?" said he, with an intonation of absurd sentiment.

"Well, and suppose an enemy came, would duty prompt not the Hay with the joke—or Winkelried on the spears?"

"Nay, why not—'It is my duty to take care of Lucy.'"

"Then Lucy ought to be broken on her own wheel."

"Not at all! It is Lucy's duty to keep her Colin from running into danger."

"I hope there are not many Lucies who would think so."

"I agree with you. Most would rather have Colin killed than disgraced."

"To be sure!" then, perceiving a knowing twinkle, as if he thought she had made an admission, she added, "but what is disgrace?"

"Some say it is misfortune," said Mr. Ogilvie.

"Is it not failure in duty? " said Ethel.

"Well!"

"Colin's first duty is to his king and country. If he fail in that, he is disgraced, in his own eyes, before Heaven and men. If he does it, there is a reward, which seems to me a better, more powerful motive for Lucy to set before him than 'My dear, I hope you will distinguish yourself,' when the fact is,

'England has forty thousand men,
We trust, as good as he.'

"'Victory or Westminster Abbey!' is a tolerable war-cry," said Mr. Ogilvie.

"Not so good as 'England expects every man to do his duty.' That serves for those who cannot look to Westminster Abbey."

"Ah! you are an English woman!"

"Only by halves. I had rather have been the Master of Glenbracken at Flodden than King James, or"—for she grew rather ashamed of having been impelled to utter the personal allusion—"better to have been the Swinton or the Gordon at Homildon than all the rest put together."

"I always thought Swinton a pig-headed old fellow, and I have little doubt that my ancestor was a young ruffian," coolly answered the Master of Glenbracken.

"Why?" was all that Ethel could say in her indignation.

"It was the normal state of Scottish gentlemen," he answered.

"If I thought you were in earnest, I should say you did not deserve to be a Scot."

"And so you wish to make me out a fause Scot!"

"Ogilvie!" called Norman, "are you fighting Scottish and English battles with Ethel there? We want you to tell us which will be the best day for going to Blenheim."

The rest of the evening was spent in arranging the programme of their lionising, in which it appeared that the Scottish cousin intended to take his full share. Ethel was not sorry, for he interested her much, while provoking her. She was obliged to put out her full strength in answering him, and felt, at the same time, that he was not making any effort in using the arguments that puzzled her—she was in earnest, while he was at play; and, though there was something teasing in this, and she knew it partook of what her brothers called chaffing, it gave her that sense of power on his side, which is always

111

attractive to women. With the knowledge that, through Norman, she had of his real character, she understood that half, at least, of what he said was jest; and the other half was enough in earnest to make it exciting to argue with him.

CHAPTER IX.

While I, thy dearest, sat apart,
And felt thy triumphs were as mine,
And lov'd them more than they were thine.

TENNYSON.

That was a week of weeks; the most memorable week in Ethel's life, spent in indefatigable sight-seeing. College Chapels, Bodleian Library, Taylor Gallery, the Museum, all were thoroughly studied, and, if Flora had not dragged the party on, in mercy to poor George's patience, Ethel would never have got through a day's work.

Indeed, Mr. Ogilvie, when annoyed at being hurried in going over Merton Chapel with her, was heard to whisper that he acted the part of policeman, by a perpetual "move on"; and as Ethel recollected the portly form and wooden face of the superintendent at Stoneborough, she was afraid that the comparison would not soon be forgotten.

Norman Ogilvie seemed to consider himself bound to their train as much as his namesake, or, as on the second morning, Norman reported his reasoning, it was that a man must walk about with somebody on Commemoration week, and that it was a comfort to do so with ladies who wore their bonnets upon their heads, instead of, like most of those he met, remind him of what Cock Robin said to Jenny Wren in that matrimonial quarrel, when

Robin, he grew angry,
Hopped upon a twig—

Flora was extremely delighted, and, in matronly fashion, told her sister that people were always respected and admired who had the strength of mind to resist unsuitable customs. Ethel laughed in answer, and said she thought it would take a great deal more strength of mind to go about with her whole visage exposed to the universal gaze; and, woman-like, they had a thorough gossip over the evils of the "backsliding" head-gear.

Norman had retreated from it into the window, when Flora returned to the charge about Harvey Anderson. She had been questioning their old friend Mr. Everard, and had learned from him that the cause of the hesitation with which his name had been received was that he had become imbued with some of the Rationalistic ideas current in some quarters. He seldom met Norman May without forcing on him debates, which were subjects of great interest to the hearers, as the two young men were considered as the most distinguished representatives of their respective causes, among their own immediate contemporaries. Norman's powers of argument, his eloquence, readiness, and clearness, were thought to rank very high, and, in the opinion of Mr. Everard, had been of great effect in preventing other youths from being carried away by the specious brilliancy of his rival.

Ethel valued this testimony far above the Newdigate prize, and she was extremely surprised by hearing Flora declare her intention of still asking Mr. Anderson to dinner, only consulting her brother as to the day.

"Why, Flora! ask him! Norman—"

Norman had turned away with the simple answer, "any day."

"Norman is wiser than you are, Ethel," said Flora. "He knows that Stoneborough would be up in arms at any neglect from us to one of the Andersons, and, considering the rivalship, it is the more graceful, and becoming."

"I do not think it right," said Ethel stoutly; "I believe that a line ought to be drawn, and that we ought not to associate with people who openly tamper with their faith."

"Never fear," smiled Flora; "I promise you that there shall be no debates at my table."

Ethel felt the force of the pronoun, and, as Flora walked out of the room, she went up to Norman, who had been resting his brow against the window.

"It is vain to argue with her," she said; "but, Norman, do not you think it is clearly wrong to seek after men who desert and deny—"

She stopped short, frightened at his pale look.

He spoke in a low clear tone that seemed to thrill her with a sort of alarm. "If the secrets of men's hearts were probed, who could cast the first stone?"

"I don't want to cast stones," she began; but he made a gesture as if he would not hear, and, at the same moment, Mr. Ogilvie entered the room.

Had Ethel been at home, she would have pondered much over her brother's meaning—here she had no leisure. Not only was she fully occupied with the new scenes around her, but her Scottish cousin took up every moment open to conversation. He was older than Norman, and had just taken his degree, and he talked with that superior aplomb, which a few years bestow at their time of life, without conceit, but more hopeful and ambitious, and with higher spirits than his cousin.

Though industrious and distinguished, he had not avoided society or amusement, was a great cricketer and tennis-player, one of the "eight" whose success in the boat races was one of Norman's prime interests, and he told stories of frolics that reminded Ethel of her father's old Cambridge adventures.

He was a new variety in her eyes, and entertained her greatly. Where the bounds of banter ended, was not easy to define, but whenever he tried a little mystification, she either entered merrily into the humour, or threw it over with keen wit that he kept constantly on the stretch. They were always discovering odd, unexpected bits of knowledge in each other, and a great deal more accordance in views and opinions than appealed on the surface, for his enthusiasm usually veiled itself in persiflage on hers, though he was too good and serious to carry it too far.

At Blenheim, perhaps he thought he had given an overdose of nonsense, and made her believe, as Meta really did, that the Duchess Sarah was his model woman; for as they walked in the park in search of Phoebe Mayflower's well, he gathered a fern leaf, to show her the Glenbracken badge, and talked to her of his home, his mother, and his sister Marjorie, and the little church in the rocky glen. He gave the history of the stolen meetings of the little knot of churchmen during the days of persecution, and showed a heart descended straight from the Ogilvie who was "out with Montrose," now that the upper structure of young England was for a little while put aside.

After this, she took his jokes much more coolly, and made thrusts beneath them, which he seemed to enjoy, and caused him to unfold himself the more. She liked him all the better for finding that he thought Norman had been a very good friend to him, and that he admired her brother heartily, watching tenderly over his tendencies to make himself unhappy. He confided to her that, much as he rejoiced in the defeats of Anderson, he feared that the reading and thought consequent on the discussions, had helped to overstrain Norman's mind, and he was very anxious to carry him away from all study, and toil, and make his brains rest, and his eyes delight themselves upon Scottish mountains.

Thereupon came vivid descriptions of the scenery, especially his own glen with the ruined tower, and ardent wishes that his cousin Ethel could see them also, and know Marjorie. She could quite echo the wish, Edinburgh and Loch Katrine had been the visions of her life, and now that she had once taken the leap and left home, absence did not seem impossible, and, with a start of delight, she hailed her own conviction that he intended his mother to invite the party to Glenbracken.

After Norman's visit, Mr. Ogilvie declared that he must come home with him and pay his long-promised visit to Stoneborough. He should have come long ago. He had been coming last winter, but the wedding had prevented him; he had always wished to know Dr. May, whom his father well remembered, and now nothing should keep him away!

Flora looked on amused and pleased at Ethel's development—her abruptness softened into piquancy, and her countenance so embellished, that the irregularity only added to the expressiveness. There was no saying what Ethel would come to! She had not said that she would not go to the intended ball, and her grimaces at the mention of it were growing fainter every day.

The discussion about Harvey Anderson was never revived; Flora sent the invitation without another word—he came with half a dozen other gentlemen—Ethel made him a civil greeting, but her head was full of boats and the procession day, about which Mr. Ogilvie was telling her, and she thought of him no more.

"A lucky step!" thought Flora. "A grand thing for Ethel—a capital connection for us all. Lady Glenbracken will not come too much into my sphere either. Yes, I am doing well by my sisters."

It would make stay-at-home people giddy to record how much pleasure, how much conversation and laughter were crowded into those ten days, and with much thought and feeling beside them, for these were not girls on whom grave Oxford could leave no impression but one of gaiety.

The whole party was very full of merriment. Norman May, especially, on whom Flora contrived to devolve that real leadership of conversation that should rightly have belonged to George Rivers, kept up the ball with wit and drollery far beyond what he usually put forth; enlivened George into being almost an agreeable man, and drew out little Meta's vivacity into sunny sparkles.

Meta generally had Norman for her share, and seemed highly contented with his lionisings, which were given much more quietly and copiously than those which his cousin bestowed upon his sister. Or if there were anything enterprising to be done, any tower to be mounted, or anything with the smallest spice of danger in it, Meta was charmed, and with her lightness and airiness of foot and figure, and perfectly feminine ways, showed a spirit of adventure that added to the general diversion. But if she were to be helped up or down anywhere, she certainly seemed to find greater security in Norman May's assistance, though it was but a feather-like touch that she ever used to aid her bounding step.

Both as being diffident, and, in a manner at home, Norman was not as constantly her cavalier as was Mr. Ogilvie to his sister; and, when supplanted, his wont was either to pioneer for Flora, or, if she did not need him, to walk alone, grave and abstracted. There was a weight on his brow, when nothing was going on to drive it away, and whether it were nervousness as to the performance in store for him, anxiety about Harry, or, as Mr. Ogilvie said, too severe application; some burden hung upon him, that was only lightened for the time by his participation in the enjoyment of the party.

On Sunday evening, when they had been entering into the almost vision-like delight of the choicest of music, and other accompaniments of church service, they went to walk in Christchurch Meadows. They had begun altogether by comparing feelings—Ethel wondering whether Stoneborough Minster would ever be used as it might be, and whether, if so, they should be practically the better for it; and proceeding with metaphysics on her side, and satire on Norman Ogilvie's, to speculate whether that which is, is best, and the rights and wrongs of striving for change and improvements, what should begin from above, and what from beneath—with illustrations often laughter-moving, though they were much in earnest, as the young heir of Glenbracken looked into his future life.

Flora had diverged into wondering who would have the living after poor old Mr. Ramsden, and walked, keeping her husband amused with instances of his blunders.

Meta, as with Norman she parted from the rest, thought her own dear Abbotstoke church, and Mr Charles Wilmot, great subjects for content and thanksgiving, though it was a wonderful treat to see and hear such as she had enjoyed to-day; and she thought it was a joy, to carry away abidingly, to know that praise and worship, as near perfection as this earth could render them, were being offered up.

Norman understood her thought, but responded by more of a sigh than was quite comfortable.

Meta went on with her own thoughts, on the connection between worship and good works, how the one leads to the other, and how praise with pure lips is, after all, the great purpose of existence.— Her last thought she spoke aloud.

"I suppose everything, our own happiness and all, are given to us to turn into praise," she said.

"Yes—" echoed Norman; but as if his thoughts were not quite with hers, or rather in another part of the same subject; then recalling himself, "Happy such as can do so."

"If one only could—" said Meta.

"You can—don't say otherwise," exclaimed Norman; "I know, at least, that you and my father can."

"Dr. May does so, more than any one I know," said Meta.

"Yes," said Norman again; "it is his secret of joy. To him, it is never, I am half sick of shadows."

"To him they are not shadows, but foretastes," said Meta. Silence again; and when she spoke, she said, "I have always thought it must be such a happiness to have power of any kind that can be used in direct service, or actual doing good."

"No," said Norman. "Whatever becomes a profession, becomes an unreality."

"Surely not, in becoming a duty," said Meta.

"Not for all," he answered; "but where the fabric erected by ourselves, in the sight of the world, is but an outer case, a shell of mere words, blown up for the occasion, strung together as mere language; then, self-convicted, we shrink within the husk, and feel our own worthlessness and hypocrisy."

"As one feels in reproving the school children for behaving ill at church?" said Meta.

"You never felt anything approaching to it!" said Norman. "To know oneself to be such a deception, that everything else seems a delusion too!"

"I don't know whether that is metaphysical," said Meta, "but I am sure I don't understand it. One must know oneself to be worse than one knows any one else to be."

"I could not wish you to understand," said Norman; and yet he seemed impelled to go on; for, after a hesitating silence, he added, "When the wanderer in the desert fears that the spring is but a mirage; or when all that is held dear is made hazy or distorted by some enchanter, what do you think are the feelings, Meta?"

"It must be dreadful," she said, rather bewildered; "but he may know it is a delusion, if he can but wake. Has he not always a spell, a charm?—"

"What is the spell?" eagerly said Norman, standing still.

"Believe—" said Meta, hardly knowing how she came to choose the words.

"I believe!" he repeated. "What—when we go beyond the province of reason—human, a thing of sense after all! How often have I so answered. But Meta, when a man has been drawn, in self-sufficient security, to look into a magic mirror, and cannot detach his eyes from the confused, misty scene—where all that had his allegiance appears shattered, overthrown, like a broken image, or at least unable to endure examination, then—"

"Oh, Norman, is that the trial to any one here? I thought old Oxford was the great guardian nurse of truth! I am sure she cannot deal in magic mirrors or such frightful things. Do you know you are talking like a very horrible dream?"

"I believe I am in one," said Norman.

"To be sure you are. Wake!" said Meta, looking up, smiling in his face. "You have read yourself into a maze, that's all—what Mary calls, muzzling your head; you don't really think all this, and when you get into the country, away from books, you will forget it. One look at our dear old purple Welsh hills will blow away all the mists!"

"I ought not to have spoken in this manner," said Norman sadly. "Forget it, Meta."

"Forget it! Of course I will. It is all nonsense, and meant to be forgotten," said Meta, laughing. "You will own that it is by-and-by."

He gave a deep sigh.

"Don't think I am unfeeling," she said; "but I know it is all a fog up from books, books, books—I should like to drive it off with a good fresh gust of wind! Oh! I wish those yellow lilies would grow in our river!"

Meta talked away gaily for the rest of the walk. She was anything but unfeeling, but she had a confidence in Norman that forbade her to see anything here but one of his variations of spirits, which always sank in the hour of triumph. She put forth her brightness to enliven him, and, in their subsequent tete-a-tetes, she avoided all that could lead to a renewal of this conversation. Ethel would not have rested till it had been fought out. Meta thought it so imaginary, that it had better die for want of the aliment of words; certainly, hers could not reach an intellect like his, and she would only soothe and amuse him. Dr. May, mind-curer as well as body-curer, would soon be here, to put the climax to the general joy and watch his own son.

He did arrive; quite prepared to enjoy, giving an excellent account of both homes; Mr. Rivers very well, and the Wilmots taking care of him, and Margaret as comfortable as usual, Mary making a most important and capable little housekeeper, Miss Bracy as good as possible. He talked as if they had all nourished the better for Ethel's absence, but he had evidently missed her greatly, as he showed, without knowing it, by his instant eagerness to have her to himself. Even Norman, prizeman as he was, was less wanted. There was proud affection, eager congratulation, for him, but it was Ethel to whom he wanted to tell everything that had passed during her absence—whom he treated as if they were meeting after a tedious separation.

They dined rather early, and went out afterwards, to walk down the High Street to Christchurch Meadow. Norman and Ethel had been anxious for this; they thought it would give their father the best idea of the tout ensemble of Oxford, and were not without hopes of beating him by his own confession, in that standing fight between him and his sons, as to the beauties of Oxford and Cambridge—a fight in which, hitherto, they had been equally matched—neither partisan having seen the rival University.

Flora stayed at home; she owned herself fairly tired by her arduous duties of following the two young ladies about, and was very glad to give her father the keeping of them. Dr. May held out his arm to Ethel—Norman secured his peculiar property. Ethel could have preferred that it should be otherwise—Norman would have no companion but George Rivers; how bored he would be!

All through the streets, while she was telling her father the names of the buildings, she was not giving her whole attention; she was trying to guess, from the sounds behind, whether Mr. Ogilvie were accompanying them. They entered the meadows—Norman turned round, with a laugh, to defy the doctor to talk of the Cam, on the banks of the Isis. The party stood still—the other two gentlemen came up. They amalgamated again—all the Oxonians conspiring to say spiteful things of the Cam, and Dr. May making a spirited defence, in which Ethel found herself impelled to join.

In the wide gravelled path, they proceeded in threes; George attached himself to his sister and Norman. Mr. Ogilvie came to Ethel's other side, and began to point out all the various notabilities. Ethel was happy again; her father was so much pleased and amused, with him, and he with her father, that it was a treat to look on.

Presently Dr. May, as usual, always meeting with acquaintances, fell in with a county neighbour, and Ethel had another pleasant aside, until her father claimed her, and Mr. Ogilvie was absorbed among another party, and lost to her sight.

He came to tea, but, by that time, Dr. May had established himself in the chair which had hitherto been appropriated to her cousin, a chair that cut her nook off from the rest of the world, and made her the exclusive possession of the occupant. There was a most interesting history for her to hear, of a meeting with the Town Council, which she had left pending, when Dr. May had been battling to save the next presentation of the living from being sold.

Few subjects could affect Ethel more nearly, yet she caught herself missing the thread of his discourse, in trying to hear what Mr. Ogilvie was saying to Flora about a visit to Glenbracken.

The time came for the two Balliol men to take their leave. Norman May had been sitting very silent all the evening, and Meta, who was near him, respected his mood. When he said good-night, he drew Ethel outside the door. "Ethel," he said, "only one thing: do ask my father not to put on his spectacles to-morrow."

"Very well," said Ethel, half smiling; "Richard did not mind them."

"Richard has more humility—I shall break down if he looks at me! I wish you were all at home."

"Thank you."

The other Norman came out of the sitting-room at the moment, and heard the last words.

"Never mind," said he to Ethel, "I'll take care of him. He shall comport himself as if you were all at Nova Zembla. A pretty fellow to talk of despising fame, and then get a fit of stage-fright!"

"Well, good-night," said Norman, sighing. "It will be over to-morrow; only remember the spectacles."

Dr. May laughed a good deal at the request, and asked if the rest of the party were to be blindfolded. Meta wondered that Ethel should have mentioned the request so publicly; she was a good deal touched by it, and she thought Dr. May ought to be so.

Good-night was said, and Dr. May put his arm round Ethel, and gave her the kiss that she had missed for seven nights. It was very homelike, and it brought a sudden flash of thought across Ethel! What had she been doing? She had been impatient of her father's monopoly of her!

She parted with Flora, and entered the room she shared with Meta, where Bellairs waited to attend her little mistress. Few words passed between the two girls, and those chiefly on the morrow's dress. Meta had some fixed ideas—she should wear pink. Norman had said he liked her pink bonnet, and then she could put down her white veil, so that he could be certain that she was not looking; Ethel vaguely believed Flora meant to wear—something—

Bellairs went away, and Meta gave expression to her eager hope that Norman would go through it well. If he would only read it as he did last Easter to her and Ethel.

"He will," said Ethel. "This nervousness always wears off when it comes to the point, and he warms with his subject."

"Oh! but think of all the eyes looking at him!"

"Our's are all that he really cares for, and he will think of none of them, when he begins. No, Meta, you must not encourage him in it. Papa says, if he did not think it half morbid—the result of the shock to his nerves—he should be angry with it as a sort of conceit!"

"I should have thought that the last thing to be said of Norman!" said Meta, with a little suppressed indignation.

"It was once in his nature," said Ethel; "and I think it is the fault he most beats down. There was a time, before you knew him, when he would have been vain and ambitious."

"Then it is as they say, conquered faults grow to be the opposite virtues!" said Meta. "How very good he is, Ethel; one sees it more when he is with other people, and one hears all these young men's stories!"

"Everything Norman does not do, is not therefore wrong," said Ethel, with her usual lucidity of expression.

"Don't you like him the better for keeping out of all these follies?"

"Norman does not call them so, I am sure."

"No, he is too good to condemn—"

"It is not only that," said Ethel. "I know papa thinks that the first grief, coming at his age, and in the manner it did, checked and subdued his spirits, so that he has little pleasure in those things. And he always meant to be a clergyman, which acted as a sort of consecration on him; but many things are innocent; and I do believe papa would like it better, if Norman were less grave."

"Yes," said Meta, remembering the Sunday talk, "but still, he would not be all he is—so different from others—"

"Of course, I don't mean less good, only, less grave," said Ethel, "and certainly less nervous. But, perhaps, it is a good thing; dear mamma thought his talents would have been a greater temptation than they seem to be, subdued as he has been. I only meant that you must not condemn all that Norman does not do. Now, goodnight."

Very different were the feelings with which those two young girls stretched themselves in their beds that night. Margaret Rivers's innocent, happy little heart was taken up in one contemplation. Admiration, sympathy, and the exultation for him, which he would not feel for himself, drew little Meta entirely out of herself—a self that never held her much. She was proud of the slender thread of connection between them; she was confident that his vague fancies were but the scruples of a sensitive mind, and, as she fell sound asleep, she murmured broken lines of Decius, mixed with promises not to look.

Etheldred heard them, for there was no sleep for her. She had a parley to hold with herself, and to accuse her own feelings of having been unkind, ungrateful, undutiful towards her father. What had a fit of vanity brought her to? that she should have been teased by what would naturally have been her greatest delight! her father's pleasure in being with her. Was this the girl who had lately vowed within herself that her father should be her first earthly object?

At first, Ethel blamed herself for her secret impatience, but another conviction crossed her, and not an unpleasing one, though it made her cheeks tingle with maidenly shame, at having called it up. Throughout this week, Norman Ogilvie had certainly sought her out. He had looked disappointed this evening—there was no doubt that he was attracted by her—by her, plain, awkward Ethel! Such a perception assuredly never gave so much pleasure to a beauty as it did to Ethel, who had always believed herself far less good-looking than she really was. It was a gleam of delight, and, though she set herself to scold it down, the conviction was elastic, and always leaped up again.

That resolution came before her, but it had been unspoken; it could not be binding, and, if her notion were really right, the misty brilliant future of mutual joy dazzled her! But there was another side: her father oppressed and lonely, Margaret ill and pining, Mary, neither companion nor authority, the children running wild; and she, who had mentally vowed never to forsake her father, far away, enjoying her own happiness. "Ah! that resolve had seemed easy enough when it was made, when," thought Ethel, "I fancied no one could care for me! Shame on me! Now is the time to test it! I must go home with papa."

It was a great struggle—on one side there was the deceitful guise of modesty, telling her it was absurd to give so much importance to the kindness of the first cousin with whom she had ever been thrown; there was the dislike to vex Flora to make a discussion, and break up the party. There was the desire to hear the concert, to go to the breakfast at — College, to return round by Warwick Castle, and Kenilworth, as designed. Should she lose all this for a mere flattering fancy? She, who had laughed at Miss Boulder, for imagining every one who spoke to her was smitten. What reason could she assign? It would be simply ridiculous, and unkind—and it was so very pleasant. Mr. Ogilvie would be too wise to think of so incongruous a connection, which would be so sure to displease his parents. It was more absurd than ever to think of it. The heir of Glenbracken, and a country physician's daughter!

That was a candid heart which owned that its own repugnance to accept this disparity as an objection, was an additional evidence that she ought to flee from further intercourse. She believed that no harm was done yet; she was sure that she loved her father better than anything else in the world, and whilst she did so, it was best to preserve her heart for him. Widowed as he was, she knew that he would sorely miss her, and that for years to come, she should be necessary at home. She had better come away while it would cost only a slight pang, for that it was pain to leave Norman Ogilvie, was symptom enough of the need of not letting her own silly heart go further. However it might be with him, another week would only make it worse with her.

"I will go home with papa!" was the ultimatum reached by each chain of mental reasonings, and borne in after each short prayer for guidance, as Ethel tossed about listening to the perpetual striking of all the Oxford clocks, until daylight had begun to shine in; when she fell asleep, and was only waked by Meta, standing over her with a sponge, looking very mischievous, as she reminded her of their appointment with Dr. May, to go to the early service in New College Chapel.

The world looked different that morning with Ethel, but the determination was fixed, and the service strengthened it. She was so silent during the walk, that her companions rallied her, and they both supposed she was anxious about Norman; but taking her opportunity, when Meta was gone to prepare for breakfast, she rushed, in her usual way, into the subject. "Papa! if you please, I should like to go home to-morrow with you."

"Eh?" said the doctor, amazed. "How is this? I told you that Miss Bracy and Mary are doing famously."

"Yes, but I had rather go back."

"Indeed!" and Dr. May looked at the door, and spoke low. "They make you welcome, I hope—"

"Oh, yes! nothing can be kinder."

"I am glad to hear it. This Rivers is such a lout, that I could not tell how it might be. I did not look to see you turn homesick all at once."

Ethel smiled. "Yes, I have been very happy; but please, papa, ask no questions—only take me home."

"Come! it is all a homesick fit, Ethel—never fear the ball. Think of the concert. If it were not for that poor baby of Mrs. Larkins, I should stay myself to hear Sonntag again. You won't have such another chance."

"I know, but I think I ought to go—"

George came in, and they could say no more. Both were silent on the subject at breakfast, but when afterwards Flora seized on Ethel, to array her for the theatre, she was able to say, "Flora, please don't be angry with me—you have been very kind to me, but I mean to go home with papa to-morrow."

"I declare!" said Flora composedly, "you are as bad as the children at the infant school, crying to go home the instant they see their mothers!"

"No, Flora, but I must go. Thank you for all this pleasure, but I shall have heard Norman's poem, and then I must go."

Flora turned her round, looked in her face kindly, kissed her, and said, "My dear, never mind, it will all come right again—only, don't run away."

"What will come right?"

"Any little misunderstanding with Norman Ogilvie."

"I don't know what you mean," said Ethel, becoming scarlet.

"My dear, you need not try to hide it. I see that you have got into a fright. You have made a discovery, but that is no reason for running away."

"Yes it is!" said Ethel firmly, not denying the charge, though reddening more than ever at finding her impression confirmed.

"Poor child! she is afraid!" said Flora tenderly; "but I will take care of you, Ethel. It is everything delightful. You are the very girl for such a heros de Roman, and it has embellished you more than all my Paris fineries."

"Hush, Flora! We ought not to talk in this way, as if —"

"As if he had done more than walk with, and talk with, nobody else! How he did hate papa last night. I had a great mind to call papa off, in pity to him."

"Don't, Flora. If there were anything in it, it would not be proper to think of it, so I am going home to prevent it." The words were spoken with averted face and heaving breath.

"Proper?" said Flora. "The Mays are a good old family, and our own grandmother was an honourable Ogilvie herself. A Scottish baron, very poor too, has no right to look down —"

"They shall not look down. Flora, it is of no use to talk. I cannot be spared from home, and I will not put myself in the way of being tempted to forsake them all."

"Tempted!" said Flora, laughing. "Is it such a wicked thing?"

"Not in others, but it would be wrong in me, with such a state of things as there is at home."

"I do not suppose he would want you for some years to come. He is only two-and-twenty. Mary will grow older."

"Margaret will either be married, or want constant care. Flora, I will not let myself be drawn from them."

"You may think so now; but it would be for their real good to relieve papa of any of us. If we were all to think as you do, how should we live? I don't know — for papa told me there will be barely ten thousand pounds, besides the houses, and what will that be among ten? I am not talking of yourself, but think of the others!"

"I know papa will not be happy without me, and I will not leave him," repeated Ethel, not answering the argument.

Flora changed her ground, and laughed. "We are getting into the heroics," she said, "when it would be very foolish to break up our plans, only because we have found a pleasant cousin. There is nothing serious in it, I dare say. How silly of us to argue on such an idea!"

Meta came in before Flora could say more, but Ethel, with burning cheeks, repeated, "It will be safer!"

Ethel had, meantime, been dressed by her sister; and, as Bellairs came to adorn Meta, and she could have no solitude, she went downstairs, thinking she heard Norman's step, and hoping to judge of his mood.

She entered the room with an exclamation, "Oh, Norman!"

"At your service!" said the wrong Norman, looking merrily up from behind a newspaper.

"Oh, I beg your pardon; I thought—"

"Your thoughts were quite right," he said, smiling. "Your brother desires me to present his respects to his honoured family, and to inform them that his stock of assurance is likely to be diminished by the pleasure of their company this morning."

"How is he?" asked Ethel anxiously.

"Pretty fair. He has blue saucers round his eyes, as he had before he went up for his little go."

"Oh, I know them," said Ethel.

"Very odd," continued her cousin; "when the end always is, that he says he has the luck of being set on in the very place he knows best. But I think it has expended itself in a sleepless night, and I have no fears, when he comes to the point."

"What is he doing?"

"Writing to his brother Harry. He said it was the day for the Pacific mail, and that Harry's pleasure would be the best of it."

"Ah!" said Ethel, glancing towards the paper, "is there any naval intelligence?"

He looked; and while she was thinking whether she ought not to depart, he exclaimed, in a tone that startled her, "Ha! No. Is your brother's ship the Alcestis?"

"Yes! Oh, what?"

"Nothing then, I assure you. See, it is merely this—she has not come into Sydney so soon as expected, which you knew before. That is all."

"Let me see," said the trembling Ethel.

It was no more than an echo of their unconfessed apprehensions, yet it seemed to give them a body; and Ethel's thoughts flew to Margaret. Her going home would be absolutely necessary now. Mr. Ogilvie kindly began to talk away her alarm, saying that there was still no reason for dread, mentioning the many causes that might have delayed the ship, and reassuring her greatly.

"But Norman!" she said.

"Ah! true. Poor May! He will break down to a certainty if he hears it. I will go at once, and keep guard over him, lest he should meet with this paper. But pray, don't be alarmed. I assure you there is no cause. You will have letters to-morrow."

Ethel would fain have thrown off her finery and hurried home at once, but no one regarded the matter as she did. Dr. May agreed with Flora that it was no worse than before, and though they now thought Ethel's return desirable, on Margaret's account, it would be better not to add to the shock by a sudden arrival, especially as they took in no daily paper at home. So the theatre was not to be given up, nor any of the subsequent plans, except so far as regarded Ethel; and, this agreed, they started for the scene of action.

They were hardly in the street before they met the ubiquitous Mr. Ogilvie, saying that Cheviot, Norman's prompter, was aware of the report, and was guarding him, while he came to escort the ladies, through what he expressively called "the bear fight." Ethel resolutely adhered to her father, and her cousin took care of Meta, who had been clinging in a tiptoe manner to the point of her brother's high elbow, looking as if the crowd might easily brush off such a little fly, without his missing her.

Inch by inch, a step at a time, the ladies were landed in a crowd of their own sex, where Flora bravely pioneered; they emerged on their benches, shook themselves out, and seated themselves. There was the swarm of gay ladies around them, and beneath the area, fast being paved with heads, black, brown, gray, and bald, a surging living sea, where Meta soon pointed out Dr. May and George; the mere sight of such masses of people was curious and interesting, reminding Ethel of Cherry Elwood having once shocked her by saying the Whit-Monday club was the most beautiful sight in the whole year. And above! that gallery of trampling undergraduates, and more than trampling! Ethel and Meta could, at first, have found it in their hearts to be frightened at those thundering shouts, but the young ladies were usually of opinions so similar, that the louder grew the cheers, the more they laughed and exulted, so carried along that no cares could be remembered.

Making a way through the thronged area, behold the procession of scarlet doctors, advancing through the midst, till the red and black vice-chancellor sat enthroned in the centre, and the scarlet line became a semicircle, dividing the flower-garden of ladies from the black mass below.

Then came the introduction of the honorary doctors, one by one, with the Latin speech, which Ethel's companions unreasonably required her to translate to them, while she was using all her ears to catch a word or two, and her eyes to glimpse at the features of men of note.

By-and-by a youth made his appearance in the rostrum, and a good deal of Latin ensued, of which Flora hoped Ethel was less tired than she was. In time, however, Meta saw the spectacles removed, and George looking straight up, and she drew down her veil, and took hold of Flora's hand, and Ethel flushed like a hot coal. Nevertheless, all contrived to see a tall figure, with face much flushed, and hands moving nervously. The world was tired, and people were departing, so that the first lines were lost, perhaps a satisfaction to Norman; but his voice soon cleared and became louder, his eyes lighted, and Ethel knew the "funny state" had come to his relief—people's attention was arrested—there was no more going away.

It was well that Norman was ignorant of the fears for Harry, for four lines had been added since Ethel had seen the poem, saying how self-sacrifice sent forth the sailor-boy from home, to the lone watch, the wave and storm, his spirit rising high, ere manhood braced his form.

Applause did not come where Ethel had expected it, and, at first, there was silence at the close, but suddenly the acclamations rose with deafening loudness, though hardly what greets some poems with more to catch the popular ear.

Ethel's great excitement was over, and presently she found herself outside of the theatre, a shower falling, and an umbrella held over her by Mr. Ogilvie, who was asking her if it was not admirable, and declaring the poem might rank with Heber's 'Palestine', or Milman's 'Apollo'.

They were bound for a great luncheon at one of the colleges, where Ethel might survey the Principal with whom Miss Rich had corresponded. Mr. Ogilvie sat next to her, told her all the names, and quizzed the dignitaries, but she had a sense of depression, and did not wish to enter into the usual strain of banter. He dropped his lively tone, and drew her out about Harry, till she was telling eagerly of her dear sailor brother, and found him so sympathising and considerate, that she did not like him less; though she felt her intercourse with him a sort of intoxication, that would only make it the worse for her by-and-by.

During that whole luncheon, and their walk through the gardens, where there was a beautiful horticultural show, something was always prompting her to say, while in this quasi-privacy, that she was on the eve of departure, but she kept her resolution against it—she thought it would have been an unwarrantable experiment. When they returned to their inn they found Norman looking fagged, but relieved, half asleep on the sofa, with a novel in his hand. He roused himself as they came in, and, to avoid any compliments on his own performance, began, "Well, Ethel, are you ready for the ball?"

"We shall spare her the ball," said Dr. May; "there is a report about the Alcestis in the newspaper that may make Margaret uncomfortable, and this good sister will not stay away from her."

Norman started up crying, "What, papa?"

"It is a mere nothing in reality," said Dr. May, "only what we knew before;" and he showed his son the paragraph, which Norman read as a death warrant; the colour ebbed from his lips and cheeks; he trembled so that he was obliged to sit down, and, without speaking, he kept his eyes fixed on the words, "Serious apprehensions are entertained with regard to H. M. S. Alcestis, Captain Gordon—"

"If you had seen as many newspaper reports come to nothing, as I have, you would not take this so much to heart," said Dr. May. "I expect to hear that this very mail has brought letters."

And Meta added that, at luncheon, she had been seated next to one of the honorary doctors—a naval captain—who had been making discoveries in the South Sea, and that he had scouted the notion of harm befalling the Alcestis, and given all manner of reassuring suppositions as to her detention, adding besides, that no one believed the Australian paper whence the report was taken. He had seen the Alcestis, knew Captain Gordon, and spoke of him as one of the safest people in the world. Had his acquaintance extended to lieutenants and midshipmen, it would have been perfect; as it was, the tidings brought back the blood to Norman's cheek, and the light to his eye.

"When do we set off?" was Norman's question.

"At five," said Ethel. "You mean it, papa?"

"I did intend it, if I had gone alone, but I shall not take you till eight; nor you, Norman, at all."

Norman was bent on returning, but his father and Flora would not hear of it. Flora could not spare him, and Dr. May was afraid of the effect of anxiety on nerves and spirits so sensitive. While this was going on, Mr. Ogilvie looked at Ethel in consternation, and said, "Are you really going home?"

"Yes, my eldest sister must not be left alone when she hears this."

He looked down—Ethel had the resolution to walk away. Flora could not give up the ball, and Meta found that she must go; but both the Normans spent a quiet evening with Dr. May and Ethel. Norman May had a bad headache, which he was allowed to have justly earned; Dr. May was very happy reviving all his Scottish recollections, and talking to young Ogilvie about Edinburgh. Once, there was a private consultation. Ethel was provoked and ashamed at the throbs that it would excite. What! on a week's acquaintance?

When alone with her father, she began to nerve herself for something heroic, and great was her shame when she heard only of her cousin's kind consideration for her brother, whom he wished to take home with him, and thence to see the Highlands, so as to divert his anxiety for Harry, as well as to call him off from the studies with which he had this term overworked himself even more than usual. Dr. May had given most grateful consent, and he spoke highly in praise of the youth; but there was no more to come, and Ethel could have beaten herself for the moment of anticipation.

Meta came home, apologising for wakening Ethel; but Ethel had not been asleep. The ball had not, it seemed, been as charming to her as most events were, and Ethel heard a sigh as the little lady lay down in her bed.

Late as it was when she went to rest, Meta rose to see the travellers off; she sent hosts of messages to her father, and wished she might go with them. George and Flora were not visible, and Dr. May was leaving messages for them, and for Norman, in her charge, when the two Balliol men walked in.

Ethel had hoped it was over, yet she could not be sorry that the two youths escorted them to the station, and, as Ethel was placed in the carriage, she believed that she heard something of never forgetting— happiest week—but in the civilities which the other occupant of the carriage was offering for the accommodation of their lesser luggage, she lost the exact words, and the last she heard were, "Good-bye; I hope you will find letters at home."

CHAPTER X.

True to the kindred points of Heaven and home.

WORDSWORTH.

Etheldred's dream was over. She had wakened to the inside of a Great Western carriage, her father beside her, and opposite a thin, foreign-looking gentleman. Her father, to whom her life was to be devoted! She looked at his profile, defined against the window, and did not repent. In a sort of impulse to do something for him, she took his hat from his hand, and was going to dispose of it in the roof, when he turned, smiling his thanks, but saying, "it was not worth while—this carriage was a very transitory resting-place."

The stranger at that moment sprang to his feet, exclaiming, "Dick himself!"

"Spencer, old fellow, is it you?" cried Dr. May, in a voice of equal amazement and joy, holding out his hand, which was grasped and wrung with a force that made Ethel shrink for the poor maimed arm.

"Ha! what is amiss with your arm?" was the immediate question. Three technical words were spoken in a matter-of-fact way, as Dr. May replaced his hand in his bosom, and then, with an eager smile, said, "Ethel, here! You have heard of him!"

Ethel had indeed, and gave her hand cordially, surprised by the bow and air of deferential politeness with which it was received, like a favour, while Dr. Spencer asked her whether she had been staying in Oxford.

"Ay; and what for, do you think?" said Dr. May joyously.

"You don't say that was your son who held forth yesterday! I thought his voice had a trick of yours—but then I thought you would have held by old Cambridge."

"What could I do?" said Dr. May deprecatingly; "the boy would go and get a Balliol scholarship—"

135

"Why! the lad is a genius! a poet—no mistake about it! but I scarcely thought you could have one of such an age."

"Of his age! His brother is in Holy Orders—one of his sisters is married. There's for you, Spencer!"

"Bless me, Dick! I thought myself a young man!"

"What! with hair of that colour?" said Dr. May, looking at his friend's milk-white locks.

"Bleached by that frightful sickly season at Poonshedagore, when I thought I was done for. But you! you—the boy of the whole lot! You think me very disrespectful to your father," added he, turning to Ethel, "but you see what old times are."

"I know," said Ethel, with a bright look.

"So you were in the theatre yesterday," continued Dr. May; "but there is no seeing any one in such a throng. How long have you been in England?"

"A fortnight. I went at once to see my sister, at Malvern; there I fell in with Rudden, the man I was with in New Guinea. He was going up to be made an honorary doctor, and made me come with him."

"And where are you bound for?" as the train showed signs of a halt.

"For London. I meant to hunt up Mat. Fleet, and hear of you, and other old friends."

"Does he expect you?"

"No one expects me. I am a regular vagabond."

"Come home with us," said Dr. May, laying his hand on his arm. "I cannot part with you so soon. Come, find your luggage. Take your ticket for Gloucester."

"So suddenly! Will it not be inconvenient?" said he, looking tempted, but irresolute.

"Oh, no, no; pray come!" said Ethel eagerly. "We shall be so glad."

He looked his courteous thanks, and soon was with them en-route for Stoneborough.

Ethel's thoughts were diverted from all she had left at Oxford. She could not but watch those two old friends. She knew enough of the traveller to enter into her father's happiness, and to have no fears is of another Sir Matthew.

They had been together at Stoneborough, at Cambridge, at Paris, at Edinburgh, always linked in the closest friendship; but, by Dr. May's own account, his friend had been the diligent one of the pair, a bright compound of principle and spirit, and highly distinguished in all his studies, and Dr. May's model of perfection. Their paths had since lain far apart, and they had not seen each other since, twenty-six years ago, they had parted in London—the one to settle at his native town, while the other accepted a situation as travelling physician. On his return, he had almost sacrificed his life, by self-devoted attendance on a fever-stricken emigrant-ship. He had afterwards received an appointment in India, and there the correspondence had died away, and Dr. May had lost traces of him, only knowing that, in a visitation of cholera, he had again acted with the same carelessness of his own life, and a severe illness, which had broken up his health, had occasioned him to relinquish his post.

It now appeared that he had thought himself coming home ever since. He had gone to recruit in the Himalayas, and had become engrossed in scientific observations on their altitudes, as well as investigations in natural history. Going to Calcutta, he had fallen in with a party about to explore the Asiatic islands and he had accompanied them, as well as going on an expedition into the interior of Australia. He had been employed in various sanitary arrangements there and in India, and had finally worked his way slowly home, overland, visiting Egypt and Palestine, and refreshing his memory with every Italian, German, or French Cathedral, or work of art, that had delighted him in early days.

He was a slight small man, much sunburned, nearly bald, and his hair snowy, but his eyes were beautiful, very dark, soft, and smiling, and yet their gaze peculiarly keen and steady, as if ready for any emergency, and his whole frame was full of alertness and vigour. His voice was clear and sweet, and his manner most refined and polished, indeed, his courtesy to Ethel, whenever there was a change of carriage, was so exemplary, that she understood it as the effect on a chivalrous mind, of living where a lady was a rare and precious article. It frightened Ethel a little at first, but, before the end of the journey, she had already begun to feel towards him like an old friend—one of those inheritances who are so much valued and loved, like a sort of uncles-in-friendship. She had an especial grateful honour for the delicate tact which asked no questions, as she saw his eye often falling anxiously on her father's left hand, where the wedding ring shone upon the little finger.

There was talk enough upon his travels, on public changes, and on old friends; but, after those first few words, home had never been mentioned.

When, at five o'clock, the engine blew its whistle, at the old familiar station, Dr. May had scarcely put his head out before Adams hastened up to him with a note.

"All well at home?"

"Yes, sir, Miss Margaret sent up the gig."

"I must go at once," said Dr May hastily—"the Larkins' child is worse. Ethel, take care of him, and introduce him. Love to Margaret. I'll be at home before tea."

He was driven off at speed, and Ethel proposed to walk home. Dr Spencer gave her his arm, and was silent, but presently said, in a low, anxious voice, "My dear, you must forgive me, I have heard nothing for many years. Your mother—"

"It was an accident," said Ethel looking straight before her. "It was when papa's arm was hurt. The carriage was over-turned."

"And—" repeated Dr Spencer earnestly

"She was killed on the spot," said Ethel, speaking shortly, and abruptly. If she was to say it at all, she could not do so otherwise.

He was dreadfully shocked—she knew it by the shudder of his arm, and a tight suppressed groan. He did not speak, and Ethel, as if a relief from the silence must be made, said what was not very consoling, and equally blunt. "Margaret had some harm done to her spine—she cannot walk."

He did not seem to hear, but walked on, as in a dream, where Ethel guided him, and she would not interrupt him again.

They had just passed Mr Bramshaw's office, when a voice was heard behind, calling, "Miss Ethel! Miss Ethel!" and Edward Anderson, now articled to Mr. Bramshaw, burst out, pen in hand, and looking shabby and inky.

"Miss Ethel!" he said breathlessly, "I beg your pardon, but have you heard from Harry?"

"No!" said Ethel. "Have they had that paper at home?"

"Not that I know of," said Edward. "My mother wanted to send it, but I would not take it—not while Dr. May was away."

"Thank you—that was very kind of you."

"And oh! Miss Ethel, do you think it is true?"

"We hope not," said Ethel kindly—"we saw a Captain at Oxford who thought it not at all to be depended on."

"I am so glad," said Edward; and, shaking hands, he went back to his high stool, Ethel feeling that he deserved the pains that Norman had taken to spare and befriend him. She spoke to her companion in explanation. "We are very anxious for news of my next brother's ship, Alcestis, in the Pacific—"

"More!" exclaimed poor Dr. Spencer, almost overpowered; "Good Heavens! I thought May, at least, was happy!"

"He is not unhappy," said Ethel, not sorry that they had arrived at the back entrance of the shrubbery.

"How long ago was this?" said he, standing still, as soon as they had passed into the garden.

"Four years, next October. I assure you, his spirits are almost always good."

"When I was at Adelaide, little thinking!" he sighed, then recollecting himself. "Forgive me, I have given you pain."

"No," she said, "or rather, I gave you more."

"I knew her—" and there he broke off, paused for a minute, then collecting himself, seemed resolutely to turn away from the subject, and said, walking on, "This garden is not much altered."

At that moment, a little shrill voice broke out in remonstrance among the laurels—"But you know, Daisy, you are the captain of the forty thieves!"

"A startling announcement!" said Dr. Spencer, looking at Ethel, and the next two steps brought them in view of the play-place in the laurels, where Aubrey lay on the ground, feigning sleep, but keeping a watchful eye over Blanche, who was dropping something into the holes of inverted flower-pots, Gertrude dancing about in a way that seemed to have called for the reproof of the more earnest actors.

"Ethel! Ethel!" screamed the children, with one voice, and, while the two girls stood in shyness at her companion, Aubrey had made a dart at her neck, and hung upon her, arms, legs, body, and all, like a wild cat.

"That will do! that will do, old man—let go! Speak to Dr. Spencer, my dear."

Blanche did so demurely, and asked where was papa?

"Coming, as soon as he has been to Mrs. Larkins's poor baby."

"George Larkins has been here," said Aubrey. "And I have finished 'Vipera et lima', Ethel, but Margaret makes such false quantities!"

"What is your name, youngster?" said Dr. Spencer, laying his hand on Aubrey's head.

"Aubrey Spencer May," was the answer.

"Hey day! where did you steal my name?" exclaimed Dr. Spencer, while Aubrey stood abashed at so mysterious an accusation.

"Oh!" exclaimed Blanche, seizing on Ethel, and whispering, "is it really the boy that climbed the market cross?"

"You see your fame lives here," said Ethel, smiling, as Dr. Spencer evidently heard.

"He was a little boy!" said Aubrey indignantly, looking at the gray-haired man.

"There!" said Ethel to Dr. Spencer.

"The tables turned!" he said, laughing heartily. "But do not let me keep you. You would wish to prepare your sister for a stranger, and I shall improve my acquaintance here. Where are the forty thieves?"

"I am all of them," said the innocent, daisy-faced Gertrude; and Ethel hastened towards the house, glad of the permission granted by his true good-breeding.

There was a shriek of welcome from Mary, who sat working beside Margaret. Ethel was certain that no evil tidings had come to her eldest sister, so joyous was her exclamation of wonder and rebuke to her home-sick Ethel. "Naughty girl! running home at once! I did think you would have been happy there!"

"So I was," said Ethel hastily; "but who do you think I have brought home?" Margaret flushed with such a pink, that Ethel resolved never to set her guessing again, and hurried to explain; and having heard that all was well, and taken her housekeeping measures, she proceeded to fetch the guest; but Mary, who had been unusually silent all this time, ran after her, and checked her.

"Ethel, have you heard?" she said.

"Have you?" said Ethel.

"George Larkins rode in this morning to see when papa would come home, and he told me. He said I had better not tell Margaret, for he did not believe it."

"And you have not! That is very good of you, Mary."

"Oh! I am glad you are come! I could not have helped telling, if you had been away a whole week! But, Ethel, does papa believe it?" Poor Mary's full lip swelled, and her eyes swam, ready to laugh or weep, in full faith in her sister's answer.

Ethel told of Meta's captain, and the smile predominated, and settled down into Mary's usual broad beamy look, like a benignant rising sun on the sign of an inn, as Ethel praised her warmly for a fortitude and consideration of which she had not thought her capable.

Dr. Spencer was discovered full in the midst of the comedy of the forty thieves, alternating, as required, between the robber-captain and the ass, and the children in perfect ecstasies with him.

They all followed in his train to the drawing-room, and were so clamorous, that he could have no conversation with Margaret. He certainly made them so, but Ethel, remembering what a blow her disclosures had been, thought it would be only a kindness to send Aubrey to show him to his room, where he might have some peace.

She was not sorry to be very busy, so as to have little time to reply to the questions on the doings at Oxford, and the cause of her sudden return; and yet it would have been a comfort to be able to sit down to understand herself, and recall her confused thoughts. But solitary reflection was a thing only to be hoped for in that house in bed, and Ethel was obliged to run up and down, and attend to everybody, under an undefined sense that she had come home to a dull, anxious world of turmoil.

Margaret seemed to guess nothing, that was one comfort; she evidently thought that her return was fully accounted for by the fascination of her papa's presence in a strange place. She gave Ethel no credit for the sacrifice, naturally supposing that she could not enjoy herself away from home. Ethel did not know whether to be glad or not; she was relieved, but it was flat. As to Norman Ogilvie, one or two inquiries whether she liked him, and if Norman were going to Scotland with him, were all that passed, and it was very provoking to be made so hot and conscious by them.

She could not begin to dress till late, and while she was unpacking, she heard her father come home, among the children's loud welcomes, and go to the drawing-room. He presently knocked at the door between their rooms.

"So Margaret does not know?" he said.

"No, Mary has been so very good;" and she told what had passed.

"Well done, Mary, I must tell her so. She is a good girl on a pinch, you see!"

"And we don't speak of it now? Or will it hurt Margaret more to think we keep things from her?"

"That is the worst risk of the two. I have seen great harm done in that way. Mention it, but without seeming to make too much of it."

"Won't you, papa?"

"You had better—it will seem of less importance. I think nothing of it myself."

Nevertheless, Ethel saw that he could not trust himself to broach the subject to Margaret.

"How was the Larkins' baby?"

"Doing better. What have you done with Spencer?"

"I put him into Richard's room. The children were eating him up! He is so kind to them."

"Ay! I say, Ethel, that was a happy consequence of your coming home with me."

"What a delightful person he is!"

"Is he not? A true knight errant, as he always was! I could not tell you what I owed to him as a boy—all my life, I may say.

Ethel," he added suddenly: "we must do our best to make him happy here. I know it now—I never guessed it then, but one is very hard and selfish when one is happy—"

"What do you mean, papa?"

"I see it now," continued Dr. May incoherently; "the cause of his wandering life—advantages thrown aside. He! the most worthy. Things I little heeded at the time have come back on me! I understand why he banished himself!"

"Why?" asked Ethel bewildered.

"She never had an idea of it; but I might have guessed from what fell from him unconsciously, for not a word would he have said—nor did he say, to show how he sacrificed himself!"

"Who was it? Aunt Flora?" said Ethel, beginning to collect his meaning.

"No, Ethel, it was your own dear mother! You will think this another romantic fancy of mine, but I am sure of it."

"So am I," said Ethel.

"How—what? Ah! I remembered after we parted that he might know nothing—"

"He asked me," said Ethel.

"And how did he bear it?"

Ethel told, and the tears filled her father's eyes.

"It was wrong and cruel in me to bring him home unprepared! and then to leave it to you. I always forget other people's feelings. Poor Spencer! And now, Ethel, you see what manner of man we have here, and how we ought to treat him."

"Indeed I do!"

"The most unselfish—the most self-sacrificing—" continued Dr. May. "And to see what it all turned on! I happened to have this place open to me—the very cause, perhaps, of my having taken things easy— and so the old Professor threw opportunities in my way; while Aubrey Spencer, with every recommendation that man could have, was set aside, and exiled himself, leaving the station, and all he might so easily have gained. Ah, Ethel, Sir Matthew Fleet never came near him in ability. But not one word to interfere with me would he say, and—how I have longed to meet him again, after parting in my selfish, unfeeling gladness; and now I have nothing to do for him, but show him how little I was to be trusted with her."

Ethel never knew how to deal with these occasional bursts of grief, but she said that she thought Dr. Spencer was very much pleased to have met with him, and delighted with the children.

"Ah! well, you are her children," said Dr. May, with his hand on Ethel's shoulder.

So they went downstairs, and found Mary making tea; and Margaret, fearing Dr. Spencer was overwhelmed with his young admirers—for Aubrey and Gertrude were one on each knee, and Blanche standing beside him, inflicting on him a catalogue of the names and ages of all the eleven.

"Ethel has introduced you, I see," said Dr. May.

"Ay, I assure you, it was an alarming introduction. No sooner do I enter your garden, than I hear that I am in the midst of the Forty Thieves. I find a young lady putting the world to death, after the fashion of Hamlet—and, looking about to find what I have lost, I find this urchin has robbed me of my name—a property I supposed was always left to unfortunate travellers, however small they might be chopped themselves."

"Well, Aubrey boy, will you make restitution?"

"It is my name," said Aubrey positively; for, as his father added, "He is not without dread of the threat being fulfilled, and himself left to be that Anon who, Blanche says, writes so much poetry."

Aubrey privately went to Ethel, to ask her if this were possible; and she had to reassure him, by telling him that they were "only in fun."

It was fun with a much deeper current though; for Dr. Spencer was saying, with a smile, between gratification and sadness, "I did not think my name would have been remembered here so long."

"We had used up mine, and the grandfathers', and the uncles', and began to think we might look a little further a-field," said Dr. May. "If I had only known where you were, I would have asked you to be the varlet's godfather; but I was much afraid you were nowhere in the land of the living."

145

"I have but one godson, and he is coffee-coloured! I ought to have written; but, you see, for seven years I thought I was coming home."

Aubrey had recovered sufficiently to observe to Blanche, "That was almost as bad as Ulysses," which, being overheard and repeated, led to the information that he was Ethel's pupil, whereupon Dr. Spencer began to inquire after the school, and to exclaim at his friend for having deserted it in the person of Tom. Dr. May looked convicted, but said it was all Norman's fault; and Dr. Spencer, shaking his head at Blanche, opined that the young gentleman was a great innovater, and that he was sure he was at the bottom of the pulling down the Market Cross, and the stopping up Randall's Alley—iniquities of the "nasty people," of which she already had made him aware.

"Poor Norman, he suffered enough anent Randall's Alley," said Dr. May; "but as to the Market Cross, that came down a year before he was born."

"It was the Town Council!" said Ethel.

"One of the ordinary stultifications of Town Councils?"

"Take care, Spencer," said Dr. May. "I am a Town Council man my-self—"

"You, Dick!" and he turned with a start of astonishment, and went into a fit of laughing, re-echoed by all the young ones, who were especially tickled by hearing, from another, the abbreviation that had, hitherto, only lived in the favourite expletive, "As sure as my name is Dick May."

"Of course," said Dr. May. "'Dost thou not suspect my place? Dost thou not suspect my years? One that hath two gowns, and everything handsome about him!'"

His friend laughed the more, and they betook themselves to the College stories, of which the quotation from Dogberry seemed to have reminded them.

There was something curious and affecting in their manner to each other. Often it was the easy bantering familiarity of the two youths they had once been together, with somewhat of elder brotherhood on Dr. Spencer's side—and of looking up on Dr. May's—and just as they had recurred to these terms, some allusion would bring back to Dr. Spencer, that the heedless, high-spirited "Dick," whom he had always had much ado to keep out of scrapes, was a householder, a man of weight and influence; a light which would at first strike him as most ludicrous, and then mirth would end in a sigh, for there was yet another aspect! After having thought of him so long as the happy husband of Margaret Mackenzie, he found her place vacant, and the trace of deep grief apparent on the countenance, once so gay—the oppression of anxiety marked on the brow, formerly so joyous, the merriment almost more touching than gravity would have been, for the former nature seemed rather shattered than altered. In merging towards this side, there was a tender respect in Dr. Spencer's manner that was most beautiful, though this evening such subjects were scrupulously kept at the utmost distance, by the constant interchange of new and old jokes and stories.

Only when bed-time had come, and Margaret had been carried off—did a silence fall on the two friends, unbroken till Dr. May rose and proposed going upstairs. When he gave his hand to wish good-night, Dr. Spencer held it this time most carefully, and said, "Oh, May! I did not expect this!"

"I should have prepared you," said his host, "but I never recollected

that you knew nothing—"

"I had dwelt on your happiness!"

"There never were two happier creatures for twenty-two years," said Dr. May, his voice low with emotion. "Sorrow spared her! Yes, think of her always in undimmed brightness—always smiling as you remember her. She was happy. She is," he concluded. His friend had turned aside and hidden his face with his hands, then looked up for a moment, "And you, Dick," he said briefly.

"Sorrow spared her," was Dr. May's first answer. "And hers are very good children!"

There was a silence again, ending in Dr. May's saying, "What do you think of my poor girl?"

They discussed the nature of the injury: Dr. Spencer could not feel otherwise than that it was a very hopeless matter. Her father owned that he had thought so from the first, and had wondered at Sir Matthew Fleet's opinion. His subdued tone of patience and resignation, struck his guest above all, as changed from what he had once been.

"You have been sorely tried," he said, when they parted at his room door.

"I have received much good!" simply answered Dr. May. "Goodnight! I am glad to have you here—if you can bear it."

"Bear it? Dick! how like that girl is to you! She is yourself!"

"Such a self as I never was! Good-night."

Ethel overcame the difficulty of giving the account of the newspaper alarm with tolerable success, by putting the story of Meta's conversation foremost. Margaret did not take it to heart as much as she had feared, nor did she appear to dwell on it afterwards. The truth was perhaps that Dr. Spencer's visit was to every one more of an excitement and amusement than it was to Ethel. Not that she did not like him extremely, but after such a week as she had been spending, the home-world seemed rather stale and unprofitable.

Miss Bracy relapsed into a state of "feelings," imagining that Ethel had distrusted her capabilities, and therefore returned; or as Ethel herself sometimes feared, there might be irritability in her own manner that gave cause of annoyance. The children were inclined to be riotous with their new friend, who made much of them continually, and especially patronised Aubrey; Mary was proud of showing how much she had learned to do for Margaret in her sister's absence; Dr. May was so much taken up with his friend, that Ethel saw less of him than usual, and she began to believe that it had been all a mistake that every one was so dependent on her, for, in fact, they did much better without her.

Meantime, she heard of the gaieties which the others were enjoying, and she could not feel heroic when they regretted her. At the end of a week, Meta Rivers was escorted home from Warwick by two servants, and came to Stoneborough, giving a lively description of all the concluding pleasures, but declaring that Ethel's departure had taken away the zest of the whole, and Mr. Ogilvie had been very disconsolate. Margaret had not been prepared to hear that Mr.

Ogilvie had been so constant a companion, and was struck by finding that Ethel had passed over one who had evidently been so great an ingredient in the delights of the expedition. Meta had, however observed nothing—she was a great deal too simple and too much engrossed for such notions to have crossed her mind; but Margaret inferred something, and hoped to learn more when she should see Flora. This would not be immediately. George and his wife were gone to London, and thence intended to pay a round of visits; and Norman had accompanied his namesake to Glenbracken.

Ethel fought hard with her own petulance and sense of tedium at home, which was, as she felt, particularly uncalled for at present; when Dr. Spencer was enlivening them so much. He was never in the way, he was always either busy in the dining-room in the morning with books and papers, or wandering about his old school-boy haunts in the town, or taking Adam's place, and driving out Dr. May, or sometimes joining the children in a walk, to their supreme delight. His sketches, for he drew most beautifully, were an endless pleasure to Margaret, with his explanations of them—she even tried to sit up to copy them, and he began to teach Blanche to draw. The evenings, when there was certain to be some entertaining talk going on between the two doctors, were very charming, and Margaret seemed quite revived by seeing her father so happy with his friend. Ethel knew she ought to be happy also, and if attention could make her so, she had it, for kind and courteous as Dr. Spencer was to all, she seemed to have a double charm for him. It was as if he found united in her the quaint brusquerie, that he had loved in her father, with somewhat of her mother; for though Ethel had less personal resemblance to Mrs. May than any other of the family, Dr. Spencer transferred to her much of the chivalrous distant devotion, with which he had regarded her mother. Ethel was very little conscious of it, but he was certainly her sworn knight, and there was an eagerness in his manner of performing every little service for her, a deference in his way of listening to her, over and above his ordinary polish of manner.

Ethel lighted up, and enjoyed herself when talking was going on — her periods of ennui were when she had to set about any home employment— when Aubrey's lessons did not go well—when she wanted to speak to her father, and could not catch him; and even when she had to go to Cocksmoor.

She did not seem to make any progress there—the room was very full, and very close, the children were dull, and she began to believe she was doing no good—it was all a weariness. But she was so heartily ashamed of her feelings, that she worked the more vehemently for them, and the utmost show that they outwardly made was, that Margaret thought her less vivacious than her wont, and she was a little too peremptory at times with Mary and Blanche. She had so much disliked the display that Flora had made about Cocksmoor, that she had imposed total silence on it upon her younger sisters, and Dr. Spencer had spent a fortnight at Stoneborough without being aware of their occupation; when there occurred such an extremely sultry day, that Margaret remonstrated with Ethel on her intention of broiling herself and Mary by walking to Cocksmoor, when the quicksilver stood at 80° in the shade.

Ethel was much inclined to stay at home, but she did not know whether this was from heat or from idleness, and her fretted spirits took the turn of determination—so she posted off at a galloping pace, that her brothers called her "Cocksmoor speed," and Mary panted by her side, humbly petitioning for the plantation path, when she answered "that it was as well to be hot in the sun as in the shade."

The school-room was unusually full, all the haymaking mothers made it serve as an infant school, and though as much window was opened as there could be, the effect was not coolness. Nevertheless, Ethel sat down and gathered her class round her, and she had just heard the chapter once read, when there was a little confusion, a frightened cry of "Ethel!" and before she could rise to her feet—a flump upon the floor—poor Mary had absolutely fainted dead away.

Ethel was much terrified, and very angry with herself; Mary was no light weight, but Mrs. Elwood coming at their cry, helped Ethel to drag her into the outer room, where she soon began to recover, and to be excessively puzzled as to what had happened to her. She said the sea was roaring, and where was Harry? and then she looked much surprised to find herself lying on Mrs. Elwood's damp flags— a circumstance extremely distressing to Mrs. Elwood, who wanted to carry her upstairs into Cherry's room, very clean and very white, but with such a sun shining full into it!

Ethel lavished all care, and reproached herself greatly, though to be sure nothing had ever been supposed capable of hurting Mary, and

Mary herself protested that nothing at all had ailed her till the children's voices began to sound funny, and turned into the waves of the sea, and therewith poor Mary burst into a great flood of tears, and asked whether Harry would ever come back. The tears did her a great deal of good, though not so much as the being petted by Ethel, and she soon declared herself perfectly well; but Ethel could not think of letting her walk home, and sent off a boy—who she trusted would not faint—with a note to Margaret, desiring her to send the gig, which fortunately was at home to-day.

Mary had partaken of some of Mrs. Elwood's tea, which, though extremely bitter, seemed a great cordial, and was sitting, quite revived, in the arbour at the door, when the gig stopped, and Dr. Spencer walked in.

"Well, and how are you?"

"Quite well now, thank you. Was Margaret frightened? Why did you come?"

"I thought it would make her happier, as your father was not at home. Here, let me feel your pulse. Do you think no one is a doctor but your papa? There's not much the matter with you, however. Where is Ethel?"

"In the school," and Mary opened the door. Dr. Spencer looked in, as Ethel came out, and his face put her in mind of Norman's look.

"No wonder!" was all he said.

Ethel was soon satisfied that he did not think Mary ill. In fact, he said fainting was the most natural and justifiable measure, under the circumstances. "How many human creatures do you keep there?" he asked.

"Forty-seven to-day," said Mary proudly.

"I shall indict you for cruelty to animals! I think I have known it hotter at Poonshedagore, but there we had punkahs!"

"It was very wrong of me," said Ethel. "I should have thought of poor Mary, in that sunny walk, but Mary never complains."

"Oh, never mind," said Mary, "it did not hurt."

"I'm not thinking of Mary," said Dr. Spencer, "but of the wretched beings you are leaving shut up there. I wonder what the mercury would be there."

"We cannot help it," said Mary. "We cannot get the ground."

And Mary, having been voted into the seat of honour and comfort by his side in the carriage, told her version of Cocksmoor and the Committee; while Ethel sat up in the little narrow seat behind, severely reproaching herself for her want of consideration towards one so good and patient as Mary, who proved to have been suffering far more on Harry's account than they had guessed, and who was so simple and thorough-going in doing her duty. This was not being a good elder sister, and, when they came home, she confessed it, and showed so much remorse that poor Mary was quite shocked, and cried so bitterly that it was necessary to quit the subject.

"Ethel, dearest," said Margaret that night, after they were in bed, "is there anything the matter?"

"No, nothing, but that Oxford has spoiled me," said Ethel, resolutely. "I am very cross and selfish!"

"It will be better by-and-by," said Margaret, "if only you are sure you have nothing to make you unhappy."

"Nothing," said Ethel. She was becoming too much ashamed of her fancy to breathe one word about it, and she had spoken the truth. Pleasure had spoiled her.

"If only we could do something for Cocksmoor!" she sighed, presently, "with that one hundred and fifty pounds lying idle."

Margaret was very glad that her thoughts were taking this channel, but it was not a promising one, for there seemed to be nothing practicable, present or future. The ground could not be had—the pig would not get over the stile—the old woman could not get home to-night. Cocksmoor must put up with its present school, and Mary must not be walked to death.

Or, as Ethel drew her own moral, sacrifice must not be selfish. One great resolution that has been costly, must not blunt us in the daily details of life.

CHAPTER XI.

If to do were as easy as to know what were good to do, Chapels
had been Churches, and poor men's cottages, princes' palaces. —

MERCHANT OF VENICE.

"Dick," said Dr. Spencer, as the friends sat together in the evening,
after Mary's swoon, "you seem to have found an expedient for
making havoc among your daughters."

"It does not hurt them," said Dr. May carelessly.

"Pretty well, after the specimen of to-day."

"That was chance."

"If you like it, I have no more to say; but I should like to make you

sit for two hours in such a temperature. If they were mine—"

"Very fine talking, but I would not take the responsibility of
hindering the only pains that have ever been taken with that unlucky
place. You don't know that girl Ethel. She began at fifteen, entirely of
her own accord, and has never faltered. If any of the children there
are saved from perdition, it is owing to her, and I am not going to be
the man to stop her. They are strong, healthy girls, and I cannot see
that it does them any harm—rather good."

"Have you any special predilection for a room eight feet by nine?"

"Can't be helped. What would you have said if you had seen the
last?"

"What is this about one hundred and fifty pounds in hand?"

"The ladies here chose to have a fancy fair, the only result of which,
hitherto, has been the taking away my Flora. There is the money, but
the land can't be had."

"Why not?"

"Tied up between the Drydale Estate and — College, and in the hands of the quarry master, Nicolson. There was an application made to the College, but they did not begin at the right end."

"Upon my word, Dick, you take it easy!" cried his friend, rather indignantly.

"I own I have not stirred in the matter," said Dr. May. "I knew nothing would come to good under the pack of silly women that our schools are ridden with—" and, as he heard a sound a little like "pish!" he continued, "and that old Ramsden, it is absolutely useless to work with such a head—or no head. There's nothing for it but to wait for better times, instead of setting up independent, insubordinate action."

"You are the man to leave venerable abuses undisturbed!"

"The cure is worse than the disease!"

"There spoke the Corporation!"

"Ah! it was not the way you set to work in Poonshedagore."

"Why, really, when the venerable abuses consisted of Hindoos praying to their own three-legged stools, and keeping sacred monkeys in honour of the ape Hanyuman, it was a question whether one could be a Christian oneself, and suffer it undisturbed. It was coming it too strong, when I was requested to lend my own step-ladder for the convenience of an exhibition of a devotee swinging on hooks in his sides."

Dr. Spencer had, in fact, never rested till he had established a mission in his former remote station; and his brown godson, once a Brahmin, now an exemplary clergyman, traced his conversion to the friendship and example of the English physician.

"Well, I have lashed about me at abuses, in my time," said Dr. May.

"I dare say you have, Dick!" and they both laughed—the inconsiderate way was so well delineated.

"Just so," replied Dr. May; "and I made enemies enough to fetter me now. I do not mean that I have done right—I have not; but there is a good deal on my hands, and I don't write easily. I have been slower to take up new matters than I ought to have been."

"I see, I see!" said Dr. Spencer, rather sorry for his implied reproach, "but must Cocksmoor be left to its fate, and your gallant daughter to hers?"

"The vicar won't stir. He is indolent enough by nature, and worse with gout; and I do not see what good I could do. I once offended the tenant, Nicolson, by fining him for cheating his unhappy labourers, on the abominable truck system; and he had rather poison me than do anything to oblige me. And, as to the copyholder, he is a fine gentleman, who never comes near the place, nor does anything for it."

"Who is he?"

"Sir Henry Walkinghame."

"Sir Henry Walkinghame! I know the man. I found him in one of the caves at Thebes, among the mummies, laid up with a fever, nearly ready to be a mummy himself! I remember bleeding him—irregular, was not it? but one does not stand on ceremony in Pharaoh's tomb. I got him through with it; we came up the Nile together, and the last I saw of him was at Alexandria. He is your man! something might be done with him!"

"I believe Flora promises to ask him if she should ever meet him in London, but he is always away. If ever we should be happy enough to get an active incumbent, we shall have a chance."

Two days after, Ethel came down equipped for Cocksmoor. It was as hot as ever, and Mary was ordered to stay at home, being somewhat pacified by a promise that she should go again as soon as the weather was fit for anything but a salamander.

Dr. Spencer was in the hall, with his bamboo, his great Panama hat, and gray loose coat, for he entirely avoided, except on Sundays, the medical suit of black. He offered to relieve Ethel of her bag of books.

"No thank you." (He had them by this time). "But I am going to Cocksmoor."

"Will you allow me to be your companion?"

"I shall be very glad of the pleasure of your company, but I am not in the least afraid of going alone," said she, smiling, however, so as to show she was glad of such pleasant company. "I forewarn you though that I have business there."

"I will find occupation."

"And you must promise not to turn against me. I have undergone a great deal already about that place. Norman was always preaching against it, and now that he has become reasonable, I can't have papa set against it again—besides, he would mind you more."

Dr. Spencer promised to do nothing but what was quite reasonable. Ethel believed that he accompanied her merely because his gallantry would not suffer her to go unescorted, and she was not sorry, for it was too long a walk for solitude to be very agreeable, when strange wagoners might be on the road, though she had never let them be "lions in the path."

The walk was as pleasant as a scorching sun would allow, and by the time they arrived at the scattered cottages, Ethel had been drawn into explaining many of her Cocksmoor perplexities.

"If you could get the land granted, where should you choose to have it?" he asked. "You know it will not do to go and say, 'Be pleased to give me a piece of land,' without specifying what, or you might chance to have one at the Land's End."

"I see, that was one of the blunders," said Ethel. "But I had often thought of this nice little square place, between two gardens, and sheltered by the old quarry."

"Ha! hardly space enough, I should say," replied Dr. Spencer, stepping it out. "No, that won't do, so confined by the quarry. Let us look farther."

A surmise crossed Ethel. Could he be going to take the work on himself, but that was too wild a supposition—she knew he had nothing of his own, only a moderate pension from the East India Company.

"What do you think of this?" he said, coming to the slope of a knoll, commanding a pretty view of the Abbotstoke woods, clear from houses, and yet not remote from the hamlet. She agreed that it would do well, and he kicked up a bit of turf, and pryed into the soil, pronouncing it dry, and fit for a good foundation. Then he began to step it out, making a circuit that amazed her, but he said, "It is of no use to do it at twice. Your school can be only the first step towards a church, and you had better have room—enough at once. It will serve as an endowment in the meantime."

He would not let her remain in the sun, and she went into school. She found him, when she came out, sitting in the arbour smoking a cigar-rather a shock to her feelings, though he threw it away the instant she appeared, and she excused him for his foreign habits.

In the evening, he brought down a traveller's case of instruments, and proceeded to draw a beautiful little map of Cocksmoor, where it seemed that he had taken all his measurements, whilst she was in school. He ended by an imaginary plan and elevation for the school, with a pretty oriel window and bell-gable, that made Ethel sigh with delight at the bare idea.

Next day, he vanished after dinner, but this he often did; he used to say he must go and have a holiday of smoking—he could not bear too much civilised society. He came back for tea, however, and had not sat down long before he said, "Now, I know all about it. I shall pack up my goods, and be off for Vienna to-morrow."

"To Vienna!" was the general and dolorous outcry, and Gertrude laid hold of him and said he should not go.

"I am coming back," he said, "if you will have me. The college holds a court at Fordholm on the 3rd, and on the last of this month, I hope to return."

"College! Court! What are you going to do at Vienna? Where have you left your senses?" asked Dr. May.

"I find Sir Henry Walkinghame is there. I have been on an exploring expedition to Drydale, found out his man of business, and where he is to be written to. The college holds a court at Fordholm, and I hope to have our business settled."

Ethel was too much confounded to speak. Her father was exclaiming on the shortness of the time.

"Plenty of time," said Dr. Spencer, demonstrating that he should be able to travel comfortably, and have four days to spare at Vienna—a journey which he seemed to think less of, than did Dr. May of going to London.

As to checking him, of that there was no possibility, nor, indeed, notion, though Ethel did not quite know how to believe in it, nor that the plan could come to good. Ethel was much better by this time: by her vigorous efforts, she had recovered her tone of mind and interest in what was passing; and though now and then Norman's letters, carrying sentences of remembrance, made her glow a little, she was so steady to her resolution that she averted all traffic in messages through her brother's correspondence, and, in that fear, allowed it to lapse into Margaret's hands more than she had ever done. Indeed, no one greatly liked writing from home, it was heartless work to say always, "No news from the Alcestis and yet they all declared they were not anxious.

Hector Ernescliffe knelt a great while beside Margaret's sofa, on the first evening of his holidays, and there was a long low-voiced talk between them. Ethel wished that she had warned him off, for Margaret looked much more harassed and anxious, after having heard the outpouring of all that was on his mind.

Dr. Spencer thought her looking worse, when he came, as come he did, on the appointed day. He had brought Sir Henry Walkinghame's full consent to the surrender of the land; drawn up in such form as could be acted upon, and a letter to his man of business. But Nicolson! He was a worse dragon nearer home, hating all schools, especially hating Dr. May.

However, said Dr. Spencer, in eastern form, "Have I encountered Rajahs, and smoked pipes with three-tailed Pachas, that I should dread the face of the father of quarrymen."

What he did with the father of quarrymen was not known, whether he talked him over, or bought him off—Margaret hoped the former; Dr. May feared the latter; the results were certain; Mr. Nicolson had agreed that the land should be given up.

The triumphant Dr. Spencer sat down to write a statement to be shown to the college authorities, when they should come to hold their court.

"The land must be put into the hands of trustees," he said. "The incumbent of course?"

"Then yourself; and we must have another. Your son-in-law?"

"You, I should think," said Dr. May.

"I! Why, I am going."

"Going, but not gone," said his friend.

"I must go! I tell you, Dick; I must have a place of my own to smoke my pipe in."

"Is that all?" said Dr. May. "I think you might be accommodated here, unless you wished to be near your sister."

"My sister is always resorting to watering-places. My nieces do nothing but play on the piano. No, I shall perhaps go off to America, the only place I have not seen yet, and I more than half engaged to go and help at Poonshedagore."

"Better order your coffin then," muttered Dr. May.

"I shall try lodgings in London, near the old hospital, perhaps—and go and turn over the British Museum library."

"Look you here, Spencer, I have a much better plan. Do you know that scrap of a house of mine, by the back gate, just big enough for you and your pipe? Set up your staff there. Ethel will never get her school built without you."

"Oh! that would be capital!" cried Ethel.

"It would be the best speculation for me. You would pay rent, and the last old woman never did," continued Dr. May. "A garden the length of this one—"

"But I say—I want to be near the British Museum."

"Take a season-ticket, and run up once a week."

"I shall teach your boys to smoke!"

"I'll see to that!"

"You have given Cocksmoor one lift," said Ethel, "and it will never go on without you."

"It is such a nice house!" added the children, in chorus; "it would be such fun to have you there."

"Daisy will never be able to spare her other doctor," said Margaret, smiling.

"Run to Mrs. Adams, Tom, and get the key," said Dr. May.

There was a putting on of hats and bonnets, and the whole party walked down the garden to inspect the house—a matter of curiosity to some—for it was where the old lady had resided on whom Harry had played so many tricks, and the subject of many myths hatched between him and George Larkins.

It was an odd, little narrow slip of a house, four stories, of two rooms all the way up, each with a large window, with a marked white eyebrow. Dr. May eagerly pointed out all the conveniences, parlour, museum, smoking den, while Dr. Spencer listened, and answered doubtfully; and the children's clamorous anxiety seemed to render him the more silent.

Hector Ernescliffe discovered a jackdaw's nest in the chimney, whereupon the whole train rushed off to investigate, leaving the two doctors and Ethel standing together in the empty parlour, Dr. May pressing, Dr. Spencer raising desultory objections; but so evidently against his own wishes, that Ethel said, "Now, indeed, you must not disappoint us all."

"No," said Dr. May, "it is a settled thing."

"No, no, thanks, thanks to you all, but it cannot be. Let me go;" and he spoke with emotion. "You are very kind, but it is not to be thought of."

"Why not?" said Dr. May. "Spencer, stay with me;" and he spoke with a pleading, almost dependent air. "Why should you go?"

"It is of no use to talk about it. You are very kind, but it will not do to encumber you with a lone man, growing old."

"We have been young together," said Dr. May.

"And you must not leave papa," added Ethel.

"No," said Dr. May. "Trouble may be at hand. Help us through with it. Remember, these children have no uncles."

"You will stay?" said Ethel.

He made a sign of assent—he could do no more, and just then Gertrude came trotting back, so exceedingly smutty, as to call everybody's attention. Hector had been shoving Tom half-way up the chimney, in hopes of reaching the nest; and the consequences of this amateur chimney-sweeping had been a plentiful bespattering of all the spectators with soot, that so greatly distressed the young ladies, that Mary and Blanche had fled away from public view.

Dr. Spencer's first act of possession was to threaten to pull Tom down by the heels for disturbing his jackdaws, whereupon there was a general acclamation; and Dr. May began to talk of marauding times, when the jackdaws in the Minster tower had been harried.

"Ah!" said Dr. Spencer, as Tom emerged, blacker than the outraged jackdaws, and half choked, "what do you know about jackdaws' nests? You that are no Whichcote scholars."

"Don't we?" cried Hector, "when there is a jackdaw's nest in Eton Chapel, twenty feet high."

"Old Grey made that!" said Tom, who usually acted the part of esprit fort to Hector's credulity.

"Why, there is a picture of it on Jesse's book," said Hector.

"But may not we get up on the roof, to see if we can get at the nest, papa? " said Tom.

"You must ask Dr. Spencer. It is his house."

Dr. Spencer did not gainsay it, and proceeded even to show the old Whichcote spirit, by leading the assault, and promising to take care of Aubrey, while Ethel retained Gertrude, and her father too; for Dr. May had such a great inclination to scramble up the ladder after them, that she, thinking it a dangerous experiment for so helpless an arm, was obliged to assure him that it would create a sensation among the gossiphood of Stoneborough, if their physician were seen disporting himself on the top of the house.

"Ah! I'm not a physician unattached, like him," said Dr. May, laughing. "Hullo! have you got up, Tom? There's a door up there.

I'll show you—"

"No, don't papa. Think of Mrs. Ledwich; and asking her to see two trustees up there!" said Ethel.

"Ah! Mrs. Ledwich; what is to be done with her, Ethel?"

"I am sure I can't tell. If Flora were but at home, she would manage it."

"Spencer can manage anything!" was the answer. "That was the happiest chance imaginable that you came home with me, and so we came to go by the same train."

Ethel was only afraid that time was being cruelly wasted; but the best men, and it is emphatically the best that generally are so—have the boy strong enough on one side or other of their natures, to be a great provocation to womankind; and Dr. Spencer did not rest from his pursuit till the brood of the jackdaws had been discovered, and two gray-headed nestlings kidnapped, which were destined to a wicker cage and education. Little Aubrey was beyond measure proud, and was suggesting all sorts of outrageous classical names for them, till politely told by Tom that he would make them as great prigs as himself, and that their names should be nothing but Jack and Jill.

"There's nothing for it but for Aubrey to go to school," cried Tom, sententiously turning round to Ethel.

"Ay, to Stoneborough," said Dr. Spencer.

Tom coloured, as if sorry for his movement, and hastened away to make himself sufficiently clean to go in quest of a prison for his captives.

Dr. Spencer began to bethink him of the paper that he had been so eagerly drawing up, and looking at his own begrimed hands, asked Ethel whether she would have him for a trustee.

"Will the other eight ladies?" said Ethel, "that's the point."

"Ha, Spencer! you did not know what you were undertaking. Do you wish to be let off?" said Dr. May.

"Not I," said the undaunted doctor. "Come, Ethel, let us hear what should be done."

"There's no time," said Ethel, bewildered. "The court will be only on the day after to-morrow."

"Ample time!" said Dr. Spencer, who seemed ready to throw himself into it with all his might. "What we have to do is this. The ladies to be propitiated are—"

"Nine Muses, to whom you will have to act Apollo," said Dr. May, who, having put his friend into the situation, had a mischievous delight in laughing at him, and watching what he would do.

"One and two, Ethel, and Mrs. Rivers!"

"Rather eight and nine," said Ethel, "though Flora may be somebody now."

"Seven then," said Dr. Spencer. "Well then, Ethel, suppose we set out on our travels this afternoon. Visit these ladies, get them to call a meeting to-morrow, and sanction their three trustees."

"You little know what a work it is to call a meeting, or how many notes Miss Rich sends out before one can be accomplished."

"Faint heart—you know the proverb, Ethel. Allons. I'll call on Mrs. Ledwich—"

"Stay," said Dr. May. "Let Ethel do that, and ask her to tea, and we will show her your drawing of the school."

So the remaining ladies were divided—Ethel was to visit Miss Anderson, Miss Boulder, and Mrs. Ledwich; Dr. Spencer, the rest, and a meeting, if possible, be appointed for the next day.

Ethel did as she was told, though rather against the grain, and her short, abrupt manner was excused the more readily, that Dr. Spencer had been a subject of much mysterious speculation in Stoneborough, and to gain any intelligence respecting him, was a great object; so that she was extremely welcome wherever she called.

Mrs. Ledwich promised to come to tea, and instantly prepared to walk to Miss Rich, and authorise her to send out the notes of summons to the morrow's meeting. Ethel offered to walk with her, and found Mrs. and Miss Rich in a flutter, after Dr. Spencer's call; the daughter just going to put on her bonnet and consult Mrs. Ledwich, and both extremely enchanted with Dr. Spencer, who "would be such an acquisition."

The hour was fixed and the notes sent out, and Ethel met Dr. Spencer at the garden gate.

"Well!" he said, smiling, "I think we have fixed them off—have not we?"

"Yes; but is it not heartless that everything should be done through so much nonsense?"

"Did you ever hear why the spire of Ulm Cathedral was never finished?" said Dr. Spencer.

"No; why not?"

"Because the citizens would accept no help from their neighbours."

"I am glad enough of help when it comes in the right way, and from good motives."

"There are more good motives in the world than you give people credit for, Ethel. You have a good father, good sense, and a good education; and you have some perception of the system by which things like this should be done. Unfortunately, the system is in bad hands here, and these good ladies have been left to work for themselves, and it is no wonder that there is plenty of little self-importance, nonsense, and the like, among them; but for their own sakes we should rather show them the way, than throw them overboard."

"If they will be shown," said Ethel.

"I can't say they seemed to me so very formidable," said Dr. Spencer.

"Gentle little women."

"Oh! it is only Mrs. Ledwich that stirs them up. I hope you are prepared for that encounter."

Mrs. Ledwich came to tea, sparkling with black bugles, and was very patronising and amiable. Her visits were generally subjects of great dread, for she talked unceasingly, laid down the law, and overwhelmed Margaret with remedies; but to-night Dr. Spencer took her in hand. It was not that he went out of his ordinary self, he was always the same simple-mannered, polished gentleman; but it was this that told— she was evidently somewhat in awe of him—the refinement kept her in check. She behaved very quietly all the evening, admired the plans, consented to everything, and was scarcely Mrs. Ledwich!

"You will get on now, Ethel," said Dr. May afterwards. "Never fear but that he will get the Ladies' Committee well in hand." "Why do you think so, papa?"

"Never you fear."

That was all she could extract from him, though he looked very arch. The Ladies' Committee accepted of their representatives with full consent; and the indefatigable Dr. Spencer next had to hunt up the fellow trustee. He finally contrived to collect every one he wanted at Fordholm, the case was laid before the College—the College was propitious, and by four o'clock in the evening, Dr. Spencer laid before Ethel the promise of the piece of land.

Mary's joy was unbounded, and Ethel blushed, and tried to thank. This would have been the summit of felicity a year ago, and she was vexed with herself for feeling that though land and money were both in such safe hands, she could not care sufficiently to feel the ecstasy the attainment of her object would once have given to her. Then she would have been frantic with excitement, and heedless of everything; now she took it so composedly as to annoy herself.

"To think of that one week at Oxford having so entirely turned this head of mine!"

Perhaps it was the less at home, because she had just heard that George and Flora had accepted an invitation to Glenbracken, but though the zest of Cocksmoor might be somewhat gone, she called herself to order, and gave her full attention to all that was planned by her champion.

Never did man plunge into business more thoroughly than he, when he had once undertaken it. He was one of those men who, from gathering particulars of every practical matter that comes under their notice, are able to accomplish well whatever they set their hand to; and building was not new to him, though his former subjects—a church and mission station in India—bore little remembrance to the present.

He bought a little round dumpling of a white pony, and trotted all over the country in search of building materials and builders, he discovered trees in distant timber-yards, he brought home specimens of stone, one in each pocket, to compare and analyse, he went to London to look at model schools, he drew plans each more neat and beautiful than the last, he compared builders' estimates, and wrote letters to the National Society, so as to be able to begin in the spring.

In the meantime he was settling himself, furnishing his new house with great precision and taste. He would have no assistance in his choice, either of servants or furniture, but made numerous journeys of inspection to Whitford, to Malvern, and to London, and these seemed to make him the more content with Stoneborough. Sir Matthew Fleet had evidently chilled him, and as he found his own few remaining relations uncongenial, he became the more ready to find a resting-place in the gray old town, the scene of his school life, beside the friend of his youth, and the children of her, for whose sake he had never sought a home of his own. Though he now and then talked of seeing America, or of going back to India, in hopes of assisting his beloved mission at Poonshedagore, these plans were fast dying away, as he formed habits and attachments, and perceived the sphere of usefulness open to him.

It was a great step when his packages arrived, and his beautiful Indian curiosities were arranged, making his drawing-room as pretty a room as could anywhere be seen; in readiness, as he used to tell Ethel, for a grand tea-party for all the Ladies' Committee, when he should borrow her and the best silver teapot to preside. Moreover, he had a chemical apparatus, a telescope, and microscope, of great power, wherewith he tried experiments that were the height of felicity to Tom and Ethel, and much interested their father. He made it his business to have full occupation for himself, with plans, books, or correspondence, so as not to be a charge on the hands of the May family, with whom he never spent an evening without special and earnest invitation.

He gave attendance at the hospital on alternate days, as well as taking off Dr. May's hands such of his gratuitous patients as were not averse to quit their old doctor, and could believe in a physician in shepherd's plaid, and Panama hat. Exceedingly sociable, he soon visited every one far and wide, and went to every sort of party, from the grand dinners of the "county families," to the tea-drinkings of the Stoneborough ladies—a welcome guest at all, and enjoying each in his own way. English life was so new to him that he entered into the little accessories with the zest of a youth; and there seemed to be a curious change between the two old fellow students, the elder and more staid of former days having come back with unencumbered freshness to enliven his friend, just beginning to grow aged under the wear of care and sorrows.

It was very droll to hear Dr. May laughing at Dr. Spencer's histories of his adventures, and at the new aspects in which his own well-trodden district appeared to travelled eyes; and not less amusing was Dr. Spencer's resolute defence of all the nine muses, generally and individually.

He certainly had no reason to think ill of them. As one woman, they were led by him, and conformed their opinions. The only seceder was Louisa Anderson, who had her brother for her oracle; and, indeed, the more youthful race, to whom Harvey was the glass of fashion, uttered disrespectful opinions as to the doctor's age, and would not accede to his being, as Mrs. Ledwich declared, "much younger than Dr. May."

Harvey Anderson had first attempted patronage, then argument, with Dr. Spencer, but found him equally impervious to both. "Very clever, but an old world man," said Harvey. "He has made up his bundle of prejudices."

"Clever sort of lad!" said Dr. Spencer, "a cool hand, but very shallow—"

Ethel wondered to hear thus lightly disposed of, the powers of argument that had been thought fairly able to compete with Norman, and which had taxed him so severely. She did not know how differently abstract questions appear to a mature mind, confirmed in principle by practice; and to one young, struggling in self-formation, and more used to theories than to realities.

CHAPTER XII.

The heart may ache, but may not burst;
Heaven will not leave thee, nor forsake.

— Christian Year.

Hector and Tom finished their holidays by a morning's shooting at the Grange, Dr. May promising to meet them, and let them drive him home.

Meta was out when he arrived; and, repairing to the library, he found Mr. Rivers sitting by a fire, though it was early in September, with the newspaper before him, but not reading. He looked depressed, and seemed much disappointed at having heard that George and Flora had accepted some further invitations in Scotland, and did not intend to return for another month. Dr. May spoke cheerfully of the hospitality and kindness they had met, but failed to enliven him, and, as if trying to assign some cause for his vexation, he lamented over fogs and frosts, and began to dread an October in Scotland for Flora, almost as if it were the Arctic regions.

He grew somewhat more animated in praising Flora, and speaking of the great satisfaction he had in seeing his son married to so admirable a person. He only wished it could be the same with his daughter.

"You are a very unselfish father," said Dr. May. "I cannot imagine you without your little fairy."

"It would be hard to part," said Mr. Rivers, sighing; "yet I should be relieved to see her in good hands, so pretty and engaging as she is, and something of an heiress. With our dear Flora, she is secure of a happy home when I am gone, but still I should be glad to have seen—" and he broke off thoughtfully.

"She is so sensible, that we shall see her make a good choice," said Dr. May, smiling; "that is, if she choose at all, for I do not know who is worthy of her."

"I am quite indifferent as to fortune," continued Mr. Rivers. "She will have enough of her own."

"Enough not to be dependent, which is the point," said Dr. May, "though I should have few fears for her any way."

"It would be a comfort," harped on Mr. Rivers, dwelling on the subject, as if he wanted to say something, "if she were only safe with a man who knew how to value her and make her happy. Such a young man as your Norman, now—I have often thought—"

Dr. May would not seem to hear, but he could not prevent himself from blushing as crimson as if he had been the very Norman, as he answered, going on with his own speech, as if Mr. Rivers's had been unmade, "She is the brightest little creature under the sun, and the sparkle is down so deep within, that however it may turn out, I should never fear for her happiness."

"Flora is my great reliance," proceeded Mr. Rivers. "Her aunt, Lady Leonora, is very kind, but somehow she does not seem to suit with Meta."

"Oh, ho," thought the doctor, "have you made that discovery, my good friend?"

The voices of the two boys were heard in the hall, explaining their achievements to Meta, and Dr. May took his departure, Hector driving him, and embarking in a long discourse on his own affairs as if he had quite forgotten that the doctor was not his father, and going on emphatically, in spite of the absence of mind now and then betrayed by his auditor, who, at Dr. Spencer's door, exclaimed, "Stop, Hector, let me out here—thank you;" and presently brought out his friend into the garden, and sat down on the grass, talking low and earnestly over the disease with which Mr. Rivers had been so long affected; for though Dr. May could not perceive any positively unfavourable symptom, he had been rendered vaguely uneasy by the unusual heaviness and depression of manner. So long did they sit conversing, that Blanche was sent out, primed with an impertinent message, that two such old doctors ought to be ashamed of themselves for sitting so late in the dew.

Dr. Spencer was dragged in to drink tea, and the meal had just been merrily concluded, when the door bell rang, and a message was brought in. "The carriage from the Grange, sir; Miss Rivers would be much obliged if you would come directly."

"There!" said Dr. May, looking at Dr. Spencer, as if to say, I told you so, in the first triumph of professional sagacity; but the next moment exclaiming, "Poor little Meta!" he hurried away.

A gloom fell on those who remained, for, besides their sympathy for Meta, and their liking for her kind old father, there was that one unacknowledged heartache, which, though in general bravely combated, lay in wait always ready to prey on them. Hector stole round to sit by Margaret, and Dr. Spencer muttered, "This will never do," and sent Tom to fetch some papers lying on his table, whence he read them some curious accounts that he had just received from his missionary friends in India.

They were interested, but in a listening mood, that caused a universal start when the bell again sounded. This time, James reported that the servant from the Grange said his master was very ill—he had brought a letter to post for Mr. George Rivers, and here was a note for Miss Ethel. It was the only note Ethel had ever received from her father, and contained these few words:

"DEAR E.—,

"I believe this attack will be the last. Come to Meta, and bring my things.

R. M."

Ethel put her hands to her forehead. It was as if she had been again plunged into the stunned dream of misery of four years ago, and her sensation was of equal bewilderment and uselessness; but it was but for a moment—the next she was in a state of over-bustle and eagerness. She wanted to fly about and hasten to help Meta, and could hardly obey the word and gesture by which Margaret summoned her to her side.

"Dear Ethel, you must calm yourself, or you will not be of use."

"I? I can't be of any use! Oh, if you could go! If Flora were but here! But I must go, Margaret."

"I will put up your father's things," said Dr. Spencer, in a soothing tone. "The carriage cannot be ready in a moment, so that there will be full time."

Mary and Miss Bracy prepared Ethel's own goods, which she would otherwise have forgotten; and Margaret, meanwhile, detained her by her side, trying to calm and encourage her with gentle words of counsel, that might hinder her from giving way to the flurry of emotion that had seized her, and prevent her from thinking herself certain to be useless.

Adams was to drive her thither in the gig, and it presently came to the door. Dr. Spencer wrapped her up well in cloaks and shawls, and spoke words of kindly cheer in her ear as she set off. The fresh night air blew pleasantly on her, the stars glimmered in full glory overhead, and now and then her eye was caught by the rocket-like track of a shooting-star. Orion was rising slowly far in the east, and bringing to her mind the sailor-boy under the southern sky; if, indeed, he were not where sun and stars no more are the light. It was strange that the thought came more as soothing than as acute pain; she could bear to think of him thus in her present frame, as long as she had not to talk of him. Under those solemn stars, the life everlasting seemed to overpower the sense of this mortal life, and Ethel's agitation was calmed away.

The old cedar-tree stood up in stately blackness against the sky, and the lights in the house glanced behind it. The servants looked rather surprised to see Ethel, as if she were not expected, and conducted her to the great drawing-room, which looked the more desolate and solitary, from the glare of lamplight, falling on the empty seats which Ethel had lately seen filled with a glad home party. She was looking round, thinking whether to venture up to Meta's room, and there summon Bellairs, when Meta came gliding in, and threw her arms round her. Ethel could not speak, but Meta's voice was more cheerful than she had expected. "How kind of you, dear Ethel!"

"Papa sent for me," said Ethel.

"He is so kind! Can Margaret spare you?"

"Oh, yes; but you must leave me. You must want to be with him."

"He never lets me come in when he has these attacks," said Meta. "If he only would! But will you come up to my room? That is nearer."

"Is papa with him?"

"Yes."

Meta wound her arms round Ethel, and led her up to her sitting-room, where a book lay on the table. She said that her father had seemed weary and torpid, and had sat still until almost their late dinner-hour, when he seemed to bethink himself of dressing, and had risen. She thought he walked weakly, and rather tottering, and had run to make him lean on her, which he did, as far as his own room door. There he had kissed her, and thanked her, and murmured a word like blessing. She had not, however, been alarmed, until his servant had come to tell her that he had another seizure.

Ethel asked whether she had seen Dr. May since he had been with her father. She had; but Ethel was surprised to find that she had not taken in the extent of his fears. She had become so far accustomed to these attacks, that, though anxious and distressed, she did not apprehend more than a few days' weakness, and her chief longing was to be of use. She was speaking cheerfully of beginning her nursing to-morrow, and of her great desire that her papa would allow her to sit up with him, when there was a slow, reluctant movement of the lock of the door, and the two girls sprang to their feet, as Dr. May opened it; and Ethel read his countenance at once.

Not so Meta. "How is he? May I go to him?" cried she.

"Not now, my dear," said Dr. May, putting his hand on her shoulder, in a gentle, detaining manner, that sent a thrill of trembling through her frame, though she did not otherwise move. She only clasped her hands together, and looked up into his face. He answered the look. "Yes, my dear, the struggle is over."

Ethel came near, and put her arm round Meta's waist, as if to strengthen her, as she stood quite passive and still.

Dr. May seemed to think it best that all should be told; but, though intently watching Meta, he directed his words to his own daughter.

"Thank Heaven, it has been shorter, and less painful, than I had dared to hope."

Meta tried to speak, but could not bring out the words, and, with an imploring look at Ethel, as if to beg her to make them clear for her, she inarticulately murmured, "Oh! why did you not call me?"

"I could not. He would not let me. His last conscious word to me was not to let you see him suffer."

Meta wrung her clasped hands together in mute anguish. Dr. May signed to Ethel to guide her back to the sofa, but the movement seemed so far to rouse her, that she said, "I should like to go to bed."

"Right—the best thing," said Dr. May; and he whispered to Ethel, "Go with her, but don't try to rouse her—don't talk to her. Come back to me, presently."

He did not even shake hands with Meta, nor wish her good-night, as she disappeared into her own room.

Bellairs undressed her, and Ethel stood watching, till the young head, under the load of sorrow, so new to it, was laid on the pillow. Bellairs asked her if she would have a light.

"No, no, thank you—the dark and alone. Good-night," said Meta. Ethel went back to the sitting-room, where her father was standing at the window, looking out into the night. He turned as she came in, folded her in his arms, and kissed her forehead. "And how is the poor little dear?" he asked.

"The same," said Ethel. "I can't bear to leave her alone, and to have said nothing to comfort her."

"It is too soon as yet," said Dr. May—"her mind has not taken it in. I hope she will sleep all night, and have more strength to look at it when she wakens."

"She was utterly unprepared."

"I could not make her understand me," said Dr. May.

"And, oh, papa, what a pity she was not there!"

175

"It was no sight for her, till the last few minutes; and his whole mind seemed bent on sparing her. What tenderness it has been."

"Must we leave her to herself all night?"

"Better so," said Dr. May. "She has been used to loneliness; and to thrust companionship on her would be only harassing."

Ethel, who scarcely knew what it was to be alone, looked as if she did not understand.

"I used to try to force consolation on people," said Dr. May, "but I know, now, that it can only be done by following their bent."

"You have seen so many sorrows," said Ethel.

"I never understood till I felt," said Dr. May. "Those few first days were a lesson."

"I did not think you knew what was passing," said Ethel.

"I doubt whether any part of my life is more distinctly before me than those two days," said Dr. May. "Flora coming in and out, and poor Alan sitting by me; but I don't believe I had any will. I could no more have moved my mind than my broken arm; and I verily think, Ethel, that, but for that merciful torpor, I should have been frantic. It taught me never to disturb grief."

"And what shall we do?"

"You must stay with her till Flora comes. I will be here as much as I can. She is our charge, till they come home. I told him, between the spasms, that I had sent for you, and he seemed pleased."

"If only I were anybody else!"

Dr. May again threw his arm round her, and looked into her face. He felt that he had rather have her, such as she was, than anybody else; and, together, they sat down, and talked of what was to be done, and what was best for Meta, and of the solemnity of being in the house of death. Ethel felt and showed it so much, in her subdued, awe-struck manner, that her father felt checked whenever he was about to return to his ordinary manner, familiarised, as he necessarily was, with the like scenes. It drew him back to the thought of their own trouble, and their conversation recurred to those days, so that each gained a more full understanding of the other, and they at length separated, certainly with the more peaceful and soft feelings for being in the abode of mourning.

Bellairs promised to call Ethel, to be with her young lady as early as might be, reporting that she was sound asleep. And sleep continued to shield her till past her usual hour, so that Ethel was up, and had been with Dr. May, before she was summoned to her, and then she found her half dressed, and hastening that she might not make Dr. May late for breakfast, and in going to his patients. There was an elasticity in the happily constituted young mind that could not be entirely struck down, nor deprived of power of taking thought for others. Yet her eyes looked wandering, and unlike themselves, and her words, now and then, faltered, as if she was not sure what she was doing or saying. Ethel told her not to mind—Dr. Spencer would take care of the patients; but she did not seem to recollect, at first, who Dr. Spencer was, nor to care for being reminded.

Breakfast was laid out in the little sitting-room. Ethel wanted to take the trouble off her hands, but she would not let her. She sat behind her urn, and asked about tea or coffee, quite accurately, in a low, subdued voice, that nearly overcame Dr. May. When the meal was over, and she had rung the bell, and risen up, as if to her daily work, she turned round, with that piteous, perplexed air, and stood for a moment, as if confused.

"Cannot we help you?" said Ethel.

"I don't know. Thank you. But, Dr. May, I must not keep you from other people—"

"I have no one to go to this morning," said Dr. May. "I am ready to stay with you, my dear."

Meta came closer to him, and murmured, "Thank you!"

The breakfast things had, by this time, been taken away, and Meta, looking to see that the door had shut for the last time, said, in a low voice, "Now tell me—"

Dr. May drew her down to sit on the sofa beside him, and, in his soft, sweet voice, told her all that she wished to learn of her father's last hours, and was glad to see showers of quiet, wholesome tears drop freely down, but without violence, and she scarcely attempted to speak. There was a pause at the end, and then she said gently, "Thank you, for it all. Dear papa!" And she rose up, and went back to her room.

"She has learned to dwell apart," said Dr. May, much moved.

"How beautiful she bears up!" said Ethel.

"It has been a life which, as she has used it, has taught her strength and self-dependence in the midst of prosperity."

"Yes," said Ethel, "she has trained herself by her dread of self-indulgence, and seeking after work. But oh! what a break up it is for her! I cannot think how she holds up. Shall I go to her?"

"I think not. She knows the way to the only Comforter. I am not afraid of her after those blessed tears."

Dr. May was right; Meta presently returned to them, in the same gentle subdued sadness, enfolding her, indeed, as a flower weighed down by mist, but not crushing nor taking away her powers. It was as if she were truly upheld; and thankful to her friends as she was, she did not throw herself on them in utter dependence or self-abandonment.

She wrote needful letters, shedding many tears over them, and often obliged to leave off to give the blinding weeping its course, but refusing to impose any unnecessary task upon Dr. May's lame arm. All that was right, she strove to do; she saw Mr. Charles Wilmot, and was refreshed by his reading to her; and when Dr. May desired it, she submissively put on her bonnet, and took several turns with Ethel in the shrubbery, though it made her cry heartily to look into the downstairs rooms. And she lay on the sofa at last, owning herself strangely tired, she did not know why, and glad that Ethel should read to her. By and by, she went to dress for the evening, and came back, full of the tidings that one of the children in the village had been badly burned. It occupied her very much—she made Ethel promise to go and see about her to-morrow, and sent Bellairs at once with every comfort that she could devise.

On the whole, those two days were to Ethel a peaceful and comfortable time. She saw more than usual of her father, and had such conversations with him as were seldom practicable at home, and that chimed in with the unavowed care which hung on their minds; while Meta was a most sweet and loving charge, without being a burden, and often saying such beautiful things in her affectionate resignation, that Ethel could only admire and lay them up in her mind. Dr. May went backwards and forwards, and brought good accounts of Margaret and fond messages; he slept at the Grange each night, and Meta used to sit in the corner of the sofa and work, or not, as best suited her, while she listened to his talk with Ethel, and now and then herself joined.

George Rivers's absence was a serious inconvenience in all arrangements; but his sister dreaded his grief as much as she wished for his return; and often were the posts and the journeys reckoned over, without a satisfactory conclusion, as to when he could arrive from so remote a part of Scotland.

At last, as the two girls had finished their early dinner, the butler brought in word that Mr. Norman May was there. Meta at once begged that he would come in, and Ethel went into the hall to meet him. He looked very wan, with the dark rings round his eyes a deeper purple than ever, and he could hardly find utterance to ask, "How is she?"

"As good and sweet as she can be," said Ethel warmly; but no more, for Meta herself had come to the dining-room door, and was holding out her hand. Norman took it in both his, but could not speak;

Meta's own soft voice was the first. "I thought you would come—he was so fond of you."

Poor Norman quite gave way, and Meta was the one to speak gentle words of soothing. "There is so much to be thankful for," she said. "He has been spared so much of the suffering Dr. May feared for him; and he was so happy about George."

Norman made a great effort to recover himself. Ethel asked for Flora and George. It appeared that they had been on an excursion when the first letter arrived at Glenbracken, and thus had received both together in the evening, on their return. George had been greatly overcome, and they had wished to set off instantly; but Lady

Glenbracken would not hear of Flora's travelling night and day, and it had at length been arranged that Norman Ogilvie should drive Norman across the country that evening, to catch the mail for Edinburgh, and he had been on the road ever since. George was following with his wife more slowly, and would be at home to-morrow evening. Meantime, he sent full authority to his father-in-law to make arrangements.

Ethel went to see the burned child, leaving Meta to take her walk in the garden under Norman's charge. He waited on her with a sort of distant reverence for a form of grief, so unlike what he had dreaded for her, when the first shock of the tidings had brought back to him the shattered bewildered feelings to which he dared not recur.

To dwell on the details was, to her, a comfort, knowing his sympathy and the affection there had been between him and her father; nor had they parted in such absolute brightness, as to make them unprepared for such a meeting as the present. The cloud of suspense was brooding lower and lower over the May family, and the need of faith and submission was as great with them as with the young orphan herself. Norman said little, but that little was so deep and fervent, that after a time Meta could not help saying, when Ethel was seen in the distance, and their talk was nearly over, "Oh, Norman, these things are no mirage!"

"It is the world that is the mirage," he answered. Ethel came up, and Dr. May also, in good time for the post. He was obliged to become very busy, using Norman for his secretary, till he saw his son's eyes so heavy, that he remembered the two nights that he had been up, and ordered him to go home and go to bed as soon as tea was over.

"May I come back to-morrow?"

"Why—yes—I think you may. No, no," he added, recollecting himself, "I think you had better not," and he did not relent, though Norman looked disappointed.

Meta had already expressed her belief that her father would be buried at the suburban church, where lay her mother; and Dr. May, having been desired to seek out the will and open it, found it was so; and fixed the day and hour with Meta, who was as submissive and reasonable as possible, though much grieved that he thought she could not be present.

Ethel, after going with Meta to her room at night, returned as usual to talk matters over with him, and again say how good Meta was.

"And I think Norman's coming did her a great deal of good," said Ethel.

"Ha! yes," said the doctor thoughtfully.

"She thinks so much of Mr. Rivers having been fond of him."

"Yes," said the doctor, "he was. I find, in glancing over the will, which was newly made on Flora's marriage, that he has remembered Norman—left him £100 and his portfolio of prints by Raffaelle."

"Has he, indeed?—how very kind, how much Norman will value it."

"It is remarkable," said Dr. May; and then, as if he could not help it, told Ethel what Mr. Rivers had said of his wishes with regard to his daughter. Ethel blushed and smiled, and looked so much touched and delighted, that he grew alarmed and said, "You know, Ethel, this must be as if it never had been mentioned."

"What! you will not tell Norman?"

"No, certainly not, unless I see strong cause. They are very fond of each other, certainly, but they don't know, and I don't know, whether it is not like brother and sister. I would not have either of them guess at this, or feel bound in any way. Why, Ethel, she has thirty thousand pounds, and I don't know how much more."

"Thirty thousand!" said Ethel, her tone one of astonishment, while his had been almost of objection.

"It would open a great prospect," continued Dr. May complacently;

"with Norman's talents, and such a lift as that, he might be one of the first men in England, provided he had nerve and hardness enough, which I doubt."

"He would not care for it," said Ethel.

"No; but the field of usefulness; but what an old fool I am, after all my resolutions not to be ambitious for that boy; to be set a-going by such a thing as this! Still Norman is something out of the common way. I wonder what Spencer thinks of him."

"And you never mean them to hear of it?"

"If they settle it for themselves," said Dr. May, "that sanction will come in to give double value to mine; or if I should see poor Norman hesitating as to the inequality, I might smooth the way; but you see, Ethel, this puts us in a most delicate situation towards this pretty little creature. What her father wanted was only to guard her from fortune-hunters, and if she should marry suitably elsewhere — why, we will be contented."

"I don't think I should be," said Ethel.

"She is the most winning of humming-birds, and what we see of her now, gives one double confidence in her. She is so far from the petted, helpless girl that he, poor man, would fain have made her! And she has a bright, brave temper and elastic spirits that would be the very thing for him, poor boy, with that morbid sensitiveness — he would not hurt her, and she would brighten him. It would be a very pretty thing — but we must never think about it again."

"If we can help it," said Ethel.

"Ah! I am sorry I have put it into your head too. We shall not so easily be unconscious now, when they talk about each other in the innocent way they do. We have had a lesson against being pleased at match-making!" But, turning away from the subject, "You shall not lose your Cocksmoor income, Ethel —"

"I had never thought of that. You have taken no fees here since we have been all one family."

"Well, he has been good enough to leave me £500, and Cocksmoor can have the interest, if you like."

"Oh, thank you, papa."

"It is only its due, for I suppose that is for attendance. Personally, to myself, he has left that beautiful Claude which he knew I admired so much. He has been very kind! But, after all, we ought not to be talking of all this — I should not have known it, if I had not been forced to read the will. Well, so we are in Flora's house, Ethel! I wonder how poor dear little Meta will feel the being a guest here, instead of the mistress. I wish that boy were three or four years older! I should like to take her straight home with us—I should like to have her for a daughter. I shall always look on her as one."

"As a Daisy!" said Ethel.

"Don't talk of it!" said Dr. May hastily; "this is no time for such things. After all, I am glad that the funeral is not here—Flora and Meta might be rather overwhelmed with these three incongruous sets of relations. By their letters, those Riverses must be quite as queer a lot as George's relations. After all, if we have nothing else, Ethel, we have the best of it, in regard to such relations as we have."

"There is Lord Cosham," said Ethel.

"Yes, he is Meta's guardian, as well as her brother; but he could not have her to live with him. She must depend upon Flora. But we shall see."

Ethel felt confident that Flora would be very kind to her little sister-in-law, and yet one of those gleams of doubt crossed her, whether Flora would not be somewhat jealous of her own authority.

Late the next evening, the carriage drove to the door, and George and Flora appeared in the hall. Their sisters went out to meet them, and George folded Meta in his arms, and kissing her again and again, called her his poor dear little sister, and wept bitterly, and even violently. Flora stood beside Ethel, and said, in a low voice, that poor George felt it dreadfully; and then came forward, touched him gently, and told him that he must not overset Meta; and, drawing her from him, kissed her, and said what a grievous time this had been for her, and how sorry they had been to leave her so long, but they knew she was in the best hands.

"Yes, I should have been so sorry you had been over-tired. I was quite well off," said Meta.

"And you must look on us as your home," added Flora.

"How can she?" thought Ethel. "This is taking possession, and making Meta a guest already!"

However, Meta did not seem so to feel it—she replied by caresses, and turned again to her brother. Poor George was by far the most struck down of all the mourners, and his whole demeanour gave his new relations a much warmer feeling towards him than they could ever have hoped to entertain. His gentle refined father had softly impressed his duller nature; and his want of attention and many extravagances came back upon him acutely now, in his changed home. He could hardly bear to look at his little orphan sister, and lavished every mark of fondness upon her; nor could he endure to sit at the bottom of his table; but when they had gone in to dinner, he turned away from the chair and hid his face. He was almost like a child in his want of self-restraint; and with all Dr. May's kind soothing manner, he could not bring him to attend to any of the necessary questions as to arrangements, and was obliged to refer to Flora, whose composed good sense was never at fault.

Ethel was surprised to find that it would be a great distress to Meta to part with her until the funeral was over, though she would hardly express a wish lest Ethel should be needed at home. As soon as Flora perceived this, she begged her sister to stay, and again Ethel felt unpleasantly that Meta might have seen, if she had chosen, that Flora took the invitation upon herself.

So, while Dr. May, with George, Norman, and Tom, went to London, she remained, though not exactly knowing what good she was doing, unless by making the numbers rather less scanty; but both sisters declared her to be the greatest comfort possible; and when Meta shut herself up in her own room, where she had long learned to seek strength in still communing with her own heart, Flora seemed to find it a relief to call her sister to hers, and talk over ordinary subjects, in a tone that struck on Ethel's ear as a little incongruous—but then Flora had not been here from the first, and the impression could not be as strong. She was very kind, and her manner, when with others, was perfect, from its complete absence of affectation; but, alone with Ethel, there was a little complacency sometimes betrayed, and some curiosity whether her father had read the will. Ethel allowed what she had heard of the contents to be extracted from her, and it certainly did not diminish Flora's secret satisfaction in being 'somebody'.

She told the whole history of her visits; first, how cordial Lady Leonora Langdale had been, and then, how happy she had been at Glenbracken. The old Lord and Lady, and Marjorie, all equally charming in their various ways; and Norman Ogilvie so good a son, and so highly thought of in his own country.

"Did I tell you, Ethel, that he desired to be remembered to you?"

"Yes, you said so."

"What has Coralie done with it?" continued Flora, seeking in her dressing-case. "She must have put it away with my brooches. Oh, no, here it is. I had been looking for Cairngorm specimens in a shop, saying I wanted a brooch that you would wear, when Norman Ogilvie came riding after the carriage, looking quite hot and eager. He had been to some other place, and hunted this one up. Is it not a beauty?"

It was one of the round Bruce brooches, of dark pebble, with a silver fern-leaf lying across it, the dots of small Cairngorm stones. "The Glenbracken badge, you know," continued Flora.

Ethel twisted it about in her fingers, and said, "Was not it meant for you?"

"It was to oblige me, if you choose so to regard it," said Flora, smiling. "He gave me no injunctions; but, you see, you must wear it now. I shall not wear coloured brooches for a year."

Ethel sighed. She felt as if her black dress ought, perhaps, to be worn for a nearer cause. She had a great desire to keep that Glenbracken brooch; and surely it could not be wrong. To refuse it would be much worse, and would only lead to Flora's keeping it, and not caring for it.

"Then it is your present, Flora?"

"If you like better to call it so, my dear. I find Norman Ogilvie is going abroad in a few months. I think we ought to ask him here on his way."

"Flora, I wish you would not talk about such things!"

"Do you really and truly, Ethel?"

"Certainly not, at such a time as this," said Ethel.

Flora was checked a little, and sat down to write to Marjorie Ogilvie. "Shall I say you like the brooch, Ethel?" she asked presently.

"Say what is proper," said Ethel impatiently. "You know what I mean, in the fullest sense of the word."

"Do I?" said Flora.

"I mean," said Ethel, "that you may say, simply and rationally, that I like the thing, but I won't have it said as a message, or that I take it as his present."

"Very well," said Flora, "the whole affair is simple enough, if you would not be so conscious, my dear."

"Flora, I can't stand your calling me my dear!"

"I am very much obliged to you," said Flora, laughing, more than she would have liked to be seen, but recalled by her sister's look. Ethel was sorry at once."

Flora, I beg your pardon; I did not mean to be cross, only please don't begin about that; indeed, I think you had better leave out about the brooch altogether. No one will wonder at your passing it over in such a return as this."

"You are right," said Flora thoughtfully.

Ethel carried the brooch to her own room, and tried to keep herself from speculating what had been Mr. Ogllvie's views in procuring it, and whether he remembered showing her, at Woodstock, which sort of fern was his badge, and how she had abstained from preserving the piece shut up in her guide-book.

Meta's patient sorrow was the best remedy for proneness to such musings. How happy poor little Meta had been! The three sisters sat together that long day, and Ethel read to the others, and by and by went to walk in the garden with them, till, as Flora was going in, Meta asked, "Do you think it would be wrong for me to cross the park to see that little burned girl, as Mr. Wilmot is away to-day, and she has no one to go to her?"

Flora could see no reason against it, and Meta and Ethel left the garden, and traversed the green park, in its quiet home beauty, not talking much, except that Meta said, "Well! I think there is quite as much sweetness as sadness in this evening."

"Because of this calm autumn sunset beauty?" said Ethel. "Look at the golden light coming in under the branches of the trees."

"Yes," said Meta, "one cannot help thinking how much more beautiful it must be—"

The two girls said no more, and came to the cottage, where so much gratitude was expressed at seeing Miss Rivers, that it was almost too much for her. She left Ethel to talk, and only said a few soft little words to her sick scholar, who seemed to want her voice and smile to convince her that the small mournful face, under all that black crape, belonged to her own dear bright teacher.

"It is odd," said Meta, as they went back; "it is seeing other people that makes one know it is all sad and altered—it seems so bewildering, though they are so kind."

"I know what you mean," said Ethel.

"One ought not to wish it to go on, because there are other people and other duties," said Meta, "but quietness is so peaceful. Do you know, Ethel, I shall always think of those two first days, before anybody came, with you and Dr. May, as something very—very—precious," she said at last, with the tears rising.

"I am sure I shall," said Ethel.

"I don't know how it is, but there is something even in this affliction that makes it like—a strange sort of happiness," said Meta musingly.

"I know what it is!" said Ethel.

"That He is so very good?" said Meta reverently.

"Yes," said Ethel, almost rebuked for the first thought, namely, that it was because Meta was so very good.

"It does make one feel more confidence," said Meta.

"'It is good for me to have been in trouble,'" repeated Ethel.

"Yes," said Meta. "I hope it is not wrong or unkind in me to feel it, for I think dear papa would wish it; but I do not feel as if— miss him always as I shall—the spring of life were gone from me. I don't think it can, for I know no more pain or trouble can reach him, and there is—don't you think, Ethel, that I may think so?—especial care for the orphan, like a compensation. And there is hope, and work here. And I am very thankful! How much worse it would have been, if George had not been married! Dear Flora! Will you tell her, Ethel, how really I do wish her to take the command of me? Tell her it will be the greatest kindness in the world to make me useful to her."

"I will,"said Ethel.

"And please tell her that I am afraid I may forget, and take upon me, as if I were still lady of the house. Tell her I do not mean it, and I hope that she will check it."

"I think there is no fear of her forgetting that," said Ethel, regretting the words before they were out of her mouth.

"I hope I shall not," said Meta. "If I do, I shall drive myself away to stay with Aunt Leonora, and I don't want to do that at all. So please to make Flora understand that she is head, and I am ready to be hand and foot;" and Meta's bright smile shone out, with the pleasure of a fresh and loving service.

Ethel understood the force of her father's words, that it was a brave, vigorous spirit.

Dr. May came back with George, and stayed to dinner, after which he talked over business with Flora, whose sagacity continually amazed him, and who undertook to make her husband understand, and do what was needed.

Meta meanwhile cross-questioned her brother on the pretty village by the Thames, of which she had a fond, childish remembrance, and heard from him of the numerous kind messages from all her relations. There were various invitations, but George repeated them unwillingly.

"You won't go, Meta," he said. "It would be a horrid nuisance to part with you."

"As long as you think so, dear George. When I am in your way, or Flora's—"

"That will never be! I say, Flora, will she ever be in our way?"

"No, indeed! Meta and I understand that," said Flora, looking up. "Well, I suppose Bruce can't be trusted to value the books and prints."

Dr. May thought it a great relief that Meta had a home with Flora, for, as he said to Ethel as they went home together, "Certainly, except Lord Cosham, I never saw such an unpresentable crew as their relations. You should have heard the boys afterwards! There was Master Tom turning up his Eton nose at them, and pronouncing that there never were such a set of snobs, and Norman taking him to task as I never heard him do before—telling him that he would never have urged his going to Eton, if he had thought it would make him despise respectable folks, probably better than himself, and that this was the last time in the world for such observations—whereat poor Tommy was quite annihilated; for a word from Norman goes further with him than a lecture from any one else."

"Well, I think Norman was right as to the unfitness of the time."

"So he was. But we had a good deal of them, waiting in the inn parlour. People make incongruities when they will have such things done in state. It could not be helped here, to be sure; but I always feel, at a grand undertaker's display like this, that, except the service itself, there is little to give peace or soothing. I hate what makes a talk! Better be little folk."

"One would rather think of our own dear cloister, and those who cared so much," said Ethel.

"Ah! you were happy to be there!" said Dr. May. "But it all comes to the same." Pausing, he looked from the window, then signed to Ethel to do the same—Orion glittered in the darkness.

"One may sleep sound without the lullaby," said Dr. May, "and the waves—"

189

"Oh! don't, papa. You don't give up hope!"

"I believe we ought, Ethel. Don't tell her, but I went to the Admirality to-day."

"And what did you hear there?"

"Great cause for fear—but they do not give up. My poor Margaret! But those stars tell us they are in the same Hand."

CHAPTER XIII.

Shall I sit alone in my chamber,
 And set the chairs by the wall,
While you sit with lords and princes,
 Yet have not a thought at all?

Shall I sit alone in my chamber,
 And duly the table lay,
Whilst you stand up in the diet,
And have not a word to say?—Old Danish Ballad.

"Oh, Norman, are you come already?" exclaimed Margaret, as her brother opened the door, bringing in with him the crisp breath of December.

"Yes, I came away directly after collections. How are you, Margaret?"

"Pretty brave, thank you;" but the brother and sister both read on each other's features that the additional three months of suspense had told. There were traces of toil and study on Norman's brow; the sunken look about his eyes, and the dejected outline of his cheek, Margaret knew betokened discouragement; and though her mild serenity was not changed, she was almost transparently thin and pale. They had long ago left off asking whether there were tidings, and seldom was the subject adverted to, though the whole family seemed to be living beneath a dark shadow.

"How is Flora?" he next asked.

"Going on beautifully, except that papa thinks she does too much in every way. She declares that she shall bring the baby to show me in another week, but I don't think it will be allowed."

"And the little lady prospers?"

"Capitally, though I get rather contradictory reports of her. First, papa declared her something surpassing—exactly like Flora, and so I suppose she is; but Ethel and Meta will say nothing for her beauty, and Blanche calls her a fright. But papa is her devoted admirer—he does so enjoy having a sort of property again in a baby!"

"And George Rivers?" said Norman, smiling.

"Poor George! he is very proud of her in his own way. He has just been here with a note from Flora, and actually talked! Between her and the election, he is wonderfully brilliant."

"The election? Has Mr. Esdaile resigned?"

"Have you not heard? He intends it, and George himself is going to stand. The only danger is that Sir Henry Walkinghame should think of it."

"Rivers in Parliament! Well, sound men are wanted."

"Fancy Flora, our member's wife. How well she will become her position."

"How soon is it likely to be?"

"Quickly, I fancy. Dr. Spencer, who knows all kinds of news (papa says he makes a scientific study of gossip, as a new branch of comparative anatomy), found out from the Clevelands that Mr. Esdaile meant to retire, and happened to mention it the last time that Flora came to see me. It was like firing a train. You would have wondered to see how it excited her, who usually shows her feelings so little. She has been so much occupied with it, and so anxious that George should be ready to take the field at once, that papa was afraid of its hurting her, and Ethel comes home declaring that the election is more to her than her baby."

"Ethel is apt to be a little hard on Flora. They are too unlike to understand each other."

"Ethel is to be godmother though, and Flora means to ask Mr. Ogilvie to come and stand."

"I think he will be gone abroad, or I should have asked him to fulfil his old promise of coming to us."

"I believe he must be lodged here, if he should come. Flora will have her house full, for Lady Leonora is coming. The baby is to be called after her."

"Indeed!" exclaimed Norman.

"Yes; I thought it unnecessary, as she is not George's aunt, but Flora is grateful to her for much kindness, and she is coming to see Meta. I am afraid papa is a little hurt, that any name but one should have been chosen."

"Has Meta been comfortable?"

"Dear little thing! Every one says how beautifully she has behaved. She brought all her housekeeping books to Flora at once, and only begged to be made helpful in whatever way might be most convenient. She explained, what we never knew before, how she had the young maids in to read with her, and asked leave to go on. Very few could have been set aside so simply and sweetly in their own house."

"Flora was sensible of it, I hope."

"Oh, yes. She took the management of course, but Meta is charmed with her having the girls in from the village, in turn, to help in the scullery. They have begun family prayers too, and George makes the stablemen go to church—a matter which had been past Meta, as you may guess, though she had been a wonderful little manager, and Flora owned herself quite astonished."

"I wonder only at her being astonished."

"Meta owned to Ethel that what had been worst of all to her was the heart sinking, at finding herself able to choose her occupations, with no one to accommodate them to. But she would not give way—she set up more work for herself at the school, and has been talking of giving singing lessons at Cocksmoor; and she forced herself to read, though it was an effort. She has been very happy lately in nursing Flora."

"Is Ethel there?"

"No; she is, as usual, at Cocksmoor. There are great councils about sending Cherry to be trained for her new school."

"Would Flora be able to see me, if I were to ride over to the Grange?"

"You may try; and, if papa is not there, I dare say she will."

"At least, I shall see Meta, and she may judge. I want to see Rivers too, so I will ask if the bay is to be had. Ah! you have the Claude, I see."

"Yes, it is too large for this room; but papa put it here that I might enjoy it, and it is almost a companion. The sky improves so in the sunset light."

Norman was soon at Abbotstoke; and, as he drew his rein, Meta's bright face nodded to him from Flora's sitting-room window; and, as he passed the conservatory, the little person met him, with a summons, at once, to his sister.

He found Flora on the sofa, with a table beside her, covered with notes and papers. She was sitting up writing; and, though somewhat pale, was very smiling and animated.

"Norman, how kind to come to me the first thing!"

"Margaret encouraged me to try whether you would be visible."

"They want to make a regular prisoner of me," said Flora, laughing. "Papa is as bad as the old nurse! But he has not been here to-day, so I have had my own way. Did you meet George?"

"No; but Margaret said he had been with her."

"I wish he would come. We expect the second post to bring the news that Mr. Esdaile has accepted the Chiltern Hundreds. If he found it so, he meant to go and talk to Mr. Bramshaw; for, though he is so dull, we must make him agent."

"Is there any danger of opposition?"

"None at all, if we are soon enough in the field. Papa's name will secure us, and there is no one else on the right side to come forward, so that it is an absolute rescue of the seat."

"It is the very moment when men of principle are most wanted," said Norman. "The questions of the day are no light matters; and it is an immense point to save Stoneborough from being represented by one of the Tomkins' set."

"Exactly so," said Flora. "I should feel it a crime to say one word to deter George, at a time when every effort must be made to support the right cause. One must make sacrifices when the highest interests are at stake."

Flora seemed to thrive upon her sacrifice—she had never appeared more brilliant and joyous. Her brother saw, in her, a Roman matron; and the ambition that was inherent in his nature, began to find compensation for being crushed, as far as regarded himself, by soaring for another. He eagerly answered that he fully agreed with her, and that she would never repent urging her husband to take on himself the duties incumbent on all who had the power.

Highly gratified, she asked him to look at a copy of George's intended address, which was lying on the table. He approved of the tenor, but saw a few phrases susceptible of a better point. "Give it," she said, putting a pen into his hand; and he began to interline and erase her fair manuscript, talking earnestly, and working up himself and the address at the same time, till it had grown into a composition far superior to the merely sensible affair it had been. Eloquence and thought were now in the language, and substance—and Flora was delighted.

"I have been very disrespectful to my niece all this time," said Norman, descending from the clouds of patriotism.

"I do not mean to inflict her mercilessly on her relations," said Flora, "but I should like you to see her. She is so like Blanche."

The little girl was brought in, and Flora made a very pretty young mother, as she held her in her arms, with so much graceful pride. Norman was perfectly entranced—he had never seen his sister so charming or so admirable, between her delight in her infant, and her self-devotion to the good of her husband and her country—acting so wisely, and speaking so considerately; and praising her dear Meta with so much warmth. He would never have torn himself away, had not the nurse hinted that Mrs. Rivers had had too much excitement and fatigue already to-day; and, besides, he suspected that he might find Meta in the drawing-room, where he might discuss the whole with her, and judge for himself of her state of spirits.

Flora's next visitor was her father, who came as the twilight was enhancing the comfortable red brightness of the fire. He was very happy in these visits—mother and child had both prospered so well, and it was quite a treat to be able to expend his tenderness on Flora. His little grandchild seemed to renew his own happy days, and he delighted to take her from her mother and fondle her. No sooner was the baby in his arms than Flora's hands were busy among the papers, and she begged him to ring for lights.

"Not yet," he said. "Why can't you sit in the dark, and give yourself a little rest?"

"I want you to hear George's address. Norman has been looking at it, and I hope you will not think it too strong," and she turned, so that the light might fall on the paper.

"Let me see," said Dr. May, holding out his hand for it.

"This is a rough copy, too much scratched for you to make out."

She read it accordingly, and her father admired it exceedingly—

Norman's touches, above all; and Flora's reading had dovetailed all so neatly together that no one knew where the joins were. "I will copy it fairly," she said, "if you will show it to Dr. Spencer, and ask whether he thinks it too strong. Mr. Dodsley too; he would be more gratified if he saw it first, in private, and thought himself consulted."

Dr. May was dismayed at seeing her take up her pen, make a desk of her blotting-book, and begin her copy by firelight.

"Flora, my dear," he said, "this must not be. Have I not told you that you must be content to rest?"

"I did not get up till ten o'clock, and have been lying here ever since."

"But what has this head of yours been doing? Has it been resting for ten minutes together? Now I know what I am saying, Flora—I warn you, that if you will not give yourself needful quiet now, you will suffer for it by and by."

Flora smiled, and said, "I thought I had been very good. But, what is to be done when one's wits will work, and there is work for them to do?"

"Is not there work enough for them here?" said Dr. May, looking at the babe. "Your mother used to value such a retirement from care."

Flora was silent for a minute, then said, "Mr. Esdaile should have put off his resignation to suit me. It is an unfortunate time for the election."

"And you can't let the election alone?"

She shook her head, and smiled a negative, as if she would, but that she was under a necessity.

"My dear, if the election cannot go on without you, it had better not go on at all."

She looked very much hurt, and turned away her head.

Her father was grieved. "My dear," he added, "I know you desire to be of use, especially to George; but do you not believe that he would rather fail, than that you, or his child, should suffer?"

No answer.

"Does he stand by his own wish, or yours, Flora?"

"He wishes it. It is his duty," said Flora, collecting her dignity.

"I can say no more, except to beg him not to let you exert yourself."

Accordingly, when George came home, the doctor read him a lecture on his wife's over-busy brain; and was listened to, as usual, with gratitude and deference. He professed that he only wished to do what was best for her, but she never would spare herself; and, going to her side, with his heavy, fond solicitude, he made her promise not to hurt herself, and she laughed and consented.

The promise was easily given, for she did not believe she was hurting herself; and, as to giving up the election, or ceasing secretly to prompt George, that was absolutely out of the question. What could be a greater duty than to incite her husband to usefulness?"

Moreover it was but proper to invite Meta's aunt and cousin to see her, and to project a few select dinners for their amusement and the gratification of her neighbours. It was only grateful and cousinly likewise, to ask the "Master of Glenbracken"; and as she saw the thrill of colour on Ethel's cheeks, at the sight of the address to the Honourable Norman Ogilvie, she thought herself the best of sisters. She even talked of Ogilvie as a second Christian name, but Meta observed that old Aunt Dorothy would call it Leonorar Rogilvie Rivers, and thus averted it, somewhat to Ethel's satisfaction.

Ethel scolded herself many times for wondering whether Mr. Ogilvie would come. What was it to her? Suppose he should; suppose the rest. What a predicament! How unreasonable and conceited, even to think of such a thing, when her mind was made up. What could result, save tossings to and fro, a passing gratification set against infinite pain, and strife with her own heart and with her father's unselfishness! Had he but come before Flora's marriage! No; Ethel hated herself for the wish that arose for the moment. Far better he should keep away, if, perhaps, without the slightest inclination towards her, his mere name could stir up such a tumult—all, it might be, founded in vanity. Rebellious feelings and sense of tedium had once been subdued—why should they be roused again?

The answer came. Norman Ogilvie was setting off for Italy, and regretted that he could not take Abbotstoke on his way. He desired his kind remembrances and warm Christmas wishes to all his cousins.

If Ethel breathed more freely, there was a sense that tranquillity is uninteresting. It was, it must be confessed, a flat end to a romance, that all the permanent present effect was a certain softening, and a degree more attention to her appearance; and after all, this might, as Flora averred, be ascribed to the Paris outfit having taught her to wear clothes; as well as to that which had awakened the feminine element, and removed that sense of not being like other women, which sometimes hangs painfully about girls who have learned to think themselves plain or awkward.

There were other causes why it should be a dreary winter to Ethel, under the anxiety that strengthened by duration, and the strain of acting cheerfulness for Margaret's sake. Even Mary was a care. Her round rosy childhood had worn into height and sallowness, and her languor and indifference fretted Miss Bracy, and was hunted down by Ethel, till Margaret convinced her that it was a case for patience and tenderness, which, thenceforth, she heartily gave, even encountering a scene with Miss Bracy, who was much injured by the suggestion that Mary was oppressed by perspective. Poor Mary, no one guessed the tears nightly shed over Harry's photograph.

Nor could Ethel quite fathom Norman. He wore the dispirited, burdened expression that she knew too well, but he would not, as formerly, seek relief in confidence to her, shunning the being alone with her, and far too much occupied to offer to walk to Cocksmoor. When the intelligence came that good old Mr. Wilmot of Settlesham had peacefully gone to his rest, after a short and painless illness, Tom was a good deal affected, in his peculiar silent and ungracious fashion; but Norman did not seek to talk over the event, and the feelings he had entertained two years ago—he avoided the subject, and threw himself into the election matters with an excitement foreign to his nature.

He was almost always at Abbotstoke, or attending George Rivers at the committee-room at the Swan, talking, writing, or consulting, concocting squibs, and perpetrating bons mots, that were the delight of friends and the confusion of foes. Flora was delighted, George adored him, Meta's eyes danced whenever he came near, Dr. Spencer admired him, and Dr. Hoxton prophesied great things of him; but Ethel did not feel as if he were the veritable Norman, and had an undefined sensation of discomfort, when she heard his brilliant repartees, and the laughter with which he accompanied them, so unlike his natural rare and noiseless laugh. She knew it was false excitement, to drive away the suspense that none dared to avow, but which did not press on them the less heavily for being endured in silence. Indeed, Dr. May could not help now and then giving way to outbursts of despondency, of which his friend, Dr. Spencer, who made it his special charge to try to lighten his troubles, was usually the kind recipient.

And though the bustle of the election was incongruous, and seemed to make the leaden weight the more heavy, there was a compensation in the tone of feeling that it elicited, which gave real and heartfelt pleasure.

Dr. May had undergone numerous fluctuations of popularity. He had always been the same man, excellent in intention, though hasty in action, and heeding neither praise nor censure; and while the main tenor of his course never varied, making many deviations by flying to the reverse of the wrong, most immediately before him, still his personal character gained esteem every year; and though sometimes his merits, and sometimes his failings, gave violent umbrage, he had steadily risen in the estimation of his fellow-townsmen, as much as his own inconsistencies and theirs would allow, and every now and then was the favourite with all, save with the few who abused him for tyranny, because he prevented them from tyrannising.

He was just now on the top of the wave, and his son-in-law had nothing to do but to float in on the tide of his favour. The opposite faction attempted a contest, but only rendered the triumph more complete, and gave the gentlemen the pleasure of canvassing, and hearing, times without number, that the constituents only wished the candidate were Dr. May himself. His sons and daughters were full of exultation—Dr. Spencer, much struck, rallied "Dick" on his influence—and Dr. May, the drops of warm emotion trembling on his eyelashes, smiled, and bade his friend see him making a church-rate.

The addresses and letters that came from the Grange were so admirable, that Dr. May often embraced Norman's steady opinion that George was a very wise man. If Norman was unconscious how much he contributed to these compositions, he knew far less how much was Flora's. In his ardour, he crammed them both, and conducted George when Flora could not be at his side. George himself was a personable man, wrote a good bold hand, would do as he was desired, and was not easily put out of countenance; he seldom committed himself by talking; and when a speech was required, was brief, and to the purpose. He made a very good figure, and in the glory of victory, Ethel herself began to grow proud of him, and the children's great object in life was to make the jackdaws cry, "Rivers for ever!"

Flora had always declared that she would be at Stoneborough for the nomination. No one believed her, until three days before, she presented herself and her daughter before the astonished Margaret, who was too much delighted to be able to scold. She had come away on her own responsibility, and was full of triumph. To come home in this manner, after having read "Rivers for ever!" on all the dead walls, might be called that for which she had lived. She made no stay—she had only come to show her child, and establish a precedent for driving out, and Margaret had begun to believe the apparition a dream, when the others came in, some from Cocksmoor, others from the committee-room at the Swan.

"So she brought the baby," exclaimed Ethel. "I should have thought she would not have taken her out before her christening."

"Ethel," said Dr. Spencer, "permit me to make a suggestion. When relations live in the same neighbourhood, there is no phrase to be more avoided than 'I should have thought—'"

The nomination-day brought Flora, Meta, baby and all to be very quiet, as was said; but how could that be? when every boy in the house was frantic, and the men scarcely less so. Aubrey and Gertrude, and the two jackdaws, each had a huge blue and orange rosette, and the two former went about roaring "Rivers for ever!" without the least consideration for the baby, who would have been decked in the same manner, if Ethel would have heard of it without indignation, at her wearing any colour before her christening white; as to Jack and Jill, though they could say their lesson, they were too much distressed by their ornaments to do ought but lurk in corners, and strive to peck them off.

Flora comported herself in her usual quiet way, and tried to talk of other things, though a carnation spot in each cheek showed her anxiety and excitement. She went with her sisters to look out from Dr. Spencer's windows towards the Town Hall. Her husband gave her his arm as they went down the garden, and Ethel saw her talking earnestly to him, and pressing his arm with her other hand to enforce her words, but if she did tutor him, it was hardly visible, and he was very glad of whatever counsel she gave.

She spoke not a word after the ladies were left with Aubrey, who was in despair at not being allowed to follow Hector and Tom, but was left, as his prematurely classical mind expressed it, like the

Gaulish women with the impedimenta in the marshes—whereas Tom had added insult to injury, by a farewell to "Jack among the maidens."

Meta tried to console him, by persuading him that he was their protector, and he began to think there was need of a guard, when a mighty cheer caused him to take refuge behind Ethel. Even when assured that it was anything but terrific, he gravely declared that he thought Margaret would want him, but he could not cross the garden without Meta to protect him.

She would not allow any one else to relieve her from the doughty champion, and thereby she missed the spectacle. It might be that she did not regret it, for though it would have been unkind to refuse to come in with her brother and sister, her wound was still too fresh for crowds, turmoil, and noisy rejoicing to be congenial. She did not withdraw her hand, which Aubrey squeezed harder at each resounding shout, nor object to his conducting her to see his museum in the dark corner of the attics, most remote from the tumult.

The loss was not great. The others could hear nothing distinctly, and see only a wilderness of heads; but the triumph was complete. Dr. May had been cheered enough to satisfy even Hector; George Rivers had made a very fair speech, and hurrahs had covered all deficiencies; Hector had shouted till he was as hoarse as the jackdaws; the opposite candidate had never come forward at all;

Tomkins was hiding his diminished head; and the gentlemen had nothing to report but success, and were in the highest spirits.

By and by Blanche was missing, and Ethel, going in quest of her, spied a hem of blue merino peeping out under all the cloaks in the hall cupboard, and found the poor little girl sobbing in such distress, that it was long before any explanation could be extracted, but at last it was revealed—when the door had been shut, and they stood in the dark, half stifled among the cloaks, that George's spirits had taken his old facetious style with Blanche, and in the very hearing of Hector! The misery of such jokes to a sensitive child, conscious of not comprehending their scope, is incalculable, and Blanche having been a baby-coquette, was the more susceptible. She hid her face again from the very sound of her own confession, and resisted Ethel's attempts to draw her out of the musty cupboard, declaring that she could never see either of them again. Ethel, in vain, assured her that George was gone to the dinner at the Swan; nothing was effectual but being told that for her to notice what had passed was the sure way to call Hector's attention thereto, when she bridled, emerged, and begged to know whether she looked as if she had been crying. Poor child, she could never again be unconscious, but, at least, she was rendered peculiarly afraid of a style of notice, that might otherwise have been a temptation.

Ethel privately begged Flora to hint to George to alter his style of wit, and the suggestion was received better than the blundering manner deserved; Flora was too exulting to take offence, and her patronage of all the world was as full-blown as her ladylike nature allowed. Ethel, she did not attempt to patronise, but she promised all the sights in London to the children, and masters to Mary and Blanche, and she perfectly overwhelmed Miss Bracy with orphan asylums for her sisters. She would have liked nothing better than dispersing cards, with Mrs. Rivers prominent among the recommenders of the case.

"A fine coming-out for you, little lady," said she to her baby, when taking leave that evening. "If it was good luck for you to make your first step in life upwards, what is this?"

"Excelsior?" said Ethel, and Flora smiled, well pleased, but she had not caught half the meaning. "May it be the right excelsior" added Ethel, in a low voice that no one heard, and she was glad they did not. They were all triumphant, and she could not tell why she had a sense of sadness, and thought of Flora's story long ago, of the girl who ascended Mont Blanc, and for what?

All she had to do at present was to listen to Miss Bracy, who was sure that Mrs. Rivers thought Mary and Blanche were not improved, and was afraid she was ungrateful for all the intended kindness to her sister.

Ethel had more sympathy here, for she had thought that Flora was giving herself airs, and she laughed and said her sister was pleased to be in a position to help her friends; and tried to turn it off, but ended by stumbling into allowing that prosperity was apt to make people over-lavish of offers of kindness.

"Dear Miss Ethel, you understand so perfectly. There is no one like you!" cried Miss Bracy, attempting to kiss her hand.

If Ethel had not spoken rightly of her sister, she was sufficiently punished.

What she did was to burst into a laugh, and exclaim, "Miss Bracy! Miss Bracy! I can't have you sentimental. I am the worst person in the world for it."

"I have offended. You cannot feel with me!"

"Yes, I can, when it is sense; but please don't treat me like a heroine. I am sure there is quite enough in the world that is worrying, without picking shades of manner to pieces. It is the sure way to make an old crab of me, and so I am going off. Only, one parting piece of advice, Miss Bracy—read 'Frank Fairlegh', and put everybody out of your head."

And, thinking she had been savage about her hand, Ethel turned back, and kissed the little governess's forehead, wished her goodnight, and ran away.

She had learned that, to be rough and merry, was the best way of doing Miss Bracy good in the end; and so she often gave herself the present pain of knowing that she was being supposed careless and hard-hearted; but the violent affection for her proved that the feeling did not last.

Ethel was glad to sit by the fire at bed-time, and think over the day, outwardly so gay, inwardly so fretting and perplexing.

It was the first time that she had seen much of her little niece. She was no great baby-handler, nor had she any of the phrases adapted to the infant mind; but that pretty little serene blue-eyed girl had been her chief thought all day, and she was abashed by recollecting how little she had dwelt on her own duties as her sponsor, in the agitations excited by the doubts about her coadjutor.

She took out her Prayer-book, and read the Service for Baptism, recollecting the thoughts that had accompanied her youngest sister's orphaned christening, "The vain pomp and glory of the world, and all covetous desires of the same." They seemed far enough off then, and now—poor little Leonora!

Ethel knew that she judged her sister hardly; yet she could not help picturing to herself the future—a young lady, trained for fashionable life, serious teaching not omitted, but right made the means of rising in the world; taught to strive secretly, but not openly, for admiration—a scheming for her marriage—a career like Flora's own. Ethel could scarcely feel that it would not be a mockery to declare, on her behalf, that she renounced the world. But, alas! where was not the world? Ethel blushed at having censured others, when, so lately, she had herself been oblivious of the higher duty. She thought of the prayer, including every Christian in holy and loving intercession—"I pray not that Thou wouldest take them out of the world, but that Thou wouldest keep them from the evil."

"Keep her from the evil—that shall be my prayer for my poor little Leonora. His grace can save her, were the surrounding evil far worse than ever it is likely to be. The intermixture with good is the trial, and is it not so everywhere—ever since the world and the Church have seemed fused together? But she will soon be the child of a Father who guards His own; and, at least, I can pray for her, and her dear mother. May I only live better, that so I may pray better, and act better, if ever I should have to act."

There was a happy family gathering on the New Year's Day, and Flora, who had kindly felt her way with Meta, finding her not yet ready to enjoy a public festivity for the village, added a supplement to the Christmas beef, that a second dinner might be eaten at home, in honour of Miss Leonora Rivers.

Lady Leonora was highly satisfied with her visit, which impressed her far more in favour of the Abbotstoke neighbourhood than in the days of poor old Mr. Rivers. Flora knew every one, and gave little select dinner-parties, which, by her good management, even George, at the bottom of the table, could not make heavy. Dr. Spencer enjoyed them greatly, and was an unfailing resource for conversation; and as to the Hoxtons, Flora felt herself amply repaying the kindness she had received in her young lady days, when she walked down to the dining-room with the portly headmaster, or saw his good lady sit serenely admiring the handsome rooms. "A very superior person, extremely pleasing and agreeable," was the universal verdict on Mrs. Rivers. Lady Leonora struck up a great friendship with her, and was delighted that she meant to take Meta to London. The only fault that could be found with her was that she had so many brothers; and Flora, recollecting that her ladyship mistrusted those brothers, avoided encouraging their presence at the Grange, and took every precaution against any opening for the suspicion that she threw them in the way of her little sister-in-law.

Nor had Flora forgotten the Ladies' Committee, or Cocksmoor. As to the muses, they gave no trouble at all. Exemplary civilities about the chair passed between the Member's lady and Mrs. Ledwich, ending in Flora's insisting that priority in office should prevail, feeling that she could well afford to yield the post of honour, since anywhere she was the leader. She did not know how much more conformable the ladies had been ever since they had known Dr. Spencer's opinion; and yet he only believed that they were grateful for good advice, and went about among them, easy, good-natured, and utterly unconscious that for him sparkled Mrs. Ledwich's bugles, and for him waved every spinster's ribbon, from Miss Rich down to Miss Boulder.

The point carried by their united influence was Charity Elwood's being sent for six months' finish at the Diocesan Training School; while a favourite pupil-teacher from Abbotstoke took her place at Cocksmoor. Dr. Spencer looked at the Training School, and talked Mrs. Ledwich into magnanimous forgiveness of Mrs. Elwood. Cherry dreaded the ordeal, but she was willing to do anything that was thought right, and likely to make her fitter for her office.

CHAPTER XIV.

'Twas a long doubt; we never heard
Exactly how the ship went down.—ARCHER GURNEY.

The tidings came at last, came when the heart-sickness of hope deferred had faded into the worse heart-sickness of fear deferred, and when spirits had been fain to rebel, and declare that they would be almost glad to part with the hope that but kept alive despair.

The Christmas holidays had come to an end, and the home party were again alone, when early in the forenoon, there was a tap at the drawing-room door, and Dr. Spencer called, "Ethel, can you come and speak to me?"

Margaret started as if those gentle tones had been a thunderclap.

"Go! go, Ethel," she said, "don't keep me waiting."

Dr. Spencer stood in the hall with a newspaper in his hand. Ethel said, "Is it?" and he made a sorrowful gesture. "Both?" she asked.

"Both," he repeated. "The ship burned—the boat lost."

"Ethel, come!" hoarsely called Margaret.

"Take it," said Dr. Spencer, putting the paper into her hand; "I will wait."

She obeyed. She could not speak, but kneeling down by her sister, they read the paragraph together; Ethel, with one eye on the words, the other on Margaret.

No doubt was left. Captain Gordon had returned, and this was his official report. The names of the missing stood below, and the list began thus:—

Lieutenant A. H. Ernescliffe.
Mr. Charles Owen, Mate.
Mr. Harry May, Midshipman.

The Alcestis had taken fire on the 12th of April of the former year. There had been much admirable conduct, and the intrepid coolness of Mr. Ernescliffe was especially recorded. The boats had been put off without loss, but they were scantily provisioned, and the nearest land was far distant. For five days the boats kept together, then followed a night of storms, and, when morning dawned, the second cutter, under command of Mr. Ernescliffe, had disappeared. There could be no doubt that she had sunk, and the captain could only record his regrets for the loss the service had experienced in the three brave young officers and their gallant seamen. After infinite toil and suffering, the captain, with the other boats' crews, had reached Tahiti, whence they had made their way home.

"Oh, Margaret, Margaret!" cried Ethel.

Margaret raised herself, and the colour came into her face.

"I did not write the letter!" she said.

"What letter?" said Ethel, alarmed.

"Richard prevented me. The letter that would have parted us. Now all is well."

"All is well, I know, if we could but feel it."

"He never had the pain. It is unbroken!" continued Margaret, her eyes brightening, but her breath, in long-drawn gasps that terrified Ethel into calling Dr. Spencer.

Mary was standing before him, with bloodless face and dilated eyes; but, as Ethel approached, she turned and rushed upstairs.

Dr. Spencer entered the drawing-room with Ethel, who tried to read his face as he saw Margaret—restored, as it seemed, to all her girlish bloom, and her eyes sparkling as they were lifted up, far beyond the present scene. Ethel had a moment's sense that his expression was as if he had seen a death-blow struck, but it was gone in a moment, as he gently shook Margaret by the hand, and spoke a word of greeting, as though to recall her.

"Thank you," she said, with her own grateful smile.

"Where is your father?" he asked of Ethel.

"Either at the hospital, or at Mr. Ramsden's," said Ethel, with a ghastly suspicion that he thought Margaret in a state to require him.

"Papa!" said Margaret. "If he were but here! But—ah! I had forgotten."

She turned aside her head, and hid her face. Dr. Spencer signed Ethel nearer to him. "This is a more natural state," he said. "Don't be afraid for her. I will find your father, and bring him home." Pressing her hand he departed.

Margaret was weeping tranquilly—Ethel knelt down beside her, without daring at first to speak, but sending up intense mental prayers to Him, who alone could bear her or her dear father through their affliction. Then she ventured to take her hand, and Margaret returned the caress, but began to blame herself for the momentary selfishness that had allowed her brother's loss and her father's grief to have been forgotten in her own. Ethel's "oh! no! no!" did not console her for this which seemed the most present sorrow, but the flow of tears was so gentle, that Ethel trusted that they were a relief. Ethel herself seemed only able to watch her, and to fear for her father, not to be able to think for herself.

The front door opened, and they heard Dr. May's step hesitating in the hall, as if he could not bear to come in.

"Go to him!" cried Margaret, wiping off her tears. Ethel stood a moment in the doorway, then sprang to him, and was clasped in his arms.

"You know it?" he whispered.

"Dr. Spencer told us. Did not you meet him?"

"No. I read it at Bramshaw's office. How—" He could not say the words, but he looked towards the room, and wrung the hand he held.

"Quiet. Like herself. Come."

He threw one arm round Ethel, and laid his hand on her head. "How much there is to be thankful for!" he said, then advancing, he hung over Margaret, calling her his own poor darling.

"Papa, you must forgive me. You said sending him to sea was giving him up."

"Did I. Well, Margaret, he did his duty. That is all we have to live for. Our yellow-haired laddie made a gallant sailor, and—"

Tears choked his utterance—Margaret gently stroked his hand.

"It falls hard on you, my poor girl," he said.

"No, papa," said Margaret, "I am content and thankful. He is spared pain and perplexity."

"You are right, I believe," said Dr. May. "He would have been grieved not to find you better."

"I ought to grieve for my own selfishness," said Margaret. "I cannot help it! I cannot be sorry the link is unbroken, and that he had not to turn to any one else."

"He never would!" cried Dr. May, almost angrily.

"I tried to think he ought," said Margaret. "His life would have been too dreary. But it is best as it is."

"It must be," said the doctor. "Where are the rest, Ethel? Call them all down."

Poor Mary, Ethel felt as if she had neglected her! She found her hanging over the nursery fire, alternating with old nurse in fond reminiscences of Harry's old days, sometimes almost laughing at his pranks, then crying again, while Aubrey sat between them, drinking in each word.

Blanche and Gertrude came from the schoolroom, where Miss Bracy seemed to have been occupying them, with much kindness and judgment. She came to the door to ask Ethel anxiously for the doctor and Miss May, and looked so affectionate and sympathising, that Ethel gave her a hearty kiss.

"Dear Miss Ethel! if you can only let me help you."

"Thank you," said Ethel with all her heart, and hurried away. Nothing was more in favour of Miss Bracy, than that there should be a hurry. Then she could be warm, and not morbid.

Dr. May gathered his children round him, and took out the great Prayer-book. He read a psalm and a prayer from the Burial Service, and the sentence for funerals at sea. Then he touched each of their heads, and, in short broken sentences, gave thanks for those still left to him, and for the blessed hope they could feel for those who were gone; and he prayed that they might so follow in their footsteps, as to come to the same holy place, and in the meantime realise the Communion of Saints. Then they said the Lord's Prayer, he blessed them, and they arose.

"Mary, my dear," he said, "you have a photograph."

She put the case into his hands, and ran away.

He went to the study, where he found Dr. Spencer awaiting him.

"I am only come to know where I shall go for you."

"Thank you, Spencer. Thank you for taking care of my poor girls."

"They took care of themselves. They have the secret of strength."

"They have—" He turned aside, and burst out, "Oh, Spencer! you have been spared a great deal. If you missed a great deal of joy, you have missed almost as much sorrow!" And, covering his face, he let his grief have a free course.

"Dick! dear old Dick, you must bear up. Think what treasures you have left."

"I do. I try to do so," said poor Dr. May; "but, Spencer, you never saw my yellow-haired laddie, with his lion look! He was the flower of them all! Not one of these other boys came near him in manliness, and with such a loving heart! An hour ago, I thought any certainty would be gain, but now I would give a lifetime to have back the hope that I might see my boy's face again! Oh, Spencer! this is the first time I could rejoice that his mother is not here!"

"She would have been your comforter," sighed his friend, as he felt his inability to contend with such grief.

"There, I can be thankful," Dr. May said, and he looked so. "She has had her brave loving boy with her all this time, while we little thought—but there are others. My poor Margaret—"

"Her patience must be blessed," said Dr. Spencer. "I think she will be better. Now that the suspense no longer preys on her, there will be more rest."

"Rest," repeated Dr. May, supporting his head on his hand; and, looking up dreamily—"there remaineth a rest—"

The large Bible lay beside him on the table, and Dr. Spencer thought that he would find more rest there than in his words. Leaving him, therefore, his friend went to undertake his day's work, and learn, once more, in the anxious inquiries and saddened countenances of the patients and their friends, how great an amount of love and sympathy that Dr. May had won by his own warmth of heart. The patients seemed to forget their complaints in sighs for their kind doctor's troubles; and the gouty Mayor of Stoneborough kept Dr. Spencer half an hour to listen to his recollections of the bright-faced boy's droll tricks, and then to the praises of the whole May family, and especially of the mother.

Poor Dr. Spencer! he heard her accident described so many times in the course of the day, that his visits were one course of shrinking and suffering; and his only satisfaction was in knowing how his friend would be cheered by hearing of the universal feeling for him and his children.

Ethel wrote letters to her brothers; and Dr. May added a few lines, begging Richard to come home, if only for a few days. Margaret would not be denied writing to Hector Ernescliffe, though she cried over her letter so much that her father could almost have taken her pen away; but she said it did her good.

When Flora came in the afternoon, Ethel was able to leave Margaret to her, and attend to Mary, with whom Miss Bracy's kindness had been inefficacious. If she was cheered for a few minutes, some association, either with the past or the vanished future, soon set her off sobbing again. "If I only knew where dear, dear Harry is lying," she sobbed, "and that it had not been very bad indeed, I could bear it better."

The ghastly uncertainty was too terrible for Ethel to have borne to contemplate it. She knew that it would haunt their pillows, and she was trying to nerve herself by faith.

"Mary," she said, "that is the worst; but, after all, God willed that we should not know. We must bear it like His good children. It makes no differences to them now—"

"I know," said Mary, trying to check her sobs.

"And, you know, we are all in the same keeping. The sea is a glorious great pure thing, you know, that man cannot hurt or defile. It seems to me," said Ethel, looking up, "as if resting there was like being buried in our baptism-tide over again, till the great new birth. It must be the next best place to a churchyard. Anywhere, they are as safe as among the daisies in our own cloister."

"Say it again—what you said about the sea," said Mary, more comforted than if Ethel had been talking down to her.

By and by Ethel discovered that the sharpest trouble to the fond simple girl was the deprivation of her precious photograph. It was like losing Harry over again, to go to bed without it, though she would not for the world seem to grudge it to her father.

Ethel found an opportunity of telling him of this distress, and it almost made him smile. "Poor Mary," he said, "is she so fond of it? It is rather a libel than a likeness."

"Don't say so to her, pray, papa. It is all the world to her. Three strokes on paper would have been the same, if they had been called by his name."

"Yes; a loving heart has eyes of its own, and she is a dear girl!"

He did not forget to restore the treasure with gratitude proportionate to what the loan had cost Mary. With a trembling voice, she proffered it to him for the whole day, and every day, if she might only have it at night; and she even looked black when he did not accept the proposal.

"It is exactly like—" said she.

"It can't help being so, in a certain sense," he answered kindly, "but after all, Mary dear, he did not pout out his chin in that way."

Mary was somewhat mortified, but she valued her photograph more than ever, because no one else would admire it, except Daisy, whom she had taught to regard it with unrivalled veneration.

A letter soon arrived from Captain Gordon, giving a fuller account of the loss of his ship, and of the conduct of his officers, speaking in the highest terms of Alan Ernescliffe, for whom he said he mourned as for his own son, and, with scarcely less warmth, of Harry, mentioning the high esteem all had felt for the boy, and the good effect which the influence of his high and truthful spirit had produced on the other youngsters, who keenly regretted him.

Captain Gordon added that the will of the late Captain Ernescliffe had made him guardian of his sons, and that he believed poor Alan had died intestate. He should therefore take upon himself the charge of young Hector, and he warmly thanked Dr. May and his family for all the kindness that the lad had received.

Though the loss of poor Hector's visits was regretted, it was, on the whole, a comforting letter, and would give still more comfort in future time.

Richard contrived to come home through Oxford and see Norman, whom he found calm, and almost relieved by the cessation from suspense; not inclined, as his father had feared, to drown sorrow in labour, but regarding his grief as an additional call to devote himself to ministerial work. In fact, the blow had fallen when he first heard the rumour of danger, and could not recur with the same force.

Richard was surprised to find that Margaret was less cast down than he could have dared to hope. It did not seem like an affliction to her. Her countenance wore the same gentle smile, and she was as ready to participate in all that passed, finding sympathy for the little pleasures of Aubrey and Gertrude, and delighting in Flora's baby; as well as going over Cocksmoor politics with a clearness and accuracy that astonished him, and asking questions about his parish and occupations, so as fully to enjoy his short visit, which she truly called the greatest possible treat.

If it had not been for the momentary consternation that she had seen upon Dr. Spencer's face, Ethel would have been perfectly satisfied; but she could not help sometimes entertaining a dim fancy that this composure came from a sense that she was too near Alan to mourn for him. Could it be true that her frame was more wasted, that there was less capability of exertion, that her hours became later in the morning, and that her nights were more wakeful? Would she fade away? Ethel longed to know what her father thought, but she could neither bear to inspire him with the apprehension, nor to ask Dr. Spencer's opinion, lest she should be confirmed in her own.

The present affliction altered Dr. May more visibly than the death of his wife, perhaps, because there was not the same need of exertion. If he often rose high in faith and resignation, he would also sink very low under the sense of bereavement and disappointment. Though Richard was his stay, and Norman his pride, there was something in Harry more congenial to his own temper, and he could not but be bowed down by the ruin of such bright hopes. With all his real submission, he was weak, and gave way to outbursts of grief, for which he blamed himself as unthankful; and his whole demeanour was so saddened and depressed, that Ethel and Dr. Spencer consulted mournfully over him, whenever they walked to Cocksmoor together.

This was not as often as usual, though the walls of the school were rising, for Dr. Spencer had taken a large share of his friend's work for the present, and both physicians were much occupied by the condition of Mr. Ramsden who was fast sinking, and, for some weeks, seemed only kept alive by their skill. The struggle ended at last, and his forty years' cure of Stoneborough was closed. It made Dr. May very sad—his affections had tendrils for anything that he had known from boyhood; and though he had often spoken strong words of the vicar, he now sat sorrowfully moralising and making excuses. "People in former times had not so high an estimate of pastoral duty—poor Mr. Ramsden had not much education—he was already old when better times came in—he might have done better in a less difficult parish with better laity to support him, etc." Yet after all, he exclaimed with one of his impatient gestures, "Better have my Harry's seventeen years than his sixty-seven!"

"Better improve a talent than lay it by!" said Ethel.

"Hush! Ethel. How do you know what he may have done? If he acted up to his own standard, he did more than most of us."

"Which is best," said Ethel, "a high standard, not acted up to, or a lower one fulfilled?"

"I think it depends on the will," said Margaret.

"Some people are angry with those whose example would show that there is a higher standard," said Ethel.

"And," said Margaret, "some who have the high one set before them content themselves with knowing that it cannot be fully attained, and will not try."

"The standard is the effect of early impression," said Dr. May. "I should be very sorry to think it could not be raised."

"Faithful in a little—" said Ethel. "I suppose all good people's standard is always going higher."

"As they comprehend more of absolute perfection," said Margaret.

CHAPTER XV.

The city's golden spire it was,
 When hope and health were strongest;
But now it is the churchyard grass,
 We look upon the longest. — E. B. BROWNING.

A disinclination for exertion or going into public hung upon Dr. May, but he was obliged to rouse himself to attend the Town Council meeting, which was held a few days after the vicar's funeral, to decide on the next appointment. If it had depended on himself alone, his choice would have been Mr. Edward Wilmot, whom the death of his good old father had uprooted from Settlesham; and the girls had much hope, but he was too much out of spirits to be sanguine. He said that he should only hear a great deal of offensive stuff from Tomkins the brewer; and that, in the desire to displease nobody, the votes should settle down on some nonentity, was the best which was likely to happen. Thus, grumbling, he set off, and his daughters watched anxiously for his return. They saw him come through the garden with a quick, light step, that made them augur well, and he entered the room with the corners of his mouth turning up. "I see," said Ethel, "it is all right."

"They were going to have made a very absurd choice."

"But you prevented it? Who was it?"

"Ah! I told you Master Ritchie was turning out a popular preacher."

"You don't mean that they chose Richard!" cried Margaret breathlessly.

"As sure as my name is Dick May, they did, every man of them, except Tomkins, and even he held his tongue; I did not think it of them," said the doctor, almost overcome; "but there is much more goodness of heart in the world than one gives it credit for."

And good Dr. May was not one to give the least credit for all that was like himself.

"But it was Richard's own doing," he continued. "Those sermons made a great impression, and they love the boy, because he has grown up among them. The old mayor waddled up to me, as I came in, telling me that they had been talking it over, and they were unanimously agreed that they could not have a parson they should like better than Mr. Richard."

"Good old Mr. Doddesley! I can see him!" cried Ethel.

"I expected it so little, that I thought he meant some Richards; but no, he said Mr. Richard May, if he had nothing better in view—they liked him, and knew he was a very steady, good young gentleman, and if he took after his fathers that went before him—and they thought we might like to have him settled near!"

"How very kind!" said Margaret, as the tears came. "We shall love our own townsfolk better than ever!"

"I always told you so, if you would but believe it. They have warm, sound hearts, every one of them! I declare, I did not know which way to look, I was so sorry to disappoint them."

"Disappoint them!" cried Margaret, in consternation.

"I was thinking," said Ethel. "I do not believe Richard would think himself equal to this place in such a state as it is. He is so diffident."

"Yes," said Dr. May, "if he were ten or twelve years older, it would be another thing; but here, where everything is to be done, he would not bring weight or force enough. He would only work himself to death, for individuals, without going to the root. Margaret, my darling, I am very sorry to have disappointed you so much—it would have been as great a pleasure as we could have had in this world to have the lad here—"

"And Cocksmoor," sighed Ethel.

"I shall be grateful all my life to those good people for thinking of it," continued the doctor; "but look you here, it was my business to get the best man chosen in my power and, though as to goodness, I believe the dear Ritchie has not many equals; I don't think we can conscientiously say he would be, at present, the best vicar for Stoneborough."

Ethel would not say no, for fear she should pain Margaret.

"Besides," continued Dr. May, "after having staved off the sale of the presentation as a sin, it would hardly have been handsome to have let my own son profit by it. It would have seemed as if we had our private ends, when Richard helped poor old Mr. Ramsden."

Margaret owned this, and Ethel said Richard would be glad to be spared the refusal.

"I was sure of it. The poor fellow would have been perplexed between the right and consideration for us. A vicar here ought to carry things with a high hand, and that is hardest to do at a man's own home, especially for a quiet lad like him."

"Yes, papa, it was quite right," said Margaret, recovering herself; "it has spared Richard a great deal."

"But are we to have Mr. Wilmot?" said Ethel. "Think of our not having heard!"

"Ay. If they would not have had Wilmot, or a man of his calibre, perhaps I might have let them offer it to Richard. I almost wish I had. With help, and Ethel—"

"No, no, papa," said Margaret. "You are making me angry with myself for my folly. It is much better for Richard himself, and for us all, as well as the town. Think how long we have wished for Mr. Wilmot!"

"He will be in time for the opening of Cocksmoor school!" cried Ethel. "How did you manage it?"

"I did not manage at all," said the doctor. "I told them exactly my mind, that Richard was not old enough for such arduous work; and though no words could tell how obliged I was, if they asked me who was the best man for it I knew, I should say Edward Wilmot, and I thought he deserved something from us, for the work he did gratis, when he was second master. Tomkins growled a little, but, fortunately, no one was prepared with another proposal, so they all came round, and the mayor is to write by this evening's post, and so shall I. If we could only have given Richard a dozen more years!"

Margaret was somewhat comforted to find that the sacrifice had cost her father a good deal; she was always slightly jealous for Richard, and now that Alan was gone, she clung to him more than ever. His soft calm manner supported her more than any other human comforter, and she always yearned after him when absent, more than for all the other brothers; but her father's decision had been too high-minded for her to dare to wish it recalled, and she could not but own that Richard would have had to undergo more toil and annoyance than perhaps his health would have endured.

Flora had discontinued comments to her sisters on her father's proceedings, finding that observations mortified Margaret, and did not tend to peace with Ethel; but she told her husband that she did not regret it much, for Richard would have exhausted his own income, and his father's likewise, in paying curates, and raising funds for charities. She scarcely expected Mr. Edward Wilmot to accept the offer, aware as he was, of the many disadvantages he should have to contend with, and unsuccessful as he had been in dealing with the Ladies' Committee.

However, Mr. Wilmot signified his thankful acceptance, and, in due time, his familiar tap was heard at the drawing-room door, at tea-time, as if he had just returned after the holidays. He was most gladly welcomed, and soon was installed in his own place, with his goddaughter, Mary, blushing with pleasure at pouring out his coffee.

"Well, Ethel, how is Cocksmoor? How like old times!"

"Oh," cried Ethel, "we are so glad you will see the beginning of the school!"

"I hear you are finishing Cherry Elwood, too."

"Much against Ethel's will," said Margaret; "but we thought Cherry not easily spoiled. And Whitford school seems to be in very good order. Dr. Spencer went and had an inspection of it, and conferred with all the authorities."

"Ah! we have a jewel of a parishioner for you," said Dr. May. "I have some hopes of Stoneborough now."

Mr. Wilmot did not look too hopeful, but he smiled, and asked after Granny Hall, and the children.

"Polly grew up quite civilised," said Ethel. "She lives at Whitford, with some very respectable people, and sends granny presents, which make her merrier than ever. Last time it was a bonnet, and Jenny persuaded her to go to church in it, though, she said, what she called the moon of it was too small."

"How do the people go on?"

"I cannot say much for them. It is disheartening. We really have done nothing. So very few go to church regularly."

"None at all went in my time," said Mr. Wilmot.

"Elwood always goes," said Mary, "and Taylor; yes, and Sam Hall, very often, and many of the women, in the evening, because they like to walk home with the children."

"The children? the Sunday scholars?"

"Oh, every one that is big enough comes to school now, here, on Sunday. If only the teaching were better—"

"Have you sent out any more pupils to service?"

"Not many. There is Willie Brown, trying to be Dr. Spencer's little groom," said Ethel.

"But I am afraid it will take a great deal of the doctor's patience to train him," added Margaret.

"It is hard," said Dr. May. "He did it purely to oblige Ethel; and, I tell her, when he lames the pony, I shall expect her to buy another for him, out of the Cocksmoor funds."

Ethel and Mary broke out in a chorus of defence of Willie Brown.

"There was Ben Wheeler," said Mary, "who went to work in the quarries; and the men could not teach him to say bad words, because the young ladies told him not."

"The young ladies have not quite done nothing," said Dr. May, smiling.

"These are only little stray things, and Cherry has done the chief of them," said Ethel. "Oh, it is grievously bad still," she added, sighing. "Such want of truth, such ungoverned tongues and tempers, such godlessness altogether! It is only surface-work, taming the children at school, while they have such homes; and their parents, even if they do come where they might learn better, are always liable to be upset, as they all it—turned out of their places in church, and they will not run the chance."

"The church must come to them," said Mr. Wilmot. "Could the school be made fit to be licensed for service."

"Ask our architect," said Dr. May. "There can be little doubt."

"I have been settling that I must have a curate specially for Cocksmoor," said Mr. Wilmot. "Can you tell me of one, Ethel—or perhaps Margaret could?"

Margaret could only smile faintly, for her heart was beating.

"Seriously," said Mr. Wilmot, turning to Dr. May, "do you think Richard would come and help us here?"

"This seems to be his destiny," said the doctor, smiling, "only it would not be fair to tell you, lest you should be jealous—that the Town Council had a great mind for him."

The matter was explained, and Mr. Wilmot was a great deal more struck by Dr. May's conduct than the good doctor thought it deserved. Every one was only too glad that Richard should come as Cocksmoor curate; and, though the stipend was very small—since Mr. Wilmot meant to have other assistance—yet, by living at home, it might be feasible.

Margaret's last words that night to Ethel were, "The last wish I had dared to make is granted!"

Mr. Wilmot wrote to Richard, who joyfully accepted his proposal, and engaged to come home as soon as his present rector could find a substitute.

Dr. Spencer was delighted, and, it appeared, had already had a view to such possibilities in designing the plan of the school.

The first good effect of Mr. Wilmot's coming was, that Dr. Spencer was cured of the vagrant habits of going to church at Abbotstoke or Fordholm, that had greatly concerned his friend. Dr. May, who could never get any answer from him except that he was not a Town Councillor, and, as to example, it was no way to set that to sleep through the sermon.

To say that Dr. May never slept under the new dynasty would be an over-statement, but slumber certainly prevailed in the minster to a far less degree than formerly. One cause might be that it was not shut up unaired from one Sunday to another, but that the chime of the bells was no longer an extraordinary sound on a week-day. It was at first pronounced that time could not be found for going to church on week-days without neglecting other things, but Mary, who had lately sat very loose to the schoolroom, began gradually to slip down to church whenever the service was neither too early nor too late; and Gertrude was often found trotting by her side—going to mamma, as the little Daisy called it, from some confusion between the church and the cloister, which Ethel was in no hurry to disturb.

Lectures in Lent filled the church a good deal, as much perhaps from the novelty as from better motives, and altogether there was a renewal of energy in parish work. The poor had become so little accustomed to pastoral care, that the doctors and the district visitors were obliged to report cases of sickness to the clergy, and vainly tried to rouse the people to send of their own accord. However, the better leaven began to work, and, of course, there was a ferment, though less violent than Ethel had expected.

Mr. Wilmot set more cautiously to work than he had done in his younger days, and did not attack prejudices so openly, and he had an admirable assistant in Dr. Spencer. Every one respected the opinion of the travelled doctor, and he had a courteous clever process of the reduction to the absurd, which seldom failed to tell, while it never gave offence. As to the Ladies' Committee, though there had been expressions of dismay, when the tidings of the appointment first went abroad, not one of the whole "Aonian choir" liked to dissent from Dr. Spencer, and he talked them over, individually, into a most conformable state, merely by taking their compliance for granted, and showing that he deemed it only the natural state of things, that the vicar should reign over the charities of the place.

The committee was not dissolved—that would have been an act of violence—but it was henceforth subject to Mr. Wilmot, and he and his curates undertook the religious instruction in the week, and chose the books—a state of affairs brought about with so much quietness, that Ethel knew not whether Flora, Dr. Spencer, or Mr. Wilmot had been the chief mover.

Mrs. Ledwich was made treasurer of a new coal club, and Miss Rich keeper of the lending-library, occupations which delighted them greatly; and Ethel was surprised to find how much unity of action was springing up, now that the period was over, of each "doing right in her own eyes."

"In fact," said Dr. Spencer, "when women have enough to do, they are perfectly tractable."

The Cocksmoor accounts were Ethel's chief anxiety. It seemed as if now there might be a school-house, but with little income to depend upon, since poor Alan Ernescliffe's annual ten pounds was at an end. However, Dr. May leaned over her as she was puzzling over her pounds, shillings, and pence, and laid a cheque upon her desk. She looked up in his face. "We must make Cocksmoor Harry's heir," he said.

By and by it appeared that Cocksmoor was not out of Hector Ernescliffe's mind. The boy's letters to Margaret had been brief, matter-of-fact, and discouraging, as long as the half-year lasted, and there was not much to be gathered about him from Tom, on his return for the Easter holidays, but soon poor Hector wrote a long dismal letter to Margaret.

Captain Gordon had taken him to Maplewood, where the recollection of his brother, and the happy hopes with which they had taken possession, came thronging upon him. The house was forlorn, and the corner that had been unpacked for their reception, was as dreary a contrast to the bright home at Stoneborough, as was the dry, stern captain, to the fatherly warm-hearted doctor. Poor Hector had little or nothing to do, and the pleasure of possession had not come yet; he had no companion of his own age, and bashfulness made him shrink with dislike from introduction to his tenants and neighbours.

There was not an entertaining book in the house, he declared, and the captain snubbed him, if he bought anything he cared to read. The captain was always at him to read musty old improving books, and talking about the position he would occupy. The evenings were altogether unbearable, and if it were not for rabbit shooting now, and the half-year soon beginning again, Hector declared he should be ready to cut and run, and leave Captain Gordon and Maplewood to each other—and very well matched too! He was nearly in a state of mind to imitate that unprecedented boy, who wrote a letter to 'The Times', complaining of extra weeks.

As to Cocksmoor, Ethel must not think it forgotten; he had spoken to the captain about it, and the old wooden-head had gone and answered that it was not incumbent on him, that Cocksmoor had no claims upon him, and he could not make it up out of his allowance; for the old fellow would not give him a farthing more than he had before, and had said that was too much.

There was a great blur over the words "wooden-head," as if Hector had known that Margaret would disapprove, and had tried to scratch it out. She wrote all the consolation in her power, and exhorted him to patience, apparently without much effect. She would not show his subsequent letters, and the reading and answering them fatigued her so much, that Hector's writing was an unwelcome sight at Stoneborough. Each letter, as Ethel said, seemed so much taken out of her, and she begged her not to think about them.

"Nothing can do me much good or harm now," said Margaret; and seeing Ethel's anxious looks, "Is it not my greatest comfort that Hector can still treat me as his sister, or, if I can only be of any use in keeping him patient? Only think of the danger of a boy, in his situation, being left without sympathy!"

There was nothing more to be said. They all felt it was good for them that the building at Cocksmoor gave full occupation to thoughts and conversation; indeed, Tom declared they never walked in any other direction, nor talked of anything else, and that without Hector, or George Rivers, he had nobody to speak to. However, he was a good deal tranquillised by an introduction to Dr. Spencer's laboratory, where he compounded mixtures that Dr. Spencer promised should do no more harm than was reasonable to himself, or any one else. Ethel suspected that, if Tom had chanced to singe his eyebrows, his friend would not have regretted a blight to his nascent coxcombry, but he was far too careful of his own beauty to do any such thing.

Richard was set at liberty just before Easter, and came home to his new charge. He was aware of what had taken place, and heartily grateful for the part his father had taken. To work at Cocksmoor, under Mr. Wilmot, and to live at home, was felicity; and he fitted at once into his old place, and resumed all the little home services for which he had been always famed. Ethel was certain that Margaret was content, when she saw her brother bending over her, and the sense of reliance and security that the presence of the silent Richard imparted to the whole family was something very peculiar, especially as they were so much more active and demonstrative than he was.

Mr. Wilmot put him at once in charge of the hamlet. The inhabitants were still a hard, rude, unpromising race, and there were many flagrant evils amongst them, but the last few years had not been without some effect—some were less obdurate, a few really touched, and, almost all, glad of instruction for their children. If Ethel's perseverance had done nothing else, it had, at least, been a witness, and her immediate scholars showed the influence of her lessons.

CHAPTER XVI.

Then out into the world, my course I did determine;
Though, to be rich was not my wish, yet to be great was charming.
My talents they were not the worst, nor yet my education;
Resolved was I, at least to try, to mend my situation.—BURNS.

In the meantime, the session of Parliament had begun, and the Rivers' party had, since February, inhabited Park Lane. Meta had looked pale and pensive, as she bade her friends at Stoneborough good-bye; but only betrayed that she had rather have stayed at home, by promising herself great enjoyment in meeting them again at Easter.

Flora was, on the other hand, in the state of calm patronage that betokened perfect satisfaction. She promised wonders for Miss Bracy's sisters—talked of inviting Mary and Blanche to see sights and take lessons; and undertook to send all the apparatus needed by Cocksmoor school; and she did, accordingly, send down so many wonderful articles, that curate and schoolmistress were both frightened; Mrs. Taylor thought the easels were new-fashioned instruments of torture; and Ethel found herself in a condition to be liberal to Stoneborough National School.

Flora was a capital correspondent, and made it her business to keep Margaret amused, so that the home-party were well informed of the doings of each of her days—and very clever her descriptions were. She had given herself a dispensation from general society until after Easter; but, in the meantime, both she and Meta seemed to find great enjoyment in country rides and drives, and in quiet little dinners at home, to George's agreeable political friends. With the help of two such ladies as Mrs. and Miss Rivers, Ethel could imagine George's house pleasant enough to attract clever people; but she was surprised to find how full her sister's letters were of political news.

It was a period when great interests were in agitation; and the details of London talk and opinions were extremely welcome. Dr. Spencer used to come in to ask after "Mrs. Rivers's Intelligencer"; and, when he heard the lucid statements, would say, she ought to have been a "special correspondent." And her father declared that her news made him twice as welcome to his patients; but her cleverest sentences always were prefaced with "George says," or "George thinks," in a manner that made her appear merely the dutiful echo of his sentiments.

In an early letter, Flora mentioned how she had been reminded of poor Harry, by finding Miss Walkinghame's card. That lady lived with her mother at Richmond, and, on returning the visit, Flora was warmly welcomed by the kind old Lady Walkinghame, who insisted on her bringing her baby and spending a long day. The sisters-in-law had been enchanted with Miss Walkinghame, whose manners, wrote Flora, certainly merited papa's encomium.

On the promised "long day," they found an unexpected addition to the party, Sir Henry Walkinghame, who had newly returned from the continent. "A fine-looking, agreeable man, about five-and-thirty," Flora described him, "very lively and entertaining. He talked a great deal of Dr. Spencer, and of the life in the caves at Thebes; and he asked me whether that unfortunate place, Cocksmoor, did not owe a great deal to me, or to one of my sisters. I left Meta to tell him that story, and they became very sociable over it."

A day or two after—"Sir Henry Walkinghame has been dining with us. He has a very good voice, and we had some delightful music in the evening."

By and by Sir Henry was the second cavalier, when they went to an oratorio, and Meta's letter overflowed with the descriptions she had heard from him of Italian church music. He always went to Rome for Easter, and had been going as usual, this spring, but he lingered, and, for once, remained in England, where he had only intended to spend a few days on necessary business.

The Easter recess was not spent at the Grange, but at Lady Leonora's pretty house in Surrey. She had invited the party in so pressing a manner that Flora did not think it right to decline. Meta expressed some disappointment at missing Easter among her school-children, but she said a great deal about the primroses and the green corn-fields, and nightingales—all which Ethel would have set down to her trick of universal content, if it had not appeared that Sir Henry was there too, and shared in all the delicious rides.

"What would Ethel say," wrote Flora, "to have our little Meta as Lady of the Manor of Cocksmoor? He has begun to talk about

Drydale, and there are various suspicious circumstances that Lady Leonora marks with the eyes of a discreet dowager. It was edifying to see how, from smiles, we came to looks, and by and by to confidential talks, which have made her entirely forgive me for having so many tall brothers. Poor dear old Mr. Rivers! Lady Leonora owns that it was the best thing possible for that sweet girl that he did not live any longer to keep her in seclusion; it is so delightful to see her appreciated as she deserves, and with her beauty and fortune, she might make any choice she pleases. In fact, I believe Lady Leonora would like to look still higher for her, but this would be mere ambition, and we should be far better satisfied with such a connection as this, founded on mutual and increasing esteem, with a man so well suited to her, and fixing her so close to us. You must not, however, launch out into an ocean of possibilities, for the good aunt has only infected me with the castle-building propensities of chaperons, and Meta is perfectly unconscious, looking on him as too hopelessly middle-aged, to entertain any such evil designs, avowing freely that she likes him, and treating him very nearly as she does papa. It is my business to keep 'our aunt,' who, between ourselves, has, below the surface, the vulgarity of nature that high-breeding cannot eradicate, from startling the little humming-bird, before the net has been properly twined round her bright little heart. As far as I can see, he is much smitten, but very cautious in his approaches, and he is wise."

Margaret did not know what dismay she conveyed, as she handed this letter to her sister. There was no rest for Ethel till she could be alone with her father. "Could nothing prevent it? Could not Flora be told of Mr. Rivers's wishes?" she asked.

"His wishes would have lain this way."

"I do not know that."

"It is no concern of ours. There is nothing objectionable here, and though I can't say it is not a disappointment, it ought not to be. The long and short of it is, that I never ought to have told you anything about it."

"Poor Norman!"

"Absurd! The lad is hardly one-and-twenty. Very few marry a first love." (Ah, Ethel!) "Poor old Rivers only mentioned it as a refuge from fortune-hunters, and it stands to reason that he would have preferred this. Anyway, it is awkward for a man with empty pockets to marry an heiress, and it is wholesomer for him to work for his living. Better that it should be out of his head at once, if it were there at all. I trust it was all our fancy. I would not have him grieved now for worlds, when his heart is sore."

"Somehow," said Ethel, "though he is depressed and silent, I like it better than I did last Christmas."

"Of course, when we were laughing out of the bitterness of our hearts," said Dr. May, sighing. "It is a luxury to let oneself alone to be sorrowful."

Ethel did not know whether she desired a tete-a-tete with Norman or not. She was aware that he had seen Flora's letter, and she did not believe that he would ever mention the hopes that must have been dashed by it; or, if he should do so, how could she ever guard her father's secret? At least, she had the comfort of recognising the accustomed Norman in his manner, low-spirited, indeed, and more than ever dreamy and melancholy, but not in the unnatural and excited state that had made her unhappy about him. She could not help telling Dr. Spencer that this was much more the real brother.

"I dare say," was the answer, not quite satisfactory in tone.

"I thought you would like it better."

"Truth is better than fiction, certainly. But I am afraid he has a tendency to morbid self-contemplation, and you ought to shake him out of it."

"What is the difference between self-contemplation and self-examination?"

"The difference between your brother and yourself. Ah! you think that no answer. Will you have a medical simile? Self-examination notes the symptoms and combats them; self-contemplation does as I did when I was unstrung by that illness at Poonshedagore, and was always feeling my own pulse. It dwells on them, and perpetually deplores itself. Oh, dear! this is no better—what a wretch I am. It is always studying its deformities in a moral looking-glass."

"Yes, I think poor Norman does that, but I thought it right and humble."

"The humility of a self-conscious mind. It is the very reverse of your father, who is the most really humble man in existence."

"Do you call self-consciousness a fault?"

"No. I call it a misfortune. In the vain, it leads to prudent vanity; in the good, to a painful effort of humility."

"I don't think I quite understand what it is."

"No, and you have so much of your father in you, that you never will. But take care of your brother, and don't let his brains work."

How Ethel was to take care of him she did not know; she could only keep a heedful eye on him, and rejoice when he took Tom out for a long walk—a companion certainly not likely to promote the working of the brain—but though it was in the opposite direction to Cocksmoor, Tom came home desperately cross, snubbed Gertrude, and fagged Aubrey; but, then, as Blanche observed, perhaps that was only because his trousers were splashed.

In her next solitary walk to Cocksmoor, Norman joined Ethel. She was gratified, but she could not think of one safe word worth saying to him, and for a mile they preserved an absolute silence, until he first began, "Ethel, I have been thinking—"

"That you have!" said she, between hope and dread, and the thrill of being again treated as his friend.

"I want to consult you. Don't you think now that Richard is settled at home, and if Tom will study medicine, that I could be spared."

"Spared!" exclaimed Ethel. "You are not much at home."

"I meant more than my present absences. It is my earnest wish—" he paused, and the continuation took her by surprise. "Do you think it would give my father too much pain to part with me as a missionary to New Zealand?"

She could only gaze at him in mute amazement.

"Do you think he could bear it?" said Norman hastily.

"He would consent," she replied. "Oh, Norman, it is the most glorious thing man can do! How I wish I could go with you."

"Your mission is here," said Norman affectionately.

"I know it is—I am contented with it," said Ethel; "but oh! Norman, after all our talks about races and gifts, you have found the more excellent way."

"Hush! Charity finds room at home, and mine are not such unmixed motives as yours."

She made a sound of inquiry.

"I cannot tell you all. Some you shall hear. I am weary of this feverish life of competition and controversy."

"I thought you were so happy with your fellowship. I thought Oxford was your delight."

"She will always be nearer my heart than any place, save this. It is not her fault that I am not like the simple and dutiful, who are not fretted or perplexed."

"Perplexed?" repeated Ethel.

"It is not so now," he replied. "God forbid! But where better men have been led astray, I have been bewildered; till, Ethel, I have felt as if the ground were slipping from beneath my feet, and I have only been able to hide my eyes, and entreat that I might know the truth."

"You knew it!" said Ethel, looking pale, and gazing searchingly at him.

"I did, I do; but it was a time of misery when, for my presumption, I suppose, I was allowed to doubt whether it were the truth."

Ethel recoiled, but came nearer, saying, very low, "It is past."

"Yes, thank Him who is Truth. You all saved me, though you did not know it."

"When was this?" she asked timidly.

"The worst time was before the Long Vacation. They told me I ought to read this book and that. Harvey Anderson used to come primed with arguments. I could always overthrow them, but when I came to glory in doing so, perhaps I prayed less. Anyway, they left a sting. It might be that I doubted my own sincerity, from knowing that I had got to argue, chiefly because I liked to be looked on as a champion."

Ethel saw the truth of what her friend had said of the morbid habit of self-contemplation.

"I read, and I mystified myself. The better I talked, the more my own convictions failed me; and, by the time you came up to Oxford, I knew how you would have shrunk from him who was your pride, if you could have seen into the secrets beneath."

Ethel took hold of his hand. "You seemed bright," she said.

"It melted like a bad dream before—before the humming-bird, and with my father. It was weeks ere I dared to face the subject again."

"How could you? Was it safe?"

"I could not have gone on as I was. Sometimes the sight of my father, or the mountains and lakes in Scotland, or—or—things at the Grange, would bring peace back; but there were dark hours, and I knew that there could be no comfort till I had examined and fought it out."

"I suppose examination was right," said Ethel, "for a man, and defender of the faith. I should only have tried to pray the terrible thought away. But I can't tell how it feels."

"Worse than you have power to imagine," said Norman, shuddering. "It is over now. I worked out their fallacies, and went over the reasoning on our side."

"And prayed—" said Ethel.

"Indeed I did; and the confidence returned, firmer, I hope, than ever. It had never gone for a whole day."

Ethel breathed freely. "It was life or death," she said, "and we never knew it!"

"Perhaps not; but I know your prayers were angel-wings ever round me. And far more than argument, was the thought of my father's heart-whole Christian love and strength."

"Norman, you believed, all the time, with your heart. This was only a bewilderment of your intellect."

"I think you are right," said Norman. "To me the doubt was cruel agony—not the amusement it seems to some."

"Because our dear home has made the truth, our joy, our union," said Ethel. "And you are sure the cloud is gone, and for ever?" she still asked anxiously.

He stood still. "For ever, I trust," he said. "I hold the faith of my childhood in all its fullness as surely as—as ever I loved my mother and Harry."

"I know you do," said Ethel. "It was only a bad dream."

"I hope I may be forgiven for it," said Norman. "I do not know how far it was sin. It was gone so far as that my mind was convinced last Christmas, but the shame and sting remained. I was not at peace again till the news of this spring came, and brought, with the grief, this compensation—that I could cast behind me and forget the criticisms and doubts that those miserable debates had connected with sacred words."

"You will be the sounder for having fought the fight," said Ethel.

"I do not dread the like shocks," said her brother, "but I long to leave this world of argument and discussion. It is right that there should be a constant defence and battle, but I am not fit for it. I argue for my own triumph, and, in heat and harassing, devotion is lost. Besides, the comparison of intellectual power has been my bane all my life."

"I thought 'praise was your penance here.'"

"I would fain render it so, but—in short, I must be away from it all, and go to the simplest, hardest work, beginning from the rudiments, and forgetting subtle arguments."

"Forgetting yourself," said Ethel.

"Right. I want to have no leisure to think about myself," said Norman. "I am never so happy as at such times."

"And you want to find work so far away?"

"I cannot help feeling drawn towards those southern seas. I am glad you can give me good-speed. But what do you think about my father?"

Ethel thought and thought. "I know he would not hinder you," she repeated.

"But you dread the pain for him? I had talked to Tom about taking his profession; but the poor boy thinks he dislikes it greatly, though, I believe, his real taste lies that way, and his aversion only arises a few grand notions he has picked up, out of which I could soon talk him."

"Tom will not stand in your place," said Ethel.

"He will be more equable and more to be depended upon," said Norman.

"None of you appreciate Tom. However, you must hear my alternative. If you think my going would be too much grief for papa, or if Tom be set against helping him in his practice, there is an evident leading of Providence, showing that I am unworthy of this work. In that case I would go abroad and throw myself, at once, with all my might, into the study of medicine, and get ready to give my father some rest. It is a shame that all his sons should turn away from his profession."

"I am more than ever amazed!" cried Ethel. "I thought you detested it. I thought papa never wished it for you. He said you had not nerve."

"He was always full of the tenderest consideration for me," said Norman. "With Heaven to help him, a man may have nerve for whatever is his duty."

"How he would like to have you to watch and help. But New Zealand would be so glorious!"

"Glory is not for me," said Norman. "Understand, Ethel, the choice is New Zealand, or going at once—at once, mind—to study at Edinburgh or Paris."

"New Zealand at once?" said Ethel.

"I suppose I mast stay for divinity lectures, but my intention must be avowed," said Norman hastily. "And now, will you sound my father? I cannot."

"I can't sound," said Ethel. "I can only do things point-blank."

"Do then," said Norman, "any way you can! Only let me know which is best for him. You get all the disagreeable things to do, good old unready one," he added kindly. "I believe you are the one who would be shoved in front, if we were obliged to face a basilisk."

The brightness that had come over Norman, when he had discharged his cares upon her, was encouragement enough for Ethel. She only asked how much she was to repeat of their conversation.

"Whatever you think best. I do not want to grieve him, but he must not think it fine in me."

Ethel privately thought that no power on earth could prevent him from doing that.

It was not consistent with cautious sounding, that Norman was always looking appealingly towards her; and, indeed, she could not wait long with such a question on her mind. She remained with her father in the drawing-room, when the rest were gone upstairs, and, plunging at once into the matter, she said, "Papa, there is something that Norman cannot bear to say to you himself."

"Humming-birds to wit?" said Dr. May.

"No, indeed, but he wants to be doing something at once. What should you think of—of—there are two things; one is—going out as a missionary—"

"Humming-birds in another shape," said the doctor, startled, but smiling, so as to pique her.

"You mean to treat it as a boy's fancy!" said she.

"It is rather suspicious," he said. "Well, what is the other of his two things?"

"The other is, to begin studying medicine at once, so as to help you."

"Heyday!" cried Dr. May, drawing up his tall vigorous figure, "does he think me so very ancient and superannuated?"

What could possess him to be so provoking and unsentimental to-night? Was it her own bad management? She longed to put an end to the conversation, and answered, "No, but he thinks it hard that none of your sons should be willing to relieve you."

"It won't be Norman," said Dr. May. "He is not made of the stuff. If he survived the course of study, every patient he lost, he would bring himself in guilty of murder, and there would soon be an end of him!"

"He says that a man can force himself to anything that is his duty."

"This is not going to be his duty, if I can make it otherwise. What is the meaning of all this? No, I need not ask, poor boy, it is what I was afraid of!"

"It is far deeper," said Ethel; and she related great part of what she had heard in the afternoon. It was not easy to make her father listen—his line was to be positively indignant, rather than compassionate, when he heard of the doubts that had assailed poor Norman. "Foolish boy, what business had he to meddle with those accursed books, when he knew what they were made of—it was tasting poison, it was running into temptation! He had no right to expect to come out safe—" and then he grasped tightly hold of Ethel's hands, and, as if the terror had suddenly flashed on him, asked her, with dilated eye and trembling voice, whether she were sure that he was safe, and held the faith.

Ethel repeated his asseveration, and her father covered his face with his hands in thanksgiving.

After this, he seemed somewhat inclined to hold poor Oxford in horror, only, as he observed, it would be going out of the frying-pan into the fire, to take refuge at Paris—a recurrence to the notion of Norman's medical studies, that showed him rather enticed by the proposal.

He sent Ethel to bed, saying he should talk to Norman and find out what was the meaning of it, and she walked upstairs, much ashamed of having so ill served her brother, as almost to have made him ridiculous.

Dr May and Norman never failed to come to an understanding, and after they had had a long drive into the country together, Dr May told Ethel that he was afraid, of what he ought not to be afraid of, that she was right, that the lad was very much in earnest now at any rate, and if he should continue in the same mind, he hoped he should not be so weak as to hold him from a blessed work.

From Norman, Ethel heard the warmest gratitude for his father's kindness. Nothing could be done yet, he must wait patiently for the present, but he was to write to his uncle, Mr. Arnott, in New Zealand, and, without pledging himself, to make inquiries as to the mission; and in the meantime, return to Oxford, where, to his other studies, he was to add a course of medical lectures, which, as Dr. May said, would do him no harm, would occupy his mind, and might turn to use wherever he was.

Ethel was surprised to find that Norman wrote to Flora an expression of his resolution, that, if he found he could be spared from assisting his father as a physician, he would give himself up to the mission in New Zealand. Why should he tell any one so unsympathetic as Flora, who would think him wasted in either case?

CHAPTER XVII.

Do not fear: Heaven is as near,
By water, as by land.—LONGFELLOW.

The fifth of May was poor Harry's eighteenth birthday, and, as usual, was a holiday. Etheldred privately thought his memory more likely to be respected, if Blanche and Aubrey were employed, than if they were left in idleness; but Mary would have been wretched had the celebration been omitted, and a leisure day was never unwelcome.

Dr. Spencer carried off Blanche and Aubrey for a walk, and Ethel found Mary at her great resort—Harry's cupboard—dusting and arranging his books, and the array of birthday gifts, to which, even to-day, she had not failed to add the marker that had been in hand at Christmas. Ethel entreated her to come down, and Mary promised, and presently appeared, looking so melancholy, that, as a sedative, Ethel set her down to the basket of scraps to find materials for a tippet for some one at Cocksmoor, intending, as soon as Margaret should be dressed, to resign her morning to the others, invite Miss Bracy to the drawing-room, and read aloud.

Gertrude was waiting for her walk, till nurse should have dressed Margaret, and was frisking about the lawn, sometimes looking in at the drawing-room window at her sisters, sometimes chattering to Adams at his work, or laughing to herself and the flowers, in that overflow of mirth, that seemed always bubbling up within her.

She was standing in rapt contemplation of a pear-tree in full blossom, her hands tightly clasped behind the back, for greater safety from the temptation, when, hearing the shrubbery gate open, she turned, expecting to see her papa, but was frightened at the sight of two strangers, and began to run off at full speed.

"Stop! Blanche! Blanche, don't you know me?" The voice was that tone of her brother's, and she stood and looked, but it came from a tall, ruddy youth, in a shabby rough blue coat, followed by a grizzled old seaman. She was too much terrified and perplexed even to run.

"What's the matter! Blanche, it is I! Why, don't you know me—Harry?"

"Poor brother Harry is drowned," she answered; and, with one bound, he was beside her, and, snatching her up, devoured her with kisses.

"Put me down—put me down, please," was all she could say.

"It is not Blanche! What? the little Daisy, I do believe!"

"Yes, I am Gertrude, but please let me go;" and, at the same time, Adams hurried up, as if he thought her being kidnapped, but his aspect changed at the glad cry, "Ha! Adams' how are you? Are they all well?"

"'Tisn't never Master Harry! Bless me!" as Harry's hand gave him sensible proof; "when we had given you up for lost!"

"My father well?" Harry asked, hurrying the words one over the other.

"Quite well, sir, but he never held up his head since he heard it, and poor Miss Mary has so moped about. If ever I thought to see the like—"

"So they did not get my letter, but I can't stop. Jennings will tell you. Take care of him. Come, Daisy—" for he had kept her unwilling hand all the time. "But what's that for?" pointing to the black ribbons, and, stopping short, startled.

"Because of poor Harry," said the bewildered child.

"Oh, that's right!" cried he, striding on, and dragging her in a breathless run, as he threw open the well-known doors; and, she escaping from him, hid her face in Mary's lap, screaming, "He says he is Harry! he says he is not drowned!"

At the same moment Ethel was in his arms, and his voice was sobbing, "Ethel! Mary! home! Where's papa?" One moment's almost agonising joy in the certainty of his identity! but ere she could look or think, he was crying, "Mary! oh, Ethel, see—"

Mary had not moved, but sat as if turned to stone, with breath suspended, wide-stretched eyes, and death-like cheeks—Ethel sprang to her, "Mary, Mary dear, it is Harry! It is himself! Don't you see? Speak to her, Harry."

He seemed almost afraid to do so, but, recovering himself, exclaimed, "Mary, dear old Polly, here I am! Oh, won't you speak to me?" he added piteously, as he threw his arm round her and kissed her, startled at the cold touch of her cheek.

The spell seemed broken, and, with a wild hoarse shriek that rang through the house, she struggled to regain her breath, but it would only come in painful, audible catches, as she held Harry's hand convulsively.

"What have I done?" he exclaimed, in distress.

"What's this! Who is this frightening my dear?" was old nurse's exclamation, as she and James came at the outcry.

"Oh, nurse, what have I done to her?" repeated Harry.

"It is joy—it is sudden joy!" said Ethel. "See, she is better now —"

"Master Harry! Well, I never!" and James, "with one wring of the hand, retreated, while old nurse was nearly hugged to death, declaring all the time that he didn't ought to have come in such a way, terrifying every one out of their senses! and as for poor Miss May—

"Where is she? " cried Harry, starting at the sight of the vacant sofa.

"Only upstairs," said Ethel; "but where's Alan? Is not he come?"

"Oh, Ethel, don't you know?" His face told but too plainly.

"Nurse! nurse, how shall we tell her?" said Ethel.

"Poor dear!" exclaimed nurse, sounding her tongue on the roof of her mouth. "She'll never abear it without her papa. Wait for him, I should say. But bless me, Miss Mary, to see you go on like that, when Master Harry is come back such a bonny man!"

"I'm better now," said Mary, with an effort. "Oh, Harry! speak to me again."

"But Margaret!" said Ethel, while the brother was holding Mary in his embrace, and she lay tremulous with the new ecstasy upon his breast—

"but Margaret. Nurse, you must go up, or she will suspect. I'll come when I can; speak quietly. Oh! poor Margaret! If Richard would but come in!"

Ethel walked up and down the room, divided between a tumult of joy, grief, dread, and perplexity. At that moment a little voice said at the door, "Please, Margaret wants Harry to come up directly."

They looked one upon another in consternation. They had never thought of the child, who, of course, had flown up at once with the tidings.

"Go up, Miss Ethel," said nurse.

"Oh! nurse, I can't be the first. Come, Harry, come."

Hand-in-hand, they silently ascended the stairs, and Ethel pushed open the door. Margaret was on her couch, her whole form and face in one throb of expectation.

She looked into Harry's face—the eagerness flitted like sunshine on the hillside, before a cloud, and, without a word, she held out her arms.

He threw himself on his knees, and her fingers were clasped among his thick curls, while his frame heaved with suppressed sobs, "Oh, if he could only have come back to you."

"Thank God," she said; then slightly pushing him back, she lay holding his hand in one of hers, and resting the other on his shoulder, and gazing in silence into his face. Each was still—she was gathering strength—he dreaded word or look.

"Tell me how and where;" she said at last.

"It was in the Loyalty Isles; it was fever—the exertions for us. His head was lying here," and he pointed to his own breast. "He sent his love to you—he bade me tell you there would be meeting by and by, in the haven where he would be. —I laid his head in the grave— under the great palm—I said some of the prayers—there are Christians round it."

He said this in short disconnected phrases, often pausing to gather voice, but forced to resume, by her inquiring looks and pressure of his hand.

She asked no more. "Kiss me," she said, and when he had done so, "Thank you, go down, please, all of you. You have brought great relief. Thank you. But I can't talk yet. You shall tell me the rest by and by."

She sent them all away, even Ethel, who would have lingered.

"Go to him, dearest. Let me be alone. Don't be uneasy. This is peace—but go."

Ethel found Mary and Harry interlaced into one moving figure, and Harry greedily asking for his father and Norman, as if famishing for the sight of them. He wanted to set out to seek the former in the town, but his movements were too uncertain, and the girls clung to the newly-found, as if they could not trust him away from them. They wandered about, speaking, all three at random, without power of attending to the answers. It was enough to see him, and touch him; they could not yet care where he had been.

Dr. May was in the midst of them ere they were aware. One look, and he flung his arms round his son, but, suddenly letting him go, he hurst away, and banged his study door. Harry would have followed.

"No, don't," said Ethel; then, seeing him disappointed, she came nearer, and murmured, "'He entered into his chamber and—'"

Harry silenced her with another embrace, but their father was with them again, to verify that he had really seen his boy, and ask, alas! whether Alan were with Margaret. The brief sad answer sent him to see how it was with her. She would not let him stay; she said it was infinite comfort, and joy was coming, but she would rather be still, and not come down till evening.

Perhaps others would fain have been still, could they have borne an instant's deprivation of the sight of their dear sailor, while greetings came thickly on him. The children burst in, having heard a report in the town, and Dr. Spencer waited at the door for the confirmation; but when Ethel would have flown out to him, he waved his hand, shut the door, and hurried away, as if a word to her would have been an intrusion.

The brothers had been summoned by a headlong apparition of Will Adams in Cocksmoor school, shouting that Master Harry was come home; and Norman's long legs out-speeding Richard, had brought him back, flushed, and too happy for one word, while, "Well, Harry," was Richard's utmost, and his care for Margaret seemed to overpower everything else, as he went up, and was not so soon sent away.

Words were few downstairs. Blanche and Aubrey agreed that they thought people would have been much happier, but, in fact, the joy was oppressive from very newness. Ethel roamed about, she could not sit still without feeling giddy, in the strangeness of the revulsion. Her father sat, as if a word would break the blest illusion; and Harry stood before each of them in turn, as if about to speak, but turned his address into a sudden caress, or blow on the shoulder, and tried to laugh. Little Gertrude, not understanding; the confusion, had taken up her station under the table, and peeped out from beneath the cover.

There was more composure as they sat at dinner, and yet there was very little talking or eating. Afterwards Dr. May and Norman exultingly walked away, to show their Harry to Dr. Spencer and Mr. Wilmot; and Ethel would gladly have tried to calm herself, and recover the balance of her mind, by giving thanks where they were due; but she did not know what to do with her sisters. Blanche was wild, and Mary still in so shaky a state of excitement, that she went off into mad laughing, when Blanche discovered that they were in mourning for Harry.

Nothing would satisfy Blanche but breaking in on Margaret, and climbing to the top of the great wardrobe to disinter the coloured raiment, beseeching that each favourite might be at once put on, to do honour to Harry. Mary chimed in with her, in begging for the wedding merinos—would not Margaret wear her beautiful blue?

"No, my dear, I cannot," said Margaret gently.

Mary looked at her and was again in a flood of tears, incoherently protesting, together with Ethel, that they would not change.

"No, dears," said Margaret. "I had rather you did so. You must not be unkind to Harry. He will not think I do not welcome him. I am only too glad that Richard would not let my impatience take away my right to wear this."

Ethel knew that it was for life.

Mary could not check her tears, and would go on making heroic protests against leaving off her black, sobbing the more at each. Margaret's gentle caresses seemed to make her worse, and Ethel, afraid that Margaret's own composure would be overthrown, exclaimed, "How can you be so silly? Come away!" and rather roughly pulled her out of the room, when she collapsed entirely at the top of the stairs, and sat crying helplessly.

"I can't think what's the use of Harry's coming home," Gertrude was heard saying to Richard. "It is very disagreeable;" whereat Mary relapsed into a giggle, and Ethel felt frantic.

"Richard! Richard! what is to be done with Mary? She can't help it,

I believe, but this is not the way to treat the mercy that—"

"Mary had better go and lie down in her own room," said Richard, tenderly and gravely.

"Oh, please! please!" began Mary, "I shall not see him when he comes back!"

"If you can't behave properly when he does come," said Richard, "there is no use in being there."

"Remember, Ritchie," said Ethel, thinking him severe, "she has not been well this long time."

Mary began to plead, but, with his own pretty persuasive manner, he took her by the hand, and drew her into his room; and when he came down, after an interval, it was to check Blanche, who would have gone up to interrupt her with queries about the perpetual blue merino. He sat down with Blanche on the staircase window-seat, and did not let her go till he had gently talked her out of flighty spirits into the soberness of thankfulness.

Ethel, meanwhile, had still done nothing but stray about, long for loneliness, find herself too unsteady to finish her letters to Flora and Tom; and, while she tried to make Gertrude think Harry a pleasant acquisition, she hated her own wild heart, that could not rejoice, nor give thanks, aright.

By and by Mary came down, with her bonnet on, quite quiet now. "I am going to church with Ritchie," she said. Ethel caught at the notion, and it spread through the house. Dr May, who just then came in with his two sons, looked at Harry, saying, "What do you think of it? Shall we go, my boy?" And Harry, as soon as he understood, declared that he should like nothing better. It seemed what they all needed, even Aubrey and Gertrude begged to come, and, when the solemn old minster was above their heads, and the hallowed stillness around them, the tightened sense of half-realised joy began to find relief in the chant of glory. The voices of the sanctuary, ever uplifting notes of praise, seemed to gather together and soften their emotions; and agitation was soothed away, and all that was oppressive and tumultuous gave place to sweet peace and thankfulness. Ethel dimly remembered the like sense of relief, when her mother had hushed her wild ecstasy, while sympathising with her joy. Richard could not trust his voice, but Mr. Wilmot offered the special thanksgiving.

Harry was, indeed, "at home," and his tears fell fast over his book, as he heard his father's "Amen," so fervent and so deep; and he gazed up and around, with fond and earnest looks, as thoughts and resolutions, formed there of old, came gathering thick upon him. And there little Gertrude seemed first to accept him. She whispered to her papa, as they stood up to go away, that it was very good in God Almighty to have sent Harry home; and, as they left the cloister, she slipped into Harry's hand a daisy from the grave, such a gift as she had never carried to any one else, save her father and Margaret, and she shrank no longer from being lifted up in his arms, and carried home through the twilight street.

He hurried into the drawing-room, and was heard declaring that all was right, for Margaret was on the sofa; but he stopped short, grieved at her altered looks. She smiled as he stooped to kiss her, and then made him stand erect, and measure himself against Norman, whose height he had almost reached. The little curly midshipman had come back, as nurse said, "a fine-growed young man," his rosy cheeks, brown and ruddy, and his countenance —

"You are much more like papa and Norman than I thought you would be," said Margaret.

"He has left his snub nose and yellow locks behind," said his father; "though the shaggy mane seems to remain. I believe lions grow darker with age. So there stand June and July together again!"

Dr. May walked backwards to look at them. It was good to see his face.

"I shall see Flora and Tom to-morrow!" said Harry, after nodding with satisfaction, as they all took their wonted places.

"Going!" exclaimed Richard.

"Why, don't you know?" said Ethel; "it is current in the nursery that he is going to be tried by court-martial for living with the King of the Cannibal Islands."

"Aubrey says he had a desert island, with Jennings for his man Friday," said Blanche.

"Harry," said little Gertrude, who had established herself on his knee, "did you really poke out the giant's eye with the top of a fir-tree?"

"Who told you so, Daisy?" was the general cry; but she became shy, and would not answer more than by a whisper about Aubrey, who indignantly declared that he never said so, only Gertrude was so foolish that she did not know Harry from Ulysses.

"After all," said Ethel, "I don't think our notions are much more defined. Papa and Norman may know more, but we have heard almost nothing. I have been waiting to hear more to close up my letters to Flora and Tom. What a shame that has not been done!"

"I'll finish," said Mary, running to the side-table.

"And tell her I'll be there to-morrow," said Harry. "I must report myself; and what fun to see Flora a member of Parliament! Come with me, June; I'll be back next day. I wish you all would come."

"Yes, I must come with you," said Norman. "I shall have to go to Oxford on Thursday;" and very reluctant he looked. "Tell Flora I am coming, Mary."

"How did you know that Flora was a married lady?" asked Blanche, in her would-be grown-up manner.

"I heard that from Aunt Flora. A famous lot of news I picked up there!"

"Aunt Flora!"

"Did you not know he had been at Auckland?" said Dr. May. "Aunt Flora had to nurse him well after all he had undergone. Did you not think her very like mamma, Harry?"

"Mamma never looked half so old!" cried Harry indignantly.

"Flora was five years younger!"

"She has got her voice and way with her," said Harry; "but you will soon see. She is coming home soon."

There was a great outcry of delight.

"Yes, there is some money of Uncle Arnott's that must be looked after, but he does not like the voyage, and can't leave his office, so perhaps Aunt Flora may come alone. She had a great mind to come with me, but there was no good berth for her in this schooner, and I could not wait for another chance. I can't think what possessed the letters not to come! She would not write by the first packet, because I was so ill, but we both wrote by the next, and I made sure you had them, or I would have written before I came."

The words were not out of his mouth before the second post was brought in, and there were two letters from New Zealand! What would they not have been yesterday? Harry would have burned his own, but the long closely-written sheets were eagerly seized, as, affording the best hope of understanding his adventures, as it had been written at intervals from Auckland, and the papers, passing from one to the other, formed the text for interrogations on further details, though much more was gleaned incidentally in tete-a-tetes, by Margaret, Norman, or his father, and no one person ever heard the whole connectedly from Harry himself.

"What was the first you knew of the fire, Harry?" asked Dr. May, looking up from the letter.

"Owen shaking me awake; and I thought it was a hoax," said Harry. "But it was true enough, and when we got on deck, there were clouds of smoke coming up the main hatch-way."

Margaret's eyes were upon him, and her lips formed the question, "And he?"

"He met us, and told us to be steady—but there was little need for that! Every man there was as cool and collected as if it had been no more than the cook's stove—and we should have scorned to be otherwise! He put his hand on my shoulder and said, 'Keep by me,' and I did."

"Then there was never much hope of extinguishing the fire?"

"No; if you looked down below the forecastle it was like a furnace, and though the pumps were at work, it was only to gain time while the boats were lowered. The first lieutenant told off the men, and they went down the side without one word, only shaking hands with those that were left."

"Oh, Harry! what were you thinking of?" cried Blanche.

"Of the powder," said Harry.

Ethel thought there was more in that answer than met the ear, and that Harry, at least, had thought of the powder to-night at church.

"Mr. Ernescliffe had the command of the second cutter. He asked to take me with him; I was glad enough; and Owen—he is mate, you know— went with us."

As to telling how he felt when he saw the good ship Alcestis blown to fragments, that was past Harry, and all but Blanche were wise enough not to ask. She had by way of answer, "Very glad to be safe out of her."

Nor was Harry willing to dwell on the subsequent days, when the unclouded sun had been a cruel foe; and the insufficient stores of food and water did, indeed, sustain life, but a life of extreme suffering. What he told was of the kindness that strove to save him, as the youngest, from all that could be spared him. "If I dropped asleep at the bottom of the boat, I was sure to find some one shading me from the sun. If there was an extra drop of water, they wanted me to have it."

"Tell me their names, Harry!" cried Dr. May. "If ever I meet one of them—"

"But the storm, Harry, the storm?" asked Blanche. "Was that not terrible?"

"Very comfortable at first, Blanche," was the answer. "Oh, that rain!"

"But when it grew so very bad?"

"We did not reck much what happened to us," said Harry. "It could not be worse than starving. When we missed the others in the morning, most of us thought them the best off."

Mary could not help coming round to kiss him, as if eyes alone were not enough to satisfy her that here he was.

Dr. May shuddered, and went on reading, and Margaret drew Harry down to her, and once more by looks craved for more minute tidings.

"All that you can think," murmured Harry; "the very life and soul of us all—so kind, and yet discipline as perfect as on board. But don't now, Margaret—"

The tone of the don't, the reddening cheek, liquid eye, and heaving chest, told enough of what the lieutenant had been to one, at least, of the desolate boat's crew.

"Oh, Harry, Harry! I can't bear it!" exclaimed Mary. "How long did it last? How did it end?"

"Fifteen days," said Harry. "It was time it should end, for all the water we had caught in the storm was gone—we gave the last drop to Jones, for we thought him dying; one's tongue was like a dry sponge."

"How did it end?" repeated Mary, in an agony.

"Jennings saw a sail. We thought it all a fancy of weakness, but 'twas true enough, and they saw our signal of distress!"

The vessel proved to be an American whaler, which had just parted with her cargo to a homeward bound ship, and was going to refit, and take in provisions and water at one of the Milanesian islands, before returning for further captures. The master was a man of the shrewd, hard money-making cast; but, at the price of Mr. Ernescliffe's chronometer, and of the services of the sailors, he undertook to convey them where they might fall in with packets bound for Australia.

The distressed Alcestes at first thought themselves in paradise, but the vessel, built with no view, save to whales, and, with a considerable reminiscence of the blubber lately parted with, proved no wholesome abode, when overcrowded, and in the tropics! Mr. Ernescliffe's science, resolution, and constancy, had saved his men so far; but with the need for exertion his powers gave way, and he fell a prey to a return of the fever which had been his introduction to Dr. May.

"There he was," said Harry, "laid up in a little bit of a stifling cabin, just like an oven, without the possibility of a breath of air! The skin-flint skipper carried no medicine; the water—shocking stuff it was—was getting so low, that there was only a pint a day served out to each, and though all of us Alcestes clubbed every drop we could spare for him—it was bad work! Owen and I never were more glad in our lives than when we heard we were to cast anchor at the Loyalty Isles! Such a place as it was! You little know what it was to see anything green! And there was this isle fringed down close to the sea with cocoa-nut trees! And the bay as clear!—you could see every shell, and wonderful fishes swimming in it! Well, every one was for going ashore, and some of the natives swam out to us, and brought things in their canoes, but not many; it is not encouraged by the mission, nor by David—for those Yankee traders are not the most edifying society—and the crew vowed they were cannibals, and had eaten a man three years ago, so they all went ashore armed."

"You stayed with him," said Margaret.

"Ay, it was my turn, and I was glad enough to have some fresh fruit and water for him, but he could not take any notice of it. Did not I want you, papa? Well, by and by, Owen came back, in a perfect rapture with the place and the people, and said it was the only hope for Mr. Ernescliffe, to take him on shore—"

"Then you did really go amongst the cannibals!" exclaimed Blanche.

"That is all nonsense," said Harry. "Some of them may once have been, and I fancy the heathens might not mind a bit of 'long pig' still; but these have been converted by the Samoans."

The Samoans, it was further explained, are the inhabitants of the Navigator Islands, who, having been converted by the Church Missionary Society, have sent out great numbers of most active and admirable teachers among the scattered islands, braving martyrdom and disease, never shrinking from their work, and, by teaching and example, preparing the way for fuller doctrine than they can yet impart. A station of these devoted men had for some years been settled in this island, and had since been visited by the missions of Newcastle and New Zealand. The young chief, whom Harry called David, and another youth, had spent two summers under instruction at New Zealand, and had been baptised. They were spending the colder part of the year at home, and hoped shortly to be called for by the mission-ship to return, and resume their course of instruction.

Owen had come to an understanding with the chief and the Samoans, and had decided on landing his lieutenant, and it was accordingly done, with very little consciousness on the patient's part. Black figures, with woolly mop-heads, and sometimes decorated with whitewash of lime, crowded round to assist in the transport of the sick man through the surf; and David himself, in a white European garb, met his guests, with dignified manners that would have suited a prince of any land, and conducted them through the grove of palms, interspersed with white huts, to a beautiful house consisting of a central room, with many others opening from it, floored with white coral lime, and lined with soft shining mats of Samoan manufacture. This, Harry learned, had been erected by them in hopes of an English missionary taking up his abode amongst them.

They were a kindly people, and had shown hospitality to other Englishmen, who had less appreciated it than these young officers could. They lavished every kindness in their power upon them, and Mr. Ernescliffe, at first, revived so much, that he seemed likely to recover.

But the ship had completed her repairs, and was ready to sail. The two midshipmen thought it would be certain death to their lieutenant to bring him back to such an atmosphere; "and so," continued Harry's letter to his father, "I thought there was nothing for it but for me to stay with him, and that you would say so. I got Owen to consent, after some trouble, as we were sure to be fetched off one time or another. We said not a word to Mr. Ernescliffe, for he was only sensible now and then, so that Owen had the command. Owen made the skipper leave me a pistol and some powder, but I was ashamed David should know it, and stowed it away. As to the quarter-master, old Jennings, whose boy you remember we picked up at the Roman camp, he had not forgotten that, and when we were shaking hands and wishing good-bye, he leaped up, and vowed 'he would never leave the young gentleman that had befriended his boy, to be eaten up by them black savage niggers. If they made roast-pork of Mr. May, he would be eaten first, though he reckoned they would find him a tougher morsel.' I don't think Owen was sorry he volunteered, and no words can tell what a blessing the good old fellow was to us both.

"So there we stayed, and, at first, Mr. Ernescliffe seemed mending. The delirium went off, he could talk quite clearly and comfortably, and he used to lie listening, when David and I had our odd sort of talks. I believe, if you had been there, or we could have strenthened him any way, he might have got over it; but he never thought he should, and he used to talk to me about all of you, and said Stoneborough had been the most blessed spot in his life; he had never had so much of a home, and that sharing our grief, and knowing you, had done him great good, just when he might have been getting elated. I cannot recollect it all, though I tried hard, for Margaret's sake, but he said Hector would have a great deal of temptation, and he hoped you would be a father to him, and Norman an elder brother. You would not think how much he talked of Cocksmoor, about a church being built there, as Ethel wished, and little Daisy laying the first stone. I remember one night, I don't know whether he was quite himself, for he looked full at me with his eyes, that had grown so large, till I did not know what was coming, and he said, 'I have seen a ship built by a sailor's vow; the roof was like the timbers of a ship—that was right. Mind, it is so. That is the ship that bears through the waves; there is the anchor that enters within the veil.' I believe that was what he said. I could not forget that—he looked at me so; but much more he said, that I dimly remember, and chiefly about poor dear Margaret. He bade me tell her—his own precious pearl, as he used to call her—that he was quite content, and believed it was best for her and him both, that all should be thus settled, for they did not part for ever, and he trusted— But I can't write all that." (There was a great tear-blot just here). "It is too good to recollect anywhere but at church. I have been there to-day, with my uncle and aunt, and I thought I could have told it when I came home, but I was too tired to write then, and now I don't seem as if it could be written anyhow. When I come home, I will try to tell Margaret. The most part was about her; only what was better seemed to swallow that up."

The narrative broke off here, but had been subsequently resumed.

"For all Mr. Ernescliffe talked as I told you, he was so quiet and happy, that I made sure he was getting well, but Jennings did not; and there came an old heathen native once to see us, who asked why we did not bury him alive, because he got no better, and gave trouble. At last, one night—it was the third of August—he was very restless, and could not breathe, nor lie easily; I lifted him up in my arms, for he was very light and thin, and tried to make him more comfortable. But presently he said, 'Is it you, Harry? God bless you;' and, in a minute, I knew he was dead. You will tell Margaret all about it. I don't think she can love him more than I did; and she did not half know him, for she never saw him on board, nor in all that dreadful time, nor in his illness. She will never know what she has lost."

There was another break here, and the story was continued.

"We buried him the next day, where one could see the sea, close under the great palm, where David hopes to have a church one of these days. David helped us, and said the Lord's Prayer and the Glory with us there. I little thought, when I used to grumble at my two verses of the psalms every day, when I should want the ninetieth, or how glad I should be to know so many by heart, for they were such a comfort to Mr. Ernescliffe.

"David got us a nice bit of wood, and Jennings carved the cross, and his name, and all about him. I should have liked to have done it, but I knocked up after that. Jennings thinks I had a sun-stroke. I don't know, but my head was so bad, whenever I moved, that I thought only Jennings would ever have come to tell you about it. Jennings looked after me as if I had been his own son; and there was David too, as kind as if he had been Richard himself—always sitting by, to bathe my forehead, or, when I was a little better, to talk to me, and ask me questions about his Christian teaching. You must not think of him like a savage, for he is my friend, and a far more perfect gentleman than I ever saw any one, but you, papa, holding the command over his people so easily and courteously, and then coming to me with little easy first questions about the Belief, and such things, like what we used to ask mamma. He liked nothing so well as for me to tell him about King David; and we had learned a good deal of each other's languages by that time. The notion of his heart—like Cocksmoor to Ethel—is to get a real English mission, and have all his people Christians. Ethel talked of good kings being Davids to their line; I think that is what he will be, if he lives; but those islanders have been dying off since Europeans came among them."

But Harry's letter could not tell what he confessed, one night, to his father, the next time he was out with him by starlight, how desolate he had been, and how he had yearned after his home, and, one evening, he had been utterly overcome by illness and loneliness, and had cried most bitterly and uncontrollably; and, though Jennings thought it was for his friend's death, it really was homesickness, and the thought of his father and Mary. Jennings had helped him out to the entrance of the hut, that the cool night air might refresh his burning brow. Orion shone clear and bright, and brought back the night when they had chosen the starry hunter as his friend. "It seemed," he said, "as if you all were looking at me, and smiling to me in the stars. And there was the Southern Cross upright, which was like the minster to me; and I recollected it was Sunday morning at home, and knew you would be thinking about me. I was so glad you had let me be confirmed, and be with you that last Sunday, papa, for it seemed to join me on so much the more; and when I thought of the words in church, they seemed, somehow, to float on me so much more than ever before, and it was like the minster, and your voice. I should not have minded dying so much after that."

At last, Harry's Black Prince had hurried into the hut with the tidings that his English father's ship was in the bay, and soon English voices again sounded in his ears, bringing the forlorn boy such warmth of kindness that he could hardly believe himself a mere stranger. If Alan could but have shared the joy with him!

He was carried down to the boat in the cool of the evening, and paused on the way, for a last farewell to the lonely grave under the palm tree-one of the many sailors' graves scattered from the tropics to the poles, and which might be the first seed in a "God's acre" to that island, becoming what the graves of holy men of old are to us.

A short space more of kind care from his new friends and his Christian chief, and Harry awoke from a feverish doze at sounds that seemed so like a dream of home, that he was unwilling to break them by rousing himself; but they approved themselves as real, and he found himself in the embrace of his mother's sister.

And here Mrs. Arnott's story began, of the note that reached her in the early morning with tidings that her nephew had been picked up by the mission-ship, and how she and her husband had hastened at once on board.

"They sent me below to see a hero," she wrote. "What I saw was a scarecrow sort of likeness of you, dear Richard; but, when he opened his eyes, there was our Maggie smiling at me. I suppose he would not forgive me for telling how he sobbed and cried, when he had his arms round my neck, and his poor aching head on my shoulder. Poor fellow, he was very weak, and I believe he felt, for the moment, as if he had found his mother.

"We brought him home with us, but when the next mail went, the fever was still so high, that I thought it would be only alarm to you to write, and I had not half a story either, though you may guess how proud I was of my nephew."

Harry's troubles were all over from that time. He had thenceforth to recover under his aunt's motherly care, while talking endlessly over the home that she loved almost as well as he did. He was well more quickly than she had ventured to hope, and nothing could check his impatience to reach his home, not even the hopes of having his aunt for a companion. The very happiness he enjoyed with her only made him long the more ardently to be with his own family; and he had taken his leave of her, and of his dear David, and sailed by the first packet leaving Auckland.

"I never knew what the old Great Bear was to me till I saw him again!" said Harry.

It was late when the elders had finished all that was to be heard at present, and the clock reminded them that they must part.

"And you go to-morrow?" sighed Margaret.

"I must. Jennings has to go on to Portsmouth, and see after his son."

"Oh, let me see Jennings!" exclaimed Margaret. "May I not, papa?"

Richard, who had been making friends with Jennings, whenever he had not been needed by his sisters that afternoon, went to fetch him from the kitchen, where all the servants, and all their particular friends, were listening to the yarn that made them hold their heads higher, as belonging to Master Harry.

Harry stepped forward, met Jennings, and said, aside, "My sister, Jennings; my sister that you have heard of."

Dr. May had already seen the sailor, but he could not help addressing him again. "Come in; come in, and see my boy among us all. Without you, we never should have had him."

"Make him come to me," said Margaret breathlessly, as the embarrassed sailor stood, sleeking down his hair; and, when he had advanced to her couch, she looked up in his face, and put her hand into his great brown one.

"I could not help saying thank you," she said.

"Mr. May, sir!" cried Jennings, almost crying, and looking round for Harry, as a sort of protector—"tell them, sir, please, it was only my duty—I could not do no less, and you knows it, sir," as if Harry had been making an accusation against him.

"We know you could not," said Margaret, "and that is what we would thank you for, if we could. I know he—Mr. Ernescliffe—must have been much more at rest for leaving my brother with so kind a friend, and—"

"Please, miss, don't say no more about it. Mr. Ernescliffe was as fine an officer as ever stepped a quarter-deck, and Mr. May here won't fall short of him; and was I to be after leaving the like of them to the mercy of the black fellows—that was not so bad neither? If it had only pleased God that we had brought them both back to you, miss; but, you see, a man can't be everything at once, and Mr. Ernescliffe was not so stout as his heart."

"You did everything, we know—" began Dr. May.

"'Twas a real pleasure," said Jennings hastily, "for two such real gentlemen as they was. Mr. May, sir, I beg your pardon if I say it to your face, never flinched, nor spoke a word of complaint, through it all; and, as to the other—"

"Margaret cannot bear this," said Richard, coming near. "It is too much."

The sailor shook his head, and was retreating, but Margaret signed him to come near again, and grasped his hand. Harry followed him out of the room, to arrange their journey, and presently returned.

"He says he is glad he has seen Margaret; he says she is the right sort of stuff for Mr. Ernescliffe."

Harry had not intended Margaret to hear, but she caught the words, smiled radiantly, and whispered, "I wish I may be!"

CHAPTER XVIII.

Margaret had borne the meeting much too well for her own good, and a wakeful night of palpitation was the consequence; but she would not allow any one to take it to heart, and declared that she should be ready to enjoy Harry by the time he should return, and meantime, she should dwell on the delight of his meeting Flora.

No one had rested too soundly that night, and Dr. May had not been able to help looking in at his sleeping boy at five in the morning, to certify himself that he had not only figured his present bliss to himself, in his ten minutes' dream. And looking in again at half-past seven, he found Harry half dressed, with his arm round Mary; laughing, almost sobbing, over the treasures in his cupboard, which he had newly discovered in their fresh order.

Dr. May looked like a new man that morning, with his brightened eye and bearing, as if there were a well-spring of joy within him, ready to brim over at once in tear and in smile, and finding an outlet in the praise and thanksgiving that his spirit chanted, and his face expressed, and in that sunny genial benevolence that must make all share his joy.

He was going to run over half the town—every one would like to hear it from him; Ethel and Mary must go to the rest—the old women in the almshouses, where lived an old cook who used to be fond of Harry— they should have a feast; all who were well enough in the hospital should have a tea-drinking; Dr. Hoxton had already granted a holiday to the school; every boy with whom they had any connection should come to dinner, and Edward Anderson should be asked to meet Harry on his return, because, poor fellow, he was so improved.

Dr. May was in such a transport of kind-hearted schemes, that he was not easily made to hear that Harry had not a sixpence wherewith to reach London.

Ethel, meanwhile, was standing beside her brother tendering to him some gold, as his last quarter.

"How did you get it, Ethel? do you keep the purse?"

"No, but papa took Cocksmoor in your stead, when—"

"Nonsense, Ethel," said Harry; "I don't want it. Have I not all my pay and allowance for the whole time I was dead? And as to robbing Cocksmoor—"

"Yes, keep it, Ethel," said her father; "do you think I would take it now, when if there were a thank-offering in the world. —And, by the bye, your Cooksmoor children must have something to remember this by—"

Every one could have envied Norman, for travelling to London with Harry, but that he must proceed to Oxford in two days, when Harry would return to them. The station-master, thinking he could not do enough for the returned mariner, put the two brothers into the coupe, as if they had been a bridal couple, and they were very glad of the privacy, having, as yet, hardly spoken to each other, when Harry's attention was dispersed among so many.

Norman asked many questions about the mission work in the southern hemisphere, and ended by telling his brother of his design, which met with Harry's hearty approbation.

"That's right, old June. There's nothing they want so much, as such as you. How glad my aunt will be! Perhaps you will see David! Oh, if you were to go out to the Loyalty group!"

"Very possibly I might," said Norman.

"Tell them you are my brother, and how they will receive you! I can see the mop-heads they will dress in honour of you, and what a feast of pork and yams you will have to eat! But there is plenty of work among the Maoris for you—they want a clergyman terribly at the next village to my uncle's place. I say, Norman, it will go hard if I don't get a ship bound for the Pacific, and come and see you."

"I shall reckon on you. That is, if I have not to stay to help my father."

"To be sure," exclaimed Harry; "I thought you would have stayed at home, and married little Miss Rivers!"

Thus broadly and boyishly did he plunge into that most tender subject, making his brother start and wince, as if he had touched a wound.

"Nonsense!" he cried, almost angrily.

"Well! you used to seem very much smitten, but so, to be sure, were some of the Alcestes with the young ladies at Valparaiso. How we used to roast Owen about that Spanish Donna, and he was as bad at Sydney about the young lady whose father, we told him, was a convict, though he kept such a swell carriage. He had no peace about his father-in-law, the house-breaker! Don't I remember how you pinched her hand the night you were righted!"

"You know nothing about it," said Norman shortly. "She is far beyond my reach."

"A fine lady? Ha! Well, I should have thought you as good as Flora any day," said Harry indignantly.

"She is what she always was," said Norman, anxious to silence him;

"but it is unreasonable to think of it. She is all but engaged to Sir Henry Walkinghame."

"Walkinghame!" cried the volatile sailor. "I have half a mind to send in my name to Flora as Miss Walkinghame!" and he laughed heartily over that adventure, ending, however, with a sigh, as he said, "It had nearly cost me a great deal! But tell me, Norman, how has that Meta, as they called her, turned out? I never saw anything prettier or nicer than she was that day of the Roman encampment, and I should be sorry if that fine fashionable aunt of hers, had made her stuck-up and disdainful."

"No such thing," said Norman.

"Ha!" said Harry to himself, "I see how it is! She has gone and made poor old June unhappy, with her scornful airs—a little impertinent puss!—I wonder Flora does not teach her better manners."

Norman, meanwhile, as the train sped over roofs, and among chimneys, was reproaching himself for running into the fascination of her presence, and then recollecting that her situation, as well as his destiny, both guaranteed that they could meet only as friendly connections.

No carriage awaited them at the station, which surprised Norman, till he recollected that the horses had probably been out all day, and it was eight o'clock. Going to Park Lane in a cab, the brothers were further surprised to find themselves evidently not expected. The butler came to speak to them, saying that Mr. and Mrs. Rivers were gone out to dinner, but would return, probably, at about eleven o'clock. He conducted them upstairs, Harry following his brother, in towering vexation and disappointment, trying to make him turn to hear that they would go directly—home—to Eton—anywhere—why would he go in at all?

The door was opened, Mr. May was announced, and they were in a silk-lined boudoir, where a little slender figure in black started up, and came forward with outstretched hand.

"Norman!" she cried, "how are you? Are you come on your way to Oxford?"

"Has not Flora had Mary's letter?"

"Yes, she said she had one. She was keeping it till she had time to read it."

As she spoke, Meta had given her hand to Harry, as it was evidently expected; she raised her eyes to his face, and said, smiling' and blushing, "I am sure I ought to know you, but I am afraid I don't."

"Look again," said Norman. "See if you have ever seen him before."

Laughing, glancing, and casting down her eyes, she raised them with a sudden start of joy, but colouring more deeply, said, "Indeed, I cannot remember. I dare say I ought."

"I think you see a likeness," said Norman.

"Oh, yes, I see," she answered, faltering; but perceiving how bright were the looks of both, "No? Impossible! Yes, it is!"

"Yes, it is," said both brothers with one voice. She clasped her hands, absolutely bounded with transport, then grasped both Harry's hands, and then Norman's, her whole countenance radiant with joy and sympathy beyond expression.

"Dear, dear Dr. May!" was her first exclamation. "Oh, how happy you must all be! And Margaret?" She looked up at Norman, and came nearer. "Is not Mr. Ernescliffe come?" she asked softly, and trembling.

"No," was the low answer, which Harry could not bear to hear, and therefore walked to the window. "No, Meta, but Margaret is much comforted about him. He died in great peace—in his arms"—as he signed towards his brother. And as Harry continued to gaze out on the stars of gas on the opposite side of the park, he was able to add a few of the particulars.

Meta's eyes glistened with tears, as she said, "Perhaps it would have been too perfect if he had come; but oh, Norman! how good she is to bear it so patiently! And how gloriously he behaved! How can we make enough of him! And Flora out! how sorry she will be!"

"And she never opened Mary's letter," said Harry, coming back to them.

"She little thought what it contained," said Meta. "Mary's letters are apt to bear keeping, you know, and she was so busy, that she laid it aside for a treat after the day's work. But there! inhospitable wretch that I am! you have had no dinner!"

A refection of tea and cold meat was preferred, and in her own pretty manner Meta lavished her welcomes, trying to cover any pain given by Flora's neglect.

"What makes her so busy?" asked Harry, looking round on the beautifully furnished apartment, which, to many eyes besides those fresh from a Milanesian hut, might have seemed a paradise of luxurious ease.

"You don't know what an important lady you have for a sister," said Meta merrily.

"But tell me, what can she have to do? I thought you London ladies had nothing to do, but to sit with your hands before you entertaining company."

Meta laughed heartily. "Shall I begin at the beginning? I'll describe to-day then, and you must understand that this is what Tom would call a mild specimen—only one evening engagement. Though, perhaps, I ought to start from last night at twelve o'clock, when she was at the Austrian Ambassador's ball, and came home at two; but she was up by eight—she always manages to get through her housekeeping matters before breakfast. At nine, breakfast, and baby—by the bye, you have never inquired for our niece."

"I have not come to believe in her yet," said Harry.

"Seeing is believing," said Meta; "but no, I won't take an unfair advantage over her mamma; and she will be fast asleep; I never knew a child sleep as she does. So to go on with our day. The papers come, and Miss Leonora is given over to me; for you must know we are wonderful politicians. Flora studies all the debates till George finds out what he has heard in the House, and baby and I profit. Baby goes out walking, and the post comes. Flora always goes to the study with George, and writes, and does all sorts of things for him.

She is the most useful wife in the world. At twelve, we had our singing lesson—"

"Singing lesson!" exclaimed Harry.

"Yes, you know she has a pretty voice, and she is glad to cultivate it. It is very useful at parties, but it takes up a great deal of time, and with all I can do to save her in note-writing, the morning is gone directly. After luncheon, she had to ride with George, and came back in a hurry to make some canvassing calls about the orphan asylum, and Miss Bracy's sister. If we get her in at all, it will be Flora's diplomacy. And there was shopping to do, and when we came in hoping for time for our letters, there were the Walkinghames, who stayed a long time, so that Flora could only despatch the most important notes, before George came in and wanted her. She was reading something for him all the time she was dressing, but, as I say, this is quite a quiet day."

"Stop!" cried Harry, with a gesture of oppression, "it sounds harder than cleaning knives, like Aunt Flora! And what is an unquiet day like?"

"You will see, for we have a great evening party to-morrow."

"Do you always stay at home?" asked Harry.

"Not always, but I do not go to large parties or balls this year," said Meta, glancing at her deep mourning; "I am very glad of a little time at home."

"So you don't like it."

"Oh, yes! it is very pleasant," said Meta. "It is so entertaining when we talk it over afterwards, and I like to hear how Flora is admired, and called the beauty of the season. I tell George, and we do so gloat over it together! There was an old French marquis the other night, a dear old man, quite of the ancien regime, who said she was exactly like the portraits of Madame de Maintenon, and produced a beautiful miniature on a snuff-box, positively like that very pretty form of face of hers. The old man even declared that Mistress Rivers was worthy to be a Frenchwoman."

"I should like to kick him!" amiably responded Harry.

"I hope you won't to-morrow! But don't let us waste our time over this; I want so much to hear about New Zealand."

Meta was well read in Australasian literature, and drew out a great deal more information from Harry than Norman had yet heard. She made him talk about the Maori pah near his uncle's farm, where the Sunday services were conducted by an old gentleman tattooed elegantly in the face, but dressed like an English clergyman; and tell of his aunt's troubles about the younger generation, whom their elders, though Christians themselves, could not educate, and who she feared would relapse into heathenism, for want of instruction, though with excellent dispositions.

"How glad you must be that you are likely to go!" exclaimed Meta to Norman, who had sat silently listening.

The sound of the door bell was the first intimation that Harry's histories had occupied them until long past twelve o'clock.

"Now, then!" cried Meta, springing forward, as if intending to meet Flora with the tidings, but checking herself, as if she ought not to be the first. There was a pause. Flora was hearing downstairs that Mr. Norman May and another gentleman had arrived, and, while vexed at her own omission, and annoyed at Norman's bringing friends without waiting for permission, she was yet prepared to be courteous and amiable. She entered in her rich black watered silk, deeply trimmed with lace, and with silver ornaments in her dark hair, so graceful and distinguished-looking, that Harry stood suspended, hesitating, for an instant, whether he beheld his own sister, especially as she made a dignified inclination towards him, offering her hand to Norman, as she said, "Meta has told you—" But there she broke off, exclaiming, "Ha! is it possible! No, surely it cannot be—"

"Miss Walkinghame?" said the sailor, who had felt at home with her at the first word, and she flew into his great rough arms.

"Harry! this is dear Harry! our own dear sailor come back," cried she, as her husband stood astonished; and, springing towards him, she put Harry's hand into his, "My brother Harry! our dear lost one."

"Your—brother—Harry," slowly pronounced George, as he instinctively gave the grasp of greeting—"your brother that was lost? Upon my word," as the matter dawned fully on him, and he became eager, "I am very glad to see you. I never was more rejoiced in my life."

"When did you come? Have you been at home?" asked Flora.

"I came home yesterday—Mary wrote to tell you."

"Poor dear old Mary! There's a lesson against taking a letter on trust. I thought it would be all Cocksmoor, and would wait for a quiet moment! How good to come to me so soon, you dear old shipwrecked mariner!"

"I was forced to come to report myself," said Harry, "or I could not have come away from my father so soon."

The usual questions and their sad answers ensued, and while Flora talked to Harry, fondly holding his hand, Norman and Meta explained the history to George, who no sooner comprehended it, that he opined it must have been a horrid nuisance, and that Harry was a gallant fellow; then striking him over the shoulder, welcomed him home with all his kind heart, told him he was proud to receive him, and falling into a state of rapturous hospitality, rang the bell, and wanted to order all sorts of eatables and drinkables, but was sadly baffled to find him already satisfied.

There was more open joy than even at home, and Flora was supremely happy as she sat between her brothers, listening and inquiring till far past one o'clock, when she perceived poor George dozing off, awakened every now and then by a great nod, and casting a wishful glance of resigned remonstrance, as if to appeal against sitting up all night.

The meeting at breakfast was a renewal of pleasure. Flora was proud and happy in showing off her little girl, a model baby, as she called her, a perfect doll for quietness, so that she could be brought in at family prayers; "and," said Flora, "I am the more glad that she keeps no one away, because we can only have evening prayers on Sunday. It is a serious thing to arrange for such a household."

"She is equal to anything," said George.

The long file of servants marched in, George read sonorously, and Flora rose from her knees, highly satisfied at the impression produced upon her brothers.

"I like to have the baby with us at breakfast," she said; "it is the only time of day when we can be sure of seeing anything of her, and I like her nurse to have some respite. Do you think her grown, Norman?"

"Not very much," said Norman, who thought her more inanimate and like a pretty little waxen toy, than when he had last seen her. "Is she not rather pale?"

"London makes children pale. I shall soon take her home to acquire a little colour. You must know Sir Henry has bitten us with his yachting tastes, and as soon as we can leave London, we are going to spend six weeks with the Walkinghames at Ryde, and rival you, Harry. I think Miss Leonora will be better at home, so we must leave her there. Lodgings and irregularities don't suit people of her age."

"Does home mean Stoneborough?" asked Norman.

"No. Old nurse has one of her deadly prejudices against Preston, and I would not be responsible for the consequences of shutting them up in the same nursery. Margaret would be distracted between them. No, miss, you shall make her a visit every day, and be fondled by your grandpapa."

George began a conversation with Harry on nautical matters, and Norman tried to discover how Meta liked the yachting project, and found her prepared to think it charming. Hopes were expressed that Harry might be at Portsmouth, and a quantity of gay scheming ensued, with reiterations of the name of Walkinghame; while Norman had a sense of being wrapped in some gray mist, excluding him from participation in their enjoyments, and condemned his own temper as frivolous for being thus excited to discontent.

Presently, he heard George insisting that he and Harry should return in time for the evening party; and, on beginning to refuse, was amazed to find Harry's only objection was on the score of lack of uniform.

"I don't want you in one, sir," said Flora.

"I have only one coat in the world, besides this," continued Harry, "and that is all over tar."

"George will see to that," said Flora. "Don't you think you would be welcome in matting, with an orange cowry round your neck?"

Norman, however, took a private opportunity of asking Harry if he was aware of what he was undertaking, and what kind of people they should meet.

"All English people behave much the same in a room," said Harry, as if all society, provided it was not cannibal, were alike to him.

"I should have thought you would prefer finding out Forder in his chambers, or going to one of the theatres."

"As you please," said Harry; "but Flora seems to want us, and I should rather like to see what sort of company she keeps."

Since Harry was impervious to shyness, Norman submitted, and George took them to a wonder-worker in cloth, who undertook that full equipments should await the young gentleman. Harry next despatched his business at the Admiralty, and was made very happy by tidings of his friend Owen's safe arrival in America.

Thence the brothers went to Eton, where home letters had been more regarded; and Dr. May having written to secure a holiday for the objects of their visit, they were met at the station by the two boys. Hector's red face and prominent light eyebrows were instantly recognised; but, as to Tom, Harry could hardly believe that the little, dusty, round-backed grub be had left had been transformed into the well-made gentlemanlike lad before him, peculiarly trim and accurate in dress, even to the extent of as much foppery as Eton taste permitted.

Ten minutes had not passed before Tom, taking a survey of the newcomer, began to exclaim at Norman, for letting him go about such a figure; and, before they knew what was doing, they had all been conducted into the shop of the "only living man who knew how to cut hair." Laughing and good-natured, Harry believed his hair was "rather long," allowed himself to be seated, and to be divested of a huge superfluous mass of sun-dried curls, which Tom, particularly resenting that "rather long," kept on taking up, and unrolling from their tight rings, to measure the number of inches.

"That is better," said he, as they issued from the shop; "but, as to that coat of yours, the rogue who made it should never make another. Where could you have picked it up?"

"At a shop at Auckland," said Harry, much amused.

"Kept by a savage?" said Tom, to whom it was no laughing matter. See that seam!"

"Have done, May!" exclaimed Hector. "He will think you a tailor's apprentice!"

"Or worse," said Norman. "Rivers's tailor kept all strictures to himself."

Tom muttered that he only wanted Harry to be fit to be seen by the fellows.

"The fellows are not such asses as you!" cried Hector. "You don't deserve that he should come to see you. If my —"

There poor Hector broke off. If his own only brother had been walking beside him, how would he not have felt? They had reached their tutor's house, and, opening his own door, he made an imploring sign to Harry to enter with him. On the table lay a letter from Margaret, and another which Harry had written to him from Auckland.

"Oh, Harry, you were with him," he said; "tell me all about him."

And he established himself, with his face hidden on the table, uttering nothing, except, "Go on," whenever Harry's voice failed in the narration. When something was said of "all for the best," he burst out, "He might say so. I suppose one ought to think so. But is not it hard, when I had nobody but him? And there was Maplewood; and I might have been so happy there, with him and Margaret."

"They say nothing could have made Margaret well," said Harry.

"I don't care; he would have married her all the same, and we should have made her so happy at Maplewood. I hate the place! I wish it were at Jericho!"

"You are captain of the ship now," said Harry, "and you must make the best of it."

"I can't. It will never be home. Home is with Margaret, and the rest of them."

"So Alan said he hoped you would make it; and you are just like one of us, you know."

"What's the use of that, when Captain Gordon will not let me go near you. Taking me to that abominable Maplewood last Easter, with half the house shut up, and all horrid! And he is as dry as a stick!"

"The captain!" cried Harry angrily. "There's not a better captain to sail with in the whole navy, and your brother would be the first to tell you so! I'm not discharged yet. Hector—you had better look out what you say!"

"Maybe he is the best to sail with, but that is not being the best to live with," said the heir of Maplewood disconsolately. "Alan himself always said he never knew what home was, till he got to your father and Margaret."

"So will you," said Harry; "why, my father is your master, or whatever you may call it."

"No, Captain Gordon is my guardian."

"Eh! what's become of the will then?"

"What will?" cried Hector. "Did Alan make one after all?"

"Ay. At Valparaiso, he had a touch of fever; I went ashore to nurse him, to a merchant's, who took us in for love of our Scottish blood. Mr. Ernescliffe made a will there, and left it in his charge."

"Do you think he made Dr. May my guardian?"

"He asked me whether I thought he would dislike it, and I told him, no."

"That's right!" cried Hector. "That's like dear old Alan! I shall get back to the doctor and Margaret after all. Mind you write to the captain, Harry!"

Hector was quite inspirited and ready to return to the others, but Harry paused to express a hope that he did not let Tom make such a fool of himself as he had done to-day.

"Not he," said Hector. "He is liked as much as any one in the house—he has been five times sent up for good. See there in the Eton list! He is a real clever fellow."

"Ay, but what's the good of all that, if you let him be a puppy?"

"Oh, he'll be cured. A fellow that has been a sloven always is a puppy for a bit," said Hector philosophically.

Norman was meantime taking Tom to task for these same airs, and, hearing it was from the desire to see his brother respectable—

Stoneborough men never cared for what they looked like, and he must have Harry do himself credit.

"You need not fear," said Norman. "He did not require Eton to make him a gentleman. How now? Why, Tom, old man, you are not taking that to heart? That's all over long ago."

For that black spot in his life had never passed out of the lad's memory, and it might be from the lurking want of self-respect that there was about him so much of self-assertion, in attention to trifles. He was very reserved, and no one except Norman had ever found the way to anything like confidence, and Norman had vexed him by the proposal he had made in the holidays.

He made no answer, but stood looking at Norman with an odd undecided gaze.

"Well, what now, old fellow?" said Norman, half fearing "that" might not be absolutely over. "One would think you were not glad to see Harry."

"I suppose he has made you all the more set upon that mad notion of yours," said Tom.

"So far as making me feel that that part of the world has a strong claim on us," replied Norman.

"I'm sure you don't look as if you found your pleasure in it," cried Tom.

"Pleasure is not what I seek," said Norman.

"What is the matter with you?" said Tom. "You said I did not seem rejoiced—you look worse, I am sure." Tom put his arm on Norman's shoulder, and looked solicitously at him—demonstrations of affection very rare with him.

"I wonder which would really make you happiest, to have your own way, and go to these black villains—"

"Remember, that but for others who have done so, Harry—"

"Pshaw," said Tom, rubbing some invisible dust from his coat sleeve. "If it would keep you at home, I would say I never would hear of doctoring."

"I thought you had said so."

"What's the use of my coming here, if I'm to be a country doctor?"

"I have told you I do not mean to victimise you. If you have a distaste to it, there's an end of it—I am quite ready."

Tom gave a great sigh. "No," he said, "if I must, I must; I don't mind the part of it that you do. I only hate the name of it, and the being tied down to a country place like that, while you go out thousands of miles off to these savages; but if it is the only thing to content you, I wont stand in your way. I can't bear your looking disconsolate."

"Don't think yourself bound, if you really dislike the profession."

"I don't," said Tom. "It is my free choice. If it were not for horrid sick people, I should like it."

Promising! it must be confessed!

Perhaps Tom had expected Norman to brighten at once, but it was a fallacious hope. The gaining his point involved no pleasant prospect, and his young brother's moody devotion to him suggested scruples whether he ought to exact the sacrifice, though, in his own mind, convinced that it was Tom's vocation; and knowing that would give him many of the advantages of an eldest son.

Eton fully justified Hector's declaration that it would not regard the cut of Harry's coat. The hero of a lost ship and savage isle was the object of universal admiration and curiosity, and inestimable were the favours conferred by Hector and Tom in giving introductions to him, till he had shaken hands with half the school, and departed amid deafening cheers.

In spite of Harry, the day had been long and heavy to Norman, and though he chid himself for his depression, he shrank from the sight of Meta and Sir Henry Walkinghame together, and was ready to plead an aching head as an excuse for not appearing at the evening party; but, besides that this might attract notice, he thought himself bound to take care of Harry in so new a world, where the boy must be at a great loss.

"I say, old June," cried a voice at his door, "are you ready?"

"I have not begun dressing yet. Will you wait?"

"Not I. The fun is beginning."

Norman heard the light foot scampering downstairs, and prepared to follow, to assume the protection of him.

Music sounded as Norman left his room, and he turned aside to avoid the stream of company flowing up the flower-decked stairs, and made his way into the rooms through Flora's boudoir. He was almost dazzled by the bright lights, and the gay murmurs of the brilliant throng. Young ladies with flowers and velvet streamers down their backs, old ladies portly and bejewelled, gentlemen looking civil, abounded wherever he turned his eyes. He could see Flora's graceful head bending as she received guest after guest, and the smile with which she answered congratulations on her brother's return; but Harry he did not so quickly perceive, and he was trying to discover in what corner he might have hidden himself, when Meta stood beside him, asking whether their Eton journey had prospered, and how poor Hector was feeling at Harry's return.

"Where is Harry?" asked Norman. "Is he not rather out of his element?"

"No, indeed," said Meta, smiling. "Why, he is the lion of the night!"

"Poor fellow, how he must hate it!"

"Come this way, into the front room. There, look at him—is it not nice to see him, so perfectly simple and at his ease, neither shy nor elated? And what a fine-looking fellow he is!"

Meta might well say so. The trim, well-knit, broad-chested form, the rosy embrowned honest face, the shining light-brown curly locks, the dancing well-opened blue eyes, and merry hearty smile showed to the best advantage, in array that even Tom would not have spurned, put on with naval neatness; and his attitude and manner were so full of manly ease, that it was no wonder that every eye rested on him with pleasure. Norman smiled at his own mistake, and asked who were the lady and gentleman conversing with him. Meta mentioned one of the most distinguished of English names, and shared his amusement in seeing Harry talking to them with the same frank unembarrassed ease as when he had that morning shaken hands with their son, in the capacity of Hector Ernescliffe's fag. No one present inspired him with a tithe of the awe he felt for a post-captain—it was simply a pleasant assembly of good-natured folks, glad to welcome home a battered sailor, and of pretty girls, for whom he had a sailor's admiration, but without forwardness or presumption—all in happy grateful simplicity.

"I suppose you cannot dance?" said Flora to him.

"I!" was Harry's interjection; and while she was looking round for a partner to whom to present him, he had turned to the young daughter of his new acquaintance, and had her on his arm, unconscious that George had been making his way to her.

Flora was somewhat uneasy, but the mother was looking on smiling, and expressed her delight in the young midshipman; and Mrs. Rivers, while listening gladly to his praises, watched heedfully, and was reassured to see that dancing was as natural to him as everything else; his steps were light as a feather, his movement all freedom and joy, without being boisterous, and his boyish chivalry as pretty a sight as any one could wish to see.

If the rest of the world enjoyed their dances a quarter as much as did "Mr. May," they were enviable people, and he contributed not a little to their pleasure, if merely by the sight of his blithe freshness and spirited simplicity, as well as the general sympathy with his sister's joy, and the interest in his adventures. He would have been a general favourite, if he had been far less personally engaging; as it was, every young lady was in raptures at dancing with him, and he did his best to dance with them all; and to try to stir up Norman, who, after Meta had been obliged to leave him, and go to act her share of the part of hostess, had disposed of himself against a wall, where he might live out the night.

"Ha! June! what makes you stand sentry there? Come and dance, and have some of the fun! Some of these girls are the nicest partners in the world. There's that Lady Alice, something with the dangling things in her hair, sitting down now—famous at a polka. Come along, I'll introduce you. It will do you good."

"I know nothing of dancing," said Norman, beginning to apprehend that he might be dragged off, as often he had been to cricket or football, and by much the same means.

"Comes by nature, when you hear the music. Ha! what a delicious polka! Come along, or I must be off! She will be waiting for me, and she is the second prettiest girl here! Come!"

"I have been trying to make something of him, Harry," said the ubiquitous Flora, "but I don't know whether it is mauvaise honte, or headache."

"I see! Poor old June!" cried Harry. "I'll get you an ice at once, old fellow! Nothing like one for setting a man going!"

Before Norman could protest, Harry had flown off.

"Flora," asked Norman, "is—are the Walkinghames here?"

"Yes. Don't you see Sir Henry. That fine-looking man with the black moustache. I want you to know him. He is a great admirer of your prize poem and of Dr. Spencer."

Harry returning, administered his ice, and then darted off to excuse himself to his partner, by explanations about his brother, whom everybody must have heard of, as he was the cleverest fellow living, and had written the best prize poem ever heard at Oxford. He firmly believed Norman a much greater lion than himself.

Norman was forced to leave his friendly corner to dispose of the glass of his ice, and thus encountered Miss Rivers, of whom Sir Henry was asking questions about a beautiful collection of cameos, which Flora had laid out as a company trap.

"Here is Norman May," said Meta; "he knows them better than I do. Do you remember which of these is the head of Diana, Norman?"

Having set the two gentlemen to discuss them, she glided away on fresh hospitable duties, while Norman repeated the comments that he had so enjoyed hearing from poor Mr. Rivers, hoping he was, at least, sparing Meta some pain, and wondering that Flora should have risked hurting her feelings by exposing these treasures to the general gaze.

If Norman were wearied by Sir Henry, it was his own fault, for the baronet was a very agreeable person, who thought a first-class man worth cultivation, so that the last half-hour might have compensated for all the rest, if conversation were always the test.

"Why, Meta," cried Harry, coming up to her, "you have not once danced! We are a sort of brother and sister, to be sure, but that is no hindrance, is it?"

"No," said Meta, smiling, "thank you, Harry, but you must find some one more worthy. I do not dance this season; at least, not in public. When we get home, who knows what we may do?"

"You don't dance! Poor little Meta! And you don't go out! What a pity!"

"I had rather not work quite so hard," said Meta. "Think what good fortune I had by staying at home last night!"

"I declare!" exclaimed Harry, bewitched by the beaming congratulation of her look, "I can't imagine why Norman had said you had turned into a fine lady! I can't see a bit of it!"

"Norman said I had turned into a fine lady!" repeated Meta. "Why?"

"Never mind! I don't think so; you are just like papa's humming-bird, as you always were, not a bit more of a fine lady than any girl here, and I am sure papa would say so. Only old June had got a bad headache, and is in one of his old dumps, such as I hoped he had left off. But he can't help it, poor fellow, and he will come out of it, by and by—so never mind. Hallo! why people are going away already. There's that girl without any one to hand her downstairs."

Away ran Harry, and presently the brothers and sisters gathered round the fire—George declaring that he was glad that nuisance was so well over, and Harry exclaiming, "Well done, Flora! It was capital fun! I never saw a lot of prettier or more good-natured people in my life. If I am at home for the Stoneborough ball, I wonder whether my father will let me go to it."

This result of Harry's successful debut in high life struck his sister and Norman as so absurd that both laughed.

"What's the matter now?" asked Harry.

"Your comparing Flora's party to a Stoneborough ball," said Norman.

"It is all the same, isn't it?" said Harry. "I'm sure you are equally disgusted at both!"

"Much you know about it," said Flora, patting him gaily. "I'm not going to put conceit in that lion head of yours, but you were as good as an Indian prince to my party. Do you know to whom you have been talking so coolly?"

"Of course. You see, Norman, it is just as I told you. All civilised people are just alike when they get into a drawing-room."

"Harry takes large views of the Genus homo," Norman exerted himself to say. "Being used to the black and brown species, he takes little heed of the lesser varieties."

"It is enough for him that he does not furnish the entertainment in another way," said Flora. "But, good-night. Meta, you look tired."

CHAPTER XIX.

Let none, henceforward, shrink from daring dreams, For earnest
hearts shall find their dreams fulfilled. —FOUQUE.

"I have it!" began Harry, as he came down to breakfast. "I don't
know how I came to forget it. The will was to be sent home to Mr.
Mackintosh's English partner. I'll go and overhaul him this very
morning. They won't mind my coming by a later train, when there is
such a reason."

"What is his name? Where shall you find him?" asked Flora.

"I can't be sure; but you've a navy list of that sort of cattle, have not
you, Flora? I'll hunt him up."

Flora supposed he meant a directory; and all possible South
American merchants having been overlooked, and the Mackintoshes
selected, he next required a chart of London, and wanted to attempt
self-navigation, but was forced to accept of George's brougham and
escort;

Flora would not trust him otherwise; and Norman was obliged to go
to Oxford at once, hurrying off to his train before breakfast was over.

Flora might have trusted Harry alone. George contributed no more
than the dignity of his presence; and, indeed, would have resigned
the pursuit at the first blunder about the firm; and still more when
the right one had been found, but the partner proved crusty, and
would not believe that any such document was in his hands. George
was consenting to let it rest till Mr. Mackintosh could be written to;
but Harry, outrunning his management, and regardless of rebuffs,
fairly teased the old gentleman into a search, as the only means of
getting rid of the troublesome sailor.

In the midst of George's civil regrets at the fruitless trouble they
were causing, forth came a bundle of papers, and forth from the
bundle fell a packet, on which Harry pounced as he read, "Will of
Alan Halliday Ernescliffe, Esquire, of Maplewood, Yorkshire,
Lieutenant in H. M. S. Alcestis," and, in the corner, the executors'

names, Captain John Gordon, of H. M. S. Alcestis; and Richard May, Esquire, M. D., Market Stoneborough.

As if in revenge, the prudent merchant would not be induced to entrust him with the document, saying he could not give it up till he had heard from the executors, and had been certified of the death of the testator. He withstood both the angry gentlemen, who finally departed in a state of great resentment—Harry declaring that the old land-lubber would not believe that he was his own father's son; and Mr. Rivers, no less incensed, that the House of Commons had been insulted in his person, because he did not carry all before him.

Flora laughed at their story, and told them that she suspected that the old gentleman was in the right; and she laid plans for having Harry to teach them yachting at Ryde, while Harry declared he would have nothing to do with such trumpery.

Harry found his home in a sort of agony of expectation, for his non-arrival at the time expected had made his first appearance seem like an unsubstantial illusion, though Dr. May, or Mary and Aubrey, had been at the station at the coming in of each train. Margaret had recovered the effects of the first shock, and the welcome was far more joyous than the first had been, with the mixed sensations that were now composed, and showed little, outwardly, but gladness.

Dr. May took Flora's view of the case, and declared that, if Harry had brought home the will, he should not have opened it without his co-executor. So he wrote to the captain, while Harry made the most of his time in learning his sisters over again. He spent a short time alone with Margaret every morning, patiently and gently allowing himself to be recalled to the sad recollections that were all the world to her. He kept Ethel and Mary merry with his droll desultory comments; he made Blanche keep up her dancing; and taught Gertrude to be a thorough little romp. As to Dr. May, his patients never were so well or so cheerful, till Dr. Spencer and Ethel suspected that the very sight of his looks brightened them—how could they help it? Dr. Spencer was as happy as a king in seeing his friend freed from the heavy weight on his spirits; and, truly, it was goodly to watch his perfect look of content, as he leaned on his lion-faced boy's arm, and walked down to the minster, whither it seemed to have become possible to go on most evenings. Good Dr. May was no musician, but Mr. Wilmot could not regret certain tones that now and then burst out in the chanting, from the very bottom of a heart that assuredly sang with the full melody of thankfulness, whatever the voice might do.

Captain Gordon not only wrote but came to Stoneborough, whence Harry was to go with him to the court-martial at Portsmouth.

The girls wondered that, after writing with so much warmth and affection, both of and to Harry, he met him without any demonstration of feeling; and his short peremptory manner removed all surprise that poor Hector had been so forlorn with him at Maplewood, and turned, with all his heart, to Dr. May. They were especially impressed at the immediate subsidence of all Harry's noise and nonsense, as if the drawing-room had been the quarter-deck of the Alcestis.

"And yet," said Margaret, "Harry will not hear a single word in dispraise of him. I do believe he loves him with all his heart."

"I think," said Ethel, "that in a strong character, there is an exulting fear in looking up to a superior, in whose justice there is perfect reliance. It is a germ of the higher feeling."

"I believe you are right," said Margaret; "but it is a serious thing for a man to have so little sympathy with those below him. You see how Hector feels it, and I now understand how it told upon Alan, and how papa's warmth was like a surprise to him."

"Because Captain Gordon had to be a father to them, and that is more than a captain. I should not wonder if there were more similarity and fellow-feeling between him and Harry than there could be with either of them. Harry, though he has all papa's tenderness, is of a rougher sort that likes to feel itself mastered. Poor Hector! I wonder if he is to be given back to us."

"Do you know—when—whether they will find out this morning?" said Margaret, catching her dress nervously, as she was moving away.

"Yes, I believe so. I was not to have told you, but—"

"There is no reason that it should do me any harm," said Margaret, almost smiling, and looking as if she was putting a restraint on something she wished to say. "Go down, dear Ethel—Aubrey will be waiting for you."

Ethel went down to the difficult task of hearing Aubrey's lessons, while Harry was pretending to write to Mrs. Arnott, but, in reality, teaching Gertrude the parts of a ship, occasionally acting mast, for her to climb.

By and by Dr. May came in. "Margaret not downstairs yet?" he said.

"She is dressed, but will not come down till the evening," said Ethel.

"I'll go to her. She will be pleased. Come up presently, Ethel. Or, where's Richard?"

"Gone out," said Harry. "What, is it anything left to her?"

"The best, the best!" said Dr. May. "Ethel, listen—twenty thousand, to build and endow a church for Cocksmoor!"

No need to bid Ethel listen. She gave a sort of leap in her chair, then looked almost ready to faint.

"My dear child," said her father, "This is your wish. I give you joy, indeed I do!"

Ethel drew his arm round her, and leaned against him. "My wish! my wish!" she repeated, as if questioning the drift of the words.

"I'm glad it is found!" cried Harry. "Now I know why he talked of Cocksmoor, and seemed to rest in planning for it. You will mind the roof is as he said."

"You must talk to Dr. Spencer about that," said Dr. May. "The captain means to leave it entirely in our hands."

"Dear Alan!" exclaimed Ethel. "My wish! Oh, yes, but how gained? Yet, Cocksmoor with a church! I don't know how to be glad enough, and yet—"

"You shall read the sentence," said Dr. May. "'In testimony of thankfulness for mercy vouchsafed to him here—' poor dear boy!"

"What does the captain say?" asked Harry.

"He is rather astounded, but he owns that the estate can bear it, for old Halliday had saved a great deal, and there will be more before Hector comes of age."

"And Hector?"

"Yes, we get him back. I am fellow-trustee with Captain Gordon, and as to personal guardianship, I fancy the captain found he could not make the boy happy, and thinks you no bad specimen of our training."

"Famous!" cried Harry. "Hector will hurrah now! Is that all?"

"Except legacies to Captain Gordon, and some Scottish relations. But poor Margaret ought to hear it. Ethel, don't be long in coming."

With all Ethel's reputation for bluntness, it was remarkable how her force of character made her always called for whenever there was the least dread of a scene.

She turned abruptly from Harry; and, going outside the window, tried to realise and comprehend the tidings, but all she could have time to discover was that Alan's memory was dearer to her than ever, and she was obliged to hasten upstairs.

Her father quitted the room by one door, as she entered by the other; she believed that it was to hide his emotion, but Margaret's fair wan face was beaming with the sweetest of congratulating smiles.

"I thought so," she said, as Ethel came in. "Dear Ethel, are you not glad?"

"I think I am," said Ethel, putting her hands to her brow.

"You think!" exclaimed Margaret, as if disappointed.

"I beg your pardon," said Ethel, with quivering lip. "Dear Margaret, I am glad—don't you believe I am, but somehow, it is harder to deal with joy than grief. It confuses one! Dear Alan—and then to have been set on it so long—to have prayed so for it, and to have it come in this way—by your—"

"Nay, Ethel, had he come home, it was his great wish to have done it. He used to make projects when he was here, but he would not let me tell you, lest he should find duties at Maplewood—whereas this would have been his pleasure."

"Dear Alan!" repeated Ethel. "If you are so kind, so dear as to be glad, Margaret, I think I shall be so presently."

Margaret almost grudged the lack of the girlish outbreak of rejoicing which would once have forgotten everything in the ecstasy of the fulfilled vision. It did not seem to be what Alan had intended; he had figured to himself unmixed joy, and she wanted to see it, and something of the wayward impatience of weakness throbbed at her heart, as Ethel paced the room, and disappeared in her own curtained recess.

Presently she came back saying, "You are sure you are glad?"

"It would be strange if I were not," said Margaret. "See, Ethel, here are blessings springing up from what I used to think had served for nothing but to bring him pain and grief. I am so thankful that he could express his desire, and so grateful to dear Harry for bringing it to light. How much better it is than I ever thought it could be! He has been spared disappointment, and surely the good that he will have done will follow him."

"And you?" said Ethel sadly.

"I shall lie here and wait," said Margaret. "I shall see the plans, and hear all about it, and oh!"—her eyes lighted up—"perhaps some day, I may hear the bell."

Richard's tap interrupted them. "Had he heard?"

"I have." The deepened colour in his cheek betrayed how much he felt, as he cast an anxious glance towards Margaret—an inquiring one on Ethel.

"She is so pleased," was all Ethel could say.

"I thought she would be," said Richard, approaching. "Captain Gordon seemed quite vexed that no special token of remembrance was left to her."

Margaret smiled in a peculiar way. "If he only knew how glad I am there was not." And Ethel knew that the church was his token to Margaret, and that any "fading frail memorial" would have lessened the force of the signification.

Ethel could speak better to her brother than to her sister. "Oh, Richard! Richard! Richard!" she cried, and a most unusual thing with both, she flung her arms round his neck. "It is come at last! If it had not been for you, this would never have been. How little likely it seemed, that dirty day, when I talked wildly, and you checked me!"

"You had faith and perseverance," said Richard, "or—"

"You are right," said Margaret, as Ethel was about to disclaim. "It was Ethel's steadiness that brought it before Alan's mind. If she had yielded when we almost wished it, in the time of the distress about Mrs. Green, I do believe that all would have died away!"

"I didn't keep steady—I was only crazy. You and Ritchie and Mr. Wilmot—" said Ethel, half crying; then, as if unable to stay, she exclaimed with a sort of petulance, "And there's Harry playing all sorts of rigs with Aubrey! I shan't get any more sense out of him to-day!"

And away she rushed to the wayfaring dust of her life of labour, to find Aubrey and Daisy half-way up the tulip tree, and Harry mischievously unwilling to help them down again, assuring her that such news deserved a holiday, and that she was growing a worse tartar than Miss Winter. She had better let the poor children alone, put on her bonnet, and come with him to tell Mr. Wilmot.

Whereat Ethel was demurring, when Dr. May came forth, and declared he should take her himself.

Poor Mr. Wilmot laboured under a great burden of gratitude, which no one would receive from him. Dr. May and Ethel repudiated thanks almost with terror; and, when he tried them with the captain, he found very doubtful approval of the whole measure, so that Harry alone was a ready acceptant of a full meed of acknowledgments for his gallant extraction of the will.

No one was more obliged to him than Hector Ernescliffe, who wrote to Margaret that it would be very jolly to come home again, and that he was delighted that the captain could not hinder either that or Cocksmoor Church. "And as to Maplewood, I shall not hate it so much, if that happens which I hope will happen." Of which oracular sentence, Margaret could make nothing.

The house of May felt more at their ease when the uncongenial captain had departed, although he carried off Harry with him. There was the better opportunity for a tea-drinking consultation with Dr. Spencer and Mr. Wilmot, when Margaret lay on her sofa, looking better than for months past, and taking the keenest interest in every arrangement.

Dr. Spencer, whose bright eyes glittered at every mention of the subject, assumed that he was to be the architect, while Dr. May was assuring him that it was a maxim that no one unpaid could be trusted; and when he talked of beautiful German churches with pierced spires, declared that the building must not make too large a hole in the twenty thousand, at the expense of future curates, because Richard was the first.

"I'll be prudent, Dick," said Dr. Spencer. "Trust me not to rival the minster."

"We shall find work next for you there," said Mr. Wilmot.

"Ay, we shall have May out of his family packing-box before many years are over his head."

"Don't mention it," said Dr. May; "I know what I exposed myself to in bringing Wilmot here."

"Yes," said Dr. Spencer, "we shall put you in the van when we attack the Corporation pen."

"I shall hold by the good old cause. As if the galleries had not been there before you were born!"

"As if poor people had a right to sit in their own church!" said Ethel.

"Sit, you may well say," said Mr. Wilmot. "As if any one could do otherwise, with those ingenious traps for hindering kneeling."

"Well, well, I know the people must have room," said Dr. May, cutting short several further attacks which he saw impending.

"Yes, you would like to build another blue gallery, blocking up another window, and with Richard May and Christopher Tomkins, Churchwardens, on it, in orange-coloured letters—the Rivers' colours. No disrespect to your father, Miss May, but, as a general observation, it is a property of Town Councillors to be conservative only where they ought not."

"I brought you here to talk of building a church, not of pulling one to pieces."

Poor Dr. May, he knew it was inevitable and quite right, but his affectionate heart and spirit of perpetuity, which had an association connected with every marble cloud, green baize pew, and square-headed panel, anticipated tortures in the general sweep, for which his ecclesiastical taste and sense of propriety would not soon compensate.

Margaret spared his feelings by bringing the Cocksmoor subject back again; Dr. Spencer seemed to comprehend the ardour with which she pressed it on, as if it were very near her heart that there should be no delay. He said he could almost promise her that the first stone should be laid before the end of the summer, and she thanked him in her own warm sweet way, hoping that it would be while Hector and Harry were at home.

Harry soon returned, having gone through the court-martial with the utmost credit, been patronised by Captain Gordon in an unheard-of manner, asked to dine with the admiral, and promised to be quickly afloat again. Ere many days had passed, he was appointed to one of the finest vessels in the fleet, commanded by a captain to whom Captain Gordon had introduced him, and who "seemed to have taken a fancy to him," as he said. The Bucephalus, now the object of his pride, was refitting, and his sisters hoped to see a good deal of him before he should again sail. Besides, Flora would be at Ryde before the end of July.

It was singular that Ethel's vision should have been fulfilled simultaneously with Flora's having obtained a position so far beyond what could have been anticipated.

She was evidently extremely happy and valuable, much admired and respected, and with full exercise for the energy and cleverness, which were never more gratified than by finding scope for action. Her husband was devotedly attached to her, and was entirely managed by her, and though her good judgment kept her from appearing visibly in matters not pertaining to her own sphere, she as, in fact, his understanding. She read, listened, and thought for him, imbued him with her own views, and composed his letters for him; ruling his affairs, both political and private, and undeniably making him fill a position which, without her, he would have left vacant; nor was there any doubt that he was far happier for finding himself of consequence, and being no longer left a charge upon his own hands. He seemed fully to suffice to her as a companion, although she was so far superior in power; for it was, perhaps, her nature to love best that which depended upon her, and gave her a sense of exercising protection; as she had always loved Margaret better than Ethel.

"Mrs. Rivers was an admirable woman." So every one felt, and her youthful beauty and success in the fashionable world made her qualities, as a wife and mistress of a household, the more appreciated. She never set aside her religious habits or principles, was an active member of various charitable associations, and found her experience of the Stoneborough Ladies' Committee applicable among far greater names. Indeed, Lady Leonora thought dear Flora Rivers's only fault, her over-strictness, which encouraged Meta in the same, but there were points that Flora could not have yielded on any account, without failing in her own eyes.

She made time for everything, and though, between business and fashion, she seemed to undertake more than mortal could accomplish, it was all effected, and excellently. She did, indeed, sigh over the briefness of the time that she could bestow on her child or on home correspondence, and declared that she should rejoice in rest; but, at the same time, her achievements were a positive pleasure to her.

Meta, in the meantime, had been living passively on the most affectionate terms with her brother and sister, and though often secretly yearning after the dear old father, whose darling she had been, and longing for power of usefulness, she took it on trust that her present lot had been ordered for her, and was thankful, like the bird of Dr. May's fable, for the pleasures in her path—culling sweet morals, and precious thoughts out of book, painting or concert, occasions for Christian charities in each courtesy of society, and opportunities for cheerful self-denial and submission, whenever any little wish was thwarted.

So Norman said she had turned into a fine lady! It was a sudden and surprising intimation, and made a change in the usually bright and calm current of her thoughts. She was not aware that there had been any alteration in herself, and it was a revelation that set her to examine where she had changed—poor little thing! She was not angry, she did not resent the charge, she took it for granted that, coming from such a source, it must be true and reasonable—and what did it mean? Did they think her too gay, or neglectful of old friends? What had they been saying to Harry about her?

"Ah!" thought Meta, "I understand it. I am living a life of ease and uselessness, and with his higher aims and nobler purposes, he shrinks from the frivolities among which I am cast. I saw his saddened countenance among our gaieties, and I know that to deep minds there is heaviness in the midst of display. He withdraws from the follies that have no charms for him, and I—ought I to be able to help being amused? I don't seek these things, but, perhaps, I ought to avoid them more than I do. If I could be quite clear what is right, I should not care what effort I made. But I was born to be one of those who have trial of riches, and such blessed tasks are not my portion. But if he sees the vanities creeping into my heart, I should be grateful for that warning."

So meditated Meta, as she copied one of her own drawings of the Grange, for her dear old governess, Mrs. Larpent, while each line and tint recalled the comments of her fond amateur father, and the scenery carried her home, in spite of the street sounds, and the scratching of Flora's pen, coursing over note-paper. Presently Sir Henry Walkinghame called, bringing a beautiful bouquet.

"Delicious," cried Meta. "See, Flora, it is in good time, for those vases were sadly shabby."

She began at once to arrange the flowers, a task that seemed what she was born for, and the choice roses and geraniums acquired fresh grace as she placed them in the slender glasses and classic vases; but Flora's discerning eyes perceived some mortification on the part of the gentleman, and, on his departure, playfully reproached Meta for ingratitude.

"Did we not thank him? I thought I did them all due honour, actually using the Dresden bowl."

"You little wretch! quite insensible to the sentiment of the thing."

"Sentiment! One would think you had been reading about the language of flowers!"

"Whatever there was, poor Sir Henry did not mean it for the Dresden bowl or Bohemian glass."

"Flora! do pray tell me whether you are in fun?"

"You ridiculous child!" said Flora, kissing her earnest forehead, ringing the bell, and gathering up her papers, as she walked out of the room, and gave her notes to the servant.

"What does she mean? Is it play? Oh, no, a hint would be far more like her. But I hope it is nonsense. He is very kind and pleasant, and I should not know what to do."

Instances of his complaisance towards herself rose before her, so as to excite some warmth and gratitude. Her lonely heart thrilled at the idea of being again the best beloved, and her energetic spirit bounded at the thought of being no longer condemned to a life of idle ease. Still it was too new a light to her to be readily accepted, after she had looked on him so long, merely as a familiar of the house, attentive to her, because she fell to his share, when Flora was occupied. She liked him, decidedly; she could possibly do more; but she was far more inclined to dread, than to desire, any disturbance of their present terms of intercourse.

"However," thought she, "I must see my way. If he should have any such thing in his head, to go on as we do now would be committing myself, and I will not do that, unless I am sure it is right. Oh, papa, you would settle it for me! But I will have it out with Flora. She will find out what I cannot—how far he is a man for whom one ought to care. I do not think Norman liked him, but then Norman has so keen a sense of the world-touched. I suppose I am that! If any other life did but seem appointed for me, but one cannot tell what is thwarting providential leading, and if this be as good a man as—

What would Ethel say? If I could but talk to Dr. May! But Flora I will catch, before I see him again, that I may know how to behave."

Catching Flora was not the easiest thing in the world, among her multifarious occupations; but Meta was not the damsel to lose an opportunity for want of decision.

Flora saw what was coming, and was annoyed with herself for having given the alarm; but, after all, it must have come some time or other, though she had rather that Meta had been more involved first.

It should be premised that Mrs. Rivers had no notion of the degree of attachment felt by her brother for Meta; she only knew that Lady Leonora had a general distrust of her family, and she felt it a point of honour to promote no dangerous meetings, and to encourage Sir Henry—a connection who would be most valuable, both as conferring importance upon George in the county, and as being himself related to persons of high influence, whose interest might push on her brothers. Preferment for Richard; promotion for Harry; nay, diplomatic appointments for Tom, came floating before her imagination, even while she smiled at her Alnaschar visions.

But the tone of Meta, as she drew her almost forcibly into her room, showed her that she had given a great shock to her basket.

"Flora, if you would only give me a minute, and would tell me—"

"What?" asked Flora, not inclined to spare her blushes.

"Whether, whether you meant anything in earnest?"

"My dear little goose, did no one ever make an innocent joke in their lives before?"

"It was very silly of me," said Meta; "but you gave me a terrible fright."

"Was it so very terrible, poor little bird?" said Flora, in commiseration. "Well then, you may safely think of him as a man tame about the house. It was much prettier of you not to appropriate the flowers, as any other damsel would have done."

"Do you really and truly think—" began Meta; but, from the colour of her cheek and the timid resolution of her tone, Flora thought it safest not to hear the interrogation, and answered, "I know what he comes here for—it is only as a refuge from his mother's friend, old Lady Drummond, who would give the world to catch him for her daughters—that's all. Put my nonsense out of your head, and be yourself, my sweet one."

Flora had never gone so near an untruth, as when she led Meta to believe this was the sole reason. But, after all, what did Flora herself know to the contrary?

Meta recovered her ease, and Flora marked, as weeks passed on, that she grew more accustomed to Sir Henry's attentions. A little while, and she would find herself so far bound by the encouragement she had given, that she could not reject him.

"My dear," said George, "when do you think of going down to take the baby to the Grange? She looks dull, I think."

"Really, I think it is hardly worth while to go down en masse," said Flora. "These last debates may be important, and it is a bad time to quit one's post. Don't you think so?"

"As you please—the train is a great bore."

"And we will send the baby down the last day before we go to Ryde, with Preston and Butts to take care of her. We can't spare him to take them down, till we shut up the house. It is so much easier for us to go to Portsmouth from hence."

The lurking conviction was that one confidential talk with Ethel would cause the humming-bird to break the toils that were being wound invisibly round her. Ethel and her father knew nothing of the world, and were so unreasonable in their requirements! Meta would consult them all, and all her scruples would awaken, and perhaps Dr. Spencer might be interrogated on Sir Henry's life abroad, where Flora had a suspicion that gossip had best not be raked up.

Not that she concealed anything positively known to her, or that she was not acting just as she would have done by her own child. She found herself happily married to one whom home notions would have rejected, and she believed Meta would be perfectly happy with a man of decided talent, honour, and unstained character, even though he should not come up to her father's or Ethel's standard.

If Meta were to marry as they would approve, she would have far to seek among "desirable connections." Meantime, was not Flora acting with exemplary judgment and self-denial?

So she wrote that she could not come home; Margaret was much disappointed, and so was Meta, who had looked to Ethel to unravel the tangles of her life.

"No, no, little miss," said Flora to herself; "you don't talk to Ethel till your fate is irrevocable. Why, if I had listened to her, I should be thankful to be singing at Mrs. Hoxton's parties at this minute! and, as for herself, look at Norman Ogilvie! No, no, after six weeks' yachting—moonlight, sea, and sympathy—I defy her to rob Sir Henry of his prize! And, with Meta lady of Cocksmoor, even Ethel herself must be charmed!"

CHAPTER XX.

We barter life for pottage, sell true bliss
For wealth or power, for pleasure or renown;
Thus, Esau-like, our Father's blessing miss,
Then wash with fruitless tears our faded crown.

—Christian Year.

"Papa, here is a message from Flora for you," said Margaret, holding up a letter; "she wants to know whom to consult about the baby."

"Ha! what's the matter?"

Margaret read—"Will you ask papa whom I had better call in to see the baby. There does not seem to be anything positively amiss, but I am not happy about her. There is a sleepiness about her which I do not understand, and, when roused, she is fretful, and will not be amused. There is a look in her eyes which I do not like, and I should wish to have some advice for her. Lady Leonora recommends Mr. —, but I always distrust people who are very much the rage, and I shall send for no one without papa's advice."

"Let me see!" said Dr. May, startled, and holding out his hand for the letter. "A look about the eyes! I shall go up and see her myself. Why has not she brought her home?"

"It would have been far better," said Margaret.

"Sleepy and dull! She was as lively a child when they took her away as I ever saw. What! is there no more about her? The letter is crammed with somebody's fete—vote of want of confidence—debate last night. What is she about? She fancies she knows everything, and, the fact is, she knows no more about infants—I could see that, when the poor little thing was a day old!"

"Do you think there is cause for fear?" said Margaret anxiously.

"I can't tell. With a first child, one can't guess what may be mamma's fancy, or what may be serious. But Flora is not too fanciful, and I must see her for my own satisfaction. Let some one write, and say I will come up to-morrow by the twelve o'clock train— and mind she opens the letter."

Dr. May kept his word, and the letter had evidently not been neglected; for George was watching for him at the station, and thanked him so eagerly for coming, that Dr. May feared that he was indeed needed, and inquired anxiously.

"Flora is uneasy about her—she seems heavy, and cries when she is disturbed," replied George. "Flora has not left her to-day, and hardly yesterday."

"Have you had no advice for her?"

"Flora preferred waiting till you should come."

Dr. May made an impatient movement, and thought the way long, till they were set down in Park Lane. Meta came to meet them on the stairs, and said that the baby was just the same, and Flora was in the nursery, and thither they hastily ascended.

"Oh, papa! I am so glad you are come!" said Flora, starting up from her low seat, beside the cradle.

Dr. May hardly paused to embrace his daughter, and she anxiously led him to the cradle, and tried to read his expression, as his eyes fell on the little face, somewhat puffed, but of a waxy whiteness, and the breathing seeming to come from the lips.

"How long has she been so?" he asked, in a rapid, professional manner.

"For about two or three hours. She was very fretful before, but I did not like to call in any one, as you were coming. Is it from her teeth?" said Flora, more and more alarmed by his manner. "Her complexion is always like that—she cannot bear to be disturbed," added she, as the child feebly moaned, on Dr. May beginning to take her from her cradle; but, without attending to the objection, he lifted her up, so that she lay as quietly as before, on his arm. Flora had trusted that hope and confidence would come with him; but, on the contrary, every lurking misgiving began to rush wildly over her, as she watched his countenance, while he carried his little granddaughter towards the light, studied her intently, raised her drooping eyelids, and looked into her eyes, scarcely eliciting another moan. Flora dared not ask a question, but looked on with eyes open, as it were, stiffened.

"This is the effect of opium," were Dr. May's first words, breaking on all with startling suddenness; but, before any one could speak, he added, "We must try some stimulant directly;" then looking round the room, "What have you nearest?"

"Godfrey's Cordial, sir," quickly suggested the nurse.

"Ay—anything to save time—she is sinking for want of the drug that has—" He broke off to apportion the dose, and to hold the child in a position to administer it—Flora tried to give it—the nurse tried— in vain.

"Do not torment her further," said the doctor, as Flora would have renewed the trial—"it cannot be done. What have you all been doing?" cried he, as, looking up, his face changed from the tender compassion with which he had been regarding his little patient, into a look of strong indignation, and one of his sentences of hasty condemnation broke from him, as it would not have done, had Flora been less externally calm. "I tell you this child has been destroyed with opium!"

They all recoiled; the father turned fiercely round on the nurse, with a violent exclamation, but Dr. May checked him. "Hush! This is no presence for the wrath of man." The solemn tone seemed to make George shrink into an awestruck quiescence; he stood motionless and transfixed, as if indeed conscious of some overwhelming presence.

Flora had come near, with an imploring gesture, to take the child in her own arms; but Dr. May, by a look of authority, prevented it; for, indeed, it would have been harassing and distressing the poor little sufferer again to move her, as she lay with feeble gasps on his arm.

So they remained, for what space no one knew—not one word was uttered, not a limb moved, and the street noises sounded far off.

Dr. May stooped his head closer to the babe's face, and seemed listening for a breath, as he once more touched the little wrist; he took away his finger, he ceased to listen, he looked up.

Flora gave one cry—not loud, not sharp, but "an exceeding bitter cry"—she would have moved forward, but reeled, and her husband's arms supported her as she sank into a swoon.

"Carry her to her room," said Dr. May. "I will come;" and, when George had borne her away, he kissed the lifeless cheek, and reverently placed the little corpse in the cradle; but, as he rose from doing so, the sobbing nurse exclaimed, "Oh, sir! oh, sir! indeed, I never did—"

"Never did what?" said Dr. May sternly.

"I never gave the dear baby anything to do her harm," cried Preston vehemently.

"You gave her this," said Dr. May, pointing to the bottle of Godfrey's Cordial.

He could say no more, for her master was hurrying back into the room. Anger was the first emotion that possessed him, and he hardly gave an answer to Dr. May's question about Flora. "Meta is with her! Where is that woman? Have you given her up to the police?"

Preston shrieked and sobbed, made incoherent exclamations, and was much disposed to cling to the doctor.

"Silence!" said Dr. May, lifting his hand, and assuming a tone and manner that awed them both, by reminding them that death was present in the chamber; and, taking his son-in-law out, and shutting the door, he said, in a low voice,

"I believe this is no case for the police—have mercy on the poor woman."

"Mercy—I'll have no mercy on my child's murderer! You said she had destroyed my child."

"Ignorantly."

"I don't care for ignorance! She destroyed her—I'll have justice," said George doggedly.

"You shall," said Dr. May, laying his hand on his arm; "but it must be investigated, and you are in no state to investigate. Go downstairs—do not do anything till I come to you."

His peremptory manner imposed on George, who, nevertheless, turned round as he went, saying, with a fierce glare in his eyes, "You will not let her escape."

"No. Go down—be quiet."

Dr. May returned to Preston, and had to assure her that Mr. Rivers was not gone to call the police, before he could bring her to any degree of coherence. She regarded him as her only friend, and soon undertook to tell the whole truth, and he perceived that it was, indeed, the truth. She had not known that the cordial was injurious, deeming it a panacea against fretfulness, precious to nurses, but against which ladies always had a prejudice, and, therefore, to be kept secret. Poor little Leonora had been very fretful and uneasy when Flora's many avocations had first caused her to be set aside, and Preston had had recourse to the remedy which, lulling her successfully, was applied with less moderation and judgment than would have been shown by a more experienced person, till gradually the poor child became dependent on it for every hour of rest. When her mother, at last, became aware of her unsatisfactory condition, and spent her time in watching her, the nurse being prevented from continuing her drug, she was, of course, so miserable without it, that Preston had ventured on proposing it, to which Mrs. Rivers had replied with displeasure sufficient to prevent her from declaring how much she had previously given. Preston was in an agony of distress for her little charge, as well as of fear for herself, and could hardly understand what her error had been. Dr. May soon saw that, though not highly principled, her sorrow was sincere, and that she still wept bitterly over the consequences of her treatment, when he told her that she had nothing to fear from the law, and that he would protect her from Mr. Rivers.

Her confession was hardly over when Meta knocked at the door, pale and frightened. "Oh, Dr. May, do come to poor Flora! I don't know what to do, and George is in such a state!"

Dr. May made a sound of sorrow and perplexity, and Meta, as she went down before him, asked, in a low, horror-stricken whisper, "Did Preston really—"

298

"Not knowingly," said Dr. May. "It is the way many children have gone; but I never thought—"

They had come to Flora's dressing-room. Her bedroom door was open, and George was pacing heavily up and down the length of both apartments, fiercely indignant. "Well!" said he, advancing eagerly on Dr. May, "has she confessed?"

"But Flora!" said Dr. May, instead of answering him. Flora lay on her bed, her face hidden on her pillow, only now and then moaning.

"Flora, my poor, poor child!" said her father, bending down to raise her, and taking her hand.

She moved away, so as to bury her face more completely; but there was life in the movement, and he was sufficiently reassured on her situation to be able to attend to George, who was only impatient to rush off to take his revenge. He led him into the outer room, where Meta was waiting, and forced upon his unwilling conviction that it was no case for the law. The child had not been killed by any one dose, but had rather sunk from the want of stimulus, to which she had been accustomed. As to any pity for the woman, George would not hear of it. She was still, in his eyes, the destroyer of bis child; and, when he found the law would afford him no vengeance, he insisted that she should be turned out of his house at once.

"George!" called a hollow voice from the next room, and hurrying back, they saw Flora sitting up, and, as well as trembling limbs allowed, endeavouring to rise to her feet, while burning spots were in her cheeks.

"George, turn me out of the house too! If Preston killed her, I did!" and she gave a ghastly laugh.

George threw his arms round her, and laid her on her bed again, with many fond words, and strength which she had not power to withstand. Dr. May, in the meantime, spoke quickly to Meta in the doorway. "She must go. They cannot see her again; but has she any friends in London?"

"I think not."

"Find out. She must not be sent adrift. Send her to the Grange, if nothing better offers. You must judge."

He felt that he could confide in Meta's discretion and promptitude, and returned to the parents.

"Is she gone?" said George, in a whisper, which he meant should be unheard by his wife, who had sunk her face in her pillows again.

"Going. Meta is seeing to it."

"And that woman gets off free!" cried George, "while my poor little girl—" and, no longer occupied by the hope of retribution, he gave way to an overpowering burst of grief.

His wife did not rouse herself to comfort him, but still lay motionless, excepting for a convulsive movement that passed over her frame at each sound from him, and her father felt her pulse bound at the same time with corresponding violence, as if each of his deep-drawn sobs were a mortal thrust. Going to him, Dr. May endeavoured to repress his agitation, and lead him from the room; but he could not, at first, prevail on him to listen or understand, still less, to quit Flora. The attempt to force on him the perception that his uncontrolled sorrow was injuring her, and that he ought to bear up for her sake, only did further harm; for, when he rose up and tried to caress her, there was the same torpid, passive resistance, the same burying her face from the light, and the only betrayal of consciousness in the agonised throbs of her pulse.

He became excessively distressed at being thus repelled, and, at last, yielded to the impatient signals of Dr. May, who drew him into the next room, and, with brief, strong, though most affectionate and pitying words, enforced on him that Flora's brain—nay, her life, was risked, and that he must leave her alone to his care for the present. Meta coming back at the same moment, Dr. May put him in her charge, with renewed orders to impress on him how much depended on tranquillity.

Dr. May went back, with his soft, undisturbing, physician's footfall, and stood at the side of the bed, in such intense anxiety as those only can endure who know how to pray, and to pray in resignation and faith.

All was still in the darkening twilight; but the distant roar of the world surged without, and a gaslight shone flickering through the branches of the trees, and fell on the rich dress spread on the couch, and the ornaments on the toilet-table. There was a sense of oppression, and of being pursued by the incongruous world, and Dr. May sighed to silence all around, and see his poor daughter in the calm of her own country air; but she had chosen for herself, and here she lay, stricken down in the midst of the prosperity that she had sought.

He could hear every respiration, tightened and almost sobbing, and he was hesitating whether to run the risk of addressing her; when, as if it had occurred to her suddenly that she was alone and deserted, she raised up her head with a startled movement, but, as she saw him, she again hid her face, as if his presence were still more intolerable than solitude.

"Flora! my own, my dearest—my poor child! you should not turn from me. Do I not carry with me the like self-reproachful conviction?"

Flora let him turn her face towards him and kiss her forehead. It was burning, and he brought water and bathed it, now and then speaking a few fond, low, gentle words, which, though she did not respond, evidently had some soothing effect; for she admitted his services, still, however, keeping her eyes closed, and her face turned towards the darkest side of the room. When he went towards the door, she murmured, "Papa!" as if to detain him.

"I am not going, darling. I only wanted to speak to George."

"Don't let him come!" said Flora.

"Not till you wish it, my dear."

George's step was heard; his hand was on the lock, and again Dr. May was conscious of the sudden rush of blood through all her veins. He quickly went forward, met him, and shut him out, persuading him, with difficulty, to remain outside, and giving him the occupation of sending out for an anodyne—since the best hope, at present, lay in encouraging the torpor that had benumbed her crushed faculties.

Her father would not even venture to rouse her to be undressed; he gave her the medicine, and let her lie still, with as little movement as possible, standing by till her regular breathings showed that she had sunk into a sleep; when he went into the other room and found that George had also forgotten his sorrows in slumber on the sofa, while Meta sat sadly presiding over the tea equipage.

She came up to meet him, her question expressed in her looks.

"Asleep," he said; "I hope the pulses are quieter. All depends on her wakening."

"Poor, poor Flora!" said Meta, wiping away her tears.

"What have you done with the woman?"

"I sent her to Mrs. Larpent's. I knew she would receive her and keep her till she could write to her friends. Bellairs took her, but I could hardly speak to her—"

"She did it ignorantly," said Dr. May.

"I could never be so merciful and forbearing as you," said Meta.

"Ah! my dear, you will never have the same cause!"

They could say no more, for George awoke, and the argument of his exclusion had to be gone through again. He could not enter into it by any means; and when Dr. May would have made him understand that poor Flora could not acquit herself of neglect, and that even his affection was too painful for her in the present state; he broke into a vehement angry defence of her devotion to her child, treating Dr. May as if the accusation came from him; and when the doctor and Meta had persuaded him out of this, he next imagined that his father-in-law feared that he was going to reproach his wife, and there was no making him comprehend more than that, if she were not kept quiet, she might have a serious illness.

Even then he insisted on going to look at her, and Dr. May could not prevent him from pressing his lips to her forehead. She half opened her eyes, and murmured "good-night," and by this he was a little comforted; but he would hear of nothing but sitting up, and Meta would have done the same, but for an absolute decree of the doctor.

It was a relief to Dr. May that George's vigil soon became a sound repose on the sofa in the dressing-room; and he was left to read and muse uninterruptedly.

It was far past two o'clock before there was any movement; then Flora drew a long breath, stirred, and, as her father came and drew her hand into his, before she was well awake, she gave a long, wondering whisper, "Oh, papa! papa!" then sitting up, and passing her hand over her eyes, "Is it all true?"

"It is true, my own poor dear," said Dr. May, supporting her, as she rested against his arm, and hid her face on his shoulder, while her breath came short, and she shivered under the renewed perception— "she is gone to wait for you."

"Hush! Oh, don't! papa!" said Flora, her voice shortened by anguish.

"Oh, think why—"

"Nay, Flora, do not, do not speak as if that should exclude peace or hope!" said Dr. May entreatingly. "Besides, it was no wilful neglect—you had other duties—"

"You don't know me, papa," said Flora, drawing her hands away from him, and tightly clenching them in one another, as thoughts far too terrible for words swept over her.

"If I do not, the most Merciful Father does," said Dr. May. Flora sat for a minute or two, her hands locked together round her knees, her head bowed down, her lips compressed. Her father was so far satisfied that the bodily dangers he had dreaded were averted; but the agony of mind was far more terrible, especially in one who expressed so little, and in whom it seemed, as it were, pent up.

"Papa!" said Flora presently, with a resolution of tone as if she would prevent resistance; "I must see her!"

"You shall, my dear," said the doctor at once; and she seemed grateful not to be opposed, speaking more gently, as she said, "May it be now—while there is no daylight?"

"If you wish it," said Dr. May.

The dawn, and a yellow waning moon, gave sufficient light for moving about, and Flora gained her feet; but she was weak and trembling, and needed the support of her father's arm, though hardly conscious of receiving it, as she mounted the same stairs, that she had so often lightly ascended in the like doubtful morning light; for never, after any party, had she omitted her visit to the nursery.

The door was locked, and she looked piteously at her father as her weak push met the resistance, and he was somewhat slow in turning the key with his left hand. The whitewashed, slightly furnished room reflected the light, and the moonbeams showed the window-frame in pale and dim shades on the blinds, the dewy air breathed in coolly from the park, and there was a calm solemnity in the atmosphere— no light, no watcher present to tend the babe. Little Leonora needed such no more; she was with the Keeper, who shall neither slumber nor sleep.

So it thrilled across her grandfather, as he saw the little cradle drawn into the middle of the room, and, on the coverlet, some pure white rosebuds and lilies of the valley, gathered in the morning by Mary and Blanche, little guessing the use that Meta would make of them ere nightfall.

The mother sank on her knees, her hands clasped over her breast, and rocking herself to and fro uneasily, with a low, irrepressible moaning.

"Will you not see her face?" whispered Dr. May.

"I may not touch her," was the answer, in the hollow voice, and with the wild eye that had before alarmed him; but trusting to the soothing power of the mute face of the innocent, he drew back the covering.

The sight was such as he anticipated, sadly lovely, smiling and tranquil—all oppression and suffering fled away for ever.

It stilled the sounds of pain, and the restless motion; the compression of the hands became less tight, and he began to hope that the look was passing into her heart. He let her kneel on without interruption, only once he said, "Of such is the kingdom of Heaven!"

She made no immediate answer, and he had had time to doubt whether he ought to let her continue in that exhausting attitude any longer, when she looked up and said, "You will all be with her there."

"She has flown on to point your aim more steadfastly," said Dr. May.

Flora shuddered, but spoke calmly—"No, I shall not meet her."

"My child!" he exclaimed, "do you know what you are saying?"

"I know, I am not in the way," said Flora, still in the same fearfully quiet, matter-of-fact tone. "I never have been"—and she bent over her child, as if taking her leave for eternity.

His tongue almost clave to the roof of his mouth, as he heard the words—words elicited by one of those hours of true reality that, like death, rend aside every wilful cloak of self-deceit, and self-approbation. He had no power to speak at first; when he recovered it, his reply was not what his heart had, at first, prompted.

"Flora! How has this dear child been saved?" he said. "What has released her from the guilt she inherited through you, through me, through all? Is not the Fountain open?"

"She never wasted grace," said Flora.

"My child! my Flora!" he exclaimed, losing the calmness he had gained by such an effort; "you must not talk thus—it is wrong! Only your own morbid feeling can treat this—this—as a charge against you, and if it were, indeed"—he sank his voice—"that such consequences destroyed hope, oh, Flora! where should I be?"

"No," said Flora, "this is not what I meant. It is that I have never set my heart right. I am not like you nor my sisters. I have seemed to myself, and to you, to be trying to do right, but it was all hollow, for the sake of praise and credit. I know it, now it is too late; and He has let me destroy my child here, lest I should have destroyed her everlasting life, like my own."

The most terrible part of this sentence was to Dr. May, that Flora spoke as if she knew it all as a certainty, and without apparent emotion, with all the calmness of despair. What she had never guessed before had come clearly and fully upon her now, and without apparent novelty, or, perhaps, there had been misgivings in the midst of her complacent self-satisfaction. She did not even seem to perceive how dreadfully she was shocking her father, whose sole comfort was in believing her language the effect of exaggerated self-reproach. His profession had rendered him not new to the sight of despondency, and, dismayed as he was, he was able at once to speak to the point.

"If it were indeed so, her removal would be the greatest blessing."

"Yes," said her mother, and her assent was in the same tone of resigned despair, owning it best for her child to be spared a worldly education, and loving her truly enough to acquiesce.

"I meant the greatest blessing to you," continued Dr. May, "if it be sent to open your eyes, and raise your thoughts upwards. Oh, Flora, are not afflictions tokens of infinite love?"

She could not accept the encouragement, and only formed, with her lips, the words, "Mercy to her—wrath to me!"

The simplicity and hearty piety which, with all Dr. May's faults, had always been part of his character, and had borne him, in faith and trust, through all his trials, had never belonged to her. Where he had been sincere, erring only from impulsiveness, she had been double-minded and calculating; and, now that her delusion had been broken down, she had nothing to rest upon. Her whole religious life had been mechanical, deceiving herself more than even others, and all seemed now swept away, except the sense of hypocrisy, and of having cut herself off, for ever, from her innocent child. Her father saw that it was vain to argue with her, and only said, "You will think otherwise by and by, my dear. Now shall I say a prayer before we go down?"

As she made no reply, he repeated the Lord's Prayer, but she did not join; and then he added a broken, hesitating intercession for the mourners, which caused her to bury her face deeper in her hands, but her dull wretchedness altered not.

Rising, he said authoritatively, "Come, Flora, you must go to bed.

See, it is morning."

"You have sat up all night with me!" said Flora, with somewhat of her anxious, considerate self.

"So has George. He had just dropped asleep on the sofa when you awoke."

"I thought he was in anger," said she.

"Not with you, dearest."

"No, I remember now, not where it was justly due. Papa," she said, pausing, as to recall her recollection, "what did I do? I must have done something very unkind to make him go away and leave me."

"I insisted on his leaving you, my dear. You seemed oppressed, and his affectionate ways were doing you harm; so I was hardhearted, and turned him out, sadly against his will."

"Poor George!" said Flora, "has he been left to bear it alone all this time? How much distressed he must have been. I must have vexed him grievously. You don't guess how fond he was of her. I must go to him at once."

"That is right, my dear."

"Don't praise me," said she, as if she could not bear it. "All that is left for me is to do what I can for him."

Dr. May felt cheered. He was sure that hope must again rise out of unselfish love and duty.

Their return awoke George, who started, half sitting up, wondering why he was spending the night in so unusual a manner, and why Flora looked so pale, in the morning light, with her loosened, drooping hair.

She went straight to him, and, kneeling by his side, said, "George, forgive!" The same moment he had caught her to his bosom; but so impressed was his tardy mind with the peril of talking to her, that he held her in his arms without a single word, till Dr. May had unclosed his lips—a sign would not suffice—he must have a sentence to assure him; and then it was such joy to have her restored, and his fondness and solicitude were so tender and eager in their clumsiness, that his father-in-law was touched to the heart.

Flora was quite herself again, in presence of mind and power of dealing with him; and Dr. May left them to each other, and went to his own room, for such rest as sorrow, sympathy, and the wakening city, would permit him.

When the house was astir in the morning, and the doctor had met Meta in the breakfast-room, and held with her a sad, affectionate conversation, George came down with a fair report of his wife, and took her father to see her.

That night had been like an illness to her, and, though perfectly composed, she was feeble and crushed, keeping the room darkened, and reluctant to move or speak. Indeed, she did not seem able to give her attention to any one's voice, except her husband's. When Dr. May, or Meta, spoke to her, she would miss what they said, beg their pardon, and ask them to repeat it; and sometimes, even then, become bewildered. They tried reading to her, but she did not seem to listen, and her half-closed eye had the expression of listless dejection, that her father knew betokened that, even as last night, her heart refused to accept promises of comfort as meant for her.

For George, however, her attention was always ready, and was perpetually claimed. He was forlorn and at a loss without her, every moment; and, in the sorrow which he too felt most acutely, could not have a minute's peace unless soothed by her presence; he was dependent on her to a degree which amazed and almost provoked the doctor, who could not bear to have her continually harassed and disturbed, and yet was much affected by witnessing so much tenderness, especially in Flora, always the cold utilitarian member of his family.

In the middle of the day she rose and dressed, because George was unhappy at having to sit without her, though only in the next room. She sat in the large arm-chair, turned away from the blinded windows, never speaking nor moving, save when he came to her, to make her look at his letters and notes, when she would, with the greatest patience and sweetness, revise them, suggest word or sentence, rouse herself to consider each petty detail, and then sink back into her attitude of listless dejection. To all besides, she appeared totally indifferent; gently courteous to Meta and to her father, when they addressed her, but otherwise showing little consciousness whether they were in the room; and yet, when something was passing about her father's staying or returning, she rose from her seat, came up to him before he was aware, and said, "Papa! papa! you will not leave me!" in such an imploring tone, that if he had ever thought of quitting her, he could not have done so.

He longed to see her left to perfect tranquillity, but such could not be in London. Though theirs was called a quiet house, the rushing stream of traffic wearied his country ears, the door bell seemed ceaselessly ringing, and though Meta bore the brunt of the notes and messages, great numbers necessarily came up to Mr. Rivers, and of these Flora was not spared one. Dr. May had his share too of messages and business, and friends and relations, the Rivers' kindred, always ready to take offence with their rich connections, and who would not be satisfied with inquiries, at the door, but must see Meta, and would have George fetched down to them—old aunts, who wanted the whole story of the child's illness, and came imagining there was something to be hushed up; Lady Leonora extremely polite, but extremely disgusted at the encounter with them; George ready to be persuaded to take every one up to see his wife, and the prohibition to be made by Dr. May over and over again—it was a most tedious, wearing afternoon, and at last, when the visitors had gone, and George had hurried back to his wife, Dr. May threw himself into an arm-chair and said, "Oh, Meta, sorrow weighs more heavily in town than in the country!"

"Yes!" said Meta. "If one only could go out and look at the flowers, and take poor Flora up a nosegay!"

"I don't think it would make much difference to her," sighed the doctor.

"Yes, I think it would," said Meta; "it did to me. The sights there speak of the better sights."

"The power to look must come from within," said Dr. May, thinking of his poor daughter.

"Ay," said Meta, "as Mr. Ernescliffe said, 'heaven is as near—!' But the skirts of heaven are more easily traced in our mountain view than here, where, if I looked out of window, I should only see that giddy string of carriages and people pursuing each other!"

"Well, we shall get her home as soon as she is able to move, and I hope it may soothe her. What a turmoil it is! There has not been one moment without noise in the twenty-two hours I have been here!"

"What would you say if you were in the city?"

"Ah! there's no talking of it; but if I had been a fashionable London physician, as my father-in-law wanted to make me, I should have been dead long ago!"

"No, I think you would have liked it very much."

"Why?"

"Love's a flower that will not die," repeated Meta, half smiling. "You would have found so much good to do —"

"And so much misery to rend one's heart," said Dr. May. "But, after all, I suppose there is only a certain capacity of feeling."

"It is within, not without, as you said," returned Meta.

"Ha, there's another!" cried Dr. May, almost petulant at the sound of the bell again, breaking into the conversation that was a great refreshment.

"It was Sir Henry Walkinghame's ring," said Meta. "It is always his time of day."

The doctor did not like it the better.

Sir Henry sent up a message to ask whether he could see Mr. or Miss Rivers.

"I suppose we must," said Meta, looking at the doctor. "Lady Walkinghame must be anxious about Flora."

She blushed greatly, fancying that Dr. May was putting his own construction on the heightened colour which she could not control. Sir Henry came in, just what he ought to be, kindly anxious, but not overwhelming, and with a ready, pleased recognition of the doctor, as an old acquaintance of his boyhood. He did not stay many minutes; but there was a perceptible difference between his real sympathy and friendly regard only afraid of obtruding, and the oppressive curiosity of their former visitors. Dr. May felt it due, both from kindness and candour, to say something in his praise when he was gone.

"That is a sensible superior man," he said. "He will be an acquisition when he takes up his abode at Drydale."

"Yes," said Meta; a very simple yes, from which nothing could be gathered.

The funeral was fixed for Monday, the next day but one, at the church where Mr. Rivers had been buried. No one was invited to be present;

Ethel wrote that, much as she wished it, she could not leave Margaret, and, as the whole party were to return home on the following day, they should soon see Flora.

Flora had laid aside all privileges of illness after the first day; she came downstairs to breakfast and dinner, and though looking wretchedly ill, and speaking very low and feebly, she was as much as ever the mistress of her house. Her father could never draw her into conversation again on the subject nearest his heart, and could only draw the sad conclusion that her state of mind was unchanged, from the dreary indifference with which she allowed every word of cheer to pass by unheeded, as if she could not bear to look beyond the grave. He had some hope in the funeral, which she was bent on attending, and more in the influence of Margaret, and the counsel of Richard, or of Mr. Wllmot.

The burial, however, failed to bring any peaceful comfort to the mourning mother. Meta's tears flowed freely, as much for her father as for her little niece; and George's sobs were deep and choking; but Flora, externally, only seemed absorbed in helping him to go through with it; she, herself, never lost her fixed, composed, hopeless look.

After her return, she went up to the nursery, and deliberately set apart and locked up every possession of her child's, then, coming down, startled Meta by laying her hand on her shoulder and saying, "Meta, dear, Preston is in the housekeeper's room. Will you go and speak to her for a moment, to reassure her before I come?"

"Oh, Flora!"

"I sent for her," said Flora, in answer. "I thought it would be a good opportunity while George is out. Will you be kind enough to prepare her, my dear?"

Meta wondered how Flora had known whither to send, but she could not but obey. Poor Preston was an ordinary sort of woman, kind-hearted, and not without a conscience; but her error had arisen from the want of any high religious principle to teach her obedience, or sincerity. Her grief was extreme, and she had been so completely overcome by the forbearance and consideration shown to her, that she was even more broken-hearted by the thought of them, than by the terrible calamity she had occasioned.

Kind-hearted Mrs. Larpent had tried to console her, as well as to turn the misfortune to the best account, and Dr. May had once seen her, and striven gently to point out the true evil of the course she had pursued. She was now going to her home, and they augured better of her, that she had been as yet too utterly downcast to say one word of that first thought with a servant, her character.

Meta found her sobbing uncontrollably at the associations of her master's house, and dreadfully frightened at hearing that she was to see Mrs. Rivers; she began to entreat to the contrary with the vehemence of a person unused to any self-government; but, in the midst, the low calm tones were heard, and her mistress stood before her—her perfect stillness of demeanour far more effective in repressing agitation, than had been Meta's coaxing attempts to soothe.

"You need not be afraid to see me, Preston," said Flora kindly. "I am very sorry for you—you knew no better, and I should not have left so much to you."

"Oh, ma'am—so kind—the dear, dear little darling—I shall never forgive myself."

"I know you did love her," continued Flora. "I am sure you intended no harm, and it was my leaving her that made her fretful."

Preston tried to thank.

"Only remember henceforth"—and the clear tone grew fainter than ever with internal anguish, though still steady—"remember strict obedience and truth henceforth; the want of them will have worse results by and by than even this. Now, Preston, I shall always wish you well. I ought not, I believe, to recommend you to the like place, without saying why you left me, but for any other I will give you a fair character. I will see what I can do for you, and if you are ever in any distress, I hope you will let me know. Have your wages been paid?"

There was a sound in the affirmative, but poor Preston could not speak. "Good-bye, then," and Flora took her hand and shook it. "Mind you let me hear if you want help. Keep this."

Meta was a little disappointed to see sovereigns instead of a book. Flora turned to go, and put her hand out to lean on her sister as for support; she stood still to gather strength before ascending the stairs, and a groan of intense misery was wrung from her.

"Dearest Flora, it has been too much!"

"No," said Flora gently.

"Poor thing, I am glad for her sake. But might she not have a book— a Bible?"

"You may give her one, if you like. I could not."

Flora reached her own room, went in, and bolted the door.

CHAPTER XXI.

Oh, where dwell ye, my ain sweet bairns?
   I'm woe and weary grown!
Oh, Lady, we live where woe never is,
   In a land to flesh unknown.—ALLAN CUNNINGHAM.

It had been with a gentle sorrow that Etheldred had expected to go and lay in her resting-place, the little niece, who had been kept from the evil of the world, in a manner of which she had little dreamt. Poor Flora! she must be ennobled, she thought, by having a child where hers is, when she is able to feel anything but the first grief; and Ethel's heart yearned to be trying, at least, to comfort her, and to be with her father, who had loved his grandchild so fondly.

It was not to be. Margaret had borne so many shocks with such calmness, that Ethel had no especial fears for her; but there are some persons who have less fortitude for others than for themselves, and she was one of these. Ethel had been her own companion-sister, and the baby had been the sunbeam of her life, during the sad winter and spring.

In the middle of the night, Ethel knocked at Richard's door. Margaret had been seized with faintness, from which they could not bring her back; and, even when Richard had summoned Dr. Spencer, it was long ere his remedies took effect; but, at last, she revived enough to thank them, and say she was glad that papa was not there.

Dr. Spencer sent them all to bed, and the rest of the night was quiet; but Margaret could not deny, in the morning, that she felt terribly shattered, and she was depressed in spirits to a degree such as they had never seen in her before. Her whole heart was with Flora; she was unhappy at being at a distance from her, almost fretfully impatient for letters, and insisting vehemently on Ethel's going to London.

Ethel had never felt so helpless and desolate, as with Margaret thus changed and broken, and her father absent.

"My dear," said Dr. Spencer, "nothing can be better for both parties than that he should be away. If he were here, he ought to leave all attendance to me, and she would suffer from the sight of his distress."

"I cannot think what he will do or feel!" sighed Ethel.

"Leave it to me. I will write to him, and we shall see her better before post time."

"You will tell him exactly how it was, or I shall," said Ethel abruptly, not to say fiercely.

"Ho! you don't trust me?" said Dr. Spencer, smiling, so that she was ashamed of her speech. "You shall speak for yourself, and I for myself; and I shall say that nothing would so much hurt her as to have others sacrificed to her."

"That is true," said Ethel; "but she misses papa."

"Of course she does; but, depend on it, she would not have him leave your sister, and she is under less restraint without him."

"I never saw her like this!"

"The drop has made it overflow. She has repressed more than was good for her, and now that her guard is broken down, she gives way under the whole weight."

"Poor Margaret! I am pertinacious; but, if she is not better by post time, papa will not bear to be away."

"I'll tell you what I think of her by that time. Send up your brother Richard, if you wish to do her good. Richard would be a much better person to write than yourself. I perceive that he is the reasonable member of the family."

"Did not you know that before?"

"All I knew of him, till last night, was, that no one could, by any possibility, call him Dick."

Dr. Spencer was glad to have dismissed Ethel smiling; and she was the better able to bear with poor Margaret's condition of petulance. She had never before experienced the effects of bodily ailments on the temper, and she was slow to understand the change in one usually so patient and submissive. She was, by turns, displeased with her sister and with her own abruptness; but, though she knew it not, her bluntness had a bracing effect. She thought she had been cross in declaring it was nonsense to harp on her going to London; but it made Margaret feel that she had been unreasonable, and keep silence.

Richard managed her much better, being gentle and firm, and less ready to speak than Ethel, and he succeeded in composing her into a sleep, which restored her balance, and so relieved Ethel, that she not only allowed Dr. Spencer to say what he pleased, but herself made light of the whole attack, little knowing how perilous was any shock to that delicate frame.

Margaret's whole purpose was to wind herself up for the first interview with Flora; and though she had returned to her usual state, she would not go downstairs on the evening the party were expected, believing it would be more grateful to her sister's feelings to meet her without witnesses.

The travellers arrived, and Dr. May hurried up to her. She barely replied to his caresses and inquiries in her eagerness to hear of Flora, and to convince him that he must not forbid the meeting. Nor had he any mind so to do. "Surely," said he, when he had seen the spiritualised look of her glistening blue eyes, the flush on her transparent cheeks, and her hands clasped over her breast— "surely poor Flora must feel as though an angel were waiting to comfort her."

Flora came, but there was sore disappointment. Fond and tender she was as ever, but, neither by word or gesture, would she admit the most remote allusion to her grief. She withdrew her hand when Margaret's pressure became expressive; she avoided her eye, and spoke incessantly of different subjects. All the time, her voice was low and hollow, her face had a settled expression of wretchedness, and her glances wandered drearily and restlessly anywhere but to Margaret's face; but her steadiness of manner was beyond her sister's power to break, and her visit was shortened on account of her husband. Poor George had quite given way at the sight of Gertrude, whom his little girl had been thought to resemble; and, though Dr. May had soothed him almost like a child, no one put any trust in his self-control, and all sat round, fearing each word or look, till Flora came downstairs, and they departed.

Richard and Ethel each offered to go with them; they could not bear to think of their spending that first evening in their childless home; but Flora gently, but decidedly, refused; and Dr. May said that, much as he wished to be with them, he believed that Flora preferred having no one but Meta. "I hope I have done Margaret no harm," were Flora's last words to him, and they seemed to explain her guarded manner; but he found Margaret weeping as she had never wept for herself, and palpitation and faintness were the consequence.

Ethel looked on at Flora as a sad and perplexing mystery during the weeks that ensued. There were few opportunities of being alone together, and Flora shrank from such as they were—nay, she checked all expression of solicitude, and made her very kisses rapid and formal.

The sorrow that had fallen on the Grange seemed to have changed none of the usual habits there—visiting, riding, driving, dinners, and music, went on with little check. Flora was sure to be found the animated, attentive lady of the house, or else sharing her husband's pursuits, helping him with his business, or assisting him in seeking pleasure, spending whole afternoons at the coachmaker's over a carriage that they were building, and, it was reported, playing ecarte in the evening.

Had grief come to be forgotten and cast aside without effecting any mission? Yet Ethel could not believe that the presence of the awful messenger was unfelt, when she heard poor George's heavy sigh, or when she looked at Flora's countenance, and heard the peculiar low, subdued tone of her voice, which, when her words were most cheerful, always seemed to Ethel the resigned accent of despair.

Ethel could not talk her over with Margaret, for all seemed to make it a point that Margaret should believe the best. Dr. May turned from the subject with a sort of shuddering grief, and said, "Don't talk of her, poor child—only pray for her!"

Ethel, though shocked by the unwonted manner of his answer, was somewhat consoled by perceiving that a double measure of tenderness had sprung up between her father and his poor daughter.

If Flora had seemed, in her girlhood, to rate him almost cheaply, this was at an end now; she met him as if his embrace were peace, the gloom was lightened, the attention less strained, when he was beside her, and she could not part with him without pressing for a speedy meeting. Yet she treated him with the same reserve; since that one ghastly revelation of the secrets of her heart, the veil had been closely drawn, and he could not guess whether it had been but a horrible thought, or were still an abiding impression. Ethel could gather no more than that her father was very unhappy about Flora, and that Richard understood why; for Richard had told her that he had written to Flora, to try to persuade her to cease from this reserve, but that he had no reply.

Norman was not at home; he had undertaken the tutorship of two schoolboys for the holidays; and his father owned, with a sigh, that he was doing wisely.

As to Meta, she was Ethel's chief consolation, by the redoubled assurances, directed to Ethel's unexpressed dread, lest Flora should be rejecting the chastening Hand. Meta had the most absolute certainty that Flora's apparent cheerfulness was all for George's sake, and that it was a most painful exertion. "If Ethel could only see how she let herself sink together, as it were, and her whole countenance relax, as soon as he was out of sight," Meta said, "she could not doubt what misery these efforts were to her."

"Why does she go on with them? " said Ethel.

"George," said Meta. "What would become of him without her? If he misses her for ten minutes he roams about lost, and he cannot enjoy anything without her. I cannot think how he can help seeing what hard work it is, and how he can be contented with those dreadful sham smiles; but as long as she can give him pleasure, poor Flora will toil for him."

"It is very selfish," Ethel caught herself saying.

"No, no, it is not," cried Meta. "It is not that he will not see, but that he cannot see. Good honest fellow, he really thinks it does her good and pleases her. I was so sorry one evening when I tried to take her place at that perpetual ecarte, and told him it teased her; he went so wistfully to her, and asked whether it did, and she exerted herself into such painful enjoyment to persuade him to the contrary; and afterwards she said to me, 'Let me alone, dearest—it is the only thing left me.'"

"There is something in being husband and wife that one cannot understand," slowly said Ethel, so much in her quaint way that Meta laughed.

Had it not been for Norman's absence, Ethel would, in the warm sympathy and accustomed manner of Meta Rivers, have forgotten all about the hopes and fears that, in brighter days, had centred on that small personage; until one day, as she came home from Cocksmoor, she found "Sir Henry Walkinghame's" card on the drawing-room table. "I should like to bite you! Coming here, are you?" was her amiable reflection.

Meta, in her riding-habit, peeped out of Margaret's room. "Oh, Ethel, there you are! It is such a boon that you did not come home sooner, or we should have had to ride home with him! I heard him asking for the Miss Mays! And now I am in hopes that he will go home without falling in with Flora and George."

"I did not know he was in these parts."

"He came to Drydale last week, but the place is forlorn, and George gave him a general invitation to the Grange."

"Do you like him?" said Ethel, while Margaret looked on, amazed at her audacity.

"I liked him very much in London," said Meta; "he is pleasant enough to talk to, but somehow, he is not congruous here—if you understand me. And I think his coming oppresses Flora—she turned quite pale when he was announced, and her voice was lower than ever when she spoke to him."

"Does he come often?" said Ethel.

"I don't think he has anything else to do," returned Meta, "for our house cannot be as pleasant as it was; but he is very kind to George, and for that we must be grateful. One thing I am afraid of, that he will persuade us off to the yachting after all."

"Oh!" was the general exclamation.

"Yes," said Meta. "George seemed to like the plan, and I very much fear that he is taking a dislike to the dear old Grange. I heard him say, 'Anything to get away.'"

"Poor George, I know he is restless," said Margaret.

"At least," said Ethel, "you can't go till after your birthday, Miss Heiress."

"No, Uncle Cosham is coming," said Meta. "Margaret, you must have your stone laid before we go!"

"Dr. Spencer promises it before Hector's holidays are over," said Margaret, blushing, as she always did, with pleasure, when they talked of the church.

Hector Ernescliffe had revived Margaret wonderfully. She was seldom downstairs before the evening, and Ethel thought his habit of making her apartment his sitting-room must be as inconvenient to her as it was to herself; but Hector could not be de trop for Margaret. She exerted herself to fulfil for him all the little sisterly offices that, with her brothers, had been transferred to Ethel and Mary; she threw herself into all his schemes, tried to make him endure Captain Gordon, and she even read his favourite book of Wild Sports, though her feelings were constantly lacerated by the miseries of the slaughtered animals. Her couch was to him as a home, and he had awakened her bright soft liveliness which had been only dimmed for a time.

The church was her other great interest, and Dr. Spencer humoured her by showing her all his drawings, consulting her on every ornament, and making many a perspective elevation, merely that she might see the effect.

Richard and Tom made it their recreation to construct a model of the church as a present for her, and Tom developed a genius for carving, which proved a beneficial interest to keep him from surliness. He had voluntarily propounded his intended profession to his father, who had been so much pleased by his choice, that he could not but be gratified; though now and then ambitious fancies, and discontent with Stoneborough, combined to bring on his ordinary moody fits, the more, because his habitual reserve prevented any one from knowing what was working in his mind.

Finally the Rivers' party announced their intention of going to the Isle of Wight as soon as Meta had come of age; and the council of Cocksmoor, meeting at tea at Dr. May's house, decided that the foundation stone of the church should be laid on the day after her birthday, when there would be a gathering of the whole family, as Margaret wished. Dr. Spencer had worked incredibly hard to bring it forward, and Margaret's sweet smiles, and liquid eyes, expressed how personally thankful she felt.

"What a blessing this church has been to that poor girl," said Dr. Spencer, as he left the house with Mr. Wilmot. "How it beguiles her out of her grief! I am glad she has the pleasure of the foundation;

I doubt if she will see the consecration."

"Indeed!" said Mr. Wilmot, shocked. "Was that attack so serious?"

"That recumbent position and want of exercise were certain to produce organic disease, and suspense and sorrow have hastened it. The death of Mrs. Rivers's poor child was the blow that called it into activity, and, if it last more than a year, I shall be surprised."

"For such as she is, one cannot presume to wish, but her father—is he aware of this?"

"He knows there is extensive damage; I think he does not open his eyes to the result, but he will bear it. Never was there a man to whom it came so naturally to live like the fowls of the air, or the lilies of the field, as it does to dear Dick May," said Dr. Spencer, his voice faltering.

"There is a strength of faith and love in him that carries him through all," said Mr. Wilmot. "His childlike nature seems to have the trustfulness that is, in itself, consolation. You said how Cocksmoor had been blessed to Margaret—I think it is the same with them all— not only Ethel and Richard, who have been immediately concerned; but that one object has been a centre and aim to elevate the whole family, and give force and unity to their efforts. Even the good doctor, much as I always looked up to him—much good as he did me in my young days—I must confess that he was sometimes very provoking."

"If you had tried to be his keeper at Cambridge, you might say so!" rejoined Dr. Spencer.

"He is so much less impetuous—more consistent—less desultory; I dare say you understand me," said Mr. Wilmot. "His good qualities do not entangle one another as they used to do."

"Exactly so. He was far more than I looked for when I came home, though I might have guessed that such a disposition, backed by such principles and such—could not but shake off all the dross."

"One thing was," said Mr. Wilmot, smiling, "that a man must take himself in hand at some time in his life, and Dr. May only began to think himself responsible for himself when he lost his wife, who was wise for both. She was an admirable person, but not easy to know well. I think you knew her at—"

"I say," interrupted Dr. Spencer, "it strikes me that we could not do better than get up our S. P. G. demonstration on the day of the stone—"

Hitherto the Stoneborough subscribers to the Society for the Propagation of the Gospel had been few and far between; but, under the new dynasty, there was a talk of forming an association, and having a meeting to bring the subject forward. Dr. Spencer's proposal, however, took the vicar by surprise.

"Never could there be a better time," he argued. "You have naturally a gathering of clergy—people ought to be liberal on such an occasion, and, as Cocksmoor is provided for, why not give the benefit to the missions, in their crying need!"

"True, but there is no time to send for any one to make a speech."

"Husband your resources. What could you have better than young Harry and his islanders?"

"Harry would never make a speech."

"Let him cram Norman. Young Lake tells me Norman made a great sensation at the Union at Oxford, and if his heart is in the work, he must not shrink from the face of his townsmen."

"No doubt he had rather they were savages," said the vicar. "And yourself—you will tell them of the Indian missions."

"With all my heart," said Dr. Spencer. "When my Brahminhee godson— the deacon I told you of, comes to pay me his promised visit, what doings we shall have! Seriously, I have just had letters from him and from others, that speak of such need, that I could feel every moment wasted that is not spent on their behalf."

Mr. Wilmot was drawn into Dr. Spencer's house, and heard the letters, till his heart burned within him.

The meeting was at once decided upon, though Ethel could not see why people could not give without speechifying, and her two younger brothers declared it was humbug—Tom saying, he wished all blackamoors were out of creation, and Harry, that he could not stand palaver about his friend David. Dr. May threatened him with being displayed on the platform as a living instance of the effects of missions, at which he took alarm, and so seriously declared that he should join the Bucephalus at once, that they pacified him by promising that he should do as he pleased.

The archdeacon promised a sermon, and the active Dr Spencer worked the nine muses and all the rest of the town and neighbourhood into a state of great enthusiasm and expectation. He went to the Grange, as he said, to collect his artillery; primed Flora that she might prime the M. P.; made the willing Meta promise to entrap the uncle, who was noted for philanthropical speeches; and himself captured Sir Henry Walkinghame, who looked somewhat rueful at what he found incumbent on him as a country gentleman, though there might be some compensation in the eagerness of Miss Rivers.

Norman had hardly set foot in Stoneborough before he was told what was in store for him, and, to the general surprise, submitted as if it were a very simple matter. As Dr. Spencer told him, it was only a foretaste of the penalty which every missionary has to pay for coming to England. Norman was altogether looking much better than when he had been last at home, and his spirits were more even. He had turned his whole soul to the career he had chosen, cast his disappointment behind him, or, more truly, made it his offering, and gathered strength and calmness, with which to set out on tasks of working for others, with thoughts too much absorbed on them, to give way to the propensity of making himself the primary object of study and contemplation. The praise of God, and love of man, were the best cures for tendencies like his, and he had found it out. His calm, though grave cheerfulness, came as a refreshment to those who had been uneasy about him, and mournfully watching poor Flora.

"Yes," said Dr. Spencer, "you have taken the best course for your own happiness."

Norman coloured, as if he understood more than met the ear. Mary and Blanche were very busy preparing presents for Meta Rivers, and every one was anxious to soften to her the thought of this first birthday without her father. Each of the family contributed some pretty little trifle, choice in workmanship or kind in device, and each was sealed and marked with the initials of the giver, and packed up by Mary, to be committed to Flora's charge. Blanche had, however, much trouble in extracting a gift from Norman, and he only yielded at last, on finding that all his brothers had sent something, so that his omission would be marked. Then he dived into the recesses of his desk, and himself sealed up a little parcel, of which he would not allow his sisters to inspect the contents.

Ethel had a shrewd guess. She remembered his having, in the flush of joy at Margaret's engagement, rather prematurely caused a seal to be cut with a daisy, and "Pearl of the meadow" as the motto; and his having said that he should keep it as a wedding present. She could understand that he was willing to part with it without remark.

Flora met Meta in her sitting-room, on the morning of the day, which rose somewhat sadly upon the young girl, as she thought of past affection and new responsibilities. If the fondness of a sister could have compensated for what she had lost, Meta received it in no scanty measure from Flora, who begged to call George, because he would be pleased to see the display of gifts.

His own was the only costly one—almost all the rest were homemade treasures of the greater price, because the skill and fondness of the maker were evident in their construction; and Meta took home the kindness as it was meant, and felt the affection that would not let her feel herself lonely. She only wished to go and thank them all at once.

"Do then," said Flora. "If Lord Cosham will spare you, and your business should be over in time, you could drive in, and try to bring papa home with you."

"Oh, thank you, Flora. That is a kind treat, in case the morning should be very awful!"

Margaret Agatha Rivers signed her documents, listened to explanations, and was complimented by her uncle on not thinking it necessary to be senseless on money matters, like her cousin, Agatha Langdale.

Still she looked a little oppressed, as she locked up the tokens of her wealth, and the sunshine of her face did not beam out again till she arrived at Stoneborough, and was dispensing her pretty thanks to the few she found at home.

"Ethel out and Norman? His seal is only too pretty —"

"They are all helping Dr. Spencer at Cocksmoor."

"What a pity! But it is so very kind of him to treat me as a daisy. In some ways I like his present for that the best of all," said Meta.

"I will tell him so," said Mary.

"Yes, no," said Meta. "I am not pretending to be anything half so nice."

Mary and Blanche fell upon her for calling herself anything but the nicest flower in the world; and she contended that she was nothing better than a parrot-tulip, stuck up in a parterre; and just as the discussion was becoming a game at romps, Dr. May came in, and the children shouted to him to say whether his humming-bird were a daisy or a tulip.

"That is as she comports herself," he said playfully.

"Which means that you don't think her quite done for," said Meta.

"Not quite," said the doctor, with a droll intonation; "but I have not seen what this morning may have done to her."

"Come and see, then," said Meta. "Flora told me to bring you home— and it is my birthday, you know. Never mind waiting to tell Ethel. Margaret will let her know that I'll keep you out of mischief."

As usual, Dr. May could not withstand her, and she carried him off in triumph in her pony carriage.

"Then you don't give me up yet?" was the first thing she said, as they were off the stones.

"What have you been doing to make me?" said he.

"Doing or not doing—one or the other," she said. "But indeed I wanted to have you to myself. I am in a great puzzle!"

"Sir Henry! I hope she won't consult me!" thought Dr. May, as he answered, "Well, my dear."

"I fear it is a lasting puzzle," she said. "What shall I do with all this money?"

"Keep it in the bank, or buy railway shares!" said Dr. May. looking arch.

"Thank you. That's a question for my cousins in the city. I want you to answer me as no one else can do. I want to know what is my duty now that I have my means in my own hands?"

"There is need enough around—"

"I do not mean only giving a little here and there, but I want you to hear a few of my thoughts. Flora and George are kindness itself— but, you see, I have no duties. They are obliged to live a gay sort of life—it is their position; but I cannot make out whether it is mine. I don't see that I am like those girls who have to go out as a matter of obedience."

Dr. May considered, but could only say, "You are very young."

"Too young to be independent," sighed Meta. "I must grow old enough to be trusted alone, and in the meantime—"

"Probably an answer will be found," said the doctor. You and your means will find their—their vocation."

"Marriage," said Meta, calmly speaking the word that he had avoided. "I think not."

"Why—" he began.

"I do not think good men like heiresses."

He became strongly interested in a corn-field, and she resumed, "Perhaps I should only do harm. It may be my duty to wait. All I wish to know is, whether it is?"

"I see you are not like girls who know their duty, and are restless, because it is not the duty they like."

"Oh! I like everything. It is my liking it so much that makes me afraid."

"Even going to Ryde?"

"Don't I like the sailing? and seeing Harry too? I don't feel as if that were waste, because I can sometimes spare poor Flora a little. We could not let her go alone."

"You need never fear to be without a mission of comfort," said Dr. May. "Your 'spirit full of glee' was given you for something. Your presence is far more to my poor Flora than you or she guess."

"I never meant to leave her now," said Meta earnestly. "I only wished to be clear whether I ought to seek for my work."

"It will seek you, when the time comes."

"And meantime I must do what comes to hand, and take it as humiliation that it is not in the more obviously blessed tasks! A call might come, as Cocksmoor did to Ethel. But oh! my money! Ought it to be laid up for myself?"

"For your call, when it comes," said Dr. May, smiling; then gravely, "There are but too many calls for the interest. The principal is your trust, till the time comes."

Meta smiled, and was pleased to think that her first-fruits would be offered to-morrow.

CHAPTER XXII.

"Oh, dear!" sighed Etheldred, as she fastened her white muslin, "I'm afraid it is my nature to hate my neighbour."

"My dear Ethel, what is coming next?" said Margaret.

"I like my neighbour at home, and whom I have to work for, very much," said Ethel, "but oh! my neighbour that I have to be civil to!"

"Poor old King! I am afraid your day will be spoiled with all your toils as lady of the house. I wish I could help you."

"Let me have my grumble out, and you will!" said Ethel.

"Indeed I am sorry you have this bustle, and so many to entertain, when I know you would rather have the peaceful feelings belonging to the day undisturbed. I should like to shelter you up here."

"It is very ungrateful of me," said Ethel, "when Dr. Spencer works so hard for us, not to be willing to grant anything to him."

"And—but then I have none of the trouble of it—I can't help liking the notion of sending out the Church to the island whence the Church came home to us."

"Yes—" said Ethel, "if we could do it without holding forth!"

"Come, Ethel, it is much better than the bazaar—it is no field for vanity."

"Certainly not," said Ethel. "What a mess every one will make! Oh, if I could but stay away, like Harry! There will be Dr. Hoxton being sonorous and prosy, and Mr. Lake will stammer, and that will be nothing to the misery of our own people's work. George will flounder, and look at Flora, and she will sit with her eyes on the ground, and Dr. Spencer will come out of his proper self, and be complimentary to people who deserve it no more!— And Norman! I wish I could run away!"

"Richard says we do not guess how well Norman speaks."

"Richard thinks Norman can do anything he can't do himself! It is all chance—he may do very well, if he gets into his 'funny state', but he always suffers for that, and he will certainly put one into an agony at the outset. I wish Dr. Spencer would have let him alone! And then there will be that Sir Henry, whom I can't abide! Oh, I wish I were more charitable, like Miss Bracy and Mary, who will think all so beautiful!"

"So will you, when you come home," said Margaret.

"If I could only be talking to Cherry, and Dame Hall! I think the school children enter into it very nicely, Margaret. Did I tell you how nicely Ellen Reid answered about the hymn, 'From Greenland's icy mountains'? She did not seem to have made it a mere geographical lesson, like Fanny Grigg—"

Ethel's misanthropy was happily conducted off via the Cocksmoor children, and any lingering remains were dissipated by her amusement at Dr. Spencer's ecstasy on seeing Dr. May assume his red robe of office, to go to the minster in state, with the Town Council. He walked round and round his friend, called him Nicholas Randall redivivus, quoted Dogberry, and affronted Gertrude, who had a dim idea that he was making game of papa.

Ethel was one of those to whom representation was such a penance, that a festival, necessitating hospitality to guests of her own rank, was burden enough seriously to disturb the repose of thankfulness for the attainment of her object, and to render difficult the recueillement which she needed for the praise and prayer that she felt due from her, and which seemed to oppress her heart, by a sense of inadequacy of her partial expression. It was well for her that the day began with the calm service in the minster, where it was her own fault if cares haunted her, and she could confess the sin of her irritated sensations, and wishes to have all her own way, and then, as ever, be led aright into thanksgiving for the unlooked-for crowning of her labours.

The archdeacon's sermon amplified what Margaret had that morning expressed, so as to carry on her sense of appropriateness in the offerings of the day being bestowed on distant lands.

But the ordeal was yet to come, and though blaming herself, she was anything but comfortable, as the world repaired to the Town Hall, the room where the same faces so often met for such diverse purposes—now an orrery displayed by a conceited lecturer, now a ball, now a magistrates' meeting, a concert or a poultry show, where rival Hamburg and Dorking uplifted their voices in the places of Mario and Grisi, all beneath the benignant portrait of Nicholas Randall, ruffed, robed, square-toed, his endowment of the scholarship in his hand, and a chequered pavement at his feet.

Who knows not an S. P. G. meeting? —the gaiety of the serious, and the first public spectacle to the young, who, like Blanche and Aubrey, gaze with admiration at the rows of bonnets, and with awe at the black coats on the platform, while the relations of the said black coats suffer, like Ethel, from nervous dread of the public speaking of their best friends.

Her expectations were realised by the archdeacon's speech, which went round in a circle, as if he could not find his way out of it. Lord Cosham was fluent, but a great many words went to very small substance; and no wonder, thought Ethel, when all they had to propose and second was the obvious fact that missions were very good things.

Dr. Hoxton pompously, Sir Henry Walkinghame creditably, assisted the ladies and gentlemen to resolve that the S. P. G. wanted help; Mr. Lake made a stammering, and Mr. Rivers, with his good-natured face, hearty manner, and good voice, came in well after him with a straightforward, speech, so brief, that Ethel gave Flora credit for the best she had yet heard.

Mr. Wilmot said something which the sharpest ears in the front row might, perhaps, have heard, and which resulted in Dr. Spencer standing up. Ethel hardly would have known who was speaking had her eyes been shut. His voice was so different, when raised and pitched, so as to show its power and sweetness; the fine polish of his manner was redoubled, and every sentence had the most graceful turn. It was like listening to a well-written book, so smooth and so fluent, and yet so earnest—his pictures of Indian life so beautiful, and his strong affection for the converts he described now and then making his eyes fill, and his voice falter, as if losing the thread of his studied composition—a true and dignified work of art, that made Dr. May whisper to Flora, "You see what he can do. They would have given anything to have had him for a lecturer."

With half a sigh, Ethel saw Norman rise, and step forward. He began, with eyes fixed on the ground, and in a low modest tone, to speak of the islands that Harry had visited; but gradually the poetic nature, inherent in him, gained the mastery; and though his language was strikingly simple, in contrast with Dr. Spencer's ornate periods, and free from all trace of "the lamp," it rose in beauty and fervour at every sentence. The feelings that had decided his lot gave energy to his discourse, and repressed as they had been by reserve and diffidence, now flowed forth, and gave earnestness to natural gifts of eloquence of the highest order. After his quiet, unobtrusive beginning, there was the more wonder to find how he seemed to raise up the audience with him, in breathless attention, as to a strain of sweet music, carrying them without thought of the scene, or of the speaker, to the lovely isles, and the inhabitants of noble promise, but withering for lack of knowledge; and finally closing his speech, when they were wrought up to the highest pitch, by an appeal that touched them all home; "for well did he know," said he, "that the universal brotherhood was drawn closest in circles nearer home, that beneath the shadow of their own old minster, gladness and mourning floated alike for all; and that all those who had shared in the welcome to one, given back as it were from the grave, would own the same debt of gratitude to the hospitable islanders."

He ceased. His father wiped his spectacles, and almost audibly murmured, "Bless him!" Ethel, who had sat like one enchanted, forgetting who spoke, forgetting all save the islanders, half turned, and met Richard's smiling eyes, and his whisper, "I told you so."

The impress of a man of true genius and power had been made throughout the whole assembly; the archdeacon put Norman out of countenance by the thanks of the meeting for his admirable speech, and all the world, except the Oxford men, were in a state of as much surprise as pleasure.

"Splendid speaker, Norman May, if he would oftener put himself out," Harvey Anderson commented. "Pity he has so many of the good doctor's prejudices!"

"Well, to be sure!" quoth Mrs. Ledwich. "I knew Mr. Norman was very clever, but I declare I never thought of such as this! I will try my poor utmost for those interesting natives."

"That youth has first-rate talents," said Lord Cosham. "Do you know what he is designed for? I should like to bring him forward."

"Ah!" said Dr. Hoxton. "The year I sent off May and Anderson was the proudest year of my life!"

"Upon my word!" declared Mrs. Elwood. "That Dr. Spencer is as good as a book, but Mr. Norman— I say, father, we will go without the new clock, but we'll send somewhat to they men that built up the church, and has no minister."

"A good move that," said Dr. Spencer. "Worth at least twenty pounds. That boy has the temperament of an orator, if the morbid were but a grain less."

"Oh, Margaret," exclaimed Blanche. "Dr. Spencer made the finest speech you ever heard, only it was rather tiresome; and Norman made everybody cry—and Mary worse than all!"

"There is no speaking of it. One should live such things, not talk over them," said Meta Rivers.

Margaret received the reports of the select few, who visited her upstairs, where she was kept quiet, and only heard the hum of the swarm, whom Dr. May, in vehement hospitality, had brought home to luncheon, to Ethel's great dread, lest there should not be enough for them to eat.

Margaret pitied her sisters, but heard that all was going well; that Flora was taking care of the elders, and Harry and Mary were making the younger fry very merry at the table on the lawn. Dr. May had to start early to see a sick gardener at Drydale before coming on to Cocksmoor, and came up to give his daughter a few minutes.

"We get on famously," he said. "Ethel does well when she is in for it, like Norman. I had no notion what was in the lad. They are perfectly amazed with his speech. It seems hard to give such as he is up to those outlandish places; but there, his speech should have taught me better—one's best—and, now and then, he seems my best."

"One comfort is," said Margaret, smiling, you would miss Ethel more."

"Gallant old King! I am glad she has had her wish. Good-bye, my Margaret, we will think of you. I wish—"

"I am very happy," was Margaret's gentle reassurance. "The dear little Daisy looks just as her godfather imagined her;" and happy was her face when her father quitted her.

Margaret's next visitor was Meta, who came to reclaim her bonnet, and, with a merry smile, to leave word that she was walking on to Cocksmoor. Margaret remonstrated on the heat.

"Let me alone," said she, making her pretty wilful gesture. "Ethel and Mary ought to have a lift, and I have had no walking to-day."

"My dear, you don't know how far it is. You can't go alone."

"I am lying in wait for Miss Bracy, or something innocent," said Meta. "In good time—here comes Tom."

Tom entered, declaring that he had come to escape from the clack downstairs.

"I'll promise not to clack if you will be so kind as to take care of me to Cocksmoor," said Meta.

"Do you intend to walk?"

"If you will let me be your companion."

"I shall be most happy," said Tom, colouring with gratification, such as he might not have felt, had he known that he was chosen for his innocence.

He took a passing glimpse at his neck-tie, screwed up the nap of his glossy hat to the perfection of its central point, armed himself with a knowing little stick, and hurried his fair companion out by the back door, as much afraid of losing the glory of being her sole protector as she was of falling in with an escort of as much consequence, in other eyes, as was Mr. Thomas in his own.

She knew him less than any of the rest, and her first amusement was keeping silence to punish him for complaining of clack; but he explained that he did not mean quiet, sensible conversation—he only referred to those foolish women's raptures over the gabble they had been hearing at the Town Hall.

She exclaimed, whereupon he began to criticise the speakers with a good deal of acuteness, exposing the weak points, but magnanimously owning that it was tolerable for the style of thing, and might go down at Stoneborough.

"I wonder you did not stay away as Harry did."

"I thought it would be marked," observed the thread-paper Tom, as if he had been at least county member.

"You did quite right," said Meta, really thinking so.

"I wished to hear Dr. Spencer, too," said Tom. "There is a man who does know how to speak! He has seen something of the world, and knows what he is talking of."

"But he did not come near Norman."

"I hated listening to Norman," said Tom. "Why should he go and set his heart on those black savages?"

"They are not savages in New Zealand."

"They are all niggers together," said Tom vehemently. "I cannot think why Norman should care for them more than for his own brothers and sisters. All I know is, that if I were my father, I would never give my consent."

"It is lucky you are not," said Meta, smiling defiance, though a tear shone in her eye. "Dr. May makes the sacrifice with a free heart and willing mind."

"Everybody goes and sacrifices somebody else," grumbled Tom.

"Who are the victims now?"

"All of us. What are we to do without Norman? He is worth all of us put together; and I—" Meta was drawn to the boy as she had never been before, as he broke off short, his face full of emotion, that made him remind her of his father.

"You might go out and follow in his steps," said she, as the most consoling hope she could suggest.

"Not I. Don't you know what is to happen to me? Ah! Flora has not told you. I thought she would not think it grand enough. She talked about diplomacy—"

"But what?" asked Meta anxiously.

"Only that I am to stick to the old shop," said Tom. "Don't tell any one; I would not have the fellows know it."

"Do you mean your father's profession?"

"Ay!"

"Oh, Tom! you don't talk of that as if you despised it?"

"If it is good enough for him, it is good enough for me, I suppose," said Tom. "I hate everything when I think of my brothers going over the world, while I, do what I will, must be tied down to this slow place all the rest of my days."

"If you were away, you would be longing after it."

"Yes; but I can't get away."

"Surely, if the notion is so unpleasant to you, Dr. May would never insist?"

"It is my free choice, and that's the worst of it."

"I don't understand."

"Don't you see? Norman told me it would be a great relief to him if I would turn my mind that way—and I can't go against Norman. I found he thought he must if I did not; and, you know, he is fit for all sorts of things that— Besides, he has a squeamishness about him, that makes him turn white, if one does but cut one's finger, and how he would ever go through the hospitals—"

Meta suspected that Tom was inclined to launch into horrors. "So you wanted to spare him," she said.

"Ay! and papa was so pleased by my offering that I can't say a word of the bore it is. If I were to back out, it would come upon Aubrey, and he is weakly, and so young, that he could not help my father for many years."

Meta was much struck at the motives that actuated the self-sacrifice, veiled by the sullen manner which she almost began to respect. "What is done for such reasons must make you happy," she said; "though there may be much that is disagreeable."

"Not the study," said Tom. "The science is famous work. I like what I see of it in my father's books, and there's a splendid skeleton at the hospital that I long to be at. If it were not for Stoneborough, it would be all very well; but, if I should get on ever so well at the examinations, it all ends there! I must come back, and go racing about this miserable circuit, just like your gold pheasant rampaging in his cage, seeing the same stupid people all my days."

"I think," said Meta, in a low, heartfelt voice, "it is a noble, beautiful thing to curb down your ambition for such causes. Tom, I like you for it."

The glance of those beautiful eyes was worth having. Tom coloured a little, but assumed his usual gruffness. "I can't bear sick people," he said.

"It has always seemed to me," said Meta, "that few lives could come up to Dr. May's. Think of going about, always watched for with hope, often bringing gladness and relief; if nothing else, comfort and kindness, his whole business doing good."

"One is paid for it," said Tom.

"Nothing could ever repay Dr. May," said Meta. "Can any one feel the fee anything but a mere form? Besides, think of the numbers and numbers that he takes nothing from; and oh! to how many he has brought the most real good, when they would have shut their doors against it in any other form! Oh, Tom, I think none of you guess how every one feels about your father. I recollect one poor woman saying, after he had attended her brother, 'He could not save his body, but, surely, ma'am, I think he was the saving of his soul.'"

"It is of no use to talk of my being like my father," said Tom.

Meta thought perhaps not, but she was full of admiration of his generosity, and said, "You will make it the same work of love, and charity is the true glory."

Any inroad on Tom's reserved and depressed nature was a benefit; and he was of an age to be susceptible of the sympathy of one so pretty and so engaging. He had never been so much gratified or encouraged, and, wishing to prolong the tete-a-tete, he chose to take the short cut through the fir-plantations, unfrequented on account of the perpendicular, spiked railings that divided it from the lane.

Meta was humming-bird enough to be undismayed. She put hand and foot wherever he desired, flattered him by letting him handily help her up, and bounded light as a feather down on the other side, congratulating herself on the change from the dusty lane to the whispering pine woods, between which wound the dark path, bestrewn with brown slippery needle-leaves, and edged with the delicate feathering ling and tufts of soft grass.

Tom had miscalculated the chances of interruption. Meta was lingering to track the royal highway of some giant ants to their fir-leaf hillock, when they were hailed from behind, and her squire felt ferocious at the sight of Norman and Harry closing the perspective of fir-trunks.

"Hallo! Tom, what a guide you are!" exclaimed Norman. "That fence which even Ethel and Mary avoid!"

"Mary climbs like a cow, and Ethel like a father-long-legs," said Tom. "Now Meta flies like a bird."

"And Tom helped me so cleverly," said Meta. "It was an excellent move, to get into the shade and this delicious pine tree fragrance."

"Halt!" said Norman—"this is too fast for Meta."

"I cannot," said Harry. "I must get there in time to set Dr. Spencer's tackle to rights. He is tolerably knowing about knots, but there is a dodge beyond him. Come on, Tom."

He drew on the reluctant Etonian, who looked repiningly back at the increasing distance between him and the other pair, till a turn in the path cut off his view.

"I am afraid you do not know what you have undertaken," said Norman.

"I am a capital walker. And I know, or do not know, how often Ethel takes the same walk."

"Ethel is no rule."

"She ought to be," said Meta. "To be like her has always been my ambition."

"Circumstances have formed Ethel."

"Circumstances! What an ambiguous word! Either Providence pointing to duty, or the world drawing us from it."

"Stepping-stones, or stumbling-blocks."

"And, oh! the difficult question, when to bend them, or to bend to them!"

"There must be always some guiding," said Norman.

"I believe there is," said Meta, "but when trumpet-peals are ringing around, it is hard to know whether one is really 'waiting beside the tent,' or only dawdling."

"It is great self-denial in the immovable square not to join the charge," said Norman.

"Yes; but they, being shot at, are not deceiving themselves."

"I suppose self-deception on those points is very common."

"Especially among young ladies," said Meta. "I hear so much of what girls would do, if they might, or could, that I long to see them like Ethel—do what they can. And then it strikes me that I am doing the same, living wilfully in indulgence, and putting my trust in my own misgivings and discontent."

"I should have thought that discontent had as little to do with you as with any living creature."

"You don't know how I could growl!" said Meta, laughing. "Though less from having anything to complain of, than from having nothing to complain of."

"You mean," he said, pausing, with a seriousness and hesitation that startled her—"do you mean that this is not the course of life that you would choose?"

A sort of bashfulness made her put her answer playfully—

"All play and no work makes Jack a mere toy.

"Toys have a kindly mission, and I may be good for nothing else; but I would have rather been a coffee-pot than a china shepherdess."

The gaiety disconcerted him, and he seemed to try to be silent, or to reply in the same tone, but he could not help returning to the subject. "Then you find no charm in the refinements to which you have been brought up?"

"Only too much," said Meta.

He was silent, and fearing to have added to his fine-lady impression, she resumed. "I mean that I never could dislike anything, and kindness gives these things a soul; but, of course, I should be better satisfied, if I lived harder, and had work to do."

"Meta!" he exclaimed, "you tempt me very much! Would you? — No, it is too unreasonable. Would you share—share the work that I have undertaken?"

He turned aside and leaned against a tree, as if not daring to watch the effect of the agitated words that had broken from him. She had little imagined whither his last sayings had been tending, and stood still, breathless with the surprise.

"Forgive me," he said hastily. "It was very wrong. I never meant to have vexed you by the betrayal of my vain affection."

He seemed to be going, and this roused her. "Stay, Norman," exclaimed she. "Why should it vex me? I should like it very much indeed."

He faced suddenly towards her— "Meta, Meta! is it possible? Do you know what you are saying?"

"I think I do."

"You must understand me," said Norman, striving to speak calmly. "You have been—words will not express what you have been to me for years past, but I thought you too far beyond my hopes. I knew I ought to be removed from you—I believed that those who are debarred from earthly happiness are marked for especial tasks. I never intended you to know what actuated me, and now the work is undertaken, and— and I cannot turn back," he added quickly, as if fearing himself.

"No indeed," was her steady reply.

"Then I may believe it!" cried Norman. "You do—you will—you deliberately choose to share it with me?"

"I will try not to be a weight on you," answered the young girl, with a sweet mixture of resolution and humility. "It would be the greatest possible privilege. I really do not think I am a fine lady ingrain, and you will teach me not to be too unworthy."

"I? Oh, Meta, you know not what I am! Yet with you, with you to inspire, to strengthen, to cheer—Meta, Meta, life is so much changed before me, that I cannot understand it yet—after the long dreary hopelessness—"

"I can't think why—" Meta had half said, when feminine dignity checked the words, consciousness and confusion suddenly assailed her, dyed her cheeks crimson, and stifled her voice.

It was the same with Norman, and bashfulness making a sudden prey of both—on they went under its dominion, in a condition partaking equally of discomfort and felicity; dreading the sound of their own voices, afraid of each other's faces, feeling they were treating each other very strangely and ungratefully, yet without an idea what to say next, or the power of speaking first; and therefore pacing onwards, looking gravely straight along the path, as if to prevent the rabbits and foxgloves from guessing that anything had been passing between them.

Dr. May had made his call at Drydale, and was driving up a rough lane, between furzy banks, leading to Cocksmoor, when he was aware of a tall gentleman on one side of the road and a little lady on the other, with the whole space of the cart-track between them, advancing soberly towards him.

"Hallo! Why, Meta! Norman! what brings you here? Where are you going?"

Norman perceived that he had turned to the left instead of to the right, and was covered with shame.

"That is all your wits are good for. It is well I met you, or you would have led poor Meta a pretty dance! You will know better than to trust yourself to the mercies of a scholar another time. Let me give you a lift."

The courteous doctor sprang out to hand Meta in, but something made him suddenly desire Adams to drive on, and then turning round to the two young people, he said, "Oh!"

"Yes," said Norman, taking her hand, and drawing her towards him.

"What, Meta, my pretty one, is it really so? Is he to be happy after all? Are you to be a Daisy of my own?"

"If you will let me," murmured Meta, clinging to her kind old friend.

"No flower on earth could come so naturally to us," said Dr. May. "And, dear child, at last I may venture to tell you that you have a sanction that you will value more than mine. Yes, my dear, on the last day of your dear father's life, when some foreboding hung upon him, he spoke to me of your prospects, and singled out this very Norman as such as he would prefer."

Meta's tears prevented all, save the two little words, "thank you;" but she put out her hand to Norman, as she still rested on the doctor's arm, more as if he had been her mother than Norman's father.

"Did he?" from Norman, was equally inexpressive of the almost incredulous gratitude and tenderness of his feeling.

It would not bear talking over at that moment, and Dr. May presently broke the silence in a playful tone. "So, Meta, good men don't like heiresses?"

"Quite true," said Meta, "it was very much against me."

"Or it may be the other way," said Norman.

"Eh? Good men don't like heiresses—here's a man who likes an heiress—therefore here's a man that is not good? Ah, ha! Meta, you can see that is false logic, though I've forgotten mine. And pray, miss, what are we to say to your uncle?"

"He cannot help it," said Meta quickly.

"Ha!" said the doctor, laughing, "we remember our twenty-one years, do we?"

"I did not mean—I hope I said nothing wrong," said Meta, in blushing distress. "Only after what you said, I can care for nothing else."

"If I could only thank him," said Norman fervently.

"I believe you know how to do that, my boy," said Dr. May, looking tenderly at the fairy figure between them, and ending with a sigh, remembering, perhaps, the sense of protection with which he had felt another Margaret lean on his arm.

The clatter of horses' hoofs caused Meta to withdraw her hand, and Norman to retreat to his own side of the lane, as Sir Henry Walkinghame and his servant overtook them.

"We will be in good time for the proceedings," called out the doctor. "Tell them we are coming."

"I did not know you were walking," said Sir Henry to Meta.

"It is pleasant in the plantations," Dr. May answered for her; "but I am afraid we are late, and our punctual friends will be in despair. Will you kindly say we are at hand?"

Sir Henry rode on, finding that he was not to be allowed to walk his horse with them, and that Miss Rivers had never looked up.

"Poor Sir Henry!" said Dr. May.

"He has no right to be surprised," said Meta, very low.

"And so you were marching right upon Drydale!" continued Dr. May, not able to help laughing. "It was a happy dispensation that I met you."

"Oh, I am so glad of it!" said Meta.

"Though to be sure you were disarming suspicion by so cautiously keeping the road between you. I should never have guessed what you had been at."

There was a little pause, then Meta said, rather tremulously, "Please—I think it should be known at once."

"Our idle deeds confessed without loss of time, miss?"

Norman came across the path, saying, "Meta is right—it should be known."

"I don't think Uncle Cosham would object, especially hearing it while he is here," said Meta— "and if he knew what you told us."

"He goes to-morrow, does he not?" said Dr. May.

A silence of perplexity ensued. Meta, brave as she was, hardly knew her uncle enough to volunteer, and Norman was privately devising a beginning by the way of George, when Dr. May said, "Well, since it is not a case for putting Ethel in the forefront, I must e'en get it over for you, I suppose."

"Oh, thank you," they cried both at once, feeling that he was the proper person in every way, and Norman added, "The sooner the better, if Meta—"

"Oh, yes, yes, the sooner the better," exclaimed Meta. "And let me tell Flora—poor dear Flora—she is always so kind."

A testimony that was welcome to Dr. May, who had once, at least, been under the impression that Flora courted Sir Henry's attentions to her sister-in-law.

Further consultation was hindered by Tom and Blanche bursting upon them from the common, both echoing Norman's former reproach of "A pretty guide!" and while Blanche explained the sufferings of all the assembly at their tardiness, Tom, without knowing it, elucidated what had been a mystery to the doctor, namely, how they ever met, by his indignation at Norman's having assumed the guidance for which he was so unfit.

"A shocking leader; Meta will never trust him again," said Dr. May.

Still Blanche thought them not nearly sufficiently sensible of their enormities, and preached eagerly about their danger of losing standing-room, when they emerged on the moor, and beheld a crowd, above whose heads rose the apex of a triangle, formed by three poles, sustaining a rope and huge stone.

"Here comes Dr. Spencer," she said. "I hope he will scold you."

Whatever Dr. Spencer might have suffered, he was far too polite to scold, and a glance between the two physicians ended in a merry twinkle of his bright eyes.

"This way," he said; "we are all ready."

"But where's my little Daisy?" said Dr. May.

"You'll see her in a minute. She is as good as gold."

He drew them on up the bank—people making way for them—till he had stationed them among the others of their own party, beside the deep trench that traced the foundation, around a space that seemed far too small.

Nearly at the same moment began the soft clear sound of chanting wafted upon the wind, then dying away—carried off by some eddying breeze, then clear, and coming nearer and nearer.

> I will not suffer mine eyes to sleep,
>> Nor mine eye-lids to slumber:

Neither the temples of my head to take any rest;
Until I find out a place for the temple of the Lord:
An habitation for the mighty God of Jacob.

Few, who knew the history of Cocksmoor, could help glancing towards the slight girl, who stood, with bent head, her hand clasped over little Aubrey's; while, all that was not prayer and thanksgiving in her mind, was applying the words to him, whose head rested in the Pacific isle, while, in the place which he had chosen, was laid the foundation of the temple that he had given unto the Lord.

There came forth the procession: the minster choristers, Dr. Spencer as architect, and, in her white dress, little Gertrude, led between Harry and Hector, Margaret's special choice for the occasion, and followed by the Stoneborough clergy.

Let thy priests be clothed with righteousness.

It came in well with the gentle, meek, steadfast face of the young curate of Cocksmoor, as he moved on in his white robe, and the sunlight shone upon his fair hair, and calm brow, thankful for the past, and hoping, more than fearing, for the future.

The prayers were said, and there was a pause, while Dr. Spencer and the foreman advanced to the machine and adjusted it. The two youths then led forward the little girl, her innocent face and large blue eyes wearing a look of childish obedient solemnity, only half understanding what she did, yet knowing it was something great.

It was very pretty to see her in the midst of the little gathering round the foundation, the sturdy workman smiling over his hod of mortar, Dr. Spencer's silver locks touching her flaxen curls as he held the shining trowel to her, and Harry's bright head and hardy face, as he knelt on one knee to guide the little soft hand, while Hector stood by, still and upright, his eyes fixed far away, as if his thoughts were roaming to the real founder.

The Victoria coins were placed—Gertrude scooped up the mass of mortar, and spread it about with increasing satisfaction, as it went so smoothly and easily, prolonging the operation, till Harry drew her back, while, slowly down creaked the ponderous corner-stone into the bed that she had prepared for it, and, with a good will, she gave three taps on it with her trowel.

Harry had taken her hand, when, at the sight of Dr. May, she broke from him, and, as if taking sudden fright at her own unwonted part, ran, at full speed, straight up to her father, and clung to him, hiding her face as he raised her in his arms and kissed her.

Meanwhile the strain arose:

> Thou heavenly, new Jerusalem,
> Vision of peace, in Prophet's dream;
> With living stones, built up on high,
> And rising to the starry sky —

The blessing of peace seemed to linger softly and gently in the fragrant summer breeze, and there was a pause ere the sounds of voices awoke again.

"Etheldred—" Mr. Wilmot stood beside her, ere going to unrobe in the school— "Etheldred, you must once let me say, God bless you for this."

As she knelt beside her sister's sofa, on her return home, Margaret pressed something into her hand. "If you please, dearest, give this to Dr. Spencer, and ask him to let it be set round the stem of the chalice," she whispered.

Ethel recognised Alan Ernescliffe's pearl hoop, the betrothal ring, and looked at her sister without a word.

"I wish it," said Margaret gently. "I shall like best to know it there."

So Margaret joined in Alan's offering, and Ethel dared say no more, as she thought how the "relic of a frail love lost" was becoming the "token of endless love begun." There was more true union in this, than in clinging to the mere tangible emblem—for broken and weak is all affection that is not knit together above in the One Infinite Love.

CHAPTER XXIII.

Of lowly fields you think no scorn,
Yet gayest gardens would adorn,
    And grace wherever set;
Home, seated in your lowly bower,
Or wedded, a transplanted flower,
    I bless you, Margaret.—CHARLES LAMB.

George Rivers had an antipathy to ladies' last words keeping the horses standing, and his wife and sister dutifully seated themselves in the carriage at once, without an attempt to linger.

Four of the young gentlemen were to walk across to Abbotstoke and dine at the Grange; and Tom, who, reasoning from analogy, had sent on his black tie and agate studs, was so dismally disconcerted on finding that Norman treated his own going as a matter of course, that Richard, whose chief use of his right of primogeniture was to set himself aside, discovered that he was wanted at home, and that Tom would be much better at the Grange, offering, at the same time, to send Norman's dressing things by Dr. Spencer.

"Which," observed Thomas, "he would never have recollected for himself."

"Tom would have had to lend him the precious studs."—"He would not have had them; who would wear imitation?" "I say, Tom, what did you give for them?" "Better ask what the Jew gave for them, that bought them at Windsor Fair; not a bad imitation, either—pity they weren't Malachite; but, no doubt, the Jew thought green would be personal." "As if they had any business to talk, who didn't know a respectable stud when they saw it—Harry, especially, with his hat set on the back of his head, like a sailor on the stage"—(a leap to set it to rights—a skirmish, knocking Tom nearly into the ditch). "Fine experience of the stage—all came from Windsor Fair." "Ay, Hector might talk, but didn't he pay a shilling to see the Irish giant. He wouldn't confess, but it was a famous take in—giant had potatoes in his shoes." "Not he; he was seven feet ten high." "Ay, when he stood upon a stool—Hector would swallow anything—even the lady of a million postage stamps had not stuck in his throat—he had made Margaret collect for her." "And, had not Tom, himself, got a bottle of ointment to get the red out of his hair?"—(great fury). "His hair wasn't red—didn't want to change the colour—not half so red as Hector's own." "What was it then? lively auburn?" But for fear of Norman's losing his bearings, Harry would fetch a carrot, to compare. "Better colour than theirs could ever be." "Then what was the ointment for? to produce whiskers? that was the reason Tom oiled himself like a Loyalty islander—his hair was so shiny, that Harry recommended a top-knot, like theirs, etc."

Norman was, like the others, in such towering glee, and took so full a share of the witticisms, that were the more noisily applauded, the worse they were, that Harry suggested that "old June had lost his way, and found his spirits in Drydale—he must have met with a private grog-shop in the plantations—would not Tom confess"— "not he; it was all in private. He thought it was laughing-gas, or the reaction of being fried all the morning, holding forth in that Town Hall. He had longed to make a speech himself—no end of the good it would have done the old stagers to come out with something to the purpose. What would old Hoxton have thought of it?

They shall dive for alligators, catch the wild goats by the beard;
Whistle to the cockatoos, and mock the hairy-faced baboon;
Worship mighty Mumbo Jumbo in the mountains of the moon.
I myself, in far Timbuctoo, leopard's blood shall daily quaff;
Ride a tiger hunting, mounted on a thoroughbred giraffe.

"Not you, Tom!" cried Hector.

You, the swell, the Eton fellow! You, to seek such horrid places.
You to haunt with squalid negroes, blubber lips, and monkey faces. Fool, again the dream, the fancy; don't I know the words are mad, For you count the gray barbarian lower than the Brocas cad!

"Nay, it is the consequence of misanthropy at the detection of the frauds of unsophisticated society," said Norman.

The edge of life is rusted;

The agate studs and whisker ointment left him very much disgusted.

"Perhaps it was Miss Rivers forsaking him. Was not that rather spider-hearted, Tom?"

"Come, Harry, it is time to have done. We are getting into civilised society—here's Abbotstoke."

"Poor Norman, he is very far gone! He takes that scarecrow for civilised society!"

"Much better clothed than the society you have been accustomed to, July." "What a prize his wardrobe would be to the Black Prince!" "Don't insult your betters!" "Which? The scarecrow, or the Black Prince?"

Norman tried to call his companions to order, for they were close upon the village, and he began to tax himself with unbecoming levity; the effect of spirits pitched rather low, which did not easily find their balance, under unwonted exhilaration, but Harry's antics were less easily repressed than excited, and if Tom had not heard the Grange clock strike half-past six, and had not been afraid of not having time to array himself, and watch over Harry's neckcloth, they would hardly have arrived in reasonable time. Dr. May had gone home, and there was no one in the drawing-room; but, as Norman was following the boys upstairs, Flora opened her sitting-room door, and attracted his attention by silently putting her cold fingers into his hand, and drawing him into the room.

"Dear Norman, this is pleasant," she said affectionately; but in a voice so sunken, that all gladness seemed to be dead within, and the effect was far more mournful than if she had not attempted to smile congratulation.

"I will give you till Dr. Spencer comes," she said. "Then Norman can dress, and you must be a good child, and come down to me."

The playfulness ill suited the wan, worn face that seemed to have caught a gray tint from her rich poplin, her full toilet making the contrast almost more painful; and, as she closed the door, her brother could only exclaim, "Poor Flora!"

"She is so kind," said the voice of the white figure that moved towards him. "Oh, if we could comfort her!"

"I trust to her own kindness working comfort to her, at last," said Norman. "But is she often thus?"

"Whenever she is not bearing up for George's sake," said Meta. "She never says anything when she is alone with me, only she does not struggle with her looks."

"It must be very trying for you."

"Nay, I feel grateful to her for even so far relaxing the restraint.

If I could but do her any good."

"You cannot help doing her good," said Norman.

Meta sighed, and shook her head slightly, as she said, "She is so gentle and considerate. I think this has been no fresh pain to her to-day, but I cannot tell. The whole day has been a strange intermixture."

"The two strands of joy and grief have been very closely twisted," said Norman. "That rose is shedding its fragrant leaves in its glory, and there is much that should have chastened the overflowing gladness of to-day."

"As I was thinking," whispered Meta, venturing nearer to him, and looking into his face with the sweet reliance of union in thought.

She meant him to proceed, but he paused, saying, "You were thinking-"

"I had rather hear it from you."

"Was it not that we were taught to-day what is enduring, and gives true permanence and blessedness to such—to what there was between Ernescliffe and Margaret?"

Her dewy eyes, and face of deep emotion, owned that he had interpreted her thought.

"Theirs would, indeed, be a disheartening example," he said, "if it did not show the strength and peace that distance, sickness, death, cannot destroy."

"Yes. To see that church making Margaret happy as she lies smiling on her couch, is a lesson of lessons."

"That what is hallowed must be blest," said Norman; "whatever the sundry and manifold changes."

Each was far too humble to deny aloud any inequality with the goodness of Alan and Margaret, knowing that it would be at once disputed, trusting to time to prevent the over-estimate, and each believing the other was the one to bring the blessing.

"But, Meta," said Norman, "have you heard nothing of—of the elders?"

"Oh, yes," said Meta, smiling, "have not you?"

"I have seen no one."

"I have!" said Meta merrily. "Uncle Cosham is delighted. That speech of yours has captivated him. He calls me a wise little woman to have found out your first-rate abilities. There's for you, sir."

"I don't understand it! Surely he must be aware of my intentions?"

"He said nothing about them; but, of course, Dr. May must have mentioned them."

"I should have thought so, but I cannot suppose—"

"That he would be willing to let me go," said Meta. "But then you know he cannot help it," added she, with a roguish look, at finding herself making one of her saucy independent speeches.

"I believe you are taking a would-be missionary instead of Norman May!" he answered, with a sort of teasing sweetness.

"All would-be missionaries did not make dear papa so fond of them," said Meta, very low; "and you would not be Norman May without such purposes."

"The purpose was not inspired at first by the highest motive," said Norman; "but it brought me peace, and, after the kind of dedication that I inwardly made of myself in my time of trouble, it would take some weighty reason, amounting to a clear duty, or physical impossibility, to make me think I ought to turn back. I believe"— the tears rose to his eyes, and he brought out the words with difficulty —

"that, if this greatest of all joys were likely to hinder me from my calling, I ought to seek strength to regard it as a temptation, and to forgo it."

"You ought, if it were so," said Meta, nevertheless holding him tighter. "I could not bear to keep back a soldier. If this were last year, and I had any tie or duty here, it would be very hard. But no one needs me, and if the health I have always had be continued to me, I don't think I shall be much in the way. There," —drawing back a little, and trying to laugh off her feeling—"only tell me at once if you think me still too much of a fine lady."

"I—you—a fine lady! Did anything ever give you the impression that I did?"

"I shall not get poor Harry into a scrape, shall I? He told me that you said so, last spring, and I feared you judged me too truly."

After a few exclamations of utter surprise, it flashed on Norman. "I know, I know—Harry interpreted my words in his own blunt fashion!"

"Then you did say something like it?"

"No, but—but— In short, Meta, these sailors' imaginations go to great lengths. Harry had guessed more than I knew myself, before he had sailed, and taxed me with it. It was a subject I could not bear then, and I answered that you were too far beyond my hopes."

"Six years ago!" said Meta slowly, blushing deeper and deeper. "Some eyes saw it all that time, and you—and," she added, laughing, though rather tearfully, "I should never have known it, if Tom had not taken me through the plantations!"

"Not if I had not discovered that your preferences did not lie—"

"Among boudoirs and balls?" said Meta. "Harry was right. You thought me a fine lady after all."

The gay taunt was cut short by a tap at the door, and Flora looked in.

"Dr. Spencer has brought your things, Norman. I am sorry to disturb you—but come down, Meta—I ran away very uncivilly to fetch you.

I hope it is not too cruel," as she drew Meta's arm into her own, and added, "I have not been able speak to George."

Meta suspected that, in the wish to spare her, Flora had abstained from seeking him.

The evening went off like any other evening—people ate and talked, thought Mrs. Rivers looking very ill, and Miss Rivers very pretty—

Flora forced herself into being very friendly to Sir Henry, commiserating the disappointment to which she had led him; and she hoped that he suspected the state of affairs, though Tom, no longer supplanted by his elder brother, pursued Meta into the sheltered nook, where Flora had favoured her seclusion, to apologise for having left her to the guidance of poor Norman, whose head was with the blackamoors. It was all Harry's fault.

"Nonsense, Tom," said Harry; "don't you think Norman is better company than you any day?"

"Then why did you not walk him off instead of me?" said Tom, turning round sharply.

"Out of consideration for Meta. She will tell you that she was very much obliged to me—"

Harry checked himself, for Meta was colouring so painfully that his own sunburned face caught the glow. He pushed Tom's slight figure aside with a commanding move of his broad hand, and said, "I beg your pardon, upon my word, though I don't know what for."

"Nor I," said Meta, rallying herself, and smiling. "You have no pardon to beg. You will know it all to-morrow."

"Then I know it now," said Harry, sheltering his face by leaning over the back of a chair, and taming the hearty gaiety of his voice. "Well done, Meta; there's nothing like old June in all the world! You may take my word for it, and I knew you would have the sense to find it out."

They were well out of sight, and Meta only answered by a good tight squeeze of his kind hand between both her own. Tom, suddenly recovering from his displeasure at being thrust aside, whisked round, dropped on a footstool before Meta, locked up in her face, and said, "Hallo!" in such utter amazement that there was nothing for it but to laugh more uncontrollably than was convenient. "Come along, Tom," said Harry, pulling him up by force, "she does not want any of your nonsense. We will not plague her now."

"Thank you, Harry," said Meta. "I cannot talk rationally just yet.

Don't think me unkind, Tom."

Tom sat in a sort of trance all the rest of the evening.

Lord Cosham talked to Norman, who felt as if he were being patronised on false pretences, drew into his shell, and displayed none of his "first-rate abilities."

Dr. Spencer discussed his architecture with the archdeacon; but his black eyes roamed heedfully after the young gentleman and lady, in the opposite corners of the room; and, as he drove home afterwards with the youths, he hummed scraps of Scottish songs, and indulged in silent smiles.

Those at home had been far more demonstrative. Dr. May had arrived, declaring himself the proudest doctor in her Majesty's dominions, and Ethel needed nothing but his face to explain why, and tell her that dear old June's troubles were over, and their pretty little Meta was their own—a joy little looked for to attend their foundation-stone.

The dreaded conference with Lord Cosham had proved highly gratifying. There might be something in the fact that he could not help it, which assisted in his ready acquiescence, but he was also a sensible right-minded man, who thought that the largeness of Meta's fortune was no reason that it should be doubled; considered that, in the matter of connection, the May family had the advantage, and saw in Norman; a young man whom any one might have pleasure in bringing forward. Oxford had established confidence both in his character and talents, and his speech had been such as to impress an experienced man, like Lord Cosham, with an opinion of his powers, that prepared a welcome for him, such as no one could have dared to expect. His lordship thought his niece not only likely to be happier, but to occupy a more distinguished position with such a man as

Norman May, than with most persons of ready-made rank and fortune.

The blushing and delighted Dr. May had thought himself bound to speak of his son's designs, but he allowed that the project had been formed under great distress of mind, and when he saw it treated by so good a man, as a mere form of disappointed love, he felt himself reprieved from the hardest sacrifice that he had ever been called on to make, loved little Meta the better for restoring his son, and once more gave a free course to the aspirations that Norman's brilliant boyhood had inspired. Richard took the same view, and the evening passed away in an argument—as if any one had been disputing with them—the father reasoning loud, the son enforcing it low, that it had become Norman's duty to stay at home to take care of Meta, whose father would have been horrified at his taking her to the Antipodes. They saw mighty tasks for her fortune to effect in England, they enhanced each other's anticipations of Norman's career, overthrew abuses before him, heaped distinctions upon him, and had made him Prime Minister and settled his policy, before ten o'clock brought their schemes to a close.

Mary gazed and believed; Margaret lay still and gently assented;

Ethel was silent at first, and only when the fabric became extremely airy and magnificent, put in her word with a vehement dash at the present abuses, which grieved her spirit above all, and, whether vulnerable or not, Norman was to dispose of, like so many giants before Mr. Great-heart.

She went upstairs, unable to analyse her sentiments. To be spared the separation would be infinite relief—all this prosperity made her exult—the fair girl at the Grange was the delight of her heart, and yet there was a sense of falling off; she disliked herself for being either glad or sorry, and could have quarrelled with the lovers for perplexing her feelings so uncomfortably.

Though she sat up till the party returned, she was inclined to be supposed in bed, so as to put off the moment of meeting; but Margaret, who she hoped was asleep, said from her pillow, "Ask dear Norman to let me give him one kiss."

She ran down headlong, clutched Norman as he was taking off his greatcoat, told him that Margaret wanted him, and dragged him up without letting him go, till she reached the first landing, where she stood still, saying breathlessly, "New Zealand."

"If I wished to fail, she would keep me to it."

"I beg your pardon," said Ethel, claiming heartily his caress. "I was wrong to doubt either of you. Now, I know how to feel! But Margaret must not wait."

The happy youth, in the flush of love and joy, bent gently, almost tearfully, down in silence to the white form, half seen in the twilight, whose hopes had fleeted away from earth, and who was calmly, softly gliding after them. Hardly a word was uttered, but of all the many heartfelt thoughts that had passed while the face was pressed into Margaret's pillow, and her sympathising arms round the neck, surely none was ever deeper, than was his prayer and vow that his affection should be like hers, unearthly, and therefore enduring.

The embrace was all; Margaret must not be agitated, and, indeed, the events of the day had been too much for her, and the ensuing morning brought the fluttering of heart and prostration of strength, no longer a novelty and occasion of immediate terror, but the token of the waning power of life.

Till she was better, her father had no thoughts for aught else, but, as with many another invalid, the relief from present distress was as cheering as if it had been recovery, and ere night, her placid look of repose had returned, and she was devising pretty greetings for her newest Daisy.

Perhaps the sobering effect of these hours of anxiety was in Norman's favour, on entering into conversation with his father. Those visions, which had had their swing the night before, belonged to the earlier, more untamed period of Dr. May's life, and had melted away in the dim room, made sacred by lingering mementos of his wife, and in the sound of that panting breath and throbbing heart. His vehemence had been, after all, chiefly against his own misgivings, and when he heard of his son's resolution, and Meta's more than acquiescence, he was greatly touched, and recurred to his kind, sorrowful promise, that he would never be a stumbling-block in the path of his children. Still he owned himself greatly allured by the career proposed by Lord Cosham, and thought Norman should consider the opportunities of doing good in, perhaps, a still more important and extensive field than that which he had chosen.

"Time was that I should have grasped at such a prospect," said Norman; "but I am not the man for it. I have too much ambition, and too little humility. You know, father, how often you have had to come to my rescue, when I was running after success as my prime object."

"Vanity fair is a dangerous place, but you who have sound principles and pure motives—"

"How long would my motives be pure?" said Norman. "Rivalry and party-spirit make me distrust my motives, and then my principles feel the shock. Other men are marked by station for such trials, and may be carried through them, but I am not."

"Yet some of these men are far from your equals."

"Not perhaps in speechifying," said Norman, smiling; "but in steadiness of aim, in patience, in callousness, in seeing one side of the question at once."

"You judge rightly for your own peace; you will be the happier; I always doubted whether you had nerve to make your wits available."

"It may be cowardice," said Norman, "but I think not. I could burn for the combat; and if I had no scruples, I could enjoy bearing down such as—"

Of course Dr. May burst in with a political name, and—"I wish you were at him!"

"Whether I could is another matter," said Norman, laughing; "but the fact is, that I stand pledged; and if I embraced what to me would be a worldly career, I should be running into temptation, and could not expect to be shielded from it."

"Your old rule," said Dr. May. "Seek to be less rather than more.

But there is another choice. Why not a parsonage at home?"

"Pleasant parishes are not in the same need," said Norman.

"I wonder what poor old Rivers would say to you, if he knew what you want to do with his daughter! Brought up as she has been — to expose her to the roughness of a colonial life, such as I should hesitate about for your sisters."

"It is her own ardent desire."

"True, but are girlish enthusiasms to be trusted? Take care, Norman, take care of her — she is a bit of the choicest porcelain of human kind, and not to be rudely dealt with."

"No, indeed, but she has the brave enterprising temper, to which I fully believe that actual work, in a good cause, is far preferable to what she calls idleness. I do not believe that we are likely to meet with more hardship than she would gladly encounter, and would almost — nay, quite enjoy."

"You do not know what your aunt has had to go through."

"A few years make a great difference in a colony. Still, it may be right for me to go out alone and judge for her; but we shall know more if my aunt comes home."

"Yes, I could trust a good deal to her. She has much of your mother's sense. Well, you must settle it as you can with Meta's people! I do not think they love the pretty creature better than I have done from the first minute we saw her — don't you remember it, Norman?"

"Remember it? Do I not? From the frosted cedar downwards! It was the first gem of spring in that dreary winter. What a Fairyland the Grange was to me!"

"You may nearly say the same of me," confessed Dr. May, smiling; "the sight of that happy little sunny spirit, full of sympathy and sweetness, always sent me brighter on my way. Wherever you may be, Norman, I am glad you have her, being one apt to need a pocket sunbeam."

"I hope my tendencies are in no danger of depressing her!" said Norman, startled. "If so—"

359

"No such thing—she will make a different man of you. You have been depressed by—that early shock, and the gap at our own fireside—all that we have shared together, Norman. To see you begin on a new score, with a bright home of your own, is the best in this world that I could wish for you, though I shall live over my own twenty-two years in thinking of you, and that sweet little fairy. But now go, Norman—she will be watching for you and news of Margaret. Give her all sorts of love from me."

Norman fared better with the uncle than he had expected. Lord Cosham, as a philanthropist, could not, with any consistency, set his face against missions, even when the cost came so near home; and he knew that opposition made the like intentions assume a heroic aspect that maintained them in greater force. He therefore went over the subject in a calm dispassionate manner, which exacted full and grateful consideration from the young man.

The final compromise was, that nothing should be settled for a year, during which Norman would complete his course of study, and the matter might be more fully weighed. Mrs. Arnott would probably return, and bring experience and judgment, which would, or ought to, decide the question—though Meta had a secret fear that it might render it more complicated than ever. However, the engagement and the mission views had both been treated so much more favourably than could have been hoped, that they felt themselves bound to be patient and forbearing. As Meta said, "If they showed themselves wilful children, they certainly did not deserve to be trusted anywhere."

Lord Cosham made his niece listen to a kind exhortation not to press her influence towards a decision that might be repented, when too late to be repaired, without a degrading sense of failure—putting her in mind of the privations that would lose romance by their pettiness, and which money could not remedy; and very sensibly representing that the effect of these on temper and health was to be duly considered as a serious impediment to usefulness.

"It would be worse for him alone," said Meta.

"That is not certain," said her uncle. "A broken-down wife is a terrible drag."

"I know it is so," said Meta firmly, "but risks must be run, and he is willing to take the chance. I do not think it can be presumption, for, you know, I am strong; and Dr. May would say if he could not warrant me. I fancy household work would be more satisfactory and less tiring than doing a season thoroughly, and I mean to go through a course of Finchley manuals in preparation."

"I hope you know what you are doing," sighed her uncle. "You see it all couleur de rose."

"I think not. It is because it is not couleur de rose that I am so much bent upon it. I have had plenty of that all my life. I expect much that will be very disagreeable and not at all heroic; but if I can only make Norman think it fun, that will be one purpose answered. I do believe he will do his work better for having me, and, at least, I shall pay his passage."

Her uncle shook his head, but did not try to say any more. George had begun by loud exclamations against the project, in which he was vehemently abetted by Tom, who primed him with all sorts of outrageous abuse of the niggers and cannibals, who would make Norman's coats out of all shape, and devour little Meta at a mouthful—predictions which Meta accepted most merrily, talking of herself so resignedly, as bound upon a spit, and calling out to be roasted slower and faster, that she safely conducted off their opposition by way of a standing joke. As to Norman's coats, she threatened to make them herself, and silenced Tom for ever by supposing, in malicious simplicity, that he must be able to teach her the most unexceptional cut.

Flora kept her opinions to herself. Only once, when urged to remonstrate, she said, "I could not—I would not."

She was gently and touchingly considerate towards the lovers, silently but unobtrusively obviating all that could jar on their feelings, and employing her exquisite tact in the kindest manner.

She released Meta from the expedition to Ryde, silencing scruples on the one hand, by a suggestion of "poor Sir Henry," and, on the other, by offering to exchange her for Mary. The first proposal made Mary take such a spring in her chair, with eyes so round, and cheeks so red, and such a shriek about Harry and the Bucephalus, that no one could have borne to say one word in opposition, even if it had not been the opinion of the Council that sea air would best repair Mary's strength.

Ethel had some private fears of a scene, since it was one of Miss Bracy's idiosyncrasies to be hurt whenever Mary was taken out of her hands; and she went to announce the design, in dread lest this shock should destroy the harmony that had prevailed for many months; nay, she almost believed, since the loss of the Alcestis had been known.

She was agreeably surprised. Miss Bracy thought Mary in need of the change, and discussed both her and Blanche in so pleasant and sensible a manner, that Ethel was quite relieved. She partook in Mary's anticipations of pleasure, forwarded her preparations, and was delighted with her promise of letters—promises that Mary bestowed so largely, in the fullness of her heart, that there were fears lest her whole time should be spent in writing.

Her soft heart indulged in a shower of tears when she wished them all good-bye; and Ethel and Blanche found the house was very empty without her; but that was only till Meta came in from a walk with Norman, and, under the plea of trying to supply Mary's place, did the work of five Maries, and a great deal besides.

Nothing could be happier than Meta's visit, brightening the house so that the Mays thought they had never known half her charms, helping whatever was going on, yet ready to play with Daisy, tell stories to Aubrey, hear Tom's confidences, talk to Margaret, read with Norman, and teach Richard singing for his school children. The only vexation was, that every one could not always engross her entirely; and Dr. May used to threaten that they should never spare her to that long-legged fellow, Norman.

She had persuaded Bellairs to go and take care of Flora and Mary, instead of the French maid—a plan which greatly satisfied Margaret, who had never liked the looks of Coralie, and which Meta held to be a grand emancipation. She persuaded old nurse to teach her to be useful, and Margaret used to declare that she witnessed scenes as good as a play in her room, where the little dexterous scholar, apparently in jest, but really in sober, earnest, wiled instruction from the old woman; and made her experiments, between smiles and blushes, and merrily glorying in results that promised that she would be a notable housewife. Whether it were novelty or not, she certainly had an aptitude and delight in domestic details, such as Ethel never could attain; and, as Dr. May said, the one performed by a little finger what the other laboured at with a great mind.

In the schoolroom, Meta was as highly appreciated. She found an hour for helping Blanche in her music, and for giving, what was still more useful, an interest and spirit to studies, where, it must be owned, poor good Mary had been a dead weight. She enlivened Miss Bracy so much, and so often contrived a walk or a talk with her, that the saucy Blanche told Hector that she thought Ethel would be quite second-fiddle with Miss Bracy.

No such thing. Miss Bracy's great delight was in having a listener for her enthusiasm about Miss Ethel. She had been lately having a correspondence with a former school-fellow, who was governess in a family less considerate than the Mays, and who poured out, in her letters, feelings much like those with which Miss Bracy had begun.

Nothing could be more salutary than to find herself repeating all Ethel's pieces of advice; and, one day, when her friend had been more distressed than usual, she called Ethel herself, to consult on her answer, owning how much she was reminded of herself.

"Indeed," she added, "I am afraid it would only tease you to hear how much I am indebted to your decision and kindness —"

"Nay," said Ethel, laughing her awkward laugh. "You have often had to forget my savage ways."

"Pray don't say that —"

"I think," said Ethel, breaking in, "the philosophy is this: I elieve that it is a trying life. I know teaching takes a great deal out of one; and loneliness may cause tendencies to dwell on fancied slights in trifles, that might otherwise be hurried over. But I think the thing is, to pass them over, and make a conscience of turning one's mind to something fresh —"

"As you made me do, when you brought me amusing books, and taught me botany —"

"And, still more, when you took to working for the infant school. Yes, I think the way to be happy and useful is to get up many interests, so as to be fresh and vigorous, and think not at all of personalities. There's a truism!"

"Very true, though," said Miss Bracy. "Indeed, all your kindness and consideration would never have done me half the good they have, dear Miss Ethel, if you had not taught me that referring all to one's own feelings and self is the way to be unhappy."

"Just so," said Ethel. "It is the surest way for any one to be miserable."

"If I could only persuade poor dear Ellen to think that even if a slight were real, it ought to be borne forgivingly, and not brooded over. Ah! you are laughing; perhaps you have said the same about me."

"You would forgive it now, I think," said Ethel.

"I never thought I did not forgive. I did not see that brooding over vexations was not pardoning them. I have told her so now; and, oh! if she could but have seen how true sorrows are borne here, she would be cured, like me, of making imaginary ones."

"None could help being better for living with papa," said Ethel.

Ethel made Miss Bracy happy by a kiss before she left her. It was a cheering belief that, whatever the future trials of her life might be, the gentle little lady would meet them with a healthier mind, more vigorous in overlooking troubles and without punctilious sensitiveness on the lookout for affronts. "Believing all things, bearing all things, hoping all things, enduring all things," would be to her the true secret of serenity of spirits.

Ethel might not have been blameless or consistent in her dealings in this difficult intercourse, but her kind heart, upright intention, and force of character, had influence far beyond her own perception. Indeed, she knew not that she had personal influence at all, but went on in her own straightforward humility.

CHAPTER XXIV.

"Enough of foresight sad, too much
    Of retrospect have I;
And well for me, that I, sometimes,
    Can put those feelings by.

There speaks the man we knew of yore,
    Well pleased, I hear them say;
Such was he, in his lighter moods,
    Before our heads were gray.

Buoyant he was in spirit, quick
    Of fancy, light of heart;
And care, and time, and change have left
    Untouch'd his better part." —SOUTHEY.

Etheldred May and Meta Rivers were together in the drawing-room. The timepiece pointed towards ten o'clock, but the tea-things were on the table, prepared for a meal, the lamp shone with a sort of consciousness, and Ethel moved restlessly about, sometimes settling her tea equipage, sometimes putting away a stray book, or resorting by turns to her book, or to work a red and gold scroll on coarse canvas, on the other end of which Meta was employed.

"Nervous, Ethel?" said Meta, looking up with a merry provoking smile, knowing how much the word would displease.

"That is for you," retorted Ethel, preferring to carry the war into the enemy's quarters. "What, don't you know that prudent people say that your fate depends on her report?"

"At least," said Meta, laughing; "she is a living instance that every one is not eaten up, and we shall see if she fulfils Tom's prediction of being tattooed, or of having a slice out of the fattest part of her cheek."

"I know very well," said Ethel, "the worst she said it would be, the more you would go."

"Not quite that," said Meta, blushing, and looking down.

"Come, don't be deceitful!" said Ethel. "You know very well that you are still more bent on it than you were last year."

"To be sure I am!" said Meta, looking up with a sudden beamy flash of her dark eyes. "Norman and I know each other so much better now," she added, rather falteringly.

"Ay! I know you are ready to go through thick and thin, and that is why I give my consent and approbation. You are not to be stopped for nonsense."

"Not for nonsense, certainly," said Meta, "but"—and her voice became tremulous—"if Dr. May deliberately said it would be wrong, and that I should be an encumbrance and perplexity, I am making up my mind to the chance."

"But what would you do?" asked Ethel.

"I don't know. You should not ask such questions, Ethel."

"Well! it won't happen, so it is no use to talk about it," said Ethel. "Fancy my having made you cry."

"Very silly of me," said Meta, brightening and laughing, but sighing. "I am only afraid Mrs. Arnott may think me individually unfit for the kind of life, as if I could not do what other women can. Do I look so?"

"You look as if you were meant to be put under a glass case!" said Ethel, surveying the little elegant figure, whose great characteristic was a look of exquisite finish, not only in the features and colouring, the turn of the head, and the shape of the small rosy-tipped fingers, but in everything she wore, from the braids of black silk hair, to the little shoe on her foot, and even in the very lightness and gaiety of her movements.

"Oh, Ethel!" cried Meta, springing up in dismay, and looking at herself in the glass. "What is the matter with me? Do tell me!"

"You'll never get rid of it," said Ethel, "unless you get yourself tattooed! Even separation from Bellairs hasn't answered. And, after all, I don't think it would be any satisfaction to Norman or papa. I assure you, Meta, whatever you may think of it, it is not so much bother to be prettier than needful, as it is to be uglier than needful."

"What is needful?" said Meta, much amused.

"I suppose to be like Mary, so that nobody should take notice of one, but that one's own people may have the satisfaction of saying, 'she is pleasing,' or 'she is in good looks.' I think Gertrude will come to that. That's one comfort."

"That is your own case, Ethel. I have heard those very things said of you."

"Of my hatchet face!" said Ethel contemptuously. "Some one must have been desperately bent on flattering the Member's family."

"I could repeat more," said Meta, "if I were to go back to the Commemoration, and to the day you went home."

Ethel crimsoned, and made a sign with her hand, exclaiming, "Hark!"

"It went past."

"It was the omnibus. She must be walking down!" Ethel breathed short, and wandered aimlessly about; Meta put her arm round her waist.

"I did not think this would be so much to you," she said.

"Oh, Meta, it seems like dear mamma coming to see how we have been going on. And then papa! I wish I had gone up to the station with him."

"He has Richard."

"Ay, but I am afraid Margaret is listening and will be restless, and have a palpitation; and I can't go and see, or I shall disturb her. Oh, I wish it were over."

Meta stroked her, and soothed her, and assured her that all would do well, and presently they heard the click of the door. Ethel flew into the hall, where she stopped short, her heart beating high at the sound of overpoweringly familiar accents.

She was almost relieved by detecting otherwise little resemblance; the height was nearly the same, but there was not the plump softness of outline. Mrs. Arnott was small, thin, brisk and active, with a vivacious countenance, once evidently very fair and pretty, but aged and worn by toil, not trouble, for the furrows were the traces of smiles around her merry mouth, and beautiful blue eyes, that had a tendency lo laugh and cry both at once. Dr. May who had led her into the light, seemed to be looking her all over, while Richard was taking the wraps from her, and Ethel tried to encourage herself to go forward.

"Ay!" said the doctor, kissing her. "I see you, Flora, now. I have found you again."

"I found you as soon as I heard your voice, Richard," said she. "And now for the bairnies."

"Here is one, but there is but a poor show forthcoming to-night. Do you know her?"

There was an unspeakable joy in being pressed in Aunt Flora's arms, like a returning beam from the sunshine of seven years ago.

"This must be Ethel! My dear, how you tower above me—you that I left in arms! And," as she advanced into the drawing-room—"why, surely this is not Margaret!"

"A Margaret—not the Margaret. I wish I were," said Meta, as Mrs. Arnott stood with an arm on her shoulder, in the midst of an embrace, Dr. May enjoying her perplexity and Meta's blushes. "See, Flora, these black locks never belonged to Calton Hill daisies, yet a daisy of my own she is. Can't you guess?"

"Miss Rivers!" exclaimed Mrs. Arnott; and though she kissed her cordially, Meta suspected a little doubt and disappointment.

"Yes," said Dr. May. "We change Mary for this little woman as Flora's lady-in-waiting, when she and her husband go out yachting and shooling."

"Flora and her husband! There's a marvellous sound! Where are they?"

"They are staying at Eccleswood Castle," said Ethel; "and Mary with them. They would have been at home to receive you, but your note yesterday took us all by surprise. Norman is away too, at a college meeting."

"And Margaret—my Margaret! Does not she come downstairs?"

"Ah! poor dear," said Dr. May, "she has not been in this room since that sultry day in July."

"The eighteenth," said Richard; the precision of the date marking but too well the consciousness that it was an epoch.

"We can keep her quieter upstairs," said Dr. May; "but you must not see her to-night. She will enjoy you very much to-morrow; but excitement at night always does her harm, so we put her to bed, and told her to think about no one."

Mrs. Arnott looked at him as if longing, but dreading, to ask further, and allowed her nephew and niece to seat her at the table, and attend to her wants, before she spoke again. "Then the babies."

"We don't keep babies, Gertrude would tell you," said Dr. May. "There are three great creatures, whom Ethel barbarously ordered off to bed. Ethel is master here, you must know, Flora—we all mind what she says."

"Oh, papa," pleaded Ethel, distressed, "you know it was because I thought numbers might be oppressive."

"I never dispute," said Dr. May. "We bow to a beneficial despotism, and never rebel, do we, Meta?"

Seeing that Ethel took the imputation to heart, Meta rejoined, "You are making Mrs. Arnott think her the strong-minded woman of the family, who winds up the clock and cuts the bread."

"No; that she makes you do, when the boys are away."

"Of course," said Ethel, "I can't be vituperated about hunches of bread. I have quite enough to bear on the score of tea."

"Your tea is very good," said Richard.

"See how they propitiate her," maliciously observed the doctor.

"Not at all; it is Richard standing up for his pupil," said Ethel. "It is all very well now, with people who know the capacities of mortal tea; but the boys expect it to last from seven o'clock to ten, through an unlimited number of cups, till I have announced that a teapot must be carved on my tombstone, with an epitaph, 'Died of unreasonable requirements.'"

Mrs. Arnott looked from one to the other, amused, observant, and perceiving that they were all under that form of shyness which brings up family wit to hide embarrassment or emotion.

"Is Harry one of these unreasonable boys?" she asked. "My dear Harry—I presume Ethel has not sent him to bed. Is there any hope of my seeing him?"

"Great hope," said Dr. May. "He has been in the Baltic fleet, a pretty little summer trip, from which we expect him to return any day. My old Lion! I am glad you had him for a little while, Flora.

"Dear fellow! his only fault was being homesick, and making me catch the infection."

"I am glad you did not put off your coming," said Dr. May gravely.

"You are in time for the consecration," said Richard.

"Ah! Cocksmoor! When will it take place?"

"On St. Andrew's Day. It is St. Andrew's Church, and the bishop fixed the day, otherwise it is a disappointment that Hector cannot be present."

"Hector?"

"Hector Ernescliffe—poor Alan's brother, whom we don't well know from ourselves."

"And you are curate, Ritchie?" said his aunt—"if I may still call you so. You are not a bit altered from the mouse you used to be."

"Church mouse to Cocksmoor," said Dr. May, "nearly as poor. We are to invest his patrimony in a parsonage as soon as our architect in ordinary can find time for it. Spencer—you remember him?"

"I remember how you and he used to be inseparable! And he has settled down, at last, by your side?"

"The two old doctors hope to bolster each other up till Mr. Tom comes down with modern science in full force. That boy will do great things—he has as clear a head as I ever knew."

"And more—" said Ethel.

"Ay, as sound a heart. I must find you his tutor's letter, Flora. They have had a row in his tutor's house at Eton, and our boys made a gallant stand for the right, Tom especially, guarding the little fellows in a way that does one good to hear of."

"'I must express my strong sense of gratitude for his truth, uprightness, and moral courage,'" quoted Meta.

"Ah, ha! you have learned it by heart! I know you copied it out for Norman, who has the best right to rejoice."

"You have a set of children to be proud of, Richard!" exclaimed Mrs. Arnott.

"To be surprised at—to be thankful for," said Dr. May, almost inarticulately.

To see her father so happy with Mrs. Arnott necessarily drew Ethel's heart towards her; and, when they had bidden him goodnight, the aunt instantly assumed a caressing confidence towards Ethel, particularly comfortable to one consciously backward and awkward, and making her feel as intimate as if the whole space of her rational life had not elapsed since their last meeting.

"Must you go, my dear?" said her aunt, detaining her over her fire.

"I can't tell how to spare you. I want to hear of your dear father. He looks aged and thin, Ethel, and yet that sweet expression is the same as ever. Is he very anxious about poor Margaret?"

"Not exactly anxious," said Ethel mournfully—"there is not much room for that."

"My dear Ethel—you don't mean?—I thought—"

"I suppose we ought to have written more fully," said Ethel; "but it has been very gradual, and we never say it to ourselves. She is as bright, and happy, and comfortable as ever, in general, and, perhaps, may be so for a long time yet, but each attack weakens her."

"What kind of attack?"

"Faintness-sinking. It is suspended action of the heart. The injury to the spine deranged the system, and then the long suspense, and the shock— It is not one thing more than another, but it must go on. Dr. Spencer will tell you. You won't ask papa too much about it?"

"No, indeed. And he bears it—"

"He bears everything. Strength comes up out of his great lovingness. But, oh! I sometimes long that he may never have any more sorrows."

"My poor child!" said Mrs. Arnott, putting her arm round her niece's waist.

Ethel rested her head on her shoulder. "Aunt Flora! Aunt Flora! If any words could tell what Margaret has been ever since we were left. Oh, don't make me talk or think of ourselves without her. It is wrong to wish. And when you see her, that dear face of hers will make you happy in the present. Then," added Ethel, not able to leave off with such a subject, "you have our Norman to see."

"Ah! Norman's project is too delightful to us; but I fear what it may be to your father."

"He gives dear Norman, as his most precious gift, the flower and pride of us all."

"But, Ethel, I am quite frightened at Miss Rivers's looks. Is it possible that—"

"Aunt Flora," broke in Ethel, "don't say a word against it. The choicest goods wear the best; and whatever woman can do, Meta Rivers can. Norman is a great tall fellow, as clever as possible, but perfectly feckless. If you had him there alone, he would be a bee without a queen."

"Well, but—"

"Listen," continued Ethel. "Meta is a concentration of spirit and energy, delights in practical matters, is twice the housewife I am, and does all like an accomplishment. Between them, they will make a noble missionary—"

"But she looks—"

"Hush," continued the niece. "You will think me domineering; but please don't give any judgment without seeing; for they look to you as an arbitrator, and casual words will weigh."

"Thank you, Ethel; perhaps you are right. When does he think of coming out?"

"When he is ordained—some time next year."

"Does she live with you?"

"I suppose she lives with Flora; but we always manage to get her when Norman is at home."

"You have told me nothing of Flora or Mary."

"I have little real to tell. Good old Mary! I dare say Harry talked to you plentifully of her. She is a—a nice old darling," said Ethel fondly. "We want her again very much, and did not quite bargain for the succession of smart visits that she has been paying."

"With Flora?"

"Yes. Unluckily George Rivers has taken an aversion to the Grange, and I have not seen Flora this whole year."

Ethel stopped short, and said that she must not keep Margaret expecting her. Perhaps her aunt guessed that she had touched the true chord of anxiety.

The morning brought a cheering account of Margaret; and Mrs. Arnott was to see her directly after breakfast. In the meantime, the firm limbs, blue eyes, and rosy face of Gertrude seemed a fair representation of the little bride's-maid, whom she remembered.

A very different niece did she find upstairs, though the smiling, overflowing eyes, and the fond, eager look of recognition, as if asking to be taken to her bosom, had in them all the familiarity of old tenderness. "Auntie! dear auntie! that you should have come back to me again!"

Mrs. Arnott fondly caressed her, but could not speak at first, for even her conversation with Ethel had not prepared her for so wasted and broken an appearance. Dr. May spoke briskly of Margaret's having behaved very well and slept like a good child, told Margaret where he had to go that morning, and pointed out to Mrs. Arnott some relics of herself still remaining; but the nervous tremulousness of manner did not much comfort her, although Margaret answered cheerfully. Nothing was so effectual in composing the aunt as Aubrey's coming headlong in to announce the gig, and to explain to Margaret his last design for a cathedral—drawing plans being just now his favourite sport.

"Architecture is all our rage at present," said Margaret, as her father hurried away.

"I am so glad to have come in time for the consecration!" said Mrs. Arnott, following her niece's lead. "Is that a model of the church?"

"Oh, yes!" cried Margaret, lighting up. "Richard made it for me."

"May I show it to Aunt Flora?" said Aubrey.

"Bring it here, if you can lift it," said Margaret; and, Aunt Flora helping, the great cumbersome thing was placed beside her, whilst she smiled and welcomed it like a child, and began an eager exhibition. Was it not a beautiful little pierced spire?—that was an extravagance of Dr. Spencer's own. Papa said he could not ask Captain Gordon to sanction it—the model did it no justice, but it was so very beautiful in the rich creamy stone rising up on the moor, and the blue sky looking through, and it caught the sunset lights so beautifully. So animated was her description, that Mrs. Arnott could not help asking, "Why, my dear, when have you seen it?"

"Never," said Margaret, with her sweet smile. "I have never seen Cocksmoor; but Dr. Spencer and Meta are always sketching it for me, and Ethel would not let an effect pass without telling me. I shall hear how it strikes you next."

"I hope to see it by and by. What a comfortable deep porch! If we could build such churches in the colonies, Margaret!"

"See what little Meta will do for you! Yes, we had the porch deep for a shelter—that is copied from the west door of the minster, and is it not a fine high-pitched roof? John Taylor, who is to be clerk, could not understand its being open; he said, when he saw the timbers, that a man and his family might live up among them. They are noble oak beams; we would not have any sham—here, Aubrey, take off the roof, and auntie will see the shape."

"Like the ribs of a ship," explained Aubrey, unconscious that the meaning was deeper than his sister could express, and he continued:

"Such fine oak beams! I rode with Dr. Spencer one day last year to choose them. It is a two-aisled church, you see, that a third may be added."

Ethel came up as Aubrey began to absorb the conversation. "Lessons, Aubrey," she said. "So, Margaret, you are over your dear model?"

"Not forestalling you too much I hope, Ethel dear," said Margaret; "as you will show her the church itself."

"You have the best right," said Ethel; "but come, Aubrey, we must not dawdle."

"I will show you the stones I laid myself, Aunt Flora," said Aubrey, running off without much reluctance.

"Ethel has him in excellent order," said Mrs. Arnott.

"That she has; she brings him on beautifully, and makes him enjoy it. She teaches him arithmetic in some wonderful scientific way that nobody can understand but Norman, and he not the details; but he says it is all coming right, and will make him a capital mathematical scholar, though he cannot add up pounds, shillings, and pence."

"I expected to be struck with Ethel," said Mrs. Arnott; "and —"

"Well," said Margaret, waiting.

"Yes, she does exceed my expectations. There is something curiously winning in that quaint, quick, decisive manner of hers. There is so much soul in the least thing she does, as if she could not be indifferent for a moment."

"Exactly—exactly so," said Margaret, delighted. "It is really doing everything with all her might. Little, simple, everyday matters did not come naturally to her as to other people, and the having had to make them duties has taught her to do them with that earnest manner, as if there were a right and a wrong to her in each little mechanical household office."

"Harry described her to me thus," said Mrs. Arnott, smiling: "'As to Ethel, she is an odd fish; but Cocksmoor will make a woman of her after all.'"

"Quite true!" cried Margaret. "I should not have thought Harry had so much discernment in those days. Cocksmoor gave the stimulus, and made Ethel what she is. Look there—over the mantelpiece, are the designs for the painted glass, all gifts, except the east window. That one of St. Andrew introducing the lad with the loaves and fishes is Ethel's window. It is the produce of the hoard she began this time seven years, when she had but one sovereign in the world. She kept steadily on with it, spending nothing on herself that she could avoid, always intending it for the church, and it was just enough to pay for this window."

"Most suitable," said Mrs. Arnott.

"Yes; Mr. Wilmot and I persuaded her into it; but I do not think she would have allowed it, if she had seen the application we made of it—the gift of her girlhood blessed and extended. Dear King Etheldred, it is the only time I ever cheated her."

"This is a beautiful east window. And this little one—St. Margaret I see."

"Ah! papa would not be denied choosing that for his subject. We reproached him with legendary saints, and overwhelmed him with antiquarianism, to show that the Margaret of the dragon was not the Margaret of the daisy; but he would have it; and said we might thank him for not setting his heart on St. Etheldreda."

"This one?"

"That is mine," said Margaret, very low; and her aunt abstained from remark, though unable to look, without tears, at the ship of the Apostles, the calming of the storm, and the scroll, with the verse:

"He bringeth them unto the haven where they would be."

Beneath were the initials, "A. H. E.," and the date of the year, the only memorials of the founder.

Margaret next drew attention to St. Andrew with his cross—Meta's gift. "And, besides," she said, "George Rivers made us a beautiful present, which Meta hunted up. Old Mr. Rivers, knowing no better, once bought all the beautiful carved fittings of a chapel in France, meaning to fit up a library with them; but, happily, he never did, and a happy notion came into Meta's head, so she found them out, and Dr. Spencer has adapted them, and set them all to rights; and they are most exquisite. You never saw such foliage."

Thus Margaret proceeded with the description of everything in the church, and all the little adventures of the building, as if she could not turn away from the subject; and her aunt listened and wondered, and, when called away, that Margaret might rest before nurse came to dress her, she expressed her wonder to Meta.

"Yes," was the answer; "it is her chief occupation and interest. I do not mean that she has not always her own dear full sympathy for every one's concerns, but Cocksmoor is her concern, almost more than even Ethel's. I think she could chronicle every stage in the building better than Dr. Spencer himself, and it is her daily delight to hear his histories of his progress. And not only with the church but the people; she knows all about every family; Richard and Ethel tell her all their news; she talks over the school with the mistress every

Sunday, and you cannot think what a feeling there is for her at Cocksmoor. A kind message from Miss May has an effect that the active workers cannot always produce."

Mrs. Arnott saw that Meta was right, when, in the afternoon, she walked with her nieces to see Cocksmoor. It was not a desolate sight as in old times, for the fair edifice, rising on the slope, gave an air of protection to the cottages, which seemed now to have a centre of unity, instead of lying forlorn and scattered. Nor were they as wretched in themselves, for the impulse of civilisation had caused windows to be mended and railings to be tidied, and Richard promoted, to the utmost, cottage gardening, so that, though there was an air of poverty, there was no longer an appearance of reckless destitution and hopeless neglect.

In the cottages, Mrs. Taylor had not entirely ceased to speak with a piteous voice, even though she told of the well-doing of her girls at service; but Granny Hall's merry content had in it something now of principle, and Sam had married a young Fordholm wife, who promised to be a pattern for Cocksmoor. Every one asked after Miss May, with a tenderness and affection that Mrs. Arnott well appreciated; and when they went into the large fresh school, where Richard was hearing a class, Cherry Elwood looked quite cheered and enlivened by hearing that she had been able to enjoy seeing her aunt. Mrs. Arnott was set to enlighten the children about the little brown girls whom she was wont to teach, and came away with a more brilliant impression of their intelligence than she might have had, if she had not come to them fresh from the Antipodes.

She had to tell Margaret all her impressions on her return, and very pretty smiles repaid her commendations. She understood better the constant dwelling on the subject, as she perceived how little capable Margaret was of any employment. The book, the writing materials, and work-basket were indeed placed by her side, but very seldom did the feeble fingers engage in any of the occupations once so familiar—now and then a pencilled note would be sent to Flora, or to Hector Ernescliffe, or a few stitches be set in her work, or a page or two turned of a book, but she was far more often perfectly still, living, assuredly in no ordinary sphere of human life, but never otherwise than cheerful, and open to the various tidings and interests which, as Ethel had formerly said, shifted before her like scenes in a magic lantern, and, perhaps, with less of substance than in those earlier days, when her work among them was not yet done, and she was not, as it were, set aside from them. They were now little more than shadows reflected from the world whence she was passing.

Yet her home was not sad. When Dr. Spencer came in the evening, and old Edinburgh stories were discussed, Dr. May talked with spirit, and laughed with the merry note that Mrs. Amott so well remembered, and Meta Rivers chimed in with her gay, saucy repartees, nor, though Richard was always silent, and Ethel's brow seemed to bear a weight of thought, did it seem as if their spirits were depressed; while there was certainly no restraint on the glee of Blanche, Aubrey, and Gertrude, who were running into Margaret's room, and making as much noise there as they chose.

Mrs. Arnott was at home with the whole family from the first, and in every one's confidence; but what she enjoyed above all was, the sitting in Margaret's room in the morning, when there was no danger of interruption, the three children being all safe captives to their lessons, and Meta, in Richard's workshop, illuminating texts on zinc scrolls for the church.

Margaret came out more in these interviews. It had been a kind of shyness that made her talk so exclusively of the church at the first meeting; she had now felt her way, and knew again—and realised—the same kind aunt with whom she had parted in her childhood, and now far dearer, since she herself was better able to appreciate her, and with a certain resemblance to her mother, that was unspeakably precious and soothing to one deprived, as Margaret had been, at the commencement of her illness and anxiety.

She could hardly see her aunt come near her, without thanking her for having come home, and saying how every time she awoke it was with the sense that something was comfortable, then remembering it was Aunt Flora's being in the house. She seemed to have a feeling, as if telling everything to her aunt were like rendering up her account to her mother, and, at different times, she related the whole, looking back on the various decisions she had had to make or to influence, and reviewing her own judgments, though often with self-blame, not with acuteness of distress, but rather with a humble trust in the Infinite Mercy that would atone for all shortcomings and infirmities, truly sorrowed for.

On the whole it was a peaceful and grateful retrospect; the brothers all doing so well in their several ways, and such a comfort to their father. Tom, concerning whom she had made the greatest mistake, might be looked upon as rescued by Norman. Aubrey, Margaret said, smiling, was Ethel's child, and had long been off her mind; Hector, to her quite a brother, would miss her almost more than her own brothers, but good honest fellow, he had a home here; and, whispered Margaret, smiling and glowing a little, "don't tell any one, for it is a secret of secrets. Hector told me one evening that, if he could be very steady, he hoped he might yet have Blanche at Maplewood. Poor little White Mayflower, it won't be for want of liking on her part, and she so blushes and watches when Hector comes near, that I sometimes think that he might have said something like it to her."

Mrs. Arnott gave no opinion on the plan for Norman and Meta; but Margaret, however, took all for granted, and expressed warm hopes for their sakes, that they would go out with Mrs. Arnott; then, when the suggestion seemed to astonish her aunt, who thought they were waiting for his ordination, she said, "The fact is, that he would like to be ordained where he is to work; but I believe they do not like to say anything about the wedding because of me. Now, of all persons, I must chiefly rejoice in what may help to teach in those islands. I cannot bear to be a hindrance. Whatever happens, Aunt Flora, will you take care that they know this?"

As to her father, Margaret was at rest. He had much more calmness than when he was more new to grief, and could bear far more patiently and hopefully than at first. He lived more on his affections above, and much as he loved those below, he did not rest in them as once, and could better afford to have been removed. "Besides," said Margaret serenely, "it has been good for him to have been gradually weaned from depending on me, so that it is Ethel who is really necessary to him."

For herself, Margaret was perfectly content and happy. She knew the temptation of her character had been to be the ruler and manager of everything, and she saw it had been well for her to have been thus assigned the part of Mary rather than of Martha. She remembered with thankful joy the engagement with Alan Ernescliffe, and though she still wore tokens of mourning for him, it was with a kind of pleasure in them. There had been so little promise of happiness from the first, that there was far more peace in thinking of him as sinking into rest in Harry's arms, than as returning to grieve over her decline; and that last gift of his, the church, had afforded her continual delight, and above all other earthly pursuits, smoothed away the languor and weariness of disease, as she slowly sank to join him. Now that her aunt had come to bring back a sunbeam of her childhood, Margaret declared that she had no more grief or care, except one, and that a very deep and sad one—namely poor Flora.

Mrs. Arnott had at first been inclined to fear that her goddaughter was neglecting her own family, since she had not been at home this whole year, but the slightest betrayal of this suspicion roused Margaret to an eager defence. She had not a doubt that Flora would gladly have been with her, but she believed that she was not acting by her own choice, or more truly, that her husband was so devoted to her, that she felt the more bound to follow his slightest wishes, however contrary to her own. The season had been spent in the same whirl that had, last year, been almost beyond human power, even when stimulated by enjoyment and success; and now, when her spirits were lowered, and her health weakened, Meta had watched and trembled for her, though never able to obtain an avowal that it was an overstrain, and while treated most affectionately, never admitted within her barrier of reserve.

"If I could see poor Flora comforted, or if even she would only let me enter into her troubles," Margaret said, sighing, "I should be content."

The consecration day came near, and the travellers began to return. Meta was in a state of restlessness, which in her was very pretty, under the disguise of a great desire to be useful. She fluttered about the house, visited Margaret, played with Gertrude, set the drawing-room ornaments to rights—a task which Ethel was very glad to depute to her, and made a great many expeditions into the garden to put together autumn nosegays for the vases—finally discovering that Ethel's potichomanie vases on the staircase window must have some red and brown leaves.

She did not come back quite so soon with them, and Mrs. Arnott, slyly looking out of window, reported, "Ha! he is come then! At least, I see the little thing has found—"

"Something extremely unlike itself," said Dr. May, laughing. "Something I could easily set down as a student at Edinburgh; thirty years ago. That's the very smile! I remember dear Maggie being more angry than I ever saw her before, because Mr. Fleet said that you smiled to show your white teeth."

"That is the best shadow of Maggie I ever saw," said Dr. May. "She has taught the lad to smile. That is what I call a pretty sight!"

"Come, Richard, it is a shame for old folks like us to stand spying them!"

"They care very little for me," said Dr. May, "but I shall have them in. Cold winds blowing about that little head! Ah! here they are. Fine leaves you gather, miss! Very red and brown."

Meta rather liked, than otherwise, those pretty teasings of Dr. May, but they always made Norman colour extremely, and he parried them by announcing news. "No, not the Bucephalus, a marriage in high life, a relation."

"Not poor Mary!" cried Ethel.

"Mary! what could make you think of her?"

"As a hen thinks of her ducklings when they go into waters beyond her ken," said Ethel. "Well, as long as it is not Mary, I don't care!"

"High life!" repeated Meta. "Oh, it can be only Agatha Langdale."

"There's only Lord Cosham further to guess," said Ethel.

"Eh! why not young Ogilvie?" said Dr. May. "I am right, I see.

Well, who is the lady?"

"A Miss Dunbar—a nice girl that I met at Glenbracken. Her property fits in with theirs, and I believe his father has been wishing it for a long time."

"It does not sound too romantic," said Meta.

"He writes as if he had the sense of having been extremely dutiful," said Norman.

"No doubt thinking it needful in addressing a namesake, who has had an eye to the main chance," said the doctor. "Don't throw stones, young people."

"Well!" exclaimed Meta; "he did not look as if he would go and do such a stupid thing as that!"

"Probably, it is anything but a stupid thing," said Dr. May.

"You are using him very ill among you," said Norman eagerly. "I believe her to be excellent in every way; he has known her from childhood; he writes as if he were perfectly contented, and saw every chance of happiness."

"None the less for having followed his father's wishes —I am glad he did," said Ethel, coming to her brother's side.

"I dare say you are right," was Meta's answer; "but I am disappointed in him. He always promised to come and stay with you, and made such friends at Oxford, and he never came."

"I fancy there was a good deal to hinder him," said Norman; and, as Mrs. Arnott proceeded to inquiries after the Ogilvies in general, the master of Glenbracken was allowed to drop.

Meta, however, renewed the subject when walking to the minster that evening with Norman.

"You may defend Mr. Ogilvie, Norman, but it is not what I should have expected from him. Why did he make promises, and then neglect his relations?"

"I believe that conscientiously he did not dare to come," said Norman. "I know that he was greatly struck with Ethel at the time of the Commemoration, and therefore I could never again press him to come here."

"Oh, Norman, you hard-hearted monster! What a bad conductor!"

"I do not wish to be a conductor," said Norman. "If you had seen Glenbracken and the old people, you would perceive that it would not have been suitable on our part to promote anything of the kind."

"Would they have been so violent?"

"Not violent, but it would have been a severe struggle. They are good, kind people, but with strong prejudices; and, though I have no doubt they would have yielded to steady attachment on their son's part, and such conduct as Ethel's would have been, I could not lead in that direction."

"Is that pride, Norman?"

"I hope not."

"It is doing by others as you were doing by yourself," half whispered Meta; "but, after all, if he had no constancy, Ethel had an escape."

"I was afraid that she had been rather touched, but I am glad to find myself mistaken."

"If you thought so, how could you make such a public announcement?"

He laughed. "I had made myself so nervous as to the effect, that, in desperation, I took her own way, and came out at once with it as unconsciously as I could."

"Very naturally you acted unconsciousness! It was better than insulting her by seeming to condole. Not that I do, though, for she deserves more steadiness than he has shown! If a man could appreciate her at all, I should have thought that it would have been once and for ever."

"Remember, he had barely known her a fortnight, and probably had no reason to believe that he had made any impression on her. He knew how such an attachment would grieve his parents, and, surely, he was acting dutifully, and with self-denial and consideration, in not putting himself in the way of being further attracted."

"Umph! You make a good defence, Norman, but I cannot forgive him for marrying somebody else, who cannot be Ethel's equal."

"She is a good little girl; he will form her, and be very happy; perhaps more so than with a great soul and strong nature like Ethel's."

"Only he is a canny Scot, and not a Dr. Spencer!"

"Too short acquaintance! besides, there were the parents. Moreover, what would become of home without Ethel?"

"The unanswerable argument to make one contented," said Meta. And, certainly, to be wife to a Member of Parliament is not so very delightful that one would covet it for her."

"Any more than she does for herself."

Norman was right in his view of his friend's motives, as well as of Ethel's present feelings. If there had ever been any disappointment about Norman Ogilvie, it had long since faded away. She had never given away the depths of her heart, though the upper surface had been stirred. All had long subsided, and she could think freely of him as an agreeable cousin, in whose brilliant public career she should always be interested, without either a wish to partake it, or a sense of injury or neglect. She had her vocation, in her father, Margaret, the children, home, and Cocksmoor; her mind and affections were occupied, and she never thought of wishing herself elsewhere.

The new church and the expected return of her sisters engrossed many more of her thoughts than did anything relating to Glenbracken.

She could not bear to talk of Flora, though almost as uneasy as was Margaret; and not able to lay aside misgivings, lest even her good simple Mary might have had her head turned by gaiety.

Mr. and Mrs. Rivers arrived on the Saturday before the Tuesday fixed for the consecration, and stopped on their way, that they might see Margaret, deposit Mary, and resume Meta.

It was a short visit, and all that Ethel could discover was, that Flora was looking very ill, no longer able to conceal the worn and fagged expression of her countenance, and evidently dreadfully shocked by the sight of the havoc made by disease on Margaret's frame. Yet she talked with composure of indifferent subjects—the yacht, the visits, the Bucephalus, the church, and the arrangements for St. Andrew's Day. She owned herself overworked, and in need of rest, and, as she was not well enough to venture on being present at the consecration, she undertook to spend the day with Margaret, thus setting the others at liberty. This settled, she took her leave, for the journey had fatigued her greatly.

During the short visit, Mary had moved and spoken so quietly, and looked so well-dressed and young-lady-like, that, in spite of her comfortable plump cheeks, Ethel felt quite afraid!

But the instant the carriage had driven off, there was a skipping, a hugging, a screaming, "Oh, it is so nice to be at home again!" —and Ethel knew she had her own Mary. It was only a much better looking and more mannerly Mary, in the full bloom of seventeen, open and honest-faced, her profuse light hair prettily disposed, her hands and arms more civilised, and her powers of conversation and self-possession developed. Mary-like were her caresses of Gertrude, Mary-like her inquiries for Cocksmoor, Mary-like her insisting on bringing her boxes into Margaret's room, her exulting exhibition of all the pretty things that Flora and George had given to her, and the still more joyous bestowal of presents upon everybody.

Her tastes were not a whit altered, nor her simplicity diminished. If she was pleased by joining a large dinner-party, her satisfaction was in the amusement of seeing well-dressed people, and a grand table; her knowledge of the world only reached to pronouncing everything unlike home, "so funny;" she had relished most freshly and innocently every pleasure that she could understand, she had learned every variety of fancy work to teach Blanche and Miss Bracy, had been the delight of every schoolroom and nursery, had struck up numberless eternal friendships, and correspondences with girls younger and shyer than herself, and her chief vexations seemed to have been first, that Flora insisted on her being called Miss May, secondly, that all her delights could not be shared by every one at home, and thirdly, that poor Flora could not bear to look at little children.

Grievous complaints were preferred by the dwellers in the attics the next morning, that Mary and Blanche had talked to an unmentionable hour of the night; but, on the whole, Blanche was rather doubtful whether Mary had made the most of her opportunities of observation.

CHAPTER XXV.

Behold, with pearls they glittering stand,
Thy peaceful gates to all expand,
By grace and strength divinely shed,
Each mortal thither may be led;
Who, kindled by Christ's love, will dare
All earthly sufferings now to bear.

By many a salutary stroke,
By many a weary blow, that broke,
Or polished, with a workman's skill,
The stones that form that glorious pile;
They all are fitly framed to lie
In their appointed place on high.

—Ancient Hymn for the Dedication of a Church.

The thirtieth of November dawned with the grave brightness of an autumn day, as the sun slowly mounted from the golden east, drinking up the mists that rose tardily, leaving the grass thickly bedewed.

The bells of Stoneborough Minster were ringing gladsome peals, and the sunshine had newly touched the lime trees, whose last bright yellow leaves were gently floating down, as the carriage, from the Grange, drew up at Dr. May's door.

Norman opened it, to claim Meta at once for the walk; Mrs. Arnott and Mary had gone on to assist Richard in his final arrangements, but even before Cocksmoor, with Ethel, was now the care of Margaret; and she had waited with her father to keep all bustle from her room, and to commit her into the charge of Flora and of nurse. Ethel seemed quite unwilling to go. There was that strange oppressed feeling on her as if the attainment of her wishes were joy too great to be real—as if she would fain hold off from it at the climax, and linger with the sister who had shared all with her, and to whom that church was even more than to herself. She came back, and back again, with fresh injunctions, sometimes forgetting the very purpose of her return, as if it had been only an excuse for looking at Margaret's countenance, and drinking in her sympathy from her face; but she was to go in George's carriage, and he was not a man to allow of loitering. He became so impatient of Ethel's delays, that she perceived that he could bear them no longer, gave her final kiss, and whispered, "In spirit with us!" then ran down and was seized on by George, who had already packed in the children and Miss Bracy, and was whirled away.

"Flora dear," said Margaret, "do you dislike having the window opened?"

Flora threw it up, protesting, in reply to her sister's scruples, that she liked the air. "You always spoiled me," said Margaret fondly. "Come and lie down by me. It is very nice to have you here," she added, as Flora complied; and she took her hand and fondled it, "It is like the old times to have you here taking care of me."

"Very unlike them in some ways," said Flora.

"It has been a great renewal of still older times," said Margaret, "to have Aunt Flora here. I hope you will get to know her, Flora, it is so like having mamma here," and she looked in her sister's face as she spoke.

Flora did not reply, but she lay quite still, as if there were a charm in the perfect rest of being alone with Margaret, making no effort, and being able to be silent. Time passed on, how long they knew not, but, suddenly, a thrill shot through Margaret's frame; she raised her hand and lifted her head, with an eager "Hark!"

Flora could hear nothing.

"The bells—his bells!" said Margaret, all one radiant look of listening, as Flora opened the window further, and the breeze wafted in the chime, softened by distance. The carnation tinted those thin white cheeks, eyes and smile beamed with joy, and uplifted finger and parted lips seemed marking every note of the cadence.

It ceased. "Alan! Alan!" said she. "It is enough! I am ready!"

The somewhat alarmed look on Flora's face recalled her, and, smiling, she held out her hands for the consecration books, saying, "Let us follow the service. It will be best for us both."

Slowly, softly, and rather monotonously, Flora read on, till she had come more than half through the first lesson. Her voice grew husky, and she sometimes paused as if she could not easily proceed.

Margaret begged her to stop, but she would not cease, and went on reading, though almost whispering, till she came to, "If they return to Thee with all their heart and with all their soul in the land of their captivity, whither they have carried them captives, and pray toward their land, which Thou gavest unto their fathers, and toward the City which Thou hast chosen, and toward the House which I have built for Thy Name; then hearing from the Heavens, even from Thy dwelling-place—"

Flora could go no further; she strove, but one of her tearless sobs cut her short. She turned her face aside, and, as Margaret began to say something tender, she exclaimed, with low, hasty utterance, "Margaret! Margaret! pray for me, for it is a hard captivity, and my heart is very, very sore. Oh! pray for me, that it may all be forgiven me—and that I may see my child again!"

"My Flora; my own poor, dear Flora! do I not pray? Oh! look up, look up. Think how He loves you. If I love you so much, how much more does not He? Come near me, Flora. Be patient, and I know peace will come!"

The words had burst from Flora uncontrollably. She was aware, the next instant, that she had given way to harmful agitation, and, resuming her quiescence, partly by her own will, partly from the soothing effect of Margaret's words and tone, she allowed herself to be drawn close to her sister, and hid her face in the pillow, while Margaret's hands were folded over her, and words of blessing and prayer were whispered with a fervency that made them broken.

Ethel, meanwhile, stood between Aubrey and Gertrude, hardly able to believe it was not a dream, as she beheld the procession enter the aisle, and heard the psalm that called on those doors to lift up their heads for Him who should enter. There was an almost bewildered feeling—could it indeed be true, as she followed the earlier part of the service, which set apart that building as a temple for ever, separate from all common uses. She had imagined the scene so often that she could almost have supposed the present, one of her many imaginations; but, by and by, the strangeness passed off, and she was able to enter into, not merely to follow, the prayers, and to feel the deep thanksgiving that such had been the crown of her feeble efforts. Margaret was in her mind the whole time, woven, as it were, into every supplication and every note of praise; and when there came the intercession for those in sickness and suffering, flowing into the commemoration of those departed in faith and fear, Ethel's spirit sank for a moment at the conviction that soon Margaret, like him, whom all must bear in mind on that day, might be included in that thanksgiving; yet, as the service proceeded, leaving more and more of earth behind, and the voices joined with angel and archangel, Ethel could lose the present grief, and only retain the certainty that, come what might, there was joy and union amid those who sung that hymn of praise. Never had Ethel been so happy—not in the sense of the finished work—no, she had lost all that, but in being more carried out of herself than ever she had been before, the free spirit of praise so bearing up her heart that the cry of glory came from her with such an exultant gladness, as might surely be reckoned as one of those foretastes of our everlasting life, not often vouchsafed even to the faithful, and usually sent to prepare strength for what may be in store.

The blessing brought the sense of peace, which hung on her even while the sounds of movement began, and the congregation were emerging. As she came out, greetings, sentences of admiration of the church, and of inquiry for her absent sisters, were crowded upon her, as people moved towards the school, where a luncheon was provided for them, to pass away the interval until evening service. The half-dozen oldest Cocksmoorites were, meantime, to have a dinner in the former schoolroom, at the Elwoods' house, and Ethel was anxious so see that all was right there; so, while the rest of her party were doing civil things, she gave her arm to Cherry, whose limping walk showed her to be very tired.

"Oh, Miss Ethel!" said Cherry, "if Miss May could only have been here!"

"Her heart is," said Ethel.

"Well, ma'am, I believe it is. You would not think, ma'am, how all the children take heed to anything about her. If I only begin to say 'Miss May told me—' they are all like mice."

"She has done more for the real good of Cocksmoor than any one else," said Ethel.

More might have been said, but they perceived that they were being overtaken by the body of clergy, who had been unrobing in the vestry. Ethel hastened to retreat within Mrs. Elwood's wicket gate, but she was arrested by Richard, and found herself being presented to the bishop, and the bishop shaking hands with her, and saying that he had much wished to be introduced to her.

Of course, that was because she was her father's daughter, and by way of something to say. She mentioned what was going on at the cottage, whereupon the bishop wished to go in and see the old people; and, entering, they found the very comfortable-looking party just sitting down to roast-beef and goose. John Taylor, in a new black coat, on account of his clerkship, presiding at one end, and Mr. Elwood at the other, and Dame Hall finding conversation for the whole assembly; while Blanche, Aubrey, Gertrude, the little Larkinses, and the Abbotstoke Wilmots were ready to act as waiters with infinite delight. Not a bit daunted by the bishop, who was much entertained by her merry manner, old granny told him "she had never seen nothing like it since the Jubilee, when the squire roasted an ox whole, and there wasn't none of it fit to eat; and when her poor father got his head broken. Well, to be sure, who would have thought what would come of Sam's bringing in the young gentleman and lady to see her the day her back was so bad!"

The bishop said grace, and left granny to the goose, while he gave Ethel his arm, which she would have thought an unaccountable proceeding if she had not recollected that Richard might be considered as host, and that she was his eldest sister forthcoming.

No sooner, however, had they come beyond the wicket than she saw her father speaking to Will Adams, and there was that in the air of both which made it no surprise when Dr. May came up, saying, "Ethel, I must carry you away;" and, in explanation to the bishop, "my poor girl at home is not so well."

All was inquiry and sympathy. Ethel was frantic to be at home, and would have rushed off at once, if Richard had not held her fast, asking what good she would do by hurrying in, breathless and exhausted, so as to add to Flora's fright and distress, the anxiety which was most upon their minds, since she had never before witnessed one of the seizures, that were only too ordinary matters in the eyes of the home party. No one but Dr. May and Ethel should go.

Richard undertook to tell the rest, and the gig making its appearance, Ethel felt that the peculiarly kind manner with which the bishop pressed her hand, and gave them all good wishes, was like a continuation of his blessing to aid her in her home scene of trial.

Perhaps, it was well for her that her part in the consecration festivities should end here; at least so thought Mr. Wilmot, who, though very sorry for the cause, could not wish her to have been present at the luncheon. She had not thought of self hitherto, the church was the gift of Alan and Margaret, the work of preparing the people belonged to all alike, and she did not guess that, in the sight of others, she was not the nobody that she believed herself. Her share in the work at Cocksmoor was pretty well known, and Dr. Hoxton could not allow a public occasion to pass without speeches, such as must either have been very painful, or very hurtful to her. The absence of herself and her father, however, permitted a more free utterance to the general feeling; and things were said, that did indeed make the rest of the family extremely hot and uncomfortable, but which gave them extreme pleasure. Norman was obliged to spare Richard the answer, and said exactly what he ought, and so beautifully, that Meta could not find it in her heart to echo the fervent wish, which he whispered as he sat down, that speechifying could be abolished by Act of Parliament.

Mrs. Arnott began to perceive that her nephew was something to be proud of, and to understand how much was sacrificed, while George Rivers expressed his opinion to her that Norman would be a crack speaker in the House, and he hoped she would say everything to hinder his going out, for it was a regular shame to waste him on the niggers.

Owing to George having constituted himself her squire, Mrs. Arnott had not arrived at an understanding of the state of affairs at home; but, as soon as they rose up from luncheon, and she learned the truth from Richard and Mary, nothing would hinder her from walking home at once to see whether she could be useful. Mary was easily persuaded to remain, for she was accustomed to Margaret's having these attacks, and had always been kept out of her room the while, so she had little uneasiness to prevent her from being very happy, in receiving in her own simple, good-humoured way all the attentions that lapsed upon her in the place of her elder sisters.

"Cocksmoor really has a church!" was note enough of joy for her, and no one could look at her round face without seeing perfect happiness. Moreover, when after evening service, the November mist turned into decided rain, she was as happy as a queen in her foresight, which had provided what seemed an unlimited supply of cloaks and umbrellas. She appeared to have an original genius for making the right people give a lift in their carriages to the distressed; and, regarding the Abbotstoke britska as her own, packed in Mrs. Anderson and Fanny, in addition to all their own little ones, Meta thrusting Miss Bracy into the demi-corner destined for herself at the last minute, and, remaining with Mary, the only ladies obliged to walk back to Stoneborough. So delighted were they "at the fun," that it might have been thought the most charming of adventures, and they laughed all the more at the lack of umbrellas. They went to Mrs. Elwood's, divested themselves of all possible finery, and tucked up the rest;

Meta was rolled up from head to foot in a great old plaid shawl of Mrs. Elwood's, and Mary had a cloak of Richard's, the one took Norman's arm, the other Dr. Spencer's, and they trudged home through the darkness and the mud in the highest glee, quite sorry when the carriage met them half-way.

It was the last mirth that they enjoyed for many weeks. When they reached home, a sense of self-reproach for their glee thrilled over them, when they found a sort of hush pervading the drawing-room, and saw the faces of awe and consternation, worn by Blanche and George Rivers.

"It was a much worse attack than usual, and it did not go off," was all that Blanche knew, but her father had desired to be told when Dr. Spencer came home, and she went up with the tidings.

This brought Flora down, looking dreadfully pale, and with her voice sunk away as it had been when she lost her child. Her husband started up, exclaiming at her aspect; she let him support her to the sofa, and gave the few particulars. Margaret had been as placid and comfortable as usual, till nurse came to dress her, but the first move had brought on the faintness and loss of breath. It did not yield to remedies, and she had neither looked nor spoken since, only moaned. Flora thought her father much alarmed; and then, after an interval, she began to entreat that they might stay there, sending Miss Bracy and the children to the Grange to make room.

Meantime, Dr. Spencer had come to the sick-room, but he could only suggest remedies that were already in course of application to the insensible sufferer. Mrs. Arnott and Ethel were watching, and trying everything to relieve her, but with little effect, and Ethel presently stood by the fire with her father, as Dr. Spencer turned towards him, and he said, in a very low, but calm voice, "It won't do—I believe it is the death-stroke."

"Not immediate," said Dr. Spencer.

"No," said Dr. May; and he quietly spoke of what the disease had effected, and what yet remained for it to do, ere the silver bowl should be broken.

Dr. Spencer put in a word of agreement.

"Will there be no rally?" said Ethel, in the same tone.

"Probably not," said Dr. May; "the brain is generally reached at this stage. I have seen it coming for a long time. The thing was done seven years ago. There was a rally for a time when youth was strong; but suspense and sorrow accelerated what began from the injury to the spine."

Dr. Spencer bowed his head, and looked at him anxiously, saying, "I do not think there will be much acute suffering."

"I fear it may be as trying," said Dr. May, sighing; and then turning to Ethel, and throwing his arm round her, "May God make it easy to her, and grant us 'patient hearts.' We will not grudge her to all that she loves best, my Ethel."

Ethel clung to him, as if to derive strength from him. But the strength that was in them then did not come from earth. Dr. Spencer wrung his hand, and stepped back to the bed to try another resource. Vain again, they only seemed to be tormenting her, and the silent helplessness prevailed again. Then Dr. May went down to Flora, told her the true state of the case, and urged on her to give up her plan of remaining. George joined with him, and she yielded submissively, but would not be refused going up once again and kissing her sister, standing beside her gazing at her, till her father came softly and drew her away. "I shall be here to-morrow," she said to Ethel, and went.

The morrow, however, brought no Flora. The agitation and distress of that day had broken her down completely, and she was so ill as to be unable to move. Her aunt went at once to see her, and finding that her presence at the Grange relieved some of Dr. May's anxieties, chiefly devoted herself to her. Flora was grateful and gentle, but as silent and impenetrable as ever, while day after day she lay on her couch, uncomplaining and undemonstrative, visited by her father, and watched over by her aunt and sister-in-law, who began to know each other much better, though Flora less than ever, in that deep fixed grief. She only roused herself to return her husband's affection, or to listen to the daily reports of Margaret. Poor George, he was very forlorn, though Meta did her best to wait on him, and he rode over twice a day to inquire at Stoneborough.

The doctors were right, and the consecration morning was her last of full consciousness. From the hour when she had heard the sound of Alan's bells, her ears were closed to earthly sounds. There was very little power of intercourse with her, as she lingered on the borders of the land very far away, where skill and tenderness could not either reach body or spirit. Often the watchers could not tell whether she was conscious, or only incapacitated from expression, by the fearful weight on her breath, which caused a restlessness most piteous in the exhausted helpless frame, wasted till the softest touch was anguish. Now and then came precious gleams when a familiar voice, or some momentary alleviation would gain a smile, or thanks, and they thought her less restless when Richard read prayers beside her, but words were very rare, only now and then a name, and when in most distress, "it will be soon over," "it will soon be over," occurred so often, that they began to think it once her solace, and now repeated habitually without a meaning.

They could not follow her into the valley of the shadow of death, but could only watch the frail earthly prison-house being broken down, as if the doom of sin must be borne, though faith could trust that it was but her full share in the Cross. Calmly did those days pass. Ethel, Richard, and Mary divided between them the watching and the household cares, and their father bore up bravely in the fullness of his love and faith, resigning her daughter to the Hands which were bearing her whither her joys had long since departed.

Hector Ernescliffe arrived when the holidays began; and his agony of sorrow, when she failed to recognise him, moved Dr. May to exert himself earnestly for his consolation; and, at the same time, Tom, in a gentle, almost humble manner, paid a sort of daughter-like attention to the smallest services for his father, as if already accepting him as his especial charge.

It was midnight, on the longest night of the year; Ethel was lying on her bed, and had fallen into a brief slumber, when her father's low, clear voice summoned her: "Ethel, she is going!"

There was a change on the face, and the breath came in labouring gasps. Richard lifted her head, and her eyes once more opened; she smiled once more.

"Papa!" she said, "dear papa!"

He threw himself on his knees beside her, but she looked beyond him, "Mamma! Alan! oh, there they are! More! more!" and, as though the unspeakable dawned on her, she gasped for utterance, then looked, with a consoling smile, on her father. "Over now!" she said—and the last struggle was ended. That which Richard laid down was no longer Margaret May.

Over now! The twenty-five years' life, the seven years' captivity on her couch, the anxious headship of the motherless household, the hopeless betrothal, the long suspense, the efforts for resignation, the widowed affections, the slow decay, the tardy, painful death agony—all was over; nothing left, save what they had rendered the undying spirit, and the impress her example had left on those around her.

The long continuance of the last suffering had softened the actual parting; and it was with thankfulness for the cessation of her pain that they turned away, and bade each other good-night.

Ethel would not have believed that her first wakening to the knowledge that Margaret was gone could have been more fraught with relief than with misery. And, for her father, it seemed as if it were a home-like, comfortable thought to him, that her mother had one of her children with her. He called her the first link of his Daisy Chain drawn up out of sight; and, during the quiet days that ensued, he seemed as it were to be lifted above grief, dwelling upon hope. His calmness impressed the same on his children, as they moved about in the solemn stillness of the house; and when Harry, pale, and shocked at the blow to him so sudden, came home, the grave silence soothed his violence of grief; and he sat beside his, father or Mary, speaking in undertones of what Margaret had loved to hear from him, of Alan Ernescliffe's last moments.

Mary gave way to a burst of weeping when she sought, in vain, for daisies in the wintry garden; but Hector Ernescliffe went down to the cloisters, and brought back the lingering blossoms to be placed on Margaret's bosom.

The dog Toby had followed him, unseen, to the cloister; and he was entering the garden, when he was struck by seeing the animal bounding, in irrepressible ecstasy, round a lad, whose tarpaulin hat, blue-bordered collar, and dark blue dress, showed him to be a sailor, as well as the broad-shouldered, grizzled, elderly man, who stood beside him.

"I say, sir," said the latter, as Hector's hand was on the door, "do you belong to Dr. May?"

Hector unhesitatingly answered that he did.

"Then, maybe, sir, you have heard of one Bill Jennings."

Hector was all in one flush, almost choking, as he told that he was Mr. Ernescliffe's brother, and gave his hand to the sailor. "What could he do for him?"

Jennings had heard from one of the crew of the Bucephalus that Mr. May had been met, on his return to Portsmouth, by the news of his sister's death. The Mays had helped his boy; he had been with Mr. May in the island; he had laid Mr. Ernescliffe in his grave; and some notion had crossed the sailor that he must be at Miss Margaret's funeral—it might be they would let him lend a hand—and, in this expedition, he was spending his time on shore.

How he was welcomed need not be told, nor how the tears came forth from full hearts, as Dr. May granted his wish, and thanked him for doing what Margaret herself would indeed have chosen; and, in his blue sailor garb, was Jennings added to the bearers, their own men, and two Cocksmoor labourers, who, early on Christmas Eve, carried her to the minster. Last time she had been there, Alan Ernescliffe had supported her. Now, what was mortal of him lay beneath the palm tree, beneath the glowing summer sky, while the first snow-flakes hung like pearls on her pall. But as they laid her by her mother's side, who could doubt that they were together?

CHAPTER XXVI.

At length I got unto the gladsome hill,
    Where lay my hope;
Where lay my heart; and, climbing still,
    When I had gained the brow and top,
A lake of brackish waters on the ground,
    Was all I found.

—GEORGE HERBERT.

Late in the evening of the same snowy 24th of December, a little daughter awoke to life at Abbotstoke Grange, and, not long after, Mrs. Arnott came to summon Dr May from the anxious vigil in the sitting-room. "Come and see if you can do anything to soothe her," she said, with much alarm. "The first sight of the baby has put her into such a state of agitation, that we do not know what to do with her."

It was so, when he came to her bedside; that fixed stony look of despair was gone; the source of tears, so long dried up, had opened again; and there she lay, weeping quietly indeed, but profusely, and with deep heaving sobs. To speak, or to leave her alone, seemed equally perilous, but he chose the first—he kissed and blessed her, and gave her joy. She looked up at him as if his blessing once more brought peace, and said faintly, "Now it is pardon—now I can die!"

"The cloud is gone! Thanks for that above all! said. Dr. May fervently. "Now, my dear, rest in thankful gladness—you are too weak to talk or think."

"I am weak—I am tired of it all," said Flora. "I am glad to be going while I am so happy—there are Margaret—my own darling—rest—peace—"

"You are not going, dearest," said her father; "at least, I trust not, if you will not give way; here is a darling given to you, instead of the first, who needs you more."

He would have taken the infant from the nurse and held her to her mother, but, recollecting how little Leonora had drawn her last breath in his arms, he feared the association, and signed to Mrs. Arnott to show her the child; but she seemed as yet only able to feel that it was not Leonora, and the long sealed-up grief would have its way. The tears burst out again. "Tell Ethel she will be the best mother to her. Name her Margaret—make her a Daisy of your own— don't call her after me," she said, with such passionate caresses, that Mrs. Arnott was glad to take the babe away.

Dr. May's next expedient was to speak to her of her husband, who needed her more than all, and to call him in. There seemed to be something tranquillising in his wistful manner of repeating, "Don't cry, Flora;" and she was at last reduced, by her extreme exhaustion, to stillness; but there were still many fears for her.

Dr. May's prediction was accomplished—that she would suffer for having over-exerted herself. Her constitution had been severely tried by the grief and despondency that she had so long endured in silence, and the fresh sorrow for her favourite sister coming at such a crisis. There was a weariness of life, and an unwillingness to resume her ordinary routine, that made her almost welcome her weakness and sinking; and now that the black terror had cleared away from the future, she seemed to long to follow Margaret at once, and to yearn after her lost child; while appeals to the affection that surrounded her often seemed to oppress her, as if there were nothing but weariness and toil in store.

The state of her mind made her father very anxious, though it was but too well accounted for. Poor Flora had voluntarily assumed the trammels that galled her; worldly motives had prompted her marriage, and though she faithfully loved her husband, he was a heavy weight on her hands, and she had made it more onerous by thrusting him into a position for which he was not calculated, and inspiring him with a self-consequence that would not recede from it. The shock of her child's death had taken away the zest and energy which had rejoiced in her chosen way of life, and opened her eyes to see what Master she had been serving; and the perception of the hollowness of all that had been apparently good in her, had filled her with remorse and despair. Her sufferings had been the more bitter because she had not parted with her proud reserve. She had refused council, and denied her confidence to those who could have guided her repentance. Her natural good sense, and the sound principle in which she had been brought up, had taught her to distrust her gloomy feelings as possibly morbid; and she had prayed, keeping her hold of faith in the Infinite Mercy, though she could not feel her own part in it; and thus that faith was beginning at last to clear her path.

It was the harder to deal with her, because her hysterical agitation was so easily excited, that her father hardly dared to let a word be spoken to her; and she was allowed to see no one else except her aunt and the dear old nurse, whose tears for her child Margaret had been checked by the urgent requirements of another of her nurslings; and whom George Rivers would have paid with her weight in gold, for taking care of his new daughter, regarding her as the only woman in the world that could be trusted.

Those were heavy days with every one, though each brought some shade of improvement. They were harder to bear than the peaceful days that had immediately followed the loss of Margaret; and Ethel was especially unhappy and forlorn under the new anxiety, where she could be of no service; and with her precious occupation gone; her father absent, instead of resting upon her; and her room deserted. She was grieved with herself, because her feelings were unable to soar at the Christmas Feast, as erst on St. Andrew's Day; and she was bewildered and distressed by the fear that she had then been only uplifted by vanity and elation.

She told Richard so, and he said, kindly, that he thought a good deal of that she complained of arose from bodily weariness.

This hurt her a little; but when he said, "I think that the blessings of St. Andrew's Day helped us through what was to follow," she owned that it had indeed been so, and added, "I am going to work again! Tell me what will be most useful to you at Cocksmoor."

Sick at heart as she was, she bravely set herself to appropriate the hours now left vacant; and manfully walked with Richard and Harry to church at Cocksmoor on St. Stephen's Day; but the church brought back the sense of contrast. Next, she insisted on fulfilling their intention of coming home by Abbotstoke to hear how Flora was, when the unfavourable account only added lead to the burden that weighed her down. Though they were sent home in the carriage, she was so completely spent, that the effect of returning home to her room, without its dear inhabitant, was quite overwhelming, and she sat on her bed for half an hour, struggling with repinings. She came downstairs without having gained the victory, and was so physically overcome with lassitude, that Richard insisted on her lying on the sofa, and leaving everything to him and Mary.

Richard seemed to make her his object in life, and was an unspeakable help and comforter to her, not only by taking every care for her for her sake, but by turning to her as his own friend and confidante, the best able to replace what they had lost. There were many plans to be put in operation for Cocksmoor, on which much consultation was needed, though every word reminded them sadly of Margaret's ever ready interest in those schemes. It was very unlike Ethel's vision of the first weeks of St. Andrew's Church; but it might be safer for her than that aught should tempt her to say, "See what my perseverance has wrought!" Perhaps her Margaret had begun to admire her too much to be her safest confidante—at any rate, it was good still to sow in tears, rather than on earth to reap in confident joy.

Norman was as brotherly and kind as possible; but it was one of the dreary feelings of those days, that Ethel then first became aware of the difference that his engagement had made, and saw that he resorted elsewhere for sympathy. She was not jealous, and acquiesced submissively and resolutely; but they had been so much to each other, that it was a trial, especially at such a time as this, when freshly deprived of Margaret.

Norman's own prospect was not cheerful. He had received a letter from New Zealand, begging him to hasten his coming out, as there was educational work much wanting him, and, according to his original wish, he could be ordained there in the autumnal Ember Week.

He was in much perplexity, since, according to this request, he ought to sail with his aunt in the last week of February, and he knew not how to reconcile the conflicting claims.

Meta was not long in finding out the whole of his trouble, as they paced up and down the terrace together on a frosty afternoon.

"You will go!" was her first exclamation.

"I ought," said Norman, "I believe I ought, and if it had only been at any other time, it would have been easy. My aunt's company would have been such a comfort for you."

"It cannot be helped," said Meta.

"Considering the circumstances," began Norman, with lingering looks at the little humming-bird on his arm, "I believe I should be justified in waiting till such time as you could go with me. I could see what Mr. Wilmot thinks."

"You don't think so yourself," said Meta. "Nobody else can give a judgment. In a thing like this, asking is, what you once called, seeking opinions as Balaam inquired."

"Turning my words against me?" said Norman, smiling. "Still, Meta, perhaps older heads would be fitter to judge what would be right for a little person not far off."

"She can be the best judge of that herself," said Meta. "Norman," and her dark eyes were steadfastly fixed, "I always resolved that, with God's help, I would not be a stumbling-block in the way of your call to your work. I will not. Go out now—perhaps you will be freer for it without me, and I suppose I have a longer apprenticeship to serve to all sorts of things before I come to help you."

"Oh, Meta, you are a rebuke to me!"

"What? when I am going to stay by my own fireside?" said Meta, trying to laugh, but not very successfully. "Seriously, I have much to do here. When poor Flora gets well, she must be spared all exertion for a long time to come; and I flatter myself that they want me at Stoneborough sometimes. If your father can bear to spare you, there is no doubt that you ought to go."

"My father is as unselfish as you are, Meta. But I cannot speak to him until he is more easy about Flora. We always think the required sacrifice the hardest, but I must own that I could not grieve if he laid his commands on me to wait till the autumn."

"Oh, that would make it a duty and all easy," said Meta, smiling;

"but I don't think he will; and Aunt Flora will be only too glad to carry you out without encumbrance."

"Has not Aunt Flora come to her senses about you?"

"I believe she would rather I belonged to any of her nephews but you. She is such a dear, sincere, kind-hearted person, and we are so comfortable together, that it will be quite like home to come out to her! I mean there, to convince her that I can be of something like use."

Meta talked so as to brighten and invigorate Norman when they were together, but they both grew low-spirited when apart. The humming-bird had hardly ever been so downcast as at present—that is, whenever she was not engaged in waiting on her brother, or in cheering up Dr. May, or in any of the many gentle offices that she was ever fulfilling. She was greatly disappointed, and full of fears for Norman, and dread of the separation, but she would not give way; and only now and then, when off her guard, would the sadness reign on her face without an effort. Alone, she fought and prayed for resignation for herself, and protection and strength for him, and chid herself for the foolish feeling that he would be safer with her.

She told Aunt Flora how it was one evening, as they sat over the fire together, speaking with a would-be tone of congratulation.

"Indeed!" exclaimed Mrs. Arnott. "But that is a great pity!"

Meta looked quite brightened by her saying so. "I thought you would be glad," she rejoined.

"Did you think me so hard-hearted?"

"I thought you believed he would be better without me."

"My dear, we have not kept house and nursed together for a month for nothing," said Mrs. Arnott, smiling.

"Thank you," said Meta, trying to answer the smile. "You have taken a load off me!"

"I don't like it at all," said Mrs. Arnott. "It is a very uncomfortable plan for every one. And yet when I know how great is the want of him out there, I can say nothing against it without high treason. Well, my dear, I'll take all the care I can of Norman, and when you come, I shall be almost as glad as if we were coming home for good. Poor Flora! she is one person who will not regret the arrangement."

"Poor Flora!—you think her really better this evening?"

"Much better, indeed; if we could only raise her spirits, I think she would recover very well; but she is so sadly depressed. I must try to talk to Ethel—she may better understand her."

"I have never understood Flora," said Meta. "She has been as kind to me as possible, and I very soon came to a certain point with her, but I never have known her thoroughly. I doubt whether any one did but dear Margaret."

Flora was, however, much softened and less reserved than she had been. She found great repose in her aunt's attendance, retracing, as it did, her mother's presence, and she responded to her tenderness with increasing reliance and comfort; while as her strength began to revive, and there was more disposition to talk, she became gradually drawn into greater confidence.

The seeing of Ethel was one of the difficult questions. Flora had begun to wish it very much, and yet the bare idea threw her into a nervous tremor, that caused it to be put off again and again. Her aunt found her one day almost faint with agitation—she had heard Ethel's voice in the next room, and had been winding up her expectations, and now was as much grieved as relieved, to find that she had been there seeing the baby, but was now gone.

"How does the dear Ethel look?" asked Flora presently.

"She is looking better to-day; she has looked very worn and harassed, but I thought her brighter to-day. She walked over by Aubrey on his pony, and I think it did her good."

"Dear old Ethel! Aunt, it is a thing that no one has told me yet. Can you tell me how she bore the news of Norman Ogilvie's engagement?"

"Do you mean—" and Mrs. Arnott stopped short in her interrogation.

"Yes," said Flora, answering the pause.

"But I thought young Ogilvie a most unexceptionable person."

"So he is," said Flora. "I was much annoyed at the time, but she was resolute."

"In rejecting him?"

"In running away as soon as she found what was likely to happen;" and Flora, in a few words, told what had passed at Oxford.

"Then it was entirely out of devotion to your father?"

"Entirely," said Flora. "No one could look at her without seeing that she liked him. I had left her to be the only effective one at home, and she sacrificed herself."

"I am glad that I have seen her," said Mrs. Arnott. "I should never have understood her by description. I always said that I must come home to set my correspondence going rightly."

"Aunt Flora," said her niece, "do you remember my dear mother's unfinished letter to you?"

"To be sure I do, my dear."

"Nothing ever was more true," said Flora. "I read it over some little time ago, when I set my papers in order, and understood it then. I never did before. I used to think it very good for the others."

"It is what one generally does with good advice."

"Do you recollect the comparison between Norman, Ethel, and me? It is so curious. Norman, who was ambitious and loved praise, but now dreads nothing so much; Ethel, who never cared for anything of the kind, but went straight on her own brave way; and oh! Aunt Flora—me—"

"Indeed, my dear, I should have thought you had her most full approbation."

"Ah! don't you see the tone, as if she were not fully satisfied, as if she only could not see surface faults in me," said Flora; "and how she said she dreaded my love of praise, and of being liked. I wonder how it would have been if she had lived. I have looked back so often in the past year, and I think the hollowness began from that time. It might have been there before, but I am not so sure. You see, at that dreadful time, after the accident, I was the eldest who was able to be efficient, and much more useful than poor Ethel. I think the credit I gained made me think myself perfection, and I never did anything afterwards but seek my own honour."

Mrs. Arnott began better to understand Flora's continued depression, but she thought her self-reproach exaggerated, and said something at once soothing and calculated to encourage her to undraw the curtain of reserve.

"You do not know," continued Flora, "how greedy I was of credit and affection. It made me jealous of Ethel herself, as long as we were in the same sphere; and when I felt that she was more to papa than I could be, I looked beyond home for praise. I don't think the things I did were bad in themselves—brought up as I have been, they could hardly be so. I knew what merits praise and blame too well for that—but oh! the motive. I do believe I cared very much for Cocksmoor. I thought it would be a grand thing to bring about; but, you see, as it has turned out, all I thought I had done for it was in vain; and Ethel has been the real person and does not know it. I used to think Ethel so inferior to me. I left her all my work at home. If it had not been for that, she might have been happy with Norman Ogilvie—for never were two people better matched, and now she has done what I never thought to have left to another—watched over our own Margaret. Oh! how shall I ever bear to see her?"

"My dear, I am sure nothing can be more affectionate than Ethel. She does not think these things."

"She does," said Flora. "She always knew me better than I did myself. Her straightforward words should often have been rebukes to me. I shall see in every look and tone the opinion I have deserved. I have shrunk from her steadfast looks ever since I myself learned what I was. I could not bear them now—and yet—oh, aunt, you must bring her! Ethel! my dear, dear old King—my darling's godmother— the last who was with Margaret!"

She had fallen into one of those fits of weeping when it was impossible to attempt anything but soothing her; but, though she was so much exhausted that Mrs. Arnott expected to be in great disgrace with Dr. May for having let her talk herself into this condition, she found that he was satisfied to find that she had so far relieved her mind, and declared that she would be better now.

The effect of the conversation was, that the next day, the last of the twelve Christmas days, when Ethel, whose yearning after her sister was almost equally divided between dread and eagerness— eagerness for her embrace, and dread of the chill of her reserve, came once again in hopes of an interview. Dr. May called her at once. "I shall take you in without any preparation," he said, "that she may not have time to be flurried. Only, be quiet and natural."

Did he know what a mountain there was in her throat when he seemed to think it so easy to be natural?

She found him leading her into a darkened room, and heard his cheerful tones saying, "I have brought Ethel to you!"

"Ethel! oh!" said a low, weak voice, with a sound as of expecting a treat, and Ethel was within a curtain, where she began, in the dimness, to see something white moving, and her hands were clasped by two long thin ones. "There!" said Dr. May, "now, if you will be good, I will leave you alone. Nurse is by to look after you, and you know she always separates naughty children."

Either the recurrence to nursery language, or the mere sisterly touch after long separation, seemed to annihilate all the imaginary mutual dread, and, as Ethel bent lower and lower, and Flora's arms were round her, the only feeling was of being together again, and both at once made the childish gesture of affection, and murmured the old pet names of "Flossy," and "King," that belonged to almost forgotten days, when they were baby sisters, then kissed each other again.

"I can't see you," said Ethel, drawing herself up a little. "Why, Flora, you look like a little white shadow!"

"I have had such weak eyes," said Flora, "and this dim light is comfortable. I see your old sharp face quite plain."

"But what can you do here?"

"Do? Oh, dear Ethel, I have not had much of doing. Papa says I have three years' rest to make up."

"Poor Flora!" said Ethel; "but I should have thought it tiresome, especially for you."

"I have only now been able to think again," said Flora; "and you will say I am taking to quoting poetry. Do you remember some lines in that drama that Norman admired so much?"

"Philip von Artevelde?"

"Yes. I can't recollect them now, though they used to be always running in my head—something about time to mend and time to mourn."

"These?" said Ethel—

"He that lacks time to mourn, lacks time to mend.
Eternity mourns that."

"I never had time before for either," said Flora. "You cannot think how I used to be haunted by those, when I was chased from one thing to another, all these long, long eighteen months. I am in no haste to take up work again."

"Mending as well as mourning," said Ethel thoughtfully.

Flora sighed.

"And now you have that dear little Christmas gift to—" Ethel paused.

"She is not nearly so fine and healthy as her sister was," said Flora, "poor little dear. You know, Ethel, even now, I shall have very little time with her in that London life. Her papa wants me so much, and I must leave her to—to the nurses." Flora's voice trembled again.

"Our own dear old nurse," said Ethel.

"Oh! I wanted to thank you all for sparing her to us," said Flora.

"George wished it so much. But how does poor little Daisy bear it?"

"Very magnanimously," said Ethel, smiling. "In fact, nurse has had but little to do with Daisy of late, and would have been very forlorn at home. It is better for Aubrey and for her, not to return to be babies to comfort poor nurse. I have been breaking up the nursery, and taking Gertrude to live with me."

"Have you gone back there again?"

"It would not have been better for waiting," said Ethel; "and Gertrude was so proud to come to me. I could not have done it without her, but papa must not have vacancy next to him."

"It has been hard on you for me to engross him," said Flora; "but oh, Ethel, I could not spare him. I don't think even you can tell what papa is."

"You have found it out," said Ethel, in an odd, dry manner; which in sound, though not in feeling, was a contrast to the soft, whispering, tearful murmurs of her sister.

"And my aunt!" continued Flora— "that I should have taken up such a great piece of her short visit!"

"Ah! it is coming to an end very fast," said Ethel, sighing; "but you had the best right to her, and she and Meta have seen so much of each other. She tells me she is quite satisfied about Meta now."

"I am sorry to see Meta looking out of spirits," said Flora. "I almost made her cry by saying something about Norman. Is there anything going wrong?"

Ethel, as usual, blundered into the subject. "Only about Norman's going out."

Flora asked further questions, and she was obliged to explain. It roused Flora's energies at once.

"This will never do!" she said. "They must marry, and go with my aunt."

Ethel was aghast. "They would not hear of it now!"

"They must. It is the only reasonable thing. Why, Norman would be miserable, and as to Meta— Imagine his going out and returning—a year's work, such an expense and loss of time, besides the missing Aunt Flora."

"If it were not wrong—"

"The waste would be the wrong thing. Besides—" and she told of Margaret's wishes.

"But, Flora, think—the last week in February—and you so ill!"

"I am not to marry them," said Flora, smiling. "If it could be in a fortnight, they could go and get their outfit afterwards, and come back to us when I am stronger. Let me see—there need be no fuss about settlements—Mr. Rivers's will arranges everything for her."

"It would be a good thing to get rid of a fine wedding," said Ethel;

"but they will never consent!"

"Yes, they will, and be grateful."

"Papa would be happier about Norman," said Ethel; "but I cannot fancy his liking it. And you—you can't spare Meta, for Aunt Flora must go to the Arnotts' in a week or two more."

"Suppose papa was to let me have you," said Flora. "If he wants you, he must come after you."

Ethel gasped at the thought that her occupation at home was gone, but she said, "If I am not too awkward for you, dear Flora. You will miss Meta terribly."

"I can't keep the humming-bird caged, with her heart far away," said Flora.

Dr. May came in to break up the conversation, and Ethel quickly guessed from his manner that Norman had been talking to him. Flora told him that she had been agreeing with Ethel that Meta had much better not miss this opportunity. He was far less startled than Ethel had expected; indeed, the proposal was rather a relief to his mind, and his chief objection was the fear that Flora would be fatigued by the extra bustle; but she promised not to trouble herself about it, otherwise than that if Norman could not persuade Meta, she would. The sisters parted, much more comfortable than before. Ethel felt as if she had found something like a dim reflection of Margaret, and Flora's fear of Ethel had fled away from the mere force of sisterhood.

As to Norman, he declared that he had not the audacity to make the proposal to Meta, though he was only too grateful; so his father carried it to the humming-bird; and, as soon as she found that it was not improper, nor would hurt any one's feelings, she gave ready consent—only begging that it might be as best suited every one, especially Flora; and ending by a whisper to her dear fatherly friend, owning that she was "very glad—she meant she was very glad there would be nobody there."

So Norman and Meta settled their plans as they walked home together from evening service, after listening to the prophecies of the blessings to be spread into the waste and desolate places, which should yet become the heritage of the Chosen, and with the evening star shining on them, like a faint reflex of the Star of the East, Who came to be a Light to lighten the Gentiles.

CHAPTER XXVII.

Euna delle facolta singolari ed incommunicabili della religione Cristiana questa, di poter dare indirizzo e quiete a chiunoque, in qualsivoglia congiuntura, a qualsivoglia termine, ricorra ad essa. Se al passato v'e rimedio, essa lo prescrive, lo somministra, presta lume e vigore per metterlo in opera a qualunque costo; se non v'e, essa da il, modo di fare realmento e in effeto, cio che 1' uom dice in proverbio, della necessita virtu. Insegna a continuare con sapienza cio che e stato intrapreso per leggerezza, piega l'animo ad abbracciare con propensione cio che e stato imposto dalla prepotenza, e da ad un elezione che fu temeraria, ma che e irrevocabile, tutta la santita, tutto il consiglio, diciamolo pur francamenta, tutte le gioje della vocazione.—MANZONI.

The wedding-day was fixed for the 20th of January, since it was less risk to Flora as an absolute invalid, than as convalescent enough to take any share in the doings.

Meta managed her correspondence with her own relatives, and obtained her uncle's kind approval, since he saw there could be nothing else; while her aunt treated her as an infatuated victim, but wished, for her mother's sake, to meet her in London before she sailed.

The worst stroke of all was to Bellairs, who had never chosen to believe that her mistress could move without her, and though mortally afraid in crossing to the Isle of Wight, and utterly abhorring all "natives," went into hysterics on finding that her young lady would take out no maid but a little hard-working village girl; and though transferred in the most flattering manner to Mrs. Rivers's service, shed a tear for every stitch she set in the trousseau, and assured her betrothed butler that, if Miss Rivers would only have heard reason, she would have followed her to the world's end, rather than that her beautiful hair should never look like anything again.

So the wedding-day came, and grass and trees wore a fitting suit of crisp hoariness. Nothing could be quieter. Meta was arrayed by the sobbing Bellairs in her simple bridal white, wrapped herself in a large shawl, took her brother's arm, and walked down the frosty path with him and Mrs. Arnott, as if going merely to the daily service.

The time had not been made known, and there was hardly an addition to the ordinary congregation, except the May family and Dr. Spencer; but the Christmas evergreens still adorned aisle and chancel, and over the altar stood the motto that Meta herself had woven of holly, on that Christmas Eve of grief and anxiety, without knowing how it would speak to her.

Fear not, for behold I bring unto you glad tidings of great joy, that shall be unto you and to all people.

Fear not, for length of voyage, for distance from kindred, for hardship, privation, misunderstanding, disappointment. The glad tidings are to all people, even to the utmost parts of the earth. Ye have your portion in the great joy—ye have freely cast in your lot with those, whose feet are beautiful on the mountains, who bear the good tidings. Fear not, for He is with you, who will never forsake.

Thus Dr. May read the words with swelling heart, as he looked at his son's clear, grave, manful look, even as it had been when he made his Confirmation vow—his natural nervous excitability quelled by a spirit not his own, and chastened into strong purpose; and the bride, her young face the more lovely for the depth of enthusiasm restrained by awe and humility, as she stood without trembling or faltering, the strength of innocence expressed in the whole bearing of her slight figure in her white drapery. Around were the four sisterly bride's-maids, their black dresses showing that these were still the twilight days of mourning, and that none would forget her, whose prayers might still bless their labour of love.

When Margaret Agatha May, on her husband's arm, turned for a last look at the altar of her own church, "Fear not," in evergreen letters, was the greeting she bore away.

Ethel was left at the Grange for the ensuing fortnight—a time of unusual leisure both to her and to Flora, which they both prized highly, for it taught them to know each other as they had never done before. Flora's confidence to her aunt had been a good thing for her, though so partial; it opened the way for further unreserve to one who knew the circumstances better, and, as to dread of Ethel, that could seldom prevail in her presence, partly from long habit, partly from her deficiency of manner, and still more from her true humility and affection. Gradually she arrived at the perception of the history of her sister's mind; understood what gloom had once overshadowed it; and how, since light had once shone upon her, she shrank not merely from the tasks that had become wearisome to her, but from the dread of losing among them her present peace.

"They are your duty," argued Ethel. "Duty brings peace."

"They were not," said Flora.

"They are now," said Ethel.

"Dinners and parties, empty talk and vain show," said Flora languidly. "Are you come to their defence, Ethel? If you could guess how sick one gets of them, and how much worse it is for them not to be hateful! And to think of bringing my poor little girl up to the like, if she is spared!"

"If they are not duties, I would not do them," said Ethel.

"Ethel," cried her sister, raising herself from her couch eagerly, "I will say it to you! What should you think of George resigning his seat, and living in peace here?"

"Would he?" said Ethel.

"If I wished it."

"But what would he do with himself?" said Ethel, not in too complimentary a strain.

"Yachting, farming, Cochin-Chinese or something," said Flora.

"Anything not so wearing as this!"

"That abominable candidate of Tomkins's would come in!" exclaimed Ethel. "Oh, Flora, that would be horrid!"

"That might be guarded against," said Flora. "Perhaps Sir Henry —

But oh! let us leave politics in peace while we can. I thought we should do some great good, but it is all a maze of confusion. It is so

415

hard to know principles from parties, and everything goes wrong! It is of no use to contend with it!"

"It is never vain to contend with evil," said Ethel.

"We are not generalising," said Flora. "There is evil nearer home than the state of parties, and I can't see that George's being in Parliament—being what he is—is anything like the benefit to things in general—that it is temptation and plague to me, besides the risk of London life for the baby, now and hereafter."

"I can't say that I think it is," said Ethel. "How nice it would be to have you here! I am so glad you are willing to give it up."

"It would have been better to have given it up untasted—like Norman," sighed Flora. "I will talk to George."

"But, Flora," said Ethel, a little startled, "you ought not to do such a thing without advice."

"There will be worry enough before it is done!" sighed Flora. "No fear of that!"

"Stop a minute," said Ethel, as if poor Flora could have done anything but lie still on her sofa. "I think you ought to consider well before you set it going."

"Have not I longed for it day and night? It is an escape from peril for ourselves and our child."

"I can't be sure!" said Ethel. "It may be more wrong to make George desert the post which—"

"Which I thrust him into," said Flora. "My father told me as much."

"I did not mean you to say that! But it is a puzzle. It seems as if it were right to give up such things; yet, when I recollect the difficulty of carrying an election right at Stoneborough, I think papa would be very sorry. I don't think his interest would bring in any sound man but his son-in-law; and George himself seems to like his parliamentary life better than anything else."

"Yes," said Flora hesitatingly; for she knew it was true—he liked to think himself important, and it gave him something to think of, and regular occupation—not too active or onerous; but she could not tell Ethel what she herself felt; that all she could do for him could not prevent him from being held cheap by the men among whom she had placed him.

"Then," said Ethel, as she heard her affirmative, "I don't think it is for his dignity, for you to put him into Parliament to please you and then take him out to please you."

"I'll take care of his dignity," said Flora shortly.

"I know you would do it well—"

"I am sick of doing things well!" said poor Flora. "You little know how I dread reading up all I must read presently! I shall lose all I have scarcely gained. I cannot find peace any way, but by throwing down the load I gave my peace for."

"Whether this is truth or fancy," said Ethel thoughtfully. "If you would ask some one competent."

"Don't you know there are some things one cannot ask?" said Flora. "I don't know why I spoke to you! Ah! come in! Why, George, that is a finer egg than ever," as he entered with a Shanghai egg in each hand, for her to mark with the date when it had been laid. Poultry was a new hobby, and Ethel had been hearing, in her tete-a-tete dinners with George, a great deal about the perfections of the hideous monsters that had obtained fabulous prices. They had been the best resource for conversation; but she watched, with something between vexation and softness, how Flora roused herself to give her full attention and interest to his prosing about his pets, really pleased as it seemed; and, at last, encouraging him actually to fetch his favourite cock to show her; when she went through the points of perfection of the ungainly mass of feathers, and did not at all allow Ethel to laugh at the unearthly sounds of disapproval which handling elicited.

"And this is our senator!" thought Ethel. "I wonder whether Honorius's hen was a Shanghai! Poor Flora is right—it is poor work to make a silk purse out of a sow's ear! but, putting him into the place is one thing, taking him out another. I wish she would take

417

advice; but I never knew her do that, except as a civil way of communicating her intentions. However, she is not quite what she was! Poor dear! Aunt Flora will never believe what a beautiful creature she used to be! It seems wrong to think of her going back to that horrid London; but I can't judge. For my part, I'd rather do work, than no work for George, and he is a good, kind-hearted fellow after all! I won't be a crab!"

So Ethel did her best, and said the cock had a bright eye—all she could say for him—and George instructed her to admire the awkward legs, and invited her to a poultry show, at Whitford, in two days' time—and they sent him away to continue his consultations with the poultry woman, which pullets should be preferred as candidates for a prize.

"Meta set him upon this," said Flora. "I hope you will go, Ethel. You see he can be very happy here."

"Still," said Ethel, "the more I think, the more sure I am that you ought to ask advice."

"I have asked yours," said Flora, as if it were a great effort. "You don't know what to say—I shall do what I see to be the only way to rest."

"I do know what to say," said Ethel; "and that is, do as the Prayer-book tells you, in any perplexity."

"I am not perplexed," said Flora.

"Don't say so. This is either the station to which God has called you, or it is not."

"He never called me to it."

"But you don't know whether you ought to leave it. If you ought not, you would be ten times more miserable. Go to Richard, Flora—he belongs to you as much as I—he has authority besides."

"Richard!"

"He is the clearest of us all in practical matters," said Ethel, preventing what she feared would be disparaging. "I don't mean only that you should ask him about this Parliament matter alone; but I am sure you would be happier and more settled if you talked things over with him before—before you go to church."

"You don't know what you propose."

"I do," said Ethel, growing bolder. "You have been going all this time by feeling. You have never cleared up, and got to the bottom of, your troubles."

"I could not talk to any one."

"Not to any one but a clergyman. Now, to enter on such a thing is most averse to your nature; and I do believe that, for that very reason, it would be what would do you most good. You say you have recovered sense of— Oh, Flora! I can't talk of what you have gone through; but if you have only a vague feeling that seems as if lying still would be the only way to keep it, I don't think it can be altogether sound, or the 'quiet conscience' that is meant."

"Oh, Ethel! Ethel! I have never told you what I have undergone, since I knew my former quietness of conscience was but sleep! I have gone on in agony, with the sense of hypocrisy and despair, because I was afraid, for George's sake, to do otherwise."

Elhel felt herself utterly powerless to advise; and, after a kind sound of sympathy, sat shocked, pondering on what none could answer; whether this were, indeed, what poor Flora imagined, or whether it had been a holding-fast to the thread through the darkness. The proud reserve was the true evil, and Ethel prayed and trusted it might give way.

She went very amiably to Whitford with George, and gained great credit with him, for admiring the prettiest speckled Hamburgh present; indeed, George was becoming very fond of "poor Ethel," as he still called her, and sometimes predicted that she would turn out a fine figure of a woman after all.

Ethel heard, on her return, that Richard had been there; and three days after, when Flora was making arrangements for going to church, a moment of confidence came over her, and she said, "I did it, Ethel! I have spoken to Richard."

"I am so glad!"

"You were right. He is as clear as he is kind," said Flora; "he showed me that, for George's sake, I must bear with my present life, and do the best I can with it, unless some leading comes for an escape; and that the glare, and weariness, and being spoken well of, must be taken as punishment for having sought after these things."

"I was afraid he would say so," said Ethel. "But you will find happiness again, Flora dear."

"Scarcely—before I come to Margaret and to my child," sighed Flora. "I suppose it was Mercy that would not let me follow when I wished it. I must work till the time of rest comes!"

"And your own little Margaret will cheer you!" said Ethel, more hopefully, as she saw Flora bend over her baby with a face that might one day be bright.

She trusted that patient continuance in well-doing would one day win peace and joy, even in the dreary world that poor Flora had chosen.

For her own part, Ethel found Flora's practical good sense and sympathy very useful, in her present need of the counsel she had always had from Margaret.

The visit to Flora lasted a fortnight, and Ethel was much benefited by the leisure for reading and the repose after the long nursing; though, before the end, her refreshed energies began to pine for Daisy and her hymns, for Aubrey and his Virgil, for Cherry and her scholars, and, above all, for her father; for, come as often as he would, it was not papa at home.

On the other hand, Mary was at a loss for Ethel every hour; Richard was putting off his affairs till Ethel should come home; Miss Bracy and Blanche longed for her to relieve the schoolroom from the children; Aubrey could not perform a lesson in comfort with any one else—never ended a sum without groaning for Ethel, and sometimes rode to Abbotstoke for the mere purpose of appealing to her; in short, no one could get on without her, and the doctor least of all.

Dr. Spencer, and Mr. Wilmot, and all his sons and daughters, had done their best for him; but, in spite of his satisfaction at seeing the two sisters so happy together, he could not help missing Ethel every minute, as the very light of his home; and when, at last, Flora brought her back, she was received with uproarious joy by Aubrey and Daisy, while the rest of the household felt a revival and refreshment of spirits—the first drawing aside of the cloud that had hung over the winter. The pearl of their home might be missed every hour, but they could thankfully rest in the trust that she was a jewel stored up in safety and peace, to shine as a star for evermore.

A few weeks more, and there were other partings, sad indeed, yet cheery. Dr. May told Mrs. Arnott that, though he grieved that so much of sorrow had come to dim her visit, he could not but own that it was the very time when her coming could be most comforting; and this, as she truly said, was satisfaction enough for her, besides that she could not rejoice enough that her arrival had been in time to see their dear Margaret. She should carry away most precious recollections; and she further told Dr. Spencer that she was far more comfortable about her brother-in-law, than if she had only known him in his youthful character, which had seemed so little calculated to bear sorrow or care. She looked at him now only to wonder at, and reverence the change that had been gradually wrought by the affections placed above.

Norman and his wife went with her—the one grave but hopeful, the other trying to wile away the pain of parting, by her tearful mirth—making all sorts of odd promises and touching requests, between jest and earnest, and clinging to the last to her dear father-in-law, as if the separation from him were the hardest of all.

"Well, humming-birds must be let fly!" said he at last. "Ah! ha! Meta, are they of no use?"

"Stay till you hear!" said Meta archly—then turning back once more. "Oh! how I have thanked you, Ethel, for those first hints you gave me how to make my life real. If I had only sat still and wished, instead of trying what could be done as I was, how unhappy I should have been!"

"Come, take your sprite away, Norman, if you don't want me to keep her for good! God bless you, my dear children! Good-bye! Who

421

knows but when Doctor Tom sets up in my place, Ethel and I may come out and pay you a visit?"

It had all been over for some weeks, and the home-party had settled down again into what was likely to be their usual course, excepting in the holidays, to which the doctor looked forward with redoubled interest, as Tom was fast becoming a very agreeable and sensible companion; for his moodiness had been charmed away by Meta, and principle was teaching him true command of temper. He seemed to take his father as a special charge, bequeathed to him by Norman, and had already acquired that value and importance at home which comes of the laying aside of all self-importance.

It was a clear evening in March, full of promise of spring, and Ethel was standing in the church porch at Cocksmoor, after making some visits in the parish, waiting for Richard, while the bell was ringing for the Wednesday evening service, and the pearly tints of a cloudless sunset were fading into the western sky.

Ethel began to wonder where Norman might be looking at the sun dipping into the western sea, and thence arose before her the visions of her girlhood, when she had first dreamt of a church on Cocksmoor, and of Richard ministering before a willing congregation. So strange did the accomplishment seem, that she even touched the stone to assure herself of the reality; and therewith came intense thanksgiving that the work had been taken out of her hands, to be the more fully blessed and accomplished—that is, as far as the building went; as to the people, there was far more labour in store, and the same Hand must be looked to for the increase.

For herself, Ethel looked back and looked on. Norman Ogilvie's marriage seemed to her to have fixed her lot in life, and what was that lot? Home and Cocksmoor had been her choice, and they were before her. Home! but her eyes had been opened to see that earthly homes may not endure, nor fill the heart. Her dear father might, indeed, claim her full-hearted devotion, but, to him, she was only one of many. Norman was no longer solely hers; and she had begun to understand that the unmarried woman must not seek undivided return of affection, and must not set her love, with exclusive eagerness, on aught below, but must be ready to cease in turn to be first with any. Ethel was truly a mother to the younger ones; but she faced the probability that they would find others to whom she would have the second place. To love each heartily, to do her utmost for each in turn, and to be grateful for their fondness, was her call; but never to count on their affection as her sole right and inalienable possession. She felt that this was the probable course, and that she might look to becoming comparatively solitary in the course of years—then tried to realise what her lonely life might be, but broke off smiling at herself, "What is that to me? What will it be when it is over? My course and aim are straight on, and He will direct my paths. I don't know that I shall be alone, and I shall have the memory—the communion with them, if not their presence. Some one there must be to be loved and helped, and the poor for certain. Only I must have my treasure above, and when I think what is there, and of— Oh! that bliss of being perfectly able to praise—with no bad old self to mar the full joy of giving thanks, and blessing, and honour, and power! Need I dread a few short years?—and they have not begun yet—perhaps they won't— Oh! here is actually papa coming home this way! how delightful! Papa, are you coming to church here?"

"Ay, Ethel. That weathercock of Spencer's is a magnet, I believe! It draws me from all parts of the country to hear Richard in St.Andrew's Church."

THE END

Lightning Source UK Ltd.
Milton Keynes UK
UKHW010631170921
390736UK00001B/21